Second Time Around

Tina Wainscott

St. Martin's Paperbacks

SECOND TIME AROUND

Copyright © 1997 by Tina Wainscott.

ISBN: 0–312–96354–8

Printed in the United States of America

St. Martin's Paperbacks edition/October 1997

St. Martin's Paperbacks are published by St. Martin's Press, 175 Fifth Avenue, New York, NY 10010.

10 9 8 7 6 5 4 3 2 1

To Sloan Steele-Perkins, my agent . . .
You know all the reasons.

And to everyone with physical disabilities . . . I wish I
could give you all a second chance.

Second Time Around

Chapter 1

$\mathcal{J}$ennie Carmichael rolled her wheelchair through the doorway of Sam's Private Eye and over to her desk by the window. Sam Magee's low, rumbly voice coming from his office was as familiar and welcoming as the scent of aged wood, the heat of the furnace, or coffee . . . which, she noticed, was absent this morning.

Darn, he'd forgotten to pick some up again. The coffeepot looked cold and impotent in the corner. The mug she'd bought Sam last Christmas sat next to the empty pot, the hound-dog face waiting patiently to be filled with the hot, strong stuff.

And speaking of hound dogs . . . she heard a jingling sound and turned to greet Romeo, the reason she'd picked that particular mug for Sam. Romeo's tail arced gracefully, and his dripping chocolate-brown layers of skin flopped this way and that as he ambled over for his rub. She always rubbed her cheek against the top of his head. He had the softest fur, but she really loved the way his eyes rolled in ecstasy. Romeo's presence meant that Sam planned to be in the office for most of the day, and Jennie felt a little like rolling her eyes at that thought, too.

She shrugged out of her coat, then her sweater, hanging both on two low hooks Sam had put in just for her. She pulled the knit cap off her head, feeling several strands of her light brown hair crackle with static. Outside snowflakes dusted the city of Chicago, making her dread leaving and dealing with the snow.

She organized the papers on her desk as Romeo settled onto his dark green pillow with a contented sigh. She put copies to be made in one pile, reports to be transcribed in another. After firing up the computer, she put the tiny tape into the transcribing machine. She might have hated transcribing, but Sam was a good speaker.

"Sam's Private Eye," she answered cheerfully when the phone rang.

Jennie put the call on hold and wheeled across the wood floor to the doorway nearby. Sam looked as if he'd been poured into that high-backed chair. He had the old leather chair he'd picked up at an auction tilted all the way back, and his sock-clad feet were perched on the desk as he dictated another report.

That huge desk would have made most men look like elves, but not Sam. Not that he was a big guy in a burly sense; his strong wide shoulders tapered to a lean waist and flat stomach, and he was tall in a lean kind of way. But he had . . . presence. His ash-blond hair was brushed back in waves, highlighting his broad forehead, high cheekbones and blue eyes. Here, the aroma of leather and the citrus cologne Sam wore almost made up for the lack of coffee.

"Upon further surveillance, the subject twice stood and—" He clicked the little recorder off. "Good morning, kiddo."

"Morning, bossman," she said, using the nickname that had started out as a joke. "There's a Petula on the line for you." Petula of the long legs and blond hair and fake eyelashes. Like most of the women Jennie had seen him with. "She says it's, er, personal."

"Tell her I'm out of the country on a case," he said, then flashed her a mischievous smile that made his mustache stretch wider. "A dangerous mission spying on Mexican drug lords in Africa trying to sell their wares to Swiss tourists. If I don't get nailed by the drug lords or the Swiss tourists, there's always the cannibals. They like white meat, I hear.''

"Mm-hm," Jennie said with a nod, trying not to look so very pleased. "That didn't last very long."

"That woman's intelligence bled out with her hair color years ago."

Jennie felt a strange whirring in her heart when she said, "Well, maybe you should change your type."

"Ah," he said with a flick of his wrist. "I don't have time to woo and court a woman. This business is hard on a relationship."

"Long hours away, rushing out on a sudden call in the middle of dinner, canceled dates . . ."

He looked at her, tilting his head a little. "Yeah, just like that."

For a second, something clicked between them, something that smacked of a deep understanding. And was she imagining something more? Probably. She snapped out of her misleading thoughts. "Oh, I'd better tell Petula. . . ." She gestured toward the phone and whirled around to give Petula the brush-off.

Afterward she mulled over what had probably been the gutsiest thing she'd ever said to him, that thing about changing his type. What made Sam's heart tick? The blues, she decided when he turned up a particularly rhythmic piece, leaned his head back and started singing the chorus of "Drowning in a Sea of Love."

Ah, she knew that feeling well. She closed her eyes for a moment, savoring the richness of his voice. She could go on forever like this.

Her eyes snapped open. She had thought that about her life before, about being able to walk and run and dance. Then twelve years ago, in one minute, it was all gone. Her whole life changed. Never again could she look at something as forever. For now, she was happy with her life, even if she was in a wheelchair. Even if she was hopelessly in love with her boss, a man she was totally wrong for.

Sam was a living-by-the-seat-of-his-pants kind of guy; Jennie would only bog him down. Paralyzed from the waist down, she wasn't bound to be much in bed, either and Sam was too sexy to put up with that. Mostly, his friendship wasn't worth risking by telling Sam how she really felt about him. He could never feel the same way about her, and her admission would put a strain on a friendship that meant everything to her.

Jennie wheeled back to Sam's office and peeked her head in the doorway. He was pacing behind the desk now, phone to his ear. "Mm-hm. Mm-hm. And what did you do?" he was saying.

"Sam, I'm going down to Shep's to make copies," she whispered, gesturing toward the door. She turned to head out. Someday Sam was going to buy them a copier, "after our first really big case," he always said. Someday he would.

"Psst!" Sam appeared in the doorway, phone scrunched between his ear and shoulder, and gestured for her to wait. He slapped his palm to his forehead. "You slept with your wife? Aw, Harry, you just blew four weeks of surveillance! I don't care if it was the greatest sex you two ever had. Don't you see? You knew she was sleeping around on you and you did the deed with her anyway. That constitutes forgiveness, and what that means, my friend, is you have no case. Her lawyer no doubt told her to hit you where your heart is, and I'm not talking about your stomach. . . . *I* should have told you this before? I didn't think you'd *sleep* with her, for Pete's sake! You're the one who told me she was lower than a toenail."

He rolled his eyes at her as she tried to stifle a giggle. "Hold on a sec, Harry. Jennie, buy us some coffee from Shep, will you?" Pulling the already stretched cord farther, he handed her a couple of dollar bills.

"Yes, bossman." Jennie looked at the bills with a wry grin. That was his way of telling her he'd forgotten coffee again. Mixed subtly into his expression was an apology.

"Thanks, kiddo. Listen, Harry, you don't have a leg to stand on, least of all your third leg. Forget the whole thing."

Jennie wheeled out into the hallway and knocked the door shut with her elbow. As she turned toward the elevator, she felt her wheels slide over something slick on the wood. Her chair slid backward toward the stairway that led down two more floors. She yelped, grabbing the railing to stop herself. Her back was to the staircase when she got the chair to stop turning. Glancing down the wood stairs, she let out a long breath and started the chair forward.

Instead, it went backward.

She lunged for the railing again. But she was already tipping over. The railing was out of reach.

The last thing she saw before she fell was Sam's horrified expression as he shot through the door and tried to grab her. She reached for him. Their fingers touched, slid apart without catching. Her stomach lurched as she fell, the steps jerking her chair to and fro.

"Sam!" she screamed out.

"Jennie! No!"

The world tilted, crushing her with pain and dizziness. Through some thick mist, she felt herself lurch down several more steps, landing on a flat, hard surface. Her body came to a jarring stop, but the dizziness kept swirling through her.

She heard voices filled with panic and exclamation. She smelled the coppery odor of blood, and heard Sam yell with a hoarse voice, "Someone help! Call an ambulance!"

Her heart thundered inside her, increasing the pain with each pulse of blood. She couldn't swallow at first. There was some kind of liquid in her mouth, warm and thick. When she forced herself to swallow it, she recognized the taste of blood. *Oh, God, I'm dying.*

Sam held her, smoothing back her hair with trembling fingers. "Jennie, don't leave me. Come on . . . oh, God. Don't close your eyes. You're going to be fine."

Sam, I love you. She tried to voice her thoughts, but her

mouth was filled with blood again. She wasn't even aware that her eyes were closing, but nothing could make them stay open. Even in the darkness, she could see Sam's face. And she could still tell what was going on around her: Sam cradling her head, other frantic voices in the stairway, Sam speaking to her, the feel of blood trickling from her mouth down her chin and neck.

She must look a wreck, she thought vaguely. Her impulse was to wipe away the blood, but nothing moved at her will. Panic gripped her. Not even a finger complied with her mental order to move. Was she completely paralyzed now?

"Jennie." Sam's voice seemed so very far away. The music he'd been listening to played through her mind: "Drowning in a Sea of Love." How odd, she thought. Then she realized she couldn't even feel him anymore, couldn't hear the other noises. It was as if the music had become a physical thing, a wave on which she rode, traveling through nothingness at a fast rate.

Sam's voice faded to a dull roar from some dark, distant place. Even the music faded away, leaving her suspended and weightless. All of her fear, hopes, dreams, frustration—everything seemed to be sucked away from her, as if an unseen vacuum cleaner was pointed at her soul. She floated in some infinite darkness, feeling her life drawing to a peaceful end.

It seemed like an eternity, and at the same time only minutes from that fall down the stairs, when Jennie opened her eyes. Time had no place here, nor did the physical. Her body was no more than an opaque mist. For the first time in many years she was free of constraints and limits. The silence was soft and comforting, rather than isolating. Yet, somehow, she knew she wasn't alone.

She felt as though she were in a fog bank suspended over a vast ocean. Through the gray mist a light as bright as the setting sun penetrated from a distance. Gentle rays of light emanated from the sun and shimmered through the mist like glowing fingers playing some giant, unseen piano. They became brighter and warmer as they moved closer. She squinted as those fingers of light enveloped her in a feeling of warmth and peace like she had never known. She reached out toward the light.

And then one word crept through the darkness, warming her even more than the light. *Sam.* She smiled, or at least thought she was smiling. But following that warmth was such a deep regret at not telling him how she felt about him, sorrow that she wasn't the kind of woman who could make him happy. *Take care of him,* she asked the light. *I love him, you know.*

A soft, sweet voice emanated from the light. Not a voice in any physical sense, but a wispy sound that seemed to penetrate her soul. *Some never get to fulfill their dreams the first time. A very chosen few get a second chance. You, Jennie, are one of those chosen. Soon you can pursue those dreams the second time around.*

Another chance! To see Sam, to continue loving him, to nag him about getting coffee. But this time she would tell him how she felt. Even if she wasn't the right woman for him—even if he could never love her that way—she wanted him to know her feelings about him. Never again could she leave her life feeling this profound regret over her silence. This was one second chance she wasn't going to waste.

Then that blower started again. Only this time, it sucked her very soul through the darkness. She was going back now! Everything happened at once. An incredible pain in her head, as if her brain had crystallized, then been dropped on a hard tile floor. Air filled her lungs so suddenly, she gasped with the force of it. Her heartbeat thudded through her, blood pulsing into every artery, every tiny vein. Her body was physical again. Gravity pulled her downward, pressing her against a hard surface below. She forced her eyes open, anxious to see what had become of her, knowing she would make the best of it.

*   *   *

The first thing Jennie saw, once her eyes focused in, was Sam's concerned face hovering over her. "Sam," she breathed, elated over the joy of smiling again—really smiling this time. Then she realized his finger was touching her neck, pressed gently against her pulse point. He looked startled as his gaze met hers. Slowly he pulled his finger away. She was lying on the wooden floor, her body sprawled out like a rag doll.

"You're alive again," he said in a low voice. "This is incredible. One minute you were gone—no pulse at all. Before I could even think about doing CPR, your pulse came back. All by itself," he finished softly.

"I did die, didn't I?" The light, the voice—it couldn't have been her imagination.

"Just a little. How are you feeling?"

The throbbing pain in her head persisted, but she was more concerned about her hands and arms. She curled her fingers, breathing in relief as they obeyed her command. She wasn't completely paralyzed.

"I think I'm okay." Her voice sounded strange, a little lower, thicker.

"I should call an ambulance."

Sam's face wavered out of focus for a second, but she willed him back. Clearing her throat, she said, "But you already asked someone to do that." Her voice still sounded strange.

"No, I didn't, but I'm going to now." Something looked different about him. Maybe it was just his concern. And his hair. It was longer, curling over his collar. "Stay put." He started to rise, but she reached out for his hand to stop him. Her whole world spun for a moment, and she squeezed his hand to steady herself.

"Just give me a minute," she whispered, letting the nausea settle down again. She put her palm on the pounding area of her head and felt something sticky. That coppery smell assaulted her senses again. The blood on her hand sent the nausea into full tilt.

She took a deep breath. "Oh, geez. What happened to me?"

"That's what I was going to ask you. I heard a noise and opened the door to find you like this."

He headed back into his office and emerged a few seconds later cutting one of his sleeves off with a pair of scissors. Very gently he pressed it to the gash on her forehead. When she put her hand there, her fingers touched his, reminding her of another moment when their hands had connected, then slipped from each other. He removed his hand, and she continued applying gentle pressure.

The pieces started coming together, shards of memories. "I remember what happened. I fell down the stairs."

Sam's eyebrow twitched. "We're on the top floor."

"I know that, but . . ." She turned behind her and was startled to see the staircase leading down. The one she'd fallen down. Well, she thought she remembered falling down the stairs. She looked down at her legs, sprawled out in front of her. She didn't even recognize the gray wool pants she had on, or the long black coat. Her feet were clad in nylons, and she squinted at what looked like red toenail polish. She'd been twelve years old the one and only time she'd ever put polish on her toes. Maybe she was seeing things.

Something else was missing. Her wheelchair. Before she could ask Sam about it, he said, "I think we've got some antiseptic in the office." A shadow darkened his eyes. "Jennie insisted we have a first-aid kit." His voice had gone softer at those words, and he got up and went into the office.

Why was he using her name in the third person? She turned around to look for her chair. Without it, she felt lost. As if a part of her were missing. Strange how she remembered falling backward down those stairs. Unless someone carried her up them and left her in front of Sam's door. No, that didn't make any sense. And neither did Sam's strange behavior. Maybe he was spooked by her coming back from the dead.

She noticed the rubber mat in front of their door. When had he put that there? She was sure no mat existed when her wheel had slipped in the puddle.

Then she felt the itch. Instinctively she leaned toward her big toe to scratch it—and stopped. Her eyes widened. *Her toe had an itch.* Her *paralyzed* toe. A cold chill washed over her. She was sure it was all in her injured head. It had been a long time since she'd sent a message to her feet. She closed her eyes and concentrated. Her toe moved. Her eyes popped open. Then she saw her toe move. She couldn't believe it!

"I found some hydrogen peroxide—What's wrong?" Sam's voice intruded in her reverie.

Her voice was squeaky with disbelief. "Sam, look! I can move my toe!" And then another amazing thing happened. She moved her leg. The whole thing!

Sam didn't look quite as thunderstruck as she did, but he did have a measure of disbelief. He crouched down beside her. "I always knew you were on the edge, but not this close. Are you sure you're all right?"

She gave him a tremulous smile. "I might be better than all right."

He just looked at her for a moment. "What were you doing here, anyway?"

Her mouth dropped open at that one. "Sam! I was getting copies and coffee at Shep's, remember?"

His face paled, then darkened with a shadow of agony. "Why the hell would you say something like that?" He stood and walked back inside their office. What had she said? What was going on here? She could hear him on the phone a moment later. "Yes, we need an ambulance. . . ."

Where was the man who had held her tenderly? Maybe she'd dreamed the whole thing. She lifted the piece of cloth from her head. Well, most of it. The bleeding seemed to have stopped. She reached for the bottle of peroxide Sam had left on the floor and poured some onto the cloth, then pressed it back to her forehead. She didn't want an ambulance, she wanted Sam to tell her why he was acting so strange.

What she needed was to find her chair. She grasped onto the railing behind her and pulled herself upward. Where could it be? It couldn't have just disappeared. After being virtually attached to it for twelve years, she felt strange without it. That black molded chair, or variations of it, was never out of her sight.

Her upper arms weren't as strong as they usually were. She struggled to hold herself upright, balancing her weight while catching her breath. The sound of the elevator's doors sliding open brought her attention to Shep. Skinny, with gray hair and beard, he looked a bit like a goat, though Jennie had come to like him an awful lot over the years. He owned a small office-supply store downstairs.

Shep's bushy eyebrows narrowed when he saw her awkward position. "Ah, see you found Sam's all right." He glanced at the open door, then back at her. "Hope everything's okay. When you came running in my office looking for Sam, I thought you were in trouble or something. Are you all right, ma'am? You look a little shaky."

Her mouth dropped open. Shep didn't seem to recognize her, either. That warm sparkle didn't light his eyes, and he didn't call her by her nickname, Speed Racer. But one of his words stuck in her brain. "Did you say I *ran* into your office?"

"Sure, don't you remember?" He shook his head, then glanced at the stairway as if it had a life of its own. "Gave me the willies when you took the stairs three at a time. Didn't you hear me yell to be careful? What with the accident last month, none of us around here hardly uses them at all." Shep's face darkened with a palpable sadness, like the pallor on Sam's face.

Her mind couldn't sort the facts fast enough. She had bounded up the steps, *three at a time.* Maybe everybody was losing their mind, asbestos in the building or something. Her brain locked on the last bit.

"What accident?" Her fingers and arms trembled with the weight of holding herself up. Where was the upper body strength she had worked on all these years?

Shep glanced in the open doorway again, then back. "Sam's assistant, Jennie. Speed Racer, I used to call her." Melancholy filled his smile. "She was a real sweetie, nicest person you could ever know. Someone spilled some lubricant on the landing there, right in front of the office door. Still haven't figured out who done it, but I think it was one of the elevator service guys. Anyway, her wheelchair caught that spill just right—or wrong, you could say."

Jennie noticed Sam's form in her peripheral vision, but kept her eyes on Shep. Her throat tightened, nearly cutting off her air. "What happened to her?" she whispered. *Jennie. He's talking about me.*

"She fell down backward, hit her head. Poor thing, only twenty-six years old, and her life is over." His shook his head, lower lip pushed out slightly.

Jennie wanted to hug him, to tell him she hadn't died. Instead, she fell to the floor amid a blizzard of black dots. No, they actually looked more like wiggly worms, all squirming this way and that. She was getting dizzier watching them.

"I've got her," Sam was saying as his arms went around her waist just before she hit the floor. "Shep, get her a glass of water, quick." He set her gently down on the floor, leaning her back against the railing she was blindly grasping for.

She was a real sweetie . . . poor thing . . . her life is over. The words floated through Jennie's mind, bits and pieces that refused to make sense to her. She had gotten a second chance, that's what the voice had told her. And she *was* there. But Shep said Jennie was dead. And neither he nor Sam seemed to know who she was.

She thought of the wool pants she didn't recognize, the long black coat. Not hers. Shep had seen her bound up the stairs. Not her legs. She opened her eyes, wiggly worms be damned. Slowly she glanced downward at the hands flattened against the floor to keep her upright. Long painted nails, strange rings on her fingers. Then farther out at the legs sprawled awkwardly.

Holy angels in Heaven—she'd gotten a second chance in someone else's body! A body that was whole, a body that could walk, run . . . dance!

Sam was trying to drape a wet, cold paper towel over her forehead when her head lurched upward.

"Get me a mirror!" Her voice gave way a little at the last word.

His forehead crinkled. "Maybe you shouldn't look. It's kinda nasty. The ambulance should be here anytime, so just calm down."

"My face is kind of nasty?" Was she some monster?

Sam shook his head, a slight smile on his face. "No, just the cut."

"Get me a mirror, or I'll get one myself."

He raised his hands. "Okay, I'll find a mirror. Vain woman," he muttered as he left.

"*Me*, vain?" She sputtered a laugh as he disappeared through the office door. "You've *got* to be kidding."

Jennie spotted a purse lying nearby, a large tapestry bag. Not her purse. Much too big and flamboyant for Jennie Carmichael. She fumbled through the contents until she found a Gucci wallet. She opened it to the driver's license. The woman in the photo had her hair pulled back, though several curls graced her forehead. Jennie's attention went to the name: Maxine Lizbon. Was she Maxine now? There had to be a mistake. Or maybe this was all a dream. Sam reappeared with the mirror he used to obliquely see who came in the door.

Jennie threw her wallet back in her purse. "Nothing's missing," she said quickly, taking the mirror from Sam.

"Were you mugged?"

She looked at her reflection. *Oh, my gosh.* Her throat constricted when she saw a stranger's face. There was no sign of Jennie there. Maxine had red hair, lots of it, curling just past her shoulders. When she lifted her bangs, she saw the gash. She quickly let them go, feeling woozy. Sam was right—it wasn't a pretty sight. Instead, she concentrated on her general appearance.

Her eyes were the prettiest shade of green she had ever seen. Her skin was pale right then, making the streaks of blush stand out like a clown's. Her upper lip twitched slightly, and she saw it move in the reflection. Even that little movement made her head ache, but she didn't care at the moment. Excitement shot through her veins, spreading a warmth through her entire body. She shoved the mirror back at Sam, not able to hide her smile.

"It doesn't look too bad." Her smile widened. She was Maxine now. Could she dare to hope this was real? And with no wheelchair in sight, that meant—had to mean—she could walk. Shep returned with the glass of water, huffing and puffing next to her.

"Couldn't find a darned cup anywhere to save my life. Or yours."

She took a drink and handed it back to him. "Thanks. I feel better now." That was an understatement. She turned to Sam. "Could you help me up, please?"

"You should stay put until the ambulance comes."

"No, I'm fine."

Sam just stared at her for a moment, expelling a short breath. Finally he extended a hand, and she grasped it, holding on for a second before pulling herself up. She had a whole new chance, a new body. Through Maxine, Jennie could now be the kind of woman Sam might fall in love with. She let her feet hold her weight for the first time in years. Her legs wavered, and she reached for Sam's strong shoulders. He steadied her with his hands, fingers tight around her waist.

"Did you hurt your legs?" he asked.

"No. I'm just a little . . . weak, that's all." Even though this body was used to walking, her mind wasn't accustomed to issuing those kinds of commands. She concentrated. Such a simple action, something she used to take for granted a long time ago. How did you walk? One foot in front of the other. Her legs wobbled, and she held tight to Sam as they walked inside the office. One, two; one, two, she chanted internally.

"Shep, why don't you wait out front for the ambulance?" Sam asked.

"Is she going to be all right?"

Sam looked at her, lifting an appraising eyebrow. "As all right as she's ever been, I suspect."

Now what did that mean? Jennie wondered. Did he know? Could he somehow tell she was really in this body? No, he would have been celebrating this blessed event of walking with her. And he would have looked at her in that familiar way. Shep set the glass of water on her desk and left to watch for the ambulance. Jennie made her slow way to the flowery couch Sam hated, the one his ex-wife had put in when she'd apparently used Sam's office as her first decorating assignment. Sam went into his office to replace the mirror he'd brought out for her. Romeo ambled cautiously over, his nose wiggling.

"Romeo!" She leaned down to rub her cheek against his head, but her head started spinning at the movement. Gripping the edge of the couch, she held her hand out to him instead. "Romeo, what's the matter?" Whoops. She knew what the matter was. He didn't know her.

Sam snapped his fingers as he reentered the front area. "Romeo, go to your pillow." Romeo gave one more glance at Jennie, then swaggered over and dropped down on his pillow with a dog sigh. "Maxine, listen to me. Did someone hit you out there? Mug you?" he asked, crouching down in front of her. "You said nothing was missing in your purse."

"No, I don't think so. I was just being paranoid, I guess." Well, she didn't think she'd been mugged. "I . . . fell. Tripped or something." She tried to laugh it off, but Sam's expression was serious.

He stood and tilted her head back, his finger gently tracing the skin around her cut. "It's deep. But the blood around the cut looks too dry for this to have just happened. I'd say it happened about half an hour ago." His eyes met hers. "Try to remember what happened before you came here."

She didn't want him to think she'd lost her memory, but it was going to be hard to bluff through this one. And then she had a sobering realization. Whatever had happened to Maxine had killed her. Whether accidental or not, this gash had probably proved fatal. She decided to tell him the truth, or as close as possible.

"I'm not sure, to be honest with you. I can't remember what happened in the last hour."

"What about before that? Do you know who you are? Maybe there's something wrong with your legs."

"No, there's nothing wrong with my legs." She couldn't keep the smile away at that statement, but she tried to downplay it. After all, she'd bounded up the steps three at a time earlier, or at least Maxine had. Bounded up the stairs! What a wonderful thought! Her legs had to work pretty good for that. She lifted each leg, flexing her foot to demonstrate their ability. "See, they work just fine. And I know who I am. I'm Maxine Lizbon, and I'm thirty years old." She recited her address, the one from the license.

Sam gave her a wry grin, jumpstarting her heart all over again. "You must have hit your head hard; I've never heard you tell anyone your age before."

"Huh?"

"But you don't remember how your head got that gash in it?" he continued.

"No. I can remember everything up until that point."

Sam tilted his head. "Why did you come to see me?"

"Uh, except for that." She swallowed. "Maybe it has something to do with this." She pointed to her forehead.

"In here," Shep's voice said. Two paramedics followed him into the office.

"I'm fine, really," she said.

The woman said, "Let us be the judge of that, okay?"

She was short and stocky, and looked like she meant business.

Jennie tilted her head back and lifted her bangs.

"Yow," the woman said. "We'd better take you in."

"No," Jennie said, almost too quickly. She had an illogical fear that the doctors would see right through her, call her an imposter or body thief. "Can't you just stitch me up here?" At the doubt in their faces, she crossed her arms and added, "I'm not going to the hospital."

"Don't be difficult," Sam said. "I know you're really good at it, but not now. Maxine, are you listening to me?"

Jennie realized he was talking to her and not the paramedic. "It's not that bad. I hate hospitals." She'd spent enough time in one after her accident.

"We can't stitch you up. All we can do is apply a butterfly stitch, which is more like a Band-Aid. Real stitches will close the wound much better, leave less of a scar."

"No hospitals. Just do what you can do here."

Sam shook his head, rolling his eyes upward. "You're asking for trouble, woman." To the paramedic, he said, "Can't you forcibly take her to the hospital?"

"No, afraid not. All we can do is make her sign a release so if something happens, we're not liable." She turned back to Jennie. "Okay, we'll apply the butterfly. But if you have any dizziness or fainting spells, you must go to the hospital right away. Head injuries are serious business."

"Yes, ma'am," Jennie said solemnly.

After running a battery of tests, including looking deep into her eyes with their flashlight, the woman said, "I don't see any signs of concussion, but I really wish you'd let us take you in." When Jennie shook her head, the woman shrugged. "All right, it's your head. We've got to cleanse it first." The other paramedic handed her a cleansing solution. When the woman pushed Maxine's hair back, she blinked. "That's strange."

"What?" both Jennie and Sam asked at the same time.

"I'd swear it looks better already. Like it's healing un-naturally fast."

Jennie smiled. "See, told you it's not that bad."

She closed her eyes while they did their ministrations on her head. Sam watched, wincing, which was why Jennie decided she couldn't keep her eyes open. Her fingers dug into the fabric of the sofa as the cleanser sent pinpricks of pain through her body.

She focused her thoughts on her old life. She could tell Sam the truth, but would he believe her? He already seemed to think she was wacky, and her actions thus far hadn't done much to dispel that. Sam wasn't into stuff that defied reason, like ghosts and UFOs. If she told him she was Jennie's soul come back in another body, she might lose him forever. That thought made her fingers curl over the arms of the sofa. She felt Sam's hand cover hers.

"It's all right. It'll be over soon."

Jennie smiled. She couldn't risk losing Sam, not now. Even if he did believe her, he'd probably still look at her as the old Jennie anyway. Just because she looked different didn't mean his feelings would change. Besides, the old Jennie was dull. She had no life, no excitement. No, it was time to let Jennie die. As Maxine, she would be exciting, sexy, everything Sam wanted in a woman. They would start fresh, the two of them. She would make Sam fall in love with her this time, and nothing would get in the way of that.

"You're all set," the woman's voice said.

"You bet I am." Jennie's eyes popped open. "I mean, I feel better already. Thank you."

The woman paramedic shone the flashlight in her eyes again, and Jennie willed her pupils to shrink properly. "Well, I have to say that you look fine. Okay, remember, any dizziness or fainting—"

"I'll go to the hospital right away," Jennie promised.

"And I would make an appointment with your doctor as soon as possible, just as a precaution."

Jennie signed the release, with Sam shaking his head the

whole time, and the medical team left. She was alone with Sam again. She'd been alone with Sam many times, but it felt different this time. The office was overly warm, and she pulled off her expensive London Fog coat and laid it on the couch.

"The heating and cooling system in this old building never did work right," he said, looking out at the snowflakes clinging to the window.

"Roasting in the winter, freezing in the summer."

He turned to look at her. "How did you know that?"

"I mean, I can tell. It's way too warm in here. The other part was a guess."

"Oh." He nodded slowly. "How are you feeling?"

"Okay. I'll live."

He looked so good, wearing his faded blue jeans and white cotton shirt. He'd cut the other sleeve off so they matched, and the muscles in his arms rippled slightly as he clenched and unclenched his fists.

"Do you remember anything more about the accident? Or why you came here?"

She shook her head, immediately regretting the action when Sam and the entire room swayed like a rolling ship. She gripped the arm of the couch again, subtly so Sam wouldn't notice.

"Are you all right?" he asked, noticing anyway.

She forced a smile. "I'm fine." And to prove it, she was going to walk to her desk and get the glass of water Shep had left there.

"What are you doing?" he asked when she started to push herself off the couch.

"I just want to stand for a minute." Oh, to feel the floor beneath her feet—the hard flatness of it. She had left her cream pumps by the door, so her feet were bare but for stockings. Her toes wiggled. Slowly she pushed herself upward, feeling all those wondrous muscles in her legs group for action. Lifting her arms out for balance, she straightened and stood there for a moment. And smiled. Sam wouldn't understand the sheer joy of simply standing, but she could hardly hide it. This was all a precious gift beyond comprehension.

"Are you sure your legs are all right?" he asked, coming closer.

"Oh, yes, I'm sure."

She eyed the water a good five feet away. She could do this. Her legs worked; it was her mind having a hard time accepting the simple motion. She took one step, then another. Like a newborn learning to walk for the first time. Her legs started to wobble. Was there any way she could ask Sam to teach her to walk without sounding crazy? No, especially in light of her history of bounding the stairs three at a time. She took another step.

"I'm a little dizzy, that's all," she said, not lying entirely.

At each movement, the dull ache in her head thrummed louder, pulsing along with her heartbeat.

Sam walked casually closer, arms at the ready. She had an errant thought about pretending to fall just so he'd wrap those arms around her again, but nixed it. And then her legs really gave way. She grabbed for the desk nearby, but Sam got to her first. She wanted to melt against him, but he steered her back to the couch and deposited her there.

"Just as stubborn as ever," he muttered as he helped her lower herself to the couch. Kneeling in front of her, he lifted one of her legs and started running his fingers over it. Chills scurried down the length of her leg, an exquisite feeling all around. But this seemed terribly forward of Sam, who was usually quite laid back and not the touchy-feely kind.

"Does this hurt?" he was saying as he pressed harder around her ankle.

"No." She watched Sam's fingers circle her calf, thinking how highly erotic something so innocent could be. Even through clothing.

"How about this?"

"Nope. Er, exactly what are you doing?"

"I think there's something wrong with your legs, and

you're too damned stubborn to admit it. How about this?"

He was at her knee now, rubbing over the bony cap. She felt a strange warmth spread through her when his fingers rubbed behind her knee.

"Maxine?"

"Hm? Oh—no, no pain there."

He went higher still, edging that warmth to more specific areas. What was going on with her body? Maxine's body? No one had ever touched her so intimately before. Tingling sensations traveled from the tips of his fingers to her most private area. She wriggled slightly, embarrassed at feeling such a thing. Embarrassed, but intrigued, too. Mid-thigh, he looked up at her. How could he look so entirely innocent and intent when she was going crazy inside?

"How about here?"

"No," she said, drawing the word out. "Sam?" He went higher, pressing his fingers into her thigh. The tingling increased, making her fidget even more. Yes, she wanted to get closer to him, but this was a little fast. Finally, she couldn't take it anymore. "Sam!"

"What? Stop moving around. What about here?" His fingers prodded at the ridge between her upper thigh and her crotch.

She jerked so hard that her bottom slipped off the couch, and she landed on the floor. Sam put his hands on his thighs, still kneeling in front of her.

"What is your problem?"

"I, well . . . don't you think you're getting a bit fresh?"

He rolled his eyes in that familiar way he had for all his loony clients. "Maxine, don't you think it's a little late to be modest now?"

"What do you mean?"

"Hell, woman, we were married for five years."

Chapter 2

*T*his wasn't happening. That had to be the explanation. Either that or someone was playing one heck of a joke on her. But that someone would have to be God, and Jennie couldn't imagine the Big Guy upstairs partaking in practical jokes.

Sam had taken a phone call, giving her a minute to think. Maybe this was all a dream then. Jennie had dreamed about walking before, and it had felt so real, she'd woken up afterward and actually tried to walk. And so she would again.

She pinched herself in the arm to start the process. This dream was too bizarre to hang around in another minute. Both bizarre and wonderful. And then she pinched herself again. A cold chill washed over her. She wasn't waking up. The smells, the sounds, everything seemed so real. Even the jingle of Romeo's tags as he scratched his ear.

Certainly the dull throbbing in her forehead felt real enough. And the weight of the concrete block Sam's words had produced in her stomach. Pushing herself up by her arms, she leaned against the arm of the couch and stood. Her legs felt sturdy, but her mind couldn't accept that so easily. She glanced toward the door in Sam's office; he was watching her in the mirror. Good grief, her legs were still tingling from his earlier touches. She took a tentative step toward her desk. Her weight held. Another step. Yes, this was working. Just like in one of those dreams.

"You ought to see a doctor, Maxine."

Sam's voice startled her, and she lunged for the corner of the desk for balance. This was silly, she knew. "I'm fine, really. You'd be surprised just how fine I am." If this was somehow real.

Sam walked up close and took her hands from the desk. She stood almost face-to-face with him, her hands tucked inside his. He was studying her eyes, probably looking for signs of insanity.

It was the first time she had ever been anywhere near his height, except when they were both sitting down. She wanted to dance. It sounded strange even to her own mind, but she wanted to dance right then with Sam. It had been her dream, to dance on her own legs, to be held by a man. By Sam. If this was a dream, she could ask him and he'd grant her request. What made sense in dreams, anyway?

"Sam, dance with me," she said, tightening her grip on his hands.

He lifted his eyebrows and looked at her as if a flock of doves had just alighted from her hair. "I'm calling a doctor."

This wasn't a dream. "I was just kidding," she said with a forced laugh. "I said it because of the way we're standing."

He glanced down, then loosened his grip on her hands. "Go sit on that couch."

"I really was kidding," she felt necessary to repeat. He was still giving her that skeptical look. "And I don't want to sit down." *I've been sitting down for twelve years.* And then she realized she was standing on her own. It was probably best to celebrate internally. She wavered a little, but caught herself. The hardwood floor felt firm beneath her feet. She flexed her toes, trying hard to keep the smile from her face.

"I really wish you'd sit down. You're worrying me, standing there wiggling your toes and grinning like that."

She'd forgotten how observant the man was. "I'm fine."

He gave her a once-over. "You haven't changed a bit, have you?"

"Oh, you'd be surprised."

He answered that in a kind of grunt, glancing out the window. She studied his profile, her heart tightening when she noticed that he looked different somehow.

"You look tired," she said, realizing that was one difference. And thin. Was he on a diet? On a heavy case? She knew the food he ate when he was on a long surveillance: junk.

He turned to her. "I am tired, Maxine. Tired to the tips of every hair on my body."

She wasn't sure if she'd ever seen him this tired before, this lackluster. Maybe it was the glum weather, which sapped everyone's energy about this time of the year. The desk calendar still read January fifteenth, the day she'd fallen down the stairs.

"Sam, what is today's date?"

He glanced at that calendar too, then looked away. "It's the fourteenth."

Wait, that couldn't be right. Jennie remembered laughing at the day's "Far Side" cartoon for the fifteenth, and she never peeked ahead. But Shep had said a month had passed since . . . Jennie's death. Her head throbbed even harder as the thoughts jumbled in her mind. She had to see for herself, in black and white.

She pretended interest in her surroundings, looking around and slowly making her way to Sam's office. She knew he had a calendar hanging in there. One step. Two steps.

"It still looks pretty much the same around here," she said, covering her own surveillance as it were.

"Unlike some people, I don't have to redecorate every six months."

Sam sounded different to her, as different as her own

voice sounded. Three steps, then four. She turned around to find Sam still standing by her desk.

"Change is good," she said with a smile. But she wasn't sure yet. And if she was Maxine, could she actually play that part enough to fool anyone? "I see you . . . kept the couch I put in."

He rolled his eyes. "I've tried to give it away a few times, but nobody'll take it."

That was true. Even on her job interview, Sam had offered it to her.

"Aw, Sam, it's not that bad. It lends a certain personality to the place."

"It does not appeal to my feminine side, wherever that may be. Admit it, Maxine. You were just getting me back for some unseen injustice. Letting my ex-wife practice her new decorating services on my office was one of the stupidest things I've ever done."

Was Maxine a spiteful person? Or just oblivious to what a man needed in his office?

When she reached Sam's doorway, the mirror directly across from her gave her a start. She'd never been high enough to notice it before. But it wasn't the mirror as much as the image of the redhead looking back at her. She had a heart-shaped face now, and her mouth was smaller. Jennie reached up to touch the curls at her cheek, and the redhead in the reflection did the same. She winked; so did the redhead. Warmth twisted and churned through her. She forced her gaze from the mirror to the calendar Sam had hung on the wall behind his desk, the one with the fancy cars on it. Plain as day it said February. A month later. She turned to Sam, feeling her face pale.

"Shep said your assistant . . . died last month." She cleared the frog from her throat. "That she fell down the stairs."

Sam's expression darkened. For a moment, she thought he wasn't going to answer. Finally he said, "Some idiot spilled oil from the elevator on the floor outside my office.

Her wheels slid across it." Sam tilted his head back, then looked at her. "Do you remember yet what you came here for? Or where you got that nasty gash on your forehead?"

Jennie was reaching blindly for the wall behind her, letting herself lean against it without looking like she was about to faint. Oh, God, Jennie really was dead. And Maxine had died, too. Jennie had gotten a second chance in her body. The blood rushed back to her face, making her feel sunburned with the heat of it.

"I don't remember. Maybe I was coming here to say hello, and did this when I fell."

"I don't think so. For one thing, you've never just come by to say hello. And the blood was too dry, remember? Something happened, and you came to me about it."

Jennie nodded slowly, having no clue about Maxine's life at all. She looked at her desk, looking exactly as she'd left it minus a few papers. It bugged her that she'd left work undone. Not that she could be blamed, but it still bugged her.

"Didn't you hire anyone else? You're so busy . . . or at least I would imagine you would be."

Sam started to follow her gaze to the desk, but stopped himself. "I'm not very busy right now."

The phone rang again, and Jennie started to walk toward her desk to answer it. Sam walked past her into his office to get it. She leaned against the solidness of the door frame and watched him. If this was real . . . and it seemed to be real . . . she had to decide who she was going to be. All she knew for sure was that she was taking this second chance to make Sam fall in love with her. As his ex-wife, she had a distinct disadvantage. But then again, maybe it wasn't. There didn't seem to be much animosity between them, the couch notwithstanding. After all, Maxine had come to him for help, even after all these years.

If she told Sam she was Jennie . . . she shook her head. Preposterous. He'd really think she was one towel short of a load, and he already thought Maxine was a little zany anyway. Worst case was she told him the truth and he'd tell her to see a shrink and get the heck away from his life. Sam seemed awfully good at shutting people away from his world, and Jennie didn't want to be one of them.

The best case was that she somehow got him to believe her. Then what? Their friendship wouldn't be the same; the boundaries were different now. But would he still view her as the old Jennie? Or get her confused with Maxine because of her body? Her heart clenched at the risks. She was certain she'd been given this second chance to fulfill her dreams of making Sam love her. The least risky proposition seemed to be winning his heart as Maxine. Sam had once loved her; maybe there was still a place in his heart for her.

Besides, the old Jennie was dull, had no life, nothing to offer Sam. Maxine looked full of possibilities. She glanced at her reflection again, a smile tugging at her lips. Well, at Maxine's lips. No, her lips now.

Jennie's whole life since the car accident had been sheltered. Her biggest risk had been getting this job. She'd never taken the chance of telling Sam she loved him; heck, she'd never taken any chances. Her gaze shifted to Sam, and a warm feeling bubbled inside her. It was time to take the biggest risk of all, to become Maxine Lizbon and win Sam's heart. She looked back at the mirror again, trying to get used to seeing green eyes and red hair and not brown eyes and brown hair. Maxine, Maxine, Maxine, she chanted internally. *It's me, Maxine. Hi, I'm Maxine. Maxine Lizbon, here. You're looking for Maxine? Oh, that's me.*

Straightening, Maxine steeled herself to walk without a wobble to the old leather chair in front of Sam's oversized desk. Romeo followed her in and sat down facing her. He studied her, his head tilted. She leaned slowly forward and scratched the folds of skin beneath his chin.

"I missed you," she whispered. "Both of you."

"This guy's really good, Ned," Sam was saying, probably to his younger brother.

She'd never met Ned, or even seen him before, but she

knew that he was an up-and-coming litigation lawyer who sometimes used Sam's services to assist in his cases. Sam rarely talked about his family, and she had always thought there was some kind of rift. But she'd never had the courage to ask him about it. *What a wimp I was. Reason enough to let Jennie go.*

"No, I'm not saying he's really injured. I'm saying he's good. But I have a few ideas about moving this case along. I'll let you know. Okay, bye." He looked up at her. "Don't keep looking around my office like that. I don't care if it lacks true taste and culture, class, or organization—it's me, it's comfortable, and I don't need your decorating services or your opinion."

She could only stare at him for a moment. "I . . . I think it looks fine," she said honestly.

"You're kidding, right? Patronizing me, then?"

"No. It really looks fine."

"Yeah, sure." He gave her that skeptical look again. It said, *You're lying; what are you up to?* Maxine realized she'd never seen that look directed at her before.

"Sam, why are you so defensive?"

"I was married to you, remember?"

Those words took her breath away for a second, but she composed herself. "Well, of course I remember." She needed to find out more about their marriage, why it hadn't worked out. "But how long has it been since we've seen each other?"

He shrugged. "Lunch a couple of years ago, I guess."

"Don't you think people can change?"

"Not you, Maxine. I *know* you haven't changed."

She gave him a wry smile. "Don't be so sure of that, Sam."

He looked at her, and she wondered if somehow he could see Jennie inside. No, he'd be smiling at her, maybe telling her a story about some goofy case that would make her giggle.

After a moment he leaned back in his chair. "How are your legs feeling?"

Her hands were resting on her thighs, and she squeezed them slightly. They were feeling! She pushed a devilish smile from her face and met his gaze. "Maybe you'd better, you know, check them again. Just to make sure." Last time he'd taken her by surprise, but she could still remember well how his hands had felt on her legs.

"Ah, I don't think that's a good idea. You feel fine. I think it's all in your head anyway."

"Well, not exactly," she answered without thinking. "No, you're probably right."

Sam walked around his desk, leaning against the edge facing her. "I know I'm right. Remember—"

"I know, you were married to me for five years," she finished for him, getting the feeling that wasn't going to be an easy block to chip away.

"Well, as fun as this has been, I think you'd better get some rest at home. You probably shouldn't drive for a day or two, and you shouldn't be alone tonight."

Home. She hadn't thought about home. Was the address on Maxine's driver's license correct? Somehow she'd thought of the apartment Jennie shared with Gabrielle. But that wasn't her home anymore. Gabrielle had probably found another roommate by now. And the place was set up for someone in a wheelchair. Maxine smiled. That wasn't her anymore.

"Maybe I should go home with you," she suggested quietly. "Just for tonight."

"I don't think your fiancé would be too hip on that."

Her mouth dropped open, but she clamped it shut again. Oh, geez, she hadn't thought about Maxine having anyone in her life. She'd been so intent on just starting a new life in between her old one and Maxine's. What about children? Friends? Job? Maxine had a life, and now Jennie would have to deal with it. But the fiancé was the immediate concern.

Sam smiled, taking her hand for a moment. Just when she thought he might do something romantic like kiss it, he held it up so she could see the huge diamond ring on her third finger.

"You didn't think I knew about that, eh? Of course, you couldn't have expected me not to find out when it was announced in the paper a month back. What's his name? Armando? No, Armand . . . Santini. The guy who owns the nightclubs all over the city. That's how I knew you hadn't changed. Some older, rich studmuffin is exactly who I'd figured you'd hook up with. That's what you wanted all along." He let go of her hand.

Maxine swallowed a dry lump in her throat. *No, no, I wanted you all along, Sam. You.*

"Hey, don't feel bad about it," Sam said, smiling. "I'm happy for you, I really am. I've never seen this guy, but he sounds sophisticated and foreign. You always did get hot for an accent. I hope it works out for you."

And he meant it. Damn. Not a speck of longing or regret lingered in his eyes. Maxine could walk right back out of his life, and he wouldn't care one bit. Except now Maxine had Jennie's soul in her, and by golly, she was going to make him care a lot more than a bit. But she first had to get rid of this exotic-sounding fiancé of hers. She'd always wanted a ring on her finger, but not this way. And not this big, either.

"I'd take you to his place, but I know how you feel about riding around in my rattletrap, as you used to so affectionately call my Chevelle. So, you want to call this guy, or do you want me to?"

She didn't want to go anywhere with some stranger!

He walked back around to the other side of the desk and lifted the phone. "What's his number?"

"I don't remember it." She pressed her fingers to her forehead. "My head hurts too much."

"Maybe you'd better go to the hospital, then."

"No, it's not that bad. I just don't remember all of the

numbers. He . . . usually calls me, so I don't use it that often.''

Sam pulled out the phone book and riffled through the pages. Then he called information. He gave her a terse look across the desk. ''Okay, thanks anyway.''

''Unlisted, huh?'' she asked, starting to feel hopeful again.

''I figured he was.'' Then he turned to his computer and started tapping keys. ''Lakeview Heights. I should have figured.''

''You found him,'' she said, trying not to sound dismal. Of course—Sam could find anyone.

He turned on the speaker and dialed the number. A man answered, ''Santini residence.'' The man's British accent made her think butler.

Sam looked at her, but her voice wouldn't cooperate. She opened her mouth, but nothing came out.

''Can I speak with Armand, please?'' Sam finally said when the man repeated the words.

''And may I inquire as to who is calling?''

Again Sam looked at her, and she forced the words out. ''This is . . . Maxine.''

The butler's voice changed. ''Maxy, what's going on? Why did some man ask for me?'' The accent was now slightly Italian.

''Armand?''

''Yes, darling. Why do you sound different?''

''I . . . I'm on a speaker phone.'' Did she sound different? ''I need you to come pick me up. I . . . had an accident.''

''Oh, my gosh, huggy buggy! Are you all right?''

She couldn't help but look at Sam, not surprised to find a smirk on his lips at the pet phrase. She tried awfully hard not to cringe. ''I'm fine. I guess. But I probably shouldn't drive. Or be alone tonight in case I faint or something. But if you're busy—''

''Of course I'm not busy, darling! And where else would

you stay, but here at home? Where are you? I'll be right there.''

Oh, geez. She lived with him. "I'm at Sam's Private Eye.'' She reluctantly recited the address.

Silence hovered on the line for a moment. "Your ex-husband's?'' Armand finally said.

"Well, yes.'' The word *ex-husband* sounded so strange to her. She'd never even been married, much less thought about having an ex. "It's a long story. I'll explain later.''

Another pause. "Well, okay, I suppose. I'll be right over. But you're all right?''

"I'll live,'' she said, those words meaning more than she could ever explain. "Good-bye.''

Sam disconnected. "Your fiancé pretends to be his own butler?''

She could only shrug. "Maybe the butler's out sick today.'' She fiddled with the little brass knobs on the arm of her chair. "So, you really think sh—I'm marrying Armand for the money?''

"I never said that.''

"You didn't have to.'' She looked down at her legs, then crossed them. Most women sat with their legs crossed, and she had envied them that. She glanced back up at Sam, who was watching her with curiosity. In a way, she wanted to share these triumphs with him. But she had made her decision, and for better or worse, she was sticking to it. "I didn't marry you for your money,'' she said, knowing that had to be true.

"Sure you did.''

Maxine's mouth dropped open. Sam had money? He'd never let on, the skunk.

"Oh, stop looking so shocked and insulted. I think you liked me well enough; enough to stick it out for five years hoping with a little fertilizer I'd grow up to be like my father.''

He propped his head against his hand. "Ah, I don't blame you. Once you saw my parents' place, and then Ned and

Sharee's place, you wanted the same. Human nature. You were the last woman I ever took over there. What? What's that expression for?''

Maxine had been absorbing his words with a tilted head, but she had no idea what her expression had been. Working with Sam day in and day out, she thought she knew him pretty well. How much else didn't she know about him? She straightened. ''I was wrong.''

''What?''

''It was wrong to try to change you, Sam. How could I have thought such a thing?''

He lifted an eyebrow. ''You do have some brain damage. I don't think I've ever heard you say anything close to the words 'I was wrong' before.''

''Well, I'm saying it now. It's so obvious that this is where you belong, that you're comfortable here. How could anyone try to change who you are?''

''With a chisel and hammer. It started with my parents and ended with you.'' He just sat there looking at her. After a minute he said, ''Don't worry. You'll feel back to yourself after a good night's rest. So, you live with him already, huh?''

''Ah, I guess I do.'' She didn't want to live with Armand. Even if he was rich, tall, and handsome and obviously in love with Maxine-the-first. She wanted the man who was not in love with her. That much hadn't changed.

''Finally going to settle down and have babies?'' Sam asked.

If only she could detect the tiniest trace of jealousy, regret, longing. Nothing. And then she realized what he'd said. ''I don't have any babies?'' Thank goodness. Not that she didn't want them, but at that moment they would make everything more complicated than it already was. ''I mean, I don't have any babies yet, and I don't know—'' Her eyes widened, and a warm rush filled her. Because of her particular injuries, having babies had been out of the question. But now . . . her hand went to her stomach. But now, maybe she could. Her eyes watered as she looked up at Sam. She wanted to have his babies, Sammies and Sammettes running around in diapers. The vision filled her mind, lots of babies crawling all over a cluttered living room. They all had Sam's ash blond hair and his blue eyes, all investigating something of interest. She stifled a giggle when she realized they all had his mustache, too. Even the girls!

"Are you all right?" he asked, leaning forward. "Geez, I didn't mean to pry or anything."

"No," she breathed wiping a bit of moisture from her eyes. "I'm fine, really." She smiled. "I'm really fine." Of course, there was still a chance Maxine-the-first had been fixed so she couldn't have babies, or was incapable of conceiving. But now she had real hope. She leaned forward, facing him over the desk. "Oh, Sam, I want to have babies."

Their eyes locked for a moment, and a slight flush crept up his face to pinken his sharp cheekbones. His mustache twitched. He cleared his throat and moved back as if propelled by rocket fuel. "That's probably something you should take up with Armand. I'm sure he'll be tickled."

"What about you? Don't you want children?"

"Well, first I figured I'd find the lady, then worry about the rugrats later."

"Didn't we ever, you know, talk about having babies?"

"Not really. And why are you asking me? You were there, too."

She glanced down at her hands, still flat on the desk. "I know that. But I don't remember if we had that particular conversation."

"Our marriage was pretty forgettable, wasn't it?" he asked with a grin.

"No, don't say that." She hoped he wouldn't test her. "There were some good things about it, weren't there?"

"Oh, a few."

Romeo's soft whining brought their attention to where he sat on the floor next to her. He was still looking at her.

Maxine patted the edge of the chair, and Romeo put his paws up.

"What's the matter, Romeo?" *Can you see that it's me?*

Sam leaned across the desk watching them. "I've never seen him like this before. I mean, he's been . . . sad since Jennie . . . left. But this is weird. Wait a minute. I know what was bugging me before. How did you know Romeo's name? When you came into the office, you called him by name. You've never seen him before."

"I, ah . . . you told me. Yeah, you told me once. You said how this lady had hired you to find out who was stealing her prize puppies, and how it was really her husband trying to pay off his gambling debts. And when the guy knew he was going to get caught, he took everything from their bank accounts and left, and she couldn't pay you except with one of her bloodhound puppies. And you said a detective ought to have a sniffer dog, so you took the deal."

That was right after she was hired. At the time, she wondered if he took in strays and hired out of pity. She realized later that Sam hired her because he believed in her. That made her believe in herself, too.

He gave her that skeptical look again. "Why would I tell you about my dog? You don't even like dogs."

Romeo tilted his head at her, those droopy eyes filled with adoration. His tail thumped against the wood floor as she continued petting him. His fur felt like silk, and she leaned slowly forward and put her cheek against the top of his head. Funny, she'd thought he'd grow into the floppy skin the way he grew into his huge feet. But the wrinkles stayed . . . well, wrinkled.

"I like dogs plenty now," she said, relishing the feel of Romeo's warmth. When she glanced up, Sam's face was pale, and his eyes looked haunted. "What's wrong?"

"What are you doing?"

"I'm . . ." She realized it was something she'd always done. Something Jennie had done. "I wasn't thinking about it, actually. I told you, I like dogs now."

The color slowly returned to Sam's face, but the haunted look remained. "I guess you do. But I still don't remember telling you about him."

"Well, if you didn't, how did I know all that, then?"

He seemed to consider that for a moment. "You got me on that one. I guess I did."

She smiled triumphantly and gave Romeo another rub with her cheek. He smelled like dog shampoo, and she pictured Sam kneeling beside the tub giving Romeo a bath. And then she closed her eyes and pictured Sam rubbing his fingers through her lathered hair. *That's a girl* his voice soothed in her mind. *Doesn't that feel good?* Could even Heaven be much better than that?

And then, *We'll get rid of those nasty fleas.* Her eyes snapped open, and it was her turn to blush as she caught sight of Sam watching her. "Daydreaming," she offered.

"Hello?" an Italian voice called from the front room a short while later.

Oh, no. The dreaded fiancé. Romeo woofed softly and ambled out to see who was there. Maxine slowly stood and followed Sam, who waited to make sure she wasn't going to fall on her face. They stopped when they saw the man standing by her desk.

"Armand?" they both said simultaneously, then looked at each other.

She had pictured an Italian Stallion. So had Sam, obviously. In actuality, Armand was more like an Italian . . . mouse. He was a bit shorter than Maxine (and a *lot* shorter than Sam), with thin, dark hair that receded from a wide, pale forehead. He wore wire-rimmed, round glasses and a Mickey Mouse bow tie with his dark jacket.

The man's concerned expression was on Maxine as he stepped forward and extended his hand to Sam. "Yes, I am Armand. You must be Sam. I have heard much about you." Then he walked over to Maxine and took her hands in his, studying her with worried gray eyes. "And you, my kis-sums. What happened? Are you okay?"

In trying to hide her astounded and amused expression, she wore an overly concerned one. "I . . . I don't remember what happened, exactly. I have a gash on my forehead." She lifted her hair and Armand made a hissing noise. When she glanced over at Sam, she saw that he wasn't trying a bit to hide his grin. Doggone it, how was she supposed to look serious when he was standing there grinning? Even if it was rather funny in a strange way.

"It looks so big," Armand was saying, staring at her bandage.

"It is. But I'll be fine."

"Did this happen at home? Perhaps in the greenhouse?"

"Why do you say that?" Sam asked, stepping closer.

Armand took a step back. "Because the flower box that was mounted beneath a window over the entrance of the greenhouse came loose and fell through the glass to the walkway below. When I returned from the city—"

"Returned?" Sam asked.

"Yes, from a meeting at one of my clubs. Apparently someone had taken down the wrong time. There was no meeting. When I returned, I saw the flower box on the floor, and my Maxine was gone. No one was even around to ask what had happened. But the blood worried me the most. I called the hospitals, but there was no one that fit your de-scription." He took her hands and buried his face against them. "I was so worried."

She looked up at Sam, who was watching the display with that same degree of amusement. He removed the smile and replaced it with his investigator's look again.

"Armand, did you look at the mounting of the flower box?"

Armand stopped smothering his face in her hands. "No, I didn't look. Why do you ask that? Are you suggesting someone dropped the box on my huggy buggy on pur-pose?"

Sam's mustache twitched, but the threatening smile didn't break loose. "I'm not suggesting anything. Just asking." He shrugged. "It's sort of an ingrained thing to get the details."

"No one would hurt my Maxine. I just can't imagine it."

She could only shrug when both men looked at her. "I don't remember what happened."

"The only reason I'm questioning it is because Maxine came here right after it happened. Armand, I can assure you she doesn't normally pop in like this, which makes me wonder why she wanted to talk to me." Sam flicked the button on an answering machine she'd never seen before, then shrugged into his coat. "I'd like to take a look at it, if you don't mind." He smiled. "For my own peace of mind."

Maxine let out an audible sigh of relief. Sam was going with them! "I'll feel better if you do," she said to cover.

Armand took her hands in his. "Whatever makes you feel better, kissums. You know that."

An immediate annullment of their engagement, she suggested mentally. She slid her feet into the pumps by the door, testing out their solidness before putting her weight on them.

"Did you drive your car, Maxine?" Sam asked as they headed out, Romeo jingling behind them.

"I, uh, don't know." Did she have a car?

"I saw it out there when I arrived," Armand said much to Maxine's relief.

Sam paused at the landing of the stairs, his knuckles white as he gripped the railing. Armand was already walking down the first step, but Maxine hesitated, too. The only time she'd gone down those stairs she'd gone backward. She hadn't walked down any stairs in twelve years. Armand stopped and looked at both of them.

"Is there something wrong with these stairs?" he asked, looking down the rest of the way with trepidation.

Sam turned abruptly. "I'll meet you at the entrance. I'm taking the elevator."

Maxine watched him walk away, then looked down the

stairs again. Something burned deep inside her as she watched his back retreat to the end of the short hallway. Those terrible moments when she'd fallen down flashed through her mind, when he'd tried to catch her hand.

"Sam!"

"Jennie! No!"

The words echoed in her mind.

"Would somebody please tell me what the big deal is with these stairs?" Armand said, stamping his foot.

"Someone died here," she said softly, her mind filled with the images of pain and screams. And Sam holding her. "Jennie died here." She blinked, bringing herself back to the present. "She's dead now. For good."

Armand's arched eyebrows knitted together. "People who die usually are gone for good. That's the way it works. Do you want to take the elevator?"

She heard the doors slide open. "Wait!" She balanced herself with the railing, but her legs carried her swiftly down the corridor where Sam held the door open. Armand followed behind her.

"What's wrong?" Sam asked as they descended two floors.

"The stairs gave her the creeps," Armand said, taking her hands in his again.

"Didn't you take them up to my office before?" Sam asked.

"Yes, but everything was different then."

Sam looked as if he were about to ask something, but the doors slid open and they walked out. Snow had piled up everywhere, filling Maxine with dread until she realized it didn't mean anything anymore. She wasn't housebound when more than a few inches of snow fell; she no longer had to call Sam and feel terrible about not being able to come in. It was beautiful, just the way it was when she was a kid. She had the sudden urge to start a snowball fight, to hear her feet crunching in the snow as she ran to hide behind a good launching site.

"Okay, where's your car?" Sam asked, scouting the area.

Maxine's expression went blank. She had a van, specially equipped for her wheelchair, but that wouldn't be there anymore. Her will stipulated that it be donated to a nonprofit handicapped transportation service.

"Right over there," Armand said, saving her from looking like a complete dunce.

He walked over to a bright aqua Sunbird convertible. A sports car. She'd never been able to own one of those before, because most of them didn't easily fit her wheelchair inside. She peered in the window. Even though she suspected it wouldn't be there, she smiled at the absence of the stick that allowed her to control the gas and brake pedals with her hand.

"How are we going to get your car home?" Armand asked. "I don't want you driving, darling. And I'm afraid to leave either of our cars here for long." He looked worriedly around, as if expecting goons to slink from every crevice.

"Ah, this area's not all that bad," Sam said. "It's in the middle of one of those neighborhood renourishment projects. But just so you and your . . . huggy buggy will feel better, I can drive Maxine's car out to your place if you'll get me back here."

Maxine didn't miss that twitch of Sam's mustache at her nickname. She narrowed her eyes at him, but he was looking at Armand, whose tightened expression relaxed at Sam's offer.

"Perfect. I'll pay for a cab to bring you back." He obviously hadn't noticed the twitch.

"Fine with me. No one will bother my car." He nodded toward the green Chevelle parked a few cars away.

Maxine gave him the set of keys from her bag, hoping he'd be able to figure out which one went with her car. Of course he would—he was a detective, after all! Her feet crunched on the icy sidewalk as she stepped around to the passenger side of the car. The pumps she wore looked expensive and elegant, even with the damp spots the snow created. Oh, to wear heels!

"Uh, huggy buggy," Armand's tentative voice asked. She paused by her car door. "Why are you riding with him?"

She looked across the roof at Sam. Because she loved him, she thought. Because she didn't know Armand. "Oops. Wasn't thinking." She walked carefully across the road to the black Mercedes where Armand held the door open for her.

Despite the overcast skies, Maxine felt sunshine surround her. Maybe Sam would determine that Armand's place was unsafe and make her go with him.

Armand's hand slipped around hers. It felt clammy, and she grimaced but didn't pull away. She wanted to break off this engagement nice and easily, so she didn't hurt Armand too much. Not that she had much experience with such things, but she'd figure a way out.

"You were going to ride with him," Armand said a few minutes later, giving her a solemn look. His lips were too thin to be considered in a pout, but it was close enough.

"I wasn't thinking." She pointed to the bandage. "You know, the head thing. I still feel a little woozy."

His fingers tightened more around her own. "Of course, darling." He glanced in the rearview mirror, making Maxine turn around to see Sam following behind them. "I thought you didn't like him."

She turned back to Armand. "I'm sure I never said that. I mean, I was married to him once."

"Well, maybe you didn't say that outright. You said he was slovenly. A Neanderthal, you called him once. You said he should have been a lawyer like his father and brother, but he insisted on throwing his life away on some private-detective ego trip."

"I said all that?"

"Yes." He lifted his chin slightly, though he didn't let

go of her hand. "So if you felt that way about him, why did you go to his office today?"

"I trust him. I must have thought there was something to talk to him about." *Why, why did she go to Sam's office?*

He squeezed her hand even more. "Kissums, you don't think there's anything to be afraid of at our home, do you? Maybe you were overreacting." He cringed. "You do that sometimes, you know. Just a tiny bit." He seemed to relax some when she didn't fly into a rage at his observation.

"Maybe I was. I mean, it was probably an accident, but I do feel better having Sam check it out. I just wish I could remember why I went to his office."

"I would like to know that, too." Armand glanced in the rearview mirror again. "He's better looking than I pictured him. I was caught up in that Neanderthal thing. You used to tell me stories about his junk-food eating habits, so I imaged someone rather, er, larger. More like that guy in the Monty Python movie who ate so much, he exploded. Your ex-husband looks . . . quite fit."

"Yeah, he does, doesn't he?" she said with a smile. "I mean, he obviously works out." Her smile faded when she turned to Armand. "But doesn't he look a little *too* thin? Especially right here in the face." She demonstrated on her own face, running her fingers along her chin. "And his eyes looked dull. They usually have a sparkle to them. I wonder if he's sick." The thought made her want to fix some home-made chicken soup like she did when he got the flu once.

Armand lifted an eyebrow at her. "I didn't realize you cared so much."

"Well, we parted on good terms, you know. It's hard not to care a little."

But something had been happening with him lately, even before her . . . death. A restlessness had permeated his content features. During their Thursday-night dinner, he'd changed his mind four times before settling on his usual anyway. And the day before her accident, he'd walked out of his office and said her name. She'd turned to see what he needed, and he'd simply stood there looking at her in the strangest way.

"What's wrong?" she'd asked him.

He seemed to be in a spell, standing there for a minute before finally asking, "Do you ever feel as though something is missing in your life, but you can't quite pinpoint what it is? Something inside, I mean."

"Sometimes," she answered, though she knew what was missing, both internally and externally.

He'd nodded slowly, then added a paragraph to the report she was typing. Sometimes he'd ask her deep questions out of the blue, but he'd never looked quite so . . . lost before. At thirty-two, he was too young to be having a mid-life crisis.

Armand finally let go of her hand when he had to maneuver in traffic, jarring her out of her memory. Five-o'clock traffic was creeping onto the main thoroughfares. She stretched her fingers, letting them dry. A minute later, he snapped up her hand again.

"Don't be mad when I say this, kissums, but honestly, I'm tired of hearing about Sam. Let him look at the flower box and leave our lives, all right?"

"Well . . ."

"And please don't tell me you've invited him to our wedding." She stiffened, and he looked over at her. "You have, haven't you?"

"No, I was only thinking about inviting him, that's all." Wedding? She couldn't marry this man. By the time it was supposed to happen, she'd be long gone from his life. But when was that? "It's not far from now, is it?"

He squeezed her hand again. "Only two months away."

"Two months?"

"Yes, isn't it exciting? And to think when we started planning, it was a whole five months away. It felt like forever. Time is flying right along, isn't it? Soon you'll be Mrs. Santini. What's the matter, darling? You look pale."

"It's my head." She pointed, then winced in pain when

she misjudged the distance and poked her bandage.

His eyebrow bobbed up and down, and he leaned closer. "Don't you worry, darling. Mr. Wiggles will make you feel better when we get home."

"Oh, joy," she said with a forced smile, cringing inside. What was a Mr. Wiggles? Her face flushed when she remembered a friend confiding that her boyfriend had named his sexual organ. *Oh, geez!* If he thought *that* was going to make her feel better, he had another think coming. Armand and Maxine were probably intimate since they were on a cutesy-name basis with his anatomy. And they did live together, after all.

She turned away so he wouldn't see the expression that emerged on her face. Well, she was going to play the headache routine to the absolute hilt.

Chapter 3

This was just too weird, Sam thought as he drove Maxine's car to Maxine and her fiancé's house. He hadn't seen her in years, and all of a sudden she shows up sprawled out on his landing. Well, it was a distraction anyway. Life had been so damned bleak and senseless lately. Most likely Maxine was overreacting, something she tended to do anyway. Still, she'd never run to him over anything else. He didn't want his conscience nagging him later, so he'd get this over with now and satisfy himself and her that it was only an accident. He glanced over at Romeo, his pancake ears swaying with the car's motion.

"Well, you sure liked her. She doesn't like dogs, you know. In fact, I'm surprised she didn't have a hissy fit when she saw you jump in her car. Don't be such a sucker for a cheek rub on your head." He didn't let himself think of other cheeks rubbing that same head. Instead he tuned in a blues station on the radio.

Romeo licked his chops and settled down onto the seat with a dog sigh. That hound hadn't looked so relaxed since—Sam cut the thought before it finished. He had thrashed himself about Jennie's death, about not being able to save her. He had raised holy hell to find out who dripped the oil outside his office door. But it didn't matter. Nothing would bring her back, not any amount of anger or guilt or blaming. He'd played the scene through his mind so many times, it invaded his dreams and his subconscious. So he'd stopped thinking about her, tried to pretend it never happened. He knew that it slighted Jennie's memory, but it was the only way he could deal with it.

Once in a while, it all rushed back on him like it did earlier when he'd looked down those stairs, and they were filled with people trying to save Jennie. Mostly he had it under control. But something else had happened when he'd finally succeeded at closing himself off. The joy of life had slipped away, too. The business he loved held no satisfaction for him. Even sitting at the Houndog Cafe listening to the blues didn't fill his soul with the sweet melancholy it used to. He just felt empty.

Now he was following his ex-wife to her fiancé's house to check out the possibility of foul play. Somewhere inside he found a smile when he remembered seeing Armand for the first time.

He turned to Romeo. "Huggy buggy! Do you think a woman actually likes being called that? A woman like Maxine? Yeah, probably. Oh, man." He scratched the dog's head. "Maxine, I hope you're happy. You're long out of my orbit." His voice grew lower. "Maybe you always were."

They weren't far from his parents' and Ned's homes when they turned down a driveway to a house that blended right in with the stark whiteness of the snow. It was a large, two-story structure with small windows and a greenhouse sprouting directly from the side. The front entrance was an alcove carved into the white stucco in a decorative oval. Scattered about what was normally the yard were several white statues that looked like cartoon figures in crazy poses. Boy, did Maxine know how to pick 'em.

She stood in front of the door, holding her coat tightly around her as she waited for him to approach. She looked a little lost, something he'd never seen on Maxine. Her cheeks were red from the cold, blending in with her hair.

She clutched at his arm when he reached the entrance.

"Thanks so much for coming," she said softly.

"No problem." Truthfully, he had nowhere else to go that evening, nothing else to do. And that's the way he liked it, nice and quiet.

She stayed there until Armand cleared his throat from just inside the doorway. She turned slowly and walked in with Sam and Romeo following.

"Oh, no you don't!" Armand shouted when he turned around at the jingling noise Romeo made. "That thing can't come in here."

"Then take us the outside way. There is an outside entrance, isn't there?"

Armand's mouth twisted. "The white orchid collection I bought a few months ago is blocking the doorway. Through the house is the only way to get to the greenhouse right now." He stared down at the dog. "But I will not have any hair-shedding, slobbery dogs in my home."

"Then we'll have to go, because I can't leave him out in the car. He'll freeze."

"Do you realize how many ... *things* live on a dog? Creatures, dander, bugs." Armand shivered violently.

"He doesn't have fleas," Sam said, feeling a little defensive. "And he had a bath two days ago."

"Doesn't matter. They still have bugs and things."

Sam leaned against the door. "I hate to tell you this, but we all have *things* on us. Microorganisms that live in our hair, our eyebrows and eyelashes, and no matter how much we clean ourselves, they never go away." Sam wiggled his fingers. "And they look real scary when they're magnified, like something out of a sci-fi movie."

"He's clean," Maxine told Armand, who looked horrified at what Sam had said. "I petted him earlier. Look how his hair shines. It looks so silky and soft."

Why was Maxine looking at him when she said those last two sentences?

Armand looked down at her hands. "With which hand did you pet him?"

She lifted the right one.

"Maxine, you should have told me," he said in a low, urgent voice. "I could have *held* that hand."

"I also rubbed my cheek against him," she said, making the little man cringe even more. "And I kissed his forehead. Armand, they're only going to walk through to the greenhouse," she pushed. "And I'll feel a lot better if Sam takes a look at things."

The woman still had a way with words, Sam thought. Only her messages were mixed. Why would she tell Armand she'd kissed Romeo when he was so adverse to the fact that she'd even touched the dog? And why did she keep flashing those glances in Sam's direction?

"Oh, all right," Armand finally relented. "But I'll have to have the place fumigated tomorrow." He turned and led the way through a house so white, Sam had to squint.

Even Romeo looked up at him, as if questioning his motives for being there. Sam could only shrug in response. White tile floors, no carpets at all; white leather furniture, white entertainment center. The only thing that broke up the vast whiteness were the marionettes and puppets, some in glass cases. Must be a hobby; some looked rather old with tiny cracks in their surface. Personally, they gave him the creeps, watching with their beady eyes as he went by.

The foursome wended through a large kitchen where Maxine paused to look around in delight. No doubt planning many a cozy meal for her and her little hubby. Not making them, mind you. Just planning them.

Romeo paused to scratch at his floppy ear, and Sam nudged him gently with the toe of his shoe. No need to freak the garbanzo bean out. Armand glanced down at the jingling sound, but missed the scratching. Romeo's foot was still poised, though, as he gave Sam a puzzled look.

Armand made a quick call to summon a cab to the house for Sam before continuing on. A glass door led out to the greenhouse, the first bit of real color he'd seen since walking in the house. There flowers bloomed left and right, easing the strain on his eyes with their pale shades of peach and yellow. Of course, the floor was a white decking. Cold air seeped down from a jagged hole above them.

"Is there some reason you don't have any colors in your house?" Sam asked, stepping around the broken flower box on the ground in front of him.

"I'm allergic to colors, particularly bright colors. Pink is my worst. Instant headache." He pinched the bridge of his nose to demonstrate.

Sam glanced at Maxine, who was giving Armand the same disbelieving look Sam probably had on his face. Well, shouldn't she know this if she was marrying the guy? He focused on the flower box instead, counting the minutes before he could put these wacky people out of his life.

Shards of glass spread out everywhere, mixed with dirt and dead plant pieces. The white metallic container was bent. Sam looked up through the star-shaped hole the box had dropped down through. On the second floor, outside one of those small windows, was the faint outline where the box had hung. It had crashed through the glass roof and hit Maxine on the forehead. He looked up at her as she stared at the mess on the ground.

"How did you survive this?" he asked.

She jerked her head upright, as if caught doing something wrong. "I don't know. It must have been a miracle."

Something bitter burned through his stomach. Why couldn't Jennie have been given a miracle, too? Heaven knew she deserved it. He pushed the thought away.

"There you are," a woman's booming voice said. "Mr. Santini, I tried to get you at the club offices, but you'd already left." She was a tall, pale-skinned woman wearing a—what else—white dress and cap. "I heard a scary crashing noise earlier and found this mess out here. And the blood. But I didn't know what had happened, or if I should call the police. So I waited until you returned."

"That's fine, Aida," Armand said to what might be the maid. "This box fell on my kissums here." He grasped Maxine's hand and pulled her so close they appeared sealed together at their side. "But thank God she's all right."

Aida's eyes widened. "My gosh, what happened?"

"She doesn't remember," Sam found himself answering for her. "That's what we're trying to figure out. Maxine was already gone when you came out here?"

"Yes. She must have gotten right up and left. It's a miracle she wasn't smooshed like a pancake," Aida said, looking up through the broken glass.

Sam didn't want to hear any more about miracles. "Let me take a look at that window."

He headed back into the house and followed Armand up the white stairs. Armand kept glancing back, giving Romeo insolent looks, but Sam ignored him. So did Romeo. Sam was too busy watching the puppets in the alcoves watching him. Until he realized Maxine wasn't following them. When he turned behind him, she was still standing at the bottom of the stairs, looking as if going up those stairs was going to be a challenge.

"Still feeling weak or dizzy?"

She shook her head. "It's . . . it's nothing. Really." She grasped the white railing and took one step, then another. Well, she was smiling. She couldn't be that hurt, he supposed. When she reached the top of the landing, she turned around and looked behind her. "I did it."

Then she turned and gave him the prettiest smile he'd ever seen on her, and he was having a hard time pulling his gaze away from her. She met his eyes squarely, her smile softening to something more intimate. His stomach tightened involuntarily. There was something about the look in her eyes, something—

"The room is in here," Armand broke in, taking Maxine's hand again and leading her into a room on the left.

The man was positively clingy, but Sam remembered

Maxine being into that touchy-feely stuff when they were married. Well, she'd found the perfect guy, then.

The windows themselves were some fancy-dangle things, and Sam had to have Armand open them. Sam leaned out the window and looked at the brackets that had held the flower box. They were rusted to nubs.

"There's the problem," he said, turning to Armand and Maxine. "The brackets deteriorated to the point where they couldn't hold the weight anymore. Maxine, you must have just had bad timing to walk under at the exact moment it gave out."

Maxine leaned out to look, too. The wool pants tightened over the curve of her buttocks, and Sam chastised himself for even noticing.

"I guess you're right," she said, pulling herself back in. "Bad luck and miracles. They seem to go hand in hand."

Sam turned away and headed out of the room. "Why don't we take a look at the other flower box just to make sure it doesn't need to be taken down?"

"That's Sally's room," Armand said, opening her door. He squinted as he took a step inside.

Sally's suite of rooms was a blitz of color. Flowered wallpaper with a matching comforter, mauve carpet, and silk flowers everywhere. It was a striking change from the stark white everywhere else.

Sam stepped over piles of clothes and magazines to the window, remembering how Armand had opened it before. The metal was cold on his bare hands as he lifted the heavy box filled with dirt and looked at the bracket holding it up.

"Yep, this one's beginning to give way, too. Better have it taken down right away." He turned to Maxine who was looking out the window. "See, just an accident. Nothing to worry about."

She breathed out in relief. "Thank goodness."

Sam headed down the stairs again. Usually in a strange place, Romeo followed literally on Sam's heels. Now the darn dog was Maxine's shadow as she slowly walked back down the stairs. And they called them faithful beasts. Hmph.

At the front door, Sam turned to Armand. "Well, good luck. I wish you and Maxine the best." Maxine was looking pale again. "You'd better lie down. Get lots of rest." And to Armand: "If she feels dizzy or disoriented, get her to the hospital immediately. I trust you'll take good care of her."

Armand had her hands tucked in his. The only time he'd let go of them was when she'd gone up and down the stairs and used the railing. "I won't let her out of my sight."

Sam swore she cringed at that, but he was probably imagining it. She tried to wriggle free. "Sam, won't you stay for dinner?"

"Oh no." He toned down his exhuberance. "No, thank you. Romeo and I have two TV dinners with our names on them at home. New and improved with honest-to-goodness dairy cheese." He smiled, because he didn't want her to feel sorry for him.

"You *and* Romeo?" Armand asked.

"He doesn't like dog food. I feed him whatever I'm eating." At Armand's surprised expression, Sam added, "Hey, would *you* eat that stuff?"

"Well, I . . . you . . . no, of course not."

"How about a drink, then?" Maxine broke in, giving him an imploring look.

Why did she sound so desperate? Armand looked a mite irritated, brows furrowed and fists clenched with Maxine's hands locked inside.

"No, I really have to get going. Besides, the cab is outside." He felt compelled to touch her arm for some reason, but held back. Armand had her firmly secured anyway. Not even a tornado would have wrenched her out of his grasp. "Everything will be fine. Take care of yourself, Maxine."

Their gazes held for a moment, giving him that strange tingling sensation in his stomach again. He broke eye contact by glancing down at Romeo, sitting at Maxine's feet.

"Ready, boy?" He stuffed his hands in his pockets and headed out the door.

During the cab ride back to the office, he mulled over the scene of the accident. It looked harmless. But something didn't sit right with him. It was because of Maxine, that was all. That personal-involvement thing tended to throw things into a different perspective. There was no reason to think it was anything but an accident.

Armand patted her hand as soon as Sam closed the door. "Well, that's done with. Do you feel better, darling?"

She was finally able to pull her hands free of his, using the excuse of pulling her hair off her neck. "Yes, I do." She wanted to go to the window and watch the cab drive away, but that seemed inappropriate. With Sam gone, she felt terribly alone.

"You don't think he was serious about things living in our eyelashes, do you?" He was rubbing his nail over his eyebrow and studying it with narrowed eyes.

"I don't know," she said with a shrug, looking around the room. Exactly fourteen pairs of eyes looked back at her. Were the puppets Maxine's or Armand's? Since this was probably Armand's house before Maxine moved in, she had to guess the puppets were his. After all, he'd had special niches built into the house for many of them.

"You didn't show Sam your collection of puppets," she ventured to confirm. She walked over to one of the glass cases where large blue eyes stared back, an openmouthed smile of perpetuity on its face. She hoped they weren't hers. They were icky.

"The man wasn't a guest, kissums. He was here on business. Now, *please,* can we stop talking about him?"

She turned to Armand from the safe distance of the puppet case. "Did I really talk about him a lot?"

"Yes. I know this probably isn't the best time to bring it up, but it has bothered me for a while now. Are you hungry?"

She wanted to keep talking about Sam, but obviously Armand wasn't into it. "A little." That kitchen was awesome. She was eager to whip up something exotic and complicated, something to take her mind off being here alone with Armand. Did Maxine cook?

"Why don't I make something for us?" She could think up a dish that she'd have to go out to get the ingredients for. Why, she could drag this dinner thing out the entire evening, going to the store, keeping busy in the kitchen and needing her hands to work so he couldn't grab them. In fact, if he got too close, she could create a little flour storm to send him away. Why, she could lose him completely in this house if he were covered in white. '

His laugh was almost a sputter. Unfortunately, her comment was somehow interpreted as an invitation for him to come over and take her hands into custody again.

"You must have bumped your brain, darling. You are the same Maxine who told me on our first date that all the cooking you do is toast, aren't you? Champagne toasts."

She tilted her head. "Well . . ."

"Come, darling." As if she had a choice, with him pulling her along as if she were some child. "Aida," he said, walking into that kitchen that made her fingers itch to pull down some of those copper pots. "Are the children due in soon?"

Children? As in young and more than one? Maybe this Sally?

Aida glanced at the clock. Yep, the white clock. "They should be home anytime, Mr. Santini. They called from the city about half an hour ago."

Armand rubbed Maxine's hands. "Good. What do you feel like eating tonight, kissums?" He walked to an enormous refrigerator that only had one door. It turned out to be a freezer crammed full with packages wrapped in cellophane. He pulled one out and read the label. "Ravioli?" He pulled out a few more. "Beef kabob. Beef burgundy. Chicken cordon bleu." Above each label was the name Anatoli's Gourmet Meals. Beneath the food type was cooking directions, both microwave and oven.

She glanced around at the fancy kitchen, then at Armand. "Nobody cooks in this kitchen?"

"Of course we cook." He lifted one of the packages. "These. Darling, you love our meal plan." He grinned. "Remember, you said it was one of the reasons you were marrying me, though I certainly hope you were kidding." He kissed the tip of her nose, then touched one of the cold packages to it. "Weren't you?"

"Oh, of course. I'm sure I was kidding."

Well, if Maxine-the-first didn't like to cook, then she could understand why the frozen meals appealed to her so much. "Ravioli is fine. But why do you have such a well-equipped kitchen?"

He rolled his eyes. "Because I like the illusion of being able to cook. Maxine, really, I wonder if that cut on your head didn't do a little more damage than you think."

"Well, I don't feel . . . normal, exactly. I'll be all right, though." As soon as she could get out of there.

She heard a noise at the front door, and Armand rubbed his hands together. "Oh, good. The children are back. Aida, why don't you start dinner? You know what James and Sally like."

Maxine turned to greet the children, bending down a little. The children turned out to be in their early twenties. The one who must be James looked like a younger version of his father, except he had more hair and was taller. Sally had waves of thick, long black hair and vivid green eyes. She must have taken after her mother.

"Maxine, I wasn't expecting to find you here," James said, hanging up his coat near the front door. His frigid gaze held her for a moment before he shifted it toward his father and forced a smile. "I thought you were both going out for dinner."

Armand took her hands in his again. "There was an accident earlier today. We're lucky to have Maxine with us now.''

"What happened, Daddykins?" Sally said, walking up to Maxine with concern in her eyes.

"The flower box fell from the guest bedroom right through the greenhouse roof and hit Maxine on the forehead. It was a miracle she survived."

"Oh, gosh. How horrible!" Sally said when Armand lifted Maxine's bangs to show her the bandage. "How did the flower box fall?"

"The brackets holding the box rusted right through." Armand shook his head. "It was a freak accident. But the future Mrs. Santini is going to be just fine." He patted her hand.

"Aren't we lucky," James muttered, going up the stairs with terse movements. So, both of the *children* lived at home still. And one of them wasn't all that thrilled that his father was marrying her. Well, he didn't have a thing to worry about. She'd play along tonight, and tomorrow she'd break it off with him and find someplace to stay.

During dinner, Maxine thought about Sam eating his TV dinner while they ate what was basically a gourmet version of the same. She'd much rather be in his apartment than this sterile dining room with these strangers. She smiled faintly when she pictured Romeo sitting at the table with Sam eating his own Salisbury steak and mashed potatoes.

James and Sally discussed a few financial aspects of opening another nightclub in a newly refurbished area of Chicago. Apparently James managed Temptations, one of the dance clubs. Sally managed Belly Aches, the comedy club next store. The more she listened, the more she realized they didn't do the hands-on managing, but oversaw various operations at all the clubs. Temptations and Belly Aches seemed to be their pet businesses.

Armand cut his ravioli into perfectly sized pieces with his fork and knife. He looked up at his children. "Neither of you called this morning and left a message with Aida about some emergency meeting at the club offices did you?''

James shook his head, setting down his bottle of Coke. ''No. I knew you were spending the afternoon with Maxine. I wouldn't have bothered you, knowing how important that was.'' His cool, gray eyes alighted on hers for a moment.

Sally tossed her black hair back over her shoulders. ''Besides, we didn't have any emergencies that I know of. James has everything running smoothly,'' she added with a proud smile.

''As much as I'm allowed to run,'' he added in a monotone voice.

If they were trying to get something across to Armand, it was lost on him.

''Aida said it sounded a little like you, James, but that the caller didn't leave a name. She probably just assumed it was you. I got to the offices and no one was looking for me. If it hadn't been for that call, I would have been here when my kissums had her run-in with the flower box.''

James shrugged. ''Wasn't me. I was in a meeting all day with the real estate people talking about the new location.''

''And I was interviewing people all day,'' Sally said. ''Now I have about a hundred people to call for references. I wish there was a way to tell if they were being honest or not.''

Maxine was going to suggest having Sam look into their backgrounds, but she decided mixing her past and present any more than she had wasn't such a good idea. But she was still concerned about the call.

''You mean someone called to summon you for some emergency meeting, and no one was there?''

Armand waved it off. ''It must have been a misunderstanding.''

A phone call that pulled Armand away just before the accident. While Maxine was perfectly happy believing it *was* an accident, she couldn't discount the coincidence. She watched Sally telling Armand about some of her stranger applicants. James tapped the tines of his fork on the table, his lips tight and eyes narrowed.

Sally chattered on. "And so this guy says, 'And if you ever have a comedian cancel at the last minute, I'm kind of funny. I can, you know, fill in.' He sounded a little like Andrew Dice Clay. Anyway, I told him that our wait staff never double as our entertainment, club policy. So he got up and walked out!"

James was looking back and forth between her and Armand. He let his fork drop to the tablecloth with a dull thud. Riveting his gaze to his father, he said, "Isn't anyone going to comment on how strange it is that the flower box decided to fall on Maxine the same way—"

"No," Armand interrupted firmly. "No one is going to comment on that."

Maxine looked around the table. Everyone had gone silent, their expressions grim.

"The same way as what?" she asked at last, forcing a light tone in her voice.

"Nothing, my sweet," Armand said, patting her hand.

Now why did she get the feeling that wasn't so? Sally launched into another conversation about something that happened at work, and the icy tension melted away. Maxine was still stuck on James's comment. Had there been another accident? Another threat to Maxine's life?

Maxine's attention was drawn back to the table when Armand said, "Sally, I'd like to do a show some night. Maybe next weekend. I'm getting the itch again."

"A show?" Maxine said, taken off guard.

"Yes. With Mr. Wiggles."

"*What?*" She'd never been to Belly Aches or Temptations, but she didn't think either place was *that* kind of club. She didn't even want to think about the itch part.

"That'd be great, Daddykins," Sally said, ignoring Maxine's look of disgust. "They love Mr. Wiggles. We'll pick a date and start distributing fliers to build the publicity.

We'll use the same promotion tape as last time for the radio spots."

Armand leaned closer to Maxine. "You can be my lovely assistant."

She moved away, her eyes widened. "That's disgusting."

When everyone looked at her as if *she* were the strange one, she placed her napkin to the side of her plate. "Excuse me. I'm not feeling well."

"That's obvious," James said, as she stood and turned from the table.

Not knowing exactly where to go in the house, and not feeling much like taking a stroll through the snow, she walked to the door leading to the greenhouse. She easily navigated the two steps down, always an obstacle in her wheelchair. She could not tolerate talking about Armand doing some sex show with his . . . children. Ugh, just the thought.

Aida was scraping up the dirt where the flower box had been. She'd already dumped the box itself in a large trash bin.

"Oh, it's you," Aida said, grunting with exertion as the shovel scraped along the white deck floor. She looked more like a wrestler than a maid, with a broad torso and thick arms. "Surprised to see you in here, of all places." The woman nodded upward where a blue tarp now covered the hole. "I wouldn't come out here with a ten-foot pole if it happened to me. Nope, no way."

"Well, it couldn't possibly happen again, could it?"

Aida dumped the last shovelful of dirt into the bin. "About as likely as lightning striking twice, I suppose." She leaned on the shovel, studying Maxine. "You seem different since the accident. More pensive than your usual bubbly self. They say a taste of death can change a person. Is that true?"

"You can't imagine how much."

"Mr. Santini would sure be broken up if you'd gone." Aida nodded upward, meaning Heaven and not the hole,

Maxine presumed. "He's rather fond of you."

And Aida sure couldn't figure out why, her tone and expression said.

"Yes, I gathered. I mean, I'm fond of him, too."

"I hope you mean that. He's a swell guy. You'll never find another one like him."

"Oh, I'm positive of that."

"I'd hate to see his little heart broken." Aida studied her for a moment, then pushed herself upright with the handle. "Well, I'm going inside now. It's a little chilly out here. Don't stay out too long. You might survive the flower box only to catch your death of a cold."

Aida passed Armand as he headed out, closing the door behind him. "Darling, what is the matter? You were acting so strange in there. What are you doing out here?" He glanced around, as if the greenhouse should host bad spirits against her. His hands deftly found hers again, a moment before she'd have tucked them in her pockets.

Did Maxine know about his little shows? Obviously. "It's just been a long day, and my head hurts. Terribly," she added, in case he entertained any thoughts of bringing out Mr. Wiggles later that night as he'd previously threatened.

"I'm sorry, kissums. How very insensitive of me; I should have known. Why don't you lie down? I'll get you some aspirin."

Escape! And sleep wasn't sounding all that bad at the moment. It had been one heck of a long day. "That sounds wonderful."

He led her past the dining room where James and Sally watched her with curiosity. "I'm just not feeling well," she offered lamely with a shrug of her shoulders.

"I hope you're feeling better soon," Sally called out.

"Darling, they understand. You know, I think they adore you as much as I do."

Sally maybe, but James didn't seem fond of Maxine. Well, she wouldn't have to deal with any of them after tomorrow. The white carpet squished silently beneath her feet as he led her from the tiled living room to a hallway off the main area. The house was bigger than it looked from the outside. Maxine hoped they had separate bedrooms. When she walked inside, she had a feeling they did not.

The room was huge, dominated by a white bed. On the walls were pictures of dummies, and if that weren't bad enough, there were several on display in here, too. Apparently Maxine hadn't yet put in her own touches. Except for the one picture of Maxine on the nightstand. She was smiling up at the camera as she sat at a little table in the sun.

"I'll get you a nightgown," he said, disappearing into an enormous closet. A moment later he emerged, holding up two lacy specimens. "Which one do you want?"

Maxine dropped down to the bed. "Er, I don't feel like anything that . . . revealing tonight." No need to give Mr. Wiggles any encouragement. Her forehead was throbbing without even having to pretend she had a headache. "Something plainer, perhaps."

He disappeared again, reemerging with a long T-shirt that made Maxine breathe out in relief. It had the swirly words *Belly Aches* on the pocket.

"That's perfect." She snatched it up and walked into the hallway leading to the master bathroom. "Er, where's the door?"

He laughed. "There's no door, you know that. You're not getting modest on me, cherry lips, are you?" He tilted his head, and the light from the bathroom glinted off his round glasses.

"I just feel . . . strange tonight, that's all. Not myself, you could say."

She stepped into the shower stall and closed the door behind her. The walls were made of glass, but at least it was frosted. She stepped out of her clothing quickly, folding them into neat squares. Everything except the thin wisps of silk that might pass for panties. Good grief, could those be legally considered undergarments?

Feeling sexy was as foreign to her, as . . . well, as sex,

she supposed. She'd only just been hitting her teens and getting interested in boys when she'd been paralyzed. She had known before that, though, that she wasn't going to be one of those teenagers who looked more mature than their years. Still, experiencing the awkwardness of hormones and dating would have been preferable to the humility of being different. The hormones had raged all the same, but she'd been afraid to act on them.

Her fingers slid beneath the silk straps that barely looked able to hold the scraps together. She arched, making the fabric tighten, then sucked in her stomach. It wasn't perfectly flat but felt firm enough. Maxine's body had a little more to it than Jennie's. A little taller (well, a lot taller considering), maybe a size or two larger in the chest, a little more filled in, especially in the legs where Jennie's had been skinny sticks. She actually had curves!

Maxine smiled, running her hands down her sides and over her stomach, then down over her legs. She wasn't as lithe and graceful as her ex-roommate Gabby was, but Maxine wasn't about to complain. Tilting her head back, she wrapped her arms around her shoulders and gave herself a hug. Life was good. Even if she was Sam's ex-wife. She couldn't expect God to hand her everything, now could she?

When she emerged from the bathroom, Armand was standing there watching her with the strangest grin on his face. Well, maybe it wasn't strange for him. She pulled the T-shirt down, past her knees. She hoped he didn't know she was wearing the tiniest, laciest little panties she had ever seen beneath it.

"You are so cute. I just want to take you away and marry you this moment." He started for her, his hands ready to ensnare hers again.

She dodged him, wrapping her arms around herself. "I, ah . . . I'm going to lie down for a while."

He dropped his hands. "Yes, of course, darling. You take all the time you need."

She climbed into bed and pulled the white comforter up

to her chin. He leaned down and kissed her. Thank goodness he didn't use his tongue. She might have gagged. When he stood, she rolled over and faced the other way. "Good night, Armand." She hated being mean. He was probably a nice guy, but she had another nice guy in her heart.

For a few minutes she reveled in the silence after he left. Glorious silence where she didn't have to answer questions or pretend to be anyone. Her breathing slowed as she relaxed.

And then she felt something touch her arm. Something that didn't feel human. Lurching around, she came face-to-face with one of the puppets. She couldn't help the scream that escaped her mouth as she shoved it away from her. The puppet's eyebrows raised and its mouth opened in surprise.

"Maxy, what's wrong?" a strange little voice said in sync with the puppet's mouth.

Maxine leaned over the edge of the bed to find Armand ducked down hiding. "Good grief, you scared me," she said, trying to cover with a smile she was having an awfully hard time finding.

The puppet, which looked a lot like Armand, reached out and touched her arm again with its curved hand. It tilted its head and said in a high-pitched voice, "You're not afraid of Mr. Wiggles, are you? You can't have hit your head that hard." It looked up at Armand. "She looks rather cute with that bandage on her forehead, doesn't she?"

Maxine's mouth dropped open, but she quickly covered it. The laugh that burst out was laden with relief. "Mr. Wiggles." Another laugh. "I'm sorry, Mr. Wiggles."

"S'all right," he said in a gangster way. "Just don't let it happen again. You nearly scared my little wooden heart right outta me when you screamed in my face like that. I was just giving you a good-night kiss, that's all."

She was actually conversing with a dummy. And now she was going to have to let it kiss her. "Why, thank you." She turned her cheek, and Mr. Wiggles pressed his wooden lips against her skin. She dropped back down on the pillow.

Armand stood there gazing down at her. "Good night, huggy buggy. I'll be in soon."

She lurched upright again. "You will?"

He took her hand. "Of course I will. Don't you worry one little bit."

She slowly lowered herself again, forcing a smile. "Oh, I won't."

When he left, she allowed herself a laugh. Mr. Wiggles was a dummy. The show, Mr. Wiggles cheering her up later . . . Armand hadn't been a lecherous fool at all.

She hardly wanted to admit to herself the mental pictures all that had conjured, Armand standing on a small, lit stage twirling a two-foot-long . . . no, she still couldn't think about it. All these years of pushing the subject of sex to the back of her mind came in handy, and she shoved the images and thoughts away.

She glanced around in the dim light of the room. Mr. Wiggles sat on a stand by the door, watching her. She rolled over so she couldn't see him. All she had to do was get through this night and she'd go back to Sam. But what was she going to tell him? That she didn't love Armand anymore, that she was in love with Sam now? Geez, why did she have to come back as Sam's ex-wife? Not that she was ungrateful, or complaining really. It was just going to make things harder, that's all.

Well, if she had once faced the challenge of living without the use of her legs, she should darn well be able to handle this setback.

When Armand returned with the glass of water and aspirin, she pretended to be sound asleep, then took it when he left. Then she closed her eyes and drifted into a mottled sleep.

Maxine dreamed about stairs, walking up them, falling down them; she dreamed of Sam holding her as she died, then kissing her gently. Then his lips turned wooden and she discovered Mr. Wiggles kissing her instead. She woke with a start, blinking to clear the fuzzies from her eyes and brain. Adding to her confusion was the man who was staring down at her.

"What are you doing out here?" James asked, standing there with consternation on his face.

Faint light streamed in through the opaque white curtains, filling the living room with softness. *The living room?* She sat up and looked around her. The couch had an inviting hollow where she'd lain.

"You and dad have a fight?" he asked, sitting down in the matching chair beside her.

"No, nothing like that." Now she remembered. She'd woken during the night to find Armand clinging to her. The man was making her claustrophobic! So she'd slipped out of his grasp and come out here. But she couldn't tell James that. "I couldn't sleep and didn't want my tossing and turning to wake Armand."

Where Armand's gray eyes were soft and kind, James's were more like chips of granite. "I know what you're up to, Maxine."

She pulled the comforter around her, creating a cocoon of security. "You do?" How could he know?

"Yes. I know a gold digger when I see one. He'll love and take care of you, and you'll use him. Probably have a lover or two on the side. And you won't be too careful about hiding them. He'll be miserable, but he won't divorce you, which is what you're counting on. He's not the divorcing kind of guy. In fact, if our mother hadn't died, he would have kept putting up with her forever. Well, I'm not going to let you make him miserable. I'm going to make sure my father sees what you really are. This wedding is not going to happen."

Well, she knew that. But she couldn't tell him he had nothing to worry about. She gathered the comforter about her as she stood. My, but it was nice to face someone at their height. It was harder to confront someone when you had to look up to them.

"Your father is a nice man. I have no intention of hurting him." She walked past him and to the bedroom, hoping Armand was still asleep.

He was. All the sheets were thrown off the bed, and he was curled up in a fetal position in the exact center of the bed. She tiptoed to the closet and found half of it filled with women's clothing. Maxine's, she presumed. She found a soft beige sweater and black pants. What she needed was some time alone to figure out her game plan. And find an excuse to see Sam again. She took a shower as quietly as possible, then pulled her clothes into the stall to change in there.

After changing, she went back out to the greenhouse. It was only a little past seven o'clock. She'd always been an early riser; that remained the same. How much of Jennie was still inside her? She again felt the triumph of taking those two steps down. One step she could handle with nary a pause in her wheelchair, but two steps were an insurmountable barrier.

The cold air and spot of muted light on the white deck made her look upward. The tarp covering the hole had blown off during the night. A slight breeze lifted her hair, and she touched the edge of the bandage on her forehead. Beneath it still felt tender, though the throbbing pain was gone. She looked up through the hole to the place the flower box had been.

"I'm sorry you had to die, Maxine," she said softly. "I promise to take good care of your body. And Sam. I . . ." She crossed her arms in front of her. "I don't like the co-incidence of Armand being called to some nonexistent meeting at the same time the box just happened to fall down as you were walking beneath it. And why did you go to Sam's?"

Maybe she was making more of this than necessary, but she couldn't put it out of her mind. Maxine walked back inside, took a breath and mounted the stairs. She passed Sally and paused to make the expected pleasantries.

"How are you feeling, Maxine?" she asked. There was a sticky sweet quality to her voice, and to her smile. It made Maxine think of cinnamon buns.

"Much better, thank you."

Sally seemed to pause for a moment, as if expecting Maxine to say something else. "Were you looking for me?"

"No, why?"

"It's just that you're never in this part of the house. Mostly you hang around either in Daddy's bedroom or the greenhouse."

"Oh. Well, I. . . ." She glanced toward the guest bedroom. "I lost an earring. I think it may have dropped off in the guest room."

Sally glanced at the closed door. "What were you doing in there?"

"Oh, just looking at the brackets on the wall. They were rusted. In fact, the ones holding up the flower box in your room are rusted, too."

"Really? Well, we'd better take it down before it falls and does even more damage."

"Armand's going to take care of that today."

Sally nodded. "Good. One accident around here is too many. Do you need some help looking for your earring?"

"No, thank you. I'm sure it'll only take a minute." She started to walk away, but paused. "Sally, do you think I'm just after your father's money?" She didn't want to think that Maxine-the-first was a gold digger.

"No, why would you ask me that?"

"Oh, it was something James said earlier."

She gave her a flip of the wrist. "He's very protective of Daddy. He's a little worried that Daddy might go overboard and give everything to you."

Ah, James was worried about his inheritance, the businesses. No wonder he was hostile. Armand could very well be the kind of man to do just that for his kissums. And Maxine-the-first probably knew that.

"And you're not worried," Maxine pressed.

"Nah. I'm pretty good about judging people's character. I have you pegged." She glanced toward the stairs. "Well, I'd better find James. He's supposed to take me to breakfast."

She ambled down the hallway, and Maxine walked into the guest bedroom. After a moment of fiddling with the cranks, she wished she'd paid more attention when Armand opened them yesterday. Finally she got the thing open and braced herself against the brisk air outside. She leaned out through the narrow space. The ragged hole was beneath her, open to the deck below. It seemed an awfully long way down. Though the glass roof had a reflective quality to it, she could see the faint outlines of what lay below.

She inspected the bent brackets, thick with rust. Just an accident. Then why did Maxine-the-first run right to Sam's office instead of going to the hospital? Was she really that flaky? Or was she afraid?

She pulled herself back in, thinking about the other window. What was that flower box hanging over? Maxine walked across the hall and looked down the stairs. No sounds from below. She knocked softly on the door, but no one answered. They'd probably left for breakfast. She pushed the door open and looked inside.

Glorious color greeted her along with the disarray. She opened the window and looked out over the box. If this one fell, it would hit the outside wall of the greenhouse. Harmless. She gripped the molding around the window to push herself back in, then pulled her hand back when she touched something sticky. A brown smudge covered the tip of her finger. That was odd.

She leaned way over and found a few more drops suspended beneath the ledge. Then she noticed that the area around the brackets had recently been wiped clean. The house was relatively clean, so it wasn't easy to see the difference. It was only the morning light shining directly on the surface that revealed the cleaner area. Since stucco didn't rust, she didn't think these drops were moist rust. But what else could they be?

A movement within the hole in the greenhouse roof caught her eye. Through the glass she could see a form moving quickly into the house. Someone had been standing there watching her, but they'd moved out of sight before Maxine had seen them. Damn, she'd been spotted in Sally's room. She wiped the brown stuff on her pants, quickly closed the window, and walked down the hallway to the top of the stairs. If it had been Sally, surely she would have come up wondering what Maxine was doing in her bedroom. No one came, nor did she hear anyone talking downstairs. She walked back to the guest bedroom.

The room was frigid now, and Maxine walked back to the open window and leaned out to look at the concrete ridge just below the window. No one stood in the greenhouse now, or at least that she could see. She focused on the wall, shifting this way and that. She could see the slight difference there, too, where someone had wiped something off the surface. But they'd missed the drops hidden beneath the ledge. She touched one. What would make metal corrode rather quickly? Something brown and sticky. She lifted the brown smudge to her nose. It smelled a little sweet. She made a face. She'd probably regret this, but she had to know. She touched the tip of her tongue to the drop. When she didn't gag or keel over, she did it again, smacking her tongue to find the taste a bit like . . . Coke.

She braced herself against the windowsill and leaned out. A dull pressure thrummed in her chest as she followed her thoughts. Someone could have poured cola on both window brackets over the last few weeks to make them look corroded. They could have waited there until Maxine-the-first took her afternoon walk in the greenhouse. They could have pushed down on the box just as she walked outside, even calling her name, to make sure she stayed there to answer. Which is what she might have seen before the box came down on her. Her heart was now pounding at the images her mind put forth. Maxine-the-first had seen her murderer, and that was why she'd run to Sam.

"Kissums, what on earth are you doing?"

Armand's voice startled her, and she lost her footing as she hung out the window. Grabbing onto the frame, she found the precious floor and pulled herself inside. Armand stood there in a white robe with Mickey Mouse stitched on the pocket, his hands stuck under his armpits against the cold. She felt cold, too, but not from the weather. Her hands were trembling as she closed the window.

"I, er . . ." What to tell him? That someone in the house had tried to kill her? That someone *had* killed Maxine-the-first? He'd probably be a little sensitive when she listed the suspects: James, Aida, or Sally. She couldn't imagine Armand himself snuffing Maxine.

He pulled her close, trapping her hands in his. "Darling, you're freezing. Are you delirious? Should I call a doctor?"

She let him lead her to the bed, but she didn't sit as he wanted her to. "No, I'm just curious. I wanted another look at the brackets."

"But why? That Sam ex-husband of yours confirmed it was only an accident. You saw the rusted brackets yourself. My poor darling, this has all been a bit much for you, hasn't it?"

She nodded. "More than you can imagine."

"Will it make you feel better knowing we won't ever hang another flower box there again?"

"Oh, much." She glanced at the window. Yeah, right. A chill settled in her bones, seizing her stomach. Someone, for some reason, had murdered Maxine-the-first. And they would try again, because they thought they hadn't succeeded.

"Come, let's go down and get you a cup of coffee. Aida has a pot brewing now."

When they reached the kitchen, Maxine looked around for James and Sally. "Are the, er, children gone already?"

Aida waved her hand toward the door. "They usually grab breakfast on the way in to work."

"How long have they been gone?" Maxine asked, eyeing the greenhouse door which was closed now.

"Only a few minutes. Why?"

Aida was watching her with open curiosity now. She followed Maxine's gaze to the door.

"I thought I saw someone out in the greenhouse just now." She shrugged, trying not to make an issue of it. "I wondered who it was."

She'd been so subtle about it that no one responded. It could have been anyone in the house. She looked at both Armand and Aida, but neither looked as though they were hiding something. Then again, Armand had known where she was.

Armand stood as Aida poured Maxine a cup of coffee. "I'm going to get dressed. You'll be all right for a few minutes? Won't climb out any windows while I'm gone, hmm?"

Maxine forced a smile at his patronizing expression. "I'll try to hold myself back."

Aida pretended not to pay any attention to them, but Maxine knew she was listening by the way her brows pinched together. Maybe it sounded strange; maybe Aida knew exactly what he was talking about.

As soon as Armand was gone, Maxine took her cup of coffee and walked out into the greenhouse again. She stood in the star-shaped spot of light and looked up at the window in Sally's room. Whoever had stood here could see anyone standing right inside that window rather well. It could have been Maxine-the-first's killer. She closed her eyes.

Maxine, did you see who murdered you? When you were lying here, did you see one of the people in this house looking down at you to make sure you were dead? You probably did see someone, and that's why you went to Sam. Something stirred inside her. *Maxine, I'm going to find out who murdered you. It's the least I can do, seeing as you've done*

a whole lot for me. Which means I can't cut ties here yet.
Maybe she could find out if Aida had been out here this morning for a start.

"Aida, the tarp isn't covering the hole in the roof anymore," Maxine said when she walked back inside. If Aida already knew, she'd probably been out there.

"The repairman will be here in less than an hour," was all she said.

"Oh. Good."

A noncommittal answer if she ever heard one. Sam was better at these things than she was. Sam! She had to tell him what she'd found. That chill inside her thawed at the thought of him. But would he think she was crazy? Was she?

Chapter 4

It took a great deal of doing, but Maxine convinced Armand to leave her alone for a little while and go into the city to practice his Mr. Wiggles routine. He and Maxine-the-first had originally planned to go car shopping; she'd talked him into buying her a Mercedes like his for her wedding present. Maxine rolled her eyes. Maybe the woman had been a gold digger. Nevertheless, Maxine-the-second had changed her mind and wanted to keep her Sunbird after all. She wasn't going to let Armand spend a penny on her.

Once Armand had left, under her promise to stay put and take it easy, she called their office. Sam's office, she amended. Her smile faded at the fourth ring, and finally she heard Sam's voice. But not his real voice. It was that answering machine he'd tried to replace Jennie with.

"Hello. You've reached Sam's Private Eye. We're—I'm not in to answer your call. Please leave a message, and I'll call you back as soon as possible. Thank you."

The beep prompted her to hang up the phone, but it didn't do a thing to dislodge the lump in her throat. He still thought of the business as *we*. Sam had always made her feel as though the business were a partnership. She'd begun to feel that way herself. There was nothing in the office she didn't have access to, even his precious client files. Sometimes he asked her for advice and even took it. But there was something in his voice. Or rather, something missing from his voice. Maybe it was the tape recording that stripped the life from his words.

Maxine wandered around the house for a while, trying Sam's office every fifteen minutes. Aida dusted and vacuumed around her, offering to make her lunch at noon. Maxine passed on that, the thought of those frozen dinners not in the least bit stimulating. She did check the cabinets and pantry for something to make lunch with, but everything was processed. When she opened one of the lower cabinet doors, she saw several twelve-packs of Coke. James drank Coke. A lot of it apparently.

Fear numbed her edges, making her ultra aware of her surroundings and any noises that sounded out of the ordinary. Finally she couldn't stand it any longer. Grabbing her car keys, she skirted the room Aida was in and headed out to her car. She had to get out of the white. It was everywhere, inside and out. Besides, she didn't want to be around when Armand returned.

Her heart was tight when she walked up those stairs to Sam's Private Eye. The images of that horrible day were fading, but she could still taste the blood in her mouth, hear Sam's voice calling her name. When she reached the top, she saw that the light was on inside the office. So she tried the doorknob. It turned, and she opened the door to find Sam putting a stack of books in one of several boxes on the floor. His jeans were stretched tight over his thighs as he knelt by the boxes.

He looked up, and she wasn't sure if it was annoyance or just surprise that filled his expression. "What are you doing here?"

"I'm fine, thank you," she said cheerfully finding herself wanting to smooth back the bit of hair that fell across his forehead. "And yourself?"

He ducked his head, though he didn't smile. "Sorry. That was kinda rude, wasn't it?" He remained crouched, curling his fingers over the top edge of the box. "How are you doing?"

"I'm okay." Now that she was here with him, she could smile again. "My head doesn't hurt much anymore."

"Glad to hear it. What are you doing here?"

A jingling sound coming from the pillow behind her desk preceded Romeo's greeting, which was a lot friendlier than Sam's had been. In fact, Sam just sat there with wonderment on his expression as he watched her rub her cheek against the dog's head. She closed her eyes, relishing the feel, amazed at how something so simple could feel so good.

After a moment, she lifted her head to the other animal in her life that made her feel that way. "And I came because . . ." She paused, wondering why she hadn't thought of this before. "I want to hire you. I think someone tried to kill me."

Sam sat back on his haunches, arms resting on his thighs. "I thought we resolved that yesterday. You think it was a case of malicious rust, maybe?"

She walked closer and sat down on the floor in front of Sam, taking great pleasure in crossing her legs Indian-style. Ignoring his smart-aleck reply she said, "I found something that makes me almost sure it wasn't an accident. And I think my life is still in danger."

She told him what she'd discovered, wishing he could hold her and make the fear go away. He smelled warm and familiar, with a touch of that citrus aftershave she loved.

He slowly rose to his full height, giving his legs a shake. "Maxine, I can't take your case."

She rose, too, finding herself facing him. "Why? You still think I'm delusional? Paranoid?"

He shook his head. "I'm not sure what to think about you, but that's nothing new. I can't take your case for two reasons. One is I never take on anything I have any personal involvement with. That includes ex-wives." His voice went lower. "And second, I'm not in the business anymore."

She almost heard her heart drop to the floor. The first

reason she could dispense with. But the second? "Sam, you can't be serious." She looked down at the boxes, then to the half-empty shelves on the far wall. "No, Sam. You can't."

His jaw tightened. "Maxine, there are other private investigators in town, some of them very good. I can refer you to one of them."

"I'm not talking about my case. I'm talking about your not doing this anymore."

"I'll still be doing this, only I'll be working for someone else. Mostly paper chases, computer work. I'm going to sit back and let the other guys pound the pavement from now on."

For a moment she wondered if someone else had come back in Sam's body. "You hate working for other people! That's why you started this business."

He narrowed his eyes at her. "Why are you so concerned about me closing up shop? You didn't want me doing this anyway, when we were married. Why the passionate appeal now?"

She wrung her hands, ducking her head before meeting his gaze. Jennie could give it to him, up one side and down the other. Maxine was a different story. "Because I know how much you love this business. *Your* business."

"Maybe I don't love it anymore. Maybe I'm tired of it." And he sounded tired, expelling the last sentence on a long breath.

"Not you, Sam. You never get tired of this." She gestured to the office in general. "Tracking down the scumbags, proving them fraudulent. You live for this."

He regarded her silently for a moment, but his expression was still shuttered. She wanted so badly to climb over the wall he'd constructed and eradicate that lack luster quality that lingered in his blue eyes.

"Do you ever wonder if it's all been worth it? You work toward something, and then one day it's all gone. Or it doesn't even mean what it used to mean anymore."

"It's what you make of your life that counts, Sam. I've never seen you like this before." Her voice grew soft. "What happened to you?"

He closed his eyes for a moment, and she saw pain when he opened them again. "I used to promise Jennie—she was my assistant—that I'd get a big case one day and buy a copier for the office, along with some of the other things we needed. Now that she's gone, it doesn't seem that important anymore. It's not the same without her. Every time I look at her desk, or see those stairs, I think about her. I think about those last moments of her life when I couldn't save her."

Maxine couldn't speak for a minute, though Sam didn't seem to notice or care. He shoved his hands in the pockets of his jeans and stared out the window over her desk. He missed her. She couldn't swallow. But there was something more important to consider. He blamed himself for her death. She reached out and touched his arm, which stiffened.

"You blame yourself, don't you?"

He moved away from her, leaning against the corner of her desk with his back to her. "Of course I blame myself. I was right there." Finally he turned to face her. "Do you know what it feels like to be a second too late? If I'd been a little faster, a little stronger—" He ran his hand through his hair, disrupting the smooth waves in back. "But I wasn't."

Those last words, spoken with such soft finality, pierced her heart. She closed the distance between them and slipped her arms around him. For a second she held her breath, waiting to see if he'd push her away.

"Sam, please don't. Don't blame yourself."

His body was stiff and unyielding at first, but at last he put his arms around her and pulled her closer. She could feel the plane of his cheek and jaw pressed against her head.

"I can't change the facts," he said, his voice muffled in her hair.

"She wouldn't want you to do this. There was nothing you could do to save her."

He pulled away. "How do you know what she would want? You didn't even know Jennie."

She took a deep breath, hoping to dispel the tightness in her chest. *Yes, I did. I did, Sam.* But the words wouldn't come. He would get over this feeling, if he'd let her help.

She let out the breath. "No, I didn't. But I know you. If you could have saved her, you would have. And I'm sure if she was any kind of friend to you, she wouldn't want you suffering over her death. She has a better life now."

"You're right about Jennie. She was a friend, and she wouldn't want this. But she's gone. She can't take this feeling of emptiness away, and neither can you."

She was still standing in front of him, close enough to feel the heat his body gave off. She placed her hands on his shoulders, enjoying for a second the strength in them. "Let me try," she said, her voice giving out to a whisper.

His blue eyes studied hers. "Why are you doing this?"

Because I love you. That was the answer of her heart, her very soul. "Because I care about you." That was true, too. "Because you don't deserve to go through this alone."

He wrapped his fingers over her wrists, but he didn't remove her hands. "Maxine, I appreciate what you're doing. But I can't help you. If you think someone is trying to hurt you, you should go to the police. Or I can refer you to a friend of mine," he added when she shook her head. "But I start my new job in three weeks, which leaves me enough time to finish up the cases I have." He lifted her hands and let them drop as he walked away from her.

The phone rang. He walked to the shelf and continued putting books in the box.

"Aren't you going to answer that?"

"No, I'll let the machine get it. Some bozo's been calling every fifteen minutes and not leaving a message."

Bozo! Hmph. She stared at the phone on her desk, her fingers tingling. After the third ring, she reached over and picked it up. "Sam's Private Eye," she said in her old way. Sam looked as though he wanted to strangle her. "And who's calling? Yes, one moment." She put them on hold. "Sam, take it. It's Paul from the insurance company."

"You had no business answering that phone."

"Yes I do."

"Who the hell appointed you as my guardian? What right do you have—"

"Sam, Paul's waiting."

After a moment he walked into his office and picked up the phone. She let out a breath. "Sam, I can't let you do this," she said very softly. "Especially not because of me."

Maxine heard Sam talking on the phone, closing her eyes and relishing the sound of that low, rumbly voice again. All the years she'd heard that sound, cherished it, and had done nothing about it. Dying hadn't only given her a whole new chance in life; it had taught her that life was too short to sit around wishing.

She walked behind her desk, standing in the empty space where a chair should be. All those wasted years. But they weren't wasted; she'd had Sam as a friend. She picked up her nameplate: Jennie Carmichael. Her fingers traced the grooves of the letters in the purple plastic. How strange it would be to go to the sign shop and request one for a Maxine Lizbon. The plate suddenly lifted from her hands as if it had wings. She sucked in a breath at the inexplicable movement and turned to find Sam standing beside her, a grim expression on his face. He held the plate in his hands for a moment, then replaced it on the desk without a word. He didn't have to say anything; his eyes said it all. *Don't touch.*

"I'm sorry," she said, feeling strange to be chastised for touching her own nameplate. But it wasn't hers anymore. Jennie was dead. And she couldn't be resurrected now.

"Listen, I'm busy. Here's the name of the guy I was telling you about."

He held the piece of paper out to her, but she didn't take

it. She gave him a determined look. After a moment, he shrugged and let the paper drift to the floor. She had never seen Sam angry with her. She'd hardly seen him angry at all. But his anger was tinged with such a sadness she wanted to cry. Mostly she wanted to slip into his arms again. Except for the annual Christmas hug (which she looked forward to all year), she'd never had any physical contact like that with him. And even then, he'd had to lean down and awkwardly hug her while she was in the chair.

"Good-bye, Maxine."

"I'm not leaving, Sam."

He ducked his head, shaking it. "You are so damned stubborn. That much hasn't changed."

"But a lot has."

"Meaning?"

Ooh, he'd trapped her in a corner. "Meaning I need your help. Only your help. Please at least take a look at the house and tell me if you think someone made the brackets look corroded."

He let out a long breath. "And if I don't think that's the case?"

"Then I won't bother you anymore." She was sure he'd agree once he saw the drips under the ledge.

He reached around and grabbed his leather bomber jacket. "Let's go." He turned to Romeo, sitting on his pillow by her desk. "Come on, boy. Back to the pristine palace."

"Should you be driving?" he asked when they emerged outside.

"I'm fine."

He gave her that skeptical look again. "That is a matter of opinion. I'll follow you out there in my car."

She wanted to ride with him, but that wasn't practical. "All right. And Sam?"

"Yeah."

She smiled. "Thanks."

"No problem." He always said that, even if it was.

*   *   *

When Maxine pulled into the mansion's driveway, she was dismayed to see Armand's black Mercedes parked out front, and a white truck parked off to the side. He wasn't going to like this, but tough! Someone in his house, most likely, was trying to kill her. Had killed her. She wasn't about to let it happen again.

Armand was waiting by the front door when she got out of the car. His expression was chagrined when he saw Sam emerge from his car, Romeo in tow. "Not again? Maxine, didn't we talk about this?"

"I'm hiring Sam as my investigator. I think that flower box was purposely dropped on me."

Sam wasn't much help in convincing Armand of that. He merely lifted his shoulder and followed her into the house. "Hope you haven't fumigated yet."

Armand caught up to Maxine as she took the stairs. "This is preposterous. Who would hurt you?"

"That's what I intend to find out."

The sun was on the far side of the house again, but she knew Sam would see the drips and the clean area since he knew what to look for. When she walked into the guest room, she stopped short. A man in coveralls was leaning out the window.

"What are you doing?" she asked, coming up behind him.

The man wore a painter's cap that covered a spray of black hair. "I removed the flower box in the next room and I'm patching where the brackets were. 'Sat all right?"

"You what?" She nudged him aside and leaned out the window. The brackets were gone, white patches where the holes were. She leaned farther out to look under the ledge, then at the ledge beneath Sally's window. Her mouth dropped open. "They're gone!"

" 'Course, ma'am. That's what I was supposed to do, 'cording to Mr. Santini."

"Did you clean beneath those ledges out there?"

"No, just around the holes."

Sam slid through the window opening next to her. Her hand slid beneath the ledge, but caught no trace of anything sticky.

"I don't believe this."

Sam ran his hand along the path hers had taken. "Nothing sticky or otherwise."

"Can you at least see where this area has been wiped clean?"

Sam studied the area. "Well, it does seem a little lighter, but that doesn't prove anything. The guy said he wiped it off." He shot her a look. "Maxine, are you sure you didn't imagine those drops there?"

"Whoever saw me from the greenhouse wiped them off."

From behind her she heard Armand say, "What a cozy picture you two make." There was a definite snideness in his tone.

She looked over at Sam. "Guess I'm off the hook," he said, one corner of his mouth lifting.

"This doesn't count. Someone sabotaged the evidence."

They both started back through the window at the same time, bodies brushing. Sam paused, putting out his hand. "Ladies first."

With an exasperated noise, she pulled herself back inside. She enjoyed the view as Sam did the same.

"Nothing there," he said to Armand's questioning gaze. "I think your wife-to-be needs to see a doctor." He tapped his finger to his temple. "If you know what I mean." Turning to Maxine, he said, "I'm outta here. Talk to my friend if you have any more revelations. Bye."

. He and Romeo walked down the stairs, and a moment later she heard the door close. She turned to Armand. "I suppose you think I'm crazy, too."

"I don't know what to think. You've acted so strange in the last day. I know the accident was frightening, but I'm not sure what to think about all these antics with your ex-husband." Before she could take countertactics, her hands were imprisoned in Armand's. "Do you really think someone is trying to hurt you?"

Her forehead started throbbing slightly again. Maybe he was squeezing the blood up into her head. "All I know is that I'm afraid."

"What can I do to make you feel safe?"

"Hire Sam to protect me."

"I don't think he wants to protect you, or investigate for you."

She let out a long breath, looking at the hallway where Sam had retreated. "I've got to change his mind."

More dreams about stairs and Sam and puppets finally woke her in the middle of the night. Maxine remained there, wondering if she'd heard something that had penetrated her consciousness. All she could hear was the soft grinding noise Armand made in his sleep. His breath was pulsing against her shoulder, and both his arms were twined around her. Claustrophobia swept in. Was this what it was like to share a bed with a man? No, it would be different if she loved Armand.

She extricated herself and slipped from the bed. She could see him in the dim light from the bathroom, looking like a small child. When Armand groped a little, she pushed the pillow toward him, and he latched onto it like a baby. After pulling the top blanket off, she crept to the living room. Shadows moved in the darkness and the silence was so thick, it hummed in her ears. Hugging the bundle of blanket to her chest, she waited for her eyes to adjust to the new level of darkness.

When she took a step toward the couch, she thought she heard another footstep nearby. Maxine froze, toes pressing down on the cold tile floor ready to launch her . . . but in what direction? Her pulse slammed against her throat. Silence thrummed again as she waited for another sound. She tried to imagine the layout of the living room, tried to place some of the shadows she saw as harmless pieces of furniture.

After what seemed like hours, her heartbeat stilled to its normal rate again. She took another step. And heard another footstep. Who else would be sneaking around down here? Everything moved within the shadows her eyes created. She debated on screaming and bringing out the entire household, but held her tongue.

Very slowly she took a step sideways, placing her foot down in increments. No other sound. She repeated the movement, not even breathing until her foot flattened. When her shoulder touched something flat, she turned to find the whites of two eyes glaring at her. A yelp escaped her lips before she could slap her hand over it. One of the puppets! Bending over in relief, she pressed her palm against her heart to still its rapid beating. The footsteps she'd heard must have been an echo of her own steps.

"Bad puppet," she whispered.

And then a real hand clamped over her wrist.

She jerked, bumping into the case that housed the puppet. Another hand clamped over her mouth.

"What are you doing sneaking around out here?" James's voice hissed in the blackness that throbbed in time to her own runaway heart.

She jerked her hand away from him, angry and afraid at the same time. "I am not sneaking around. I came out here to sleep on the couch again."

Silence. Had she imagined the whole episode? Not likely. When he finally spoke, his voice made her jump again.

"I think you're using that as an excuse."

For avoiding sleeping with his father, yes. "What are you talking about?"

He leaned closer, and even though she couldn't see anything but a large, dark shadow in front of her, she could feel his body heat. And she smelled something in his breath that went a little beyond the sweet tang of the Coke.

"You're scavenging for hidden treasure, looking for

booty. Maybe even a safe. Forget it. There's nothing here."

"Leave me alone. I just want to get some sleep."

James lingered for a moment before snorting something that sounded a bit like a laugh. "You're so transparent."

"And you're afraid of me." She wasn't going to mention that the feeling was mutual.

He moved closer again, leaning right into her face. "Why would I be afraid of you? I'm bigger than you. And I'm meaner than you."

She took a step back, crossing her arms in front of her to create a barrier with the blanket. "You're afraid your father's going to give me more than he's given you. You're afraid to lose to me."

"I've known women like you, women who try to take what they can without giving anything in return. But I'm smart enough to toss them out when I'm tired of them. My father isn't that smart. But you didn't count on me, did you?" He pinched her chin between his fingers. "It isn't a done deal yet, lady. Not until I say it's done."

Before she could shove his hand away, he disappeared into the darkness the same way he'd come. Her heart hadn't stopped pounding since the puppet encounter. She stood there for a long time, not sure of the silence anymore. Finally fatigue won over her fright, and she felt her way to the couch. Mental pictures of James sneaking down with a knife didn't present the kind of thoughts she wanted to go to sleep with. Tugging the blanket around her, she slid behind the couch after pulling it away from the wall a bit.

Instead of James haunting her nightmares, Sam invaded her sleep. She had dreams of telling Sam the truth, and he kept saying, "I'm outta here." But maybe she was making a mistake by not telling him. She felt she was making the right decision in burying Jennie, but seeing the pain in Sam's eyes made her wonder. She needed to talk to someone about this, someone who could tell her she wasn't doing the wrong thing. That person was not in this house. Obviously that person wasn't Sam. In her small world of friends, that left only one person: Gabrielle, her former roommate.

Voices pulled her thoughts to her surroundings, and Maxine opened her eyes to find blissful light instead of that horrid darkness where evil lurked. She could tell it was only just getting light outside. She tried to identify the people behind the voices.

"I think she's playing this whole accident up," James said from another room.

"You don't think anyone dropped that flower box on her, do you?" Sally asked.

"Of course not. She just wants Dad's sympathy. And it's working. He's already talking about moving up the wedding."

"Moving it up? Why?"

"He thinks the upcoming wedding is putting a strain on her. I think he's really afraid she's going to back away."

"You think you'll talk Daddy into making her sign the prenup before then?"

Maxine heard the voices coming closer.

"I'd better," James said in a grim tone of voice. "I'm heading into the city early to take care of some paperwork."

"I'll go with you. I've got a few things to take care of, too, and then we can grab lunch."

Their steps took them out the front door, and Maxine finally let out the breath she'd been holding. James was calling the accident just that, but she had a feeling he knew it wasn't. And Armand was talking about moving the wedding up? Oh, geez. She glanced down at the ring on her finger. It looked so wrong there. But she had to keep up the charade, at least for a while longer. Then she'd give it back to Armand. She quickly extricated herself from her place and went into the bedroom to get dressed before Armand woke.

She was in the closet looking through the rack of clothes when a high-pitched voice startled her into a yelp.

"You're not thinkin' of runnin' away, are you?"

That wicked little puppet leaned around the corner, its eerie grin moving realistically up and down with its words.

"Good grief, Armand, you scared me! Get out of here!" She tossed a shirt in its direction, but it ducked out of the way.

"I'm not Armand. He's still sleeping. So you can tell me. Mr. Wiggles is your friend, remember?"

Mr. Wiggles was giving her the creeps. She stalked to the doorway and found Armand ducked around the corner. He jumped when she appeared so suddenly and gave her a sheepish look. "Mr. Wiggles wanted to talk to you."

"Well, I don't want to talk to Mr. Wiggles, okay? Nothing personal."

He was taking it very personally indeed. He set the dummy on the edge of the bed. "Why are you getting up so early? You always used to sleep in with me. And where did you go in the middle of the night?"

"I can't sleep at night, and I don't want to wake you with my tossing and turning, that's all." This was not going to be easy. She had two injured men in her life, but Sam was the only one in her heart. "So I went out into the living room. And I'm not the only one who gets up early around here. Sally and James get up earlier than I do, I think."

"They always have. They're more like twins, even though they're four years apart." He glanced at the puppet, then back at her. "Maxine, I'd like to talk to you about something."

"I can't," she said a little too quickly. She didn't want to talk about moving up their wedding date. And if she skirted the conversation, she wouldn't have to reject him when he asked. "I have some running around to do today. You know, wedding stuff," she added because she felt compelled to for some reason. "Don't worry, I'll be fine. I made an appointment with a doctor to take a look at my forehead." She'd made an appointment with her old doctor. "And I have an old friend to look up. Gabrielle."

He looked more like a little boy as he shrugged. "All right, I guess. I'll probably go into the city, too." He perked up. "Can I give you a ride in? You can drop me off and take the car?"

"No, thank you. I don't know how long I'll be. I'll see you later."

She stopped in the utility room on the way out, where Aida was loading sheets into a large washing machine. After the usual morning greeting, she asked, "Aida, what time was it when you heard the crash of the flower box?"

"I'm not sure exactly. About one-thirty, I think."

"Do you know who was here? In the house, I mean."

Aida knitted her pale eyebrows together. "No one but me. I was back here at the time."

"Could someone have come home without you knowing it?"

"I suppose. Can't hear too much back here, and I was busy for a couple of hours, just like I am every week on wash day. But as far as I know, you and I were the only ones here. Mr. Santini was called in for that meeting. James and Sally were already in the city."

Maxine nodded. "All right. Thanks."

She breathed a sigh of relief as she left the house. Maybe there was some way to make Armand break off their engagement. His ego would be preserved, and she'd feel a lot better about the whole thing. Yeah, that was it. She'd stay out late and not give him an explanation. He'd tell her she was selfish and thoughtless and say they were through. Maxine was almost giddy with the thought. Then she'd talk Sam into keeping his agency; then she'd make him fall in love with her. And not necessarily in that order.

Sam dropped another two books in the box he'd started before Maxine had barged in and dragged him out to that godawful white prison. He was having a hard time figuring her out lately. After talking to her maybe a dozen times over the last five years, he couldn't get rid of her now.

And she'd been so broken up about his closing down the shop. He could still see the disappointment in her face years ago when he'd told her he wanted to open his own investigative agency. Now she was trying to get him to keep it open. He'd thought she wanted it kept open so she could hire him, but he had a feeling it went deeper than that. If he didn't know her better, he'd think she really cared. But Maxine seldom cared about anything that didn't help her. See, even his intuition was dull these days. No way could he keep the agency open.

He finally finished with the box and started on another one. Jennie's desk was going to be the hardest. His throat clogged up just thinking about it. Why was this sadness so debilitating? She had been part of his work life for four years, yes. She had also been his friend. Since her death, he hadn't been all that interested in life anymore. Even when he wasn't thinking about her, his heart still felt heavy.

And now Maxine had stormed into his life again. She'd held him, tried to comfort him. He couldn't understand it at all. Hopefully he wouldn't have to worry about it anymore. She was overreacting, though something in his gut told him otherwise. But he couldn't trust his gut anymore.

"Hi, Sam," Maxine's voice said from the doorway.

He dropped his head for a moment before looking up, hoping he was only conjuring up her voice with his thoughts. "You again," he said when he saw that wasn't the case.

She closed the door behind her. "How are you?"

"How do I look?" he asked from his position on the floor, hoping to get his irritation across.

She just stared at him, several emotions running across her expression. Her throat convulsed in a nervous swallow. "You look a little thin, actually. Are you eating enough?"

Sam stood up and walked over to her, sticking his hands in his pockets. He opened his mouth to give her a wisecrack answer, but stopped before a word emerged. Her eyes were filled with real concern, and it made his stomach twist. "I'm okay." He nodded toward her forehead. "You have a smaller bandage now."

She touched the bandage beneath her red hair. "You noticed? Well, I keep forgetting what a great detective you are."

He narrowed his eyes at her. "I seem to remember you having a different opinion of my choice of career. What did the doctor say?"

"He said it was nearly healed, a miraculous recovery. Hardly even a scar." She looked down at the box he'd been filling. "You're still packing up."

"Yes. I thought you weren't going to bug me anymore. Are you welshing on our deal?"

"But the evidence was tampered with. That didn't count."

"You always were a liar, Maxine. Or a conniver."

She wrapped her arms around herself, as if she'd never been called a liar before. He knew she had because he'd called her that a few times during and after their marriage. "I'm not conniving you, Sam. Or lying to you. I need your help. But if you're not going to help me, I'll conduct the investigation on my own."

He laughed. "And you're such an expert."

"I worked for—" Her eyes widened a little. "I worked it all out in my head. I'm going to talk to the people at the club offices James oversees, and see if he has an alibi. I think he's the one behind it. But I didn't come here about that. Sam, I can't let you do this." She gestured to his office.

"That's pretty obvious. You keep interrupting me. Well, I'm not running off to look at some window again. Or anything else."

"Sam, this is your dream. You can't work for some other guy. Not after all these years of being your own boss. You'll have to keep certain hours. You'll be making money for someone else. Someone will be looking over your shoulder, telling you what to do. You won't get that spark in your eyes when you're on a lead." Her fists were balled up at her sides. "You won't get to wear your disguises anymore."

He ducked his head. "Are you finished?"

She mirrored his action. "For now."

He nodded. "I thought about everything you just mentioned."

"And it doesn't matter to you?"

"It doesn't matter."

She reached out and touched his arm. "Sam, promise me you won't make this kind of decision in haste. You know you love this agency. Pretty soon the pain will go away and things will look different. Give it a few months."

He looked down at where she held his arm. Her touch had never felt like that before. She interpreted his look as meaning hands-off and let go. He almost felt like telling her to go ahead and put it back, but he rethought that one and put a skeptical look on his face.

"That's all you want from me? To give this a few months?" Somehow that didn't seem so hard. If he had to admit it, the thought of working for his buddy wasn't changing his outlook one bit. But he had already made the commitment, and he wasn't the welshing type, even if some people he knew were.

She nodded. "You don't even have to take on my case."

"Aw, you gotta want something. This just isn't like you, Maxine."

She lifted her hands. "I don't. Promise."

"I'll think about it."

And then she smiled, pulling her lower lip up between her teeth the way Jennie sometimes did. He turned away for a moment, and when he looked back at her, the smile was gone. Maybe he'd only imagined it.

They stood there for a few awkward moments, and he didn't know what else to say to her. Finally he thought of something. "Did you tell the doctor about the disappearing Coca-Cola drips or the paranoia you've been experiencing since the accident?"

She wrinkled her nose in a way that made her look incredibly cute. "No, I didn't tell him any of that."

"I figured."

She remained there, looking at him with the strangest expression on her face. Like a deep melancholy.

"Maxine, is there something wrong with your life?"

His question jarred that expression. "No, why?"

"Seems like you have everything you ever wanted. You're marrying a rich guy, got a beautiful, if strange, home to live in, even a maid. Why are you so interested in fixing my life all of a sudden?"

She gave him a tentative smile. "Don't you want me around?"

"No. That's why we got divorced in the first place. Neither of us wanted the other around all that much."

Her fingers tightened on the strap of her big purse. "I thought we were still friends," she said in a small voice that gripped him by the throat.

Aw, when had he gone soft with Maxine? "Hell, Maxine, we were never friends to begin with." After a moment, he added, "Okay, we can still be friends. Now will you stop bugging me about my life?"

"But that's what friends are for."

"Real friends let you live your life the way you want. They don't try to fix you."

"Even if it's for your own good?"

"Especially if it's for your own good."

Again they lapsed into that awkward silence. Hell, he'd never had any trouble talking to her before. Even when their marriage was failing, they'd always had plenty to say to each other.

She glanced down at her shoes, then back up at him. "Well, I guess I'd better get going."

"Good luck with your investigation."

"Thanks."

She hesitated a moment before turning and walking out the door. He stared after her for a while, wondering if he wasn't the one who was delusional. He rubbed his arm where he still felt remnants of her touch. That was probably the last he'd hear of her. Except maybe the picture in the paper, bride and groom. Hopefully she wouldn't take this friend thing too far and invite him to the wedding. He'd probably get her a wedding present anyway, just to show her there were no hard feelings, but he sure as heck wasn't going to attend. Because, no matter what he'd agreed to, they could never be friends.

Chapter 5

*E*ven though their conversation had gone all right, Maxine left the building feeling a little blue. She wanted to go back in and talk to him some more, but they'd run out of things to say. And he'd made it clear that he didn't want her to touch him. Why was it so complicated? It was never this hard when they worked together.

Well, of course, things were different. He hadn't looked at Jennie as anything more than a friend and coworker. Maybe there was a reason for that. Maybe whatever it was in her soul that made her who she was didn't appeal to Sam. Inside this new body, she felt more confident, more of a woman. Could it be that she wasn't enough for Sam either way?

She shook her head as she crossed the street to her car. It didn't matter—she wasn't giving up on him. Too much was at stake. She glanced up at the window next to her desk. Maxine-the-first had given up on him. She'd let him go. How could any woman let Sam go? He was warm and considerate and open—or at least he had been with Jennie. How could Maxine-the-first not have been his friend? His friendship had meant so much to Jennie, she wouldn't have risked it for anything. Now, as Maxine, she would risk it all to make Sam love her. She just had a few layers of old hurts and time to peel away first.

* * *

Maxine made the familiar drive to the apartment building she'd lived in for two years. The ground floor was tailored for people in wheelchairs by the man who owned it. Because Rick was also in a wheelchair, he saw the need for housing to accommodate those with special requirements.

She started to pull into the apartment's parking slot, then realized she didn't live there anymore. She maneuvered into one of the guest slots instead. It felt strange to be back, walking up the ramp to the front door. She no longer belonged there. But Gabrielle was her friend, and that was one part of Jennie's life she couldn't cut away. She rang the doorbell.

Gabrielle opened the door a minute later, a suspicious look in her eyes. Maxine couldn't see much of her beyond the five-inch space the chain allowed. She smiled, glad to see another familiar face she cared about.

"Hi, my name is Maxine."

"Whatever you're selling, I'm not interested." She started to close the door.

"Gabby, wait! I'm a . . . friend of Jennie's. I need to talk to you."

Gabby hesitated, her face going expressionless. Maxine went on. "I knew her for a long time. She lived here with you, and you were one of her closest friends. You're the only one I can talk to about this."

Gabby's distrust was etched all over her pretty face, a distrust she had good reason to harbor. But she relented and finally closed the door and reopened it without the chain. She rolled out of the way, and Maxine walked inside. It looked the same as it always had, and yet it looked vastly different. She felt so . . . tall. Everything here was made for someone in a chair. The island in the kitchen still had copper pots hanging above it, the large rack of spices and the pantry that used to be filled with cookie fixings. Even this modest kitchen made her fingers itch to create something edible, as she had many times.

"You said you needed to talk to me," Gabby said in a voice that leaked impatience. She was still the prettiest girl Maxine had ever known. She had sea-green eyes and a perfect complexion. Her straight brown hair was long, except for the wispy bangs over her forehead.

It was so hard to sidestep around Sam; she didn't want to do that with Gabby. Maxine turned with a nervous smile, pressing her palms together. "Gabby, it's me. Jennie."

Gabby's expression hardly changed at all. Except that her lip twitched. "This isn't funny."

Maxine knelt down beside her. "I know it's hard to believe, but it's true. When I died during the fall down the stairs, I went—I don't know, someplace. Then this voice said I was getting a second chance, and I woke up outside Sam's office. I thought I was in my own body, but I wasn't. I came back in Maxine's body. This body."

Gabby's face went white. "This is creepy. I don't know who you are or what you're up to, but I want you to leave. Now. Or I'll press the panic button."

Maxine took a quick breath. "I used to drive you crazy on the weekends by waiting until I watched the cooking shows before telling you what we were having for dinner. You loved my chocolate eclairs. You always blamed me if you got a pimple, but you never turned down anything I made with chocolate. I used to envy you because you're so poised and pretty, but maybe you didn't know that. You sometimes have nightmares about your ex-boyfriend's attack. I'd wheel into your room and wake you up and hold your hand until you stopped crying, and chanting 'bastard, bastard, bastard.' "

Gabby's face went even whiter. "You can't know all these things. No one knows about my nightmares."

"Except me. It was our secret. It still is."

Maxine went on while she had a line. "Our other secret was how I felt about my boss, Sam. You used to lecture me about telling him how I felt. I was afraid to lose my friendship with him, so I never did. I was never as daring and confident as you, Gabby. I was afraid to take the risk.''

"Because your mother overprotected you," Gabby said in a whisper, her gaze moving over her face, searching perhaps for a visible sign of Jennie.

"Yes. You were teaching me to be more confident."

"And you were teaching me not to be so bitchy about being in a wheelchair." Gabby took a deep breath, her eyes wide. "Jennie, is that really you?"

Maxine leaned forward and hugged her. "It's me. I don't know why, but I got a second chance. A bizarre, wonderful second chance. I think it has to do with Sam. *Because* I never told him how I felt. When I was dying, all I felt was regret over not telling him. And not being what he needed." She waved her hands over herself. "And now I am."

"You've talked to him?"

"Yes." She decided not to get into the whole flower box incident or Maxine's death. She stood, her legs aching from crouching. "I tried to hire him, but he's closing his business. He blames himself for my death."

"But you told him you're still here."

"No. Don't give me that look, Gabby. I want Jennie to stay dead. She was dull, self-conscious. If I tell Sam I'm Jennie, then I'll feel like Jennie. I want Sam to see me as a new person, and I want to see myself as a new person. Only there's, ah, one little hitch. I'm his ex-wife." Maxine realized she felt awkward looking down at Gabby. Was that how people felt around her? She sat down at one of the two chairs at the kitchen table.

"I can't believe this. I can't believe you're here, that we're talking like this." Gabby's eyes widened. "You came back as his ex-wife?" Even she couldn't keep the smile from her face at the irony.

Maxine nodded. "Not that I'm complaining. It just makes things a little more complicated. That and my rich fiancé."

"You have a fiancé?"

"Maxine-the-first did. Does. That's what I call her, Maxine-the-first. This fiancé is very . . . interesting. But I want

Sam. So I have to break it off with Armand—he's the fiancé—and put it back on with Sam.''

"Wait a minute. What about this Maxine-the-first person? What happened to her?''

Maxine held her mouth in a tight line. ''She died. Okay, I wasn't going to get into this, but I think she was murdered. That's why I want to hire Sam. Maxine was going to see him in the first place. That's where she died and I came in. She was scared, I think. I want Sam to find out who did her in. I'm pretty sure it was Armand's son, James. I keep thinking that if I just walk away from Armand, it'll go away. But I also want to find out who killed Maxine. I owe it to her, you know.''

Gabby sat there, hands demurely folded in her lap. ''Do you know how crazy all this sounds?''

Maxine nodded. ''I could go on *Oprah* with this.''

Gabby laughed. ''You could do the whole talk-show circuit!'' Her expression sobered. ''What about the first Maxine's life? I mean, you can't just walk away from an entire life. What about her friends? Her family?''

"But I'm not here for them. I'm here for Sam.''

"I know that, Jennie, but it's not fair to the other people in her life.''

Maxine wasn't there to talk about the other Maxine's life. She wanted affirmation that her decision was right. ''Well, for one thing, Armand seemed to be her life. She'd just moved in with him a few weeks ago. They're—we're supposed to be getting married in two months. I can't keep him in my life.'' She rolled her eyes, thinking of the way Sam did that. ''I don't want to keep him in my life. I found out that Maxine had a decorating business, but she closed it down when Armand proposed. Apparently she wanted to be a lady of leisure for a while. She'd planned to make the man her entire life. Right now I have no home and no job.''

"What about family?''

Maxine shrugged. ''I don't know. I mean, I can't ask Armand or Sam whether or not I have family.'' She took

Gabby's hands in her own. "You see, it's perfect. Yes, I feel bad about dumping Armand, but I have a sneaking suspicion Maxine-the-first was only marrying him for the life he could give her. James called me a gold digger. Armand will be better off without me."

Gabby merely shook her head. "I don't believe this."

"It's a little hard for me to take, too. But I'm doing okay. And I'm being so rude. How are you doing?"

Gabby twisted her mouth, which constituted a shrug. "I'm all right. Same as always. Except for feeling awful that my best friend died."

"And she's still dead."

"Jennie—Maxine, why do you want her to be dead? You know, she wasn't that bad a person. She was sweet, honest . . ." She threw her hands up. "What am I saying? You *are* sweet and honest. And you are still Jennie."

"I don't want to be Jennie anymore. I want a new life." She squeezed Gabby's hand. "But I'd still like you in it."

Gabby smiled. "I'd like to be in it. Once I get used to all this."

"Did you get a new roommate?"

"No. I can manage on my own."

"Gabby, don't shut yourself in." Gabby's accident—as they referred to it—had only happened two years ago. She'd had much less time to adapt than Jennie had.

"That's easy for you to say. What happened to you was an accident. What happened to me—"

"I know," Maxine cut in, knowing how painful it was for Gabby to talk about it.

"You don't live in fear, wondering if the man who took away your life is going to return to finish the job. I feel safer here in my apartment with my alarm."

"But he's probably not going to come after you here. Don't let him take from you more than he already has. You can be careful without becoming a shut-in."

After a moment, the brittleness from Gabby's face disappeared, and she smiled. "Here we are, arguing and giving advice as usual. You sure sound like the Jennie I knew.''

"Okay, I still am. In a way. But I want to be different, too. I want to be exciting, daring, confident."

"Confidence comes from within, you know."

"I'm still working on that. I've hardly had a chance to get used to this new body."

"What was the first thing you did when you realized you could walk?" Gabby asked, a wistful expression on her face.

"I fell down. Don't laugh. I've been in a wheelchair so long, I had to reprogram my brain for walking. I was all wobbly like a newborn colt." She grimaced. "I still am. But I'm getting used to it. The first thing I wanted to do was dance. It was so romantic. Sam was holding me—because I'd lost my balance—and I asked him to dance with me. That was what I dreamed about the entire time I was in the wheelchair. I wanted to dance."

"And did he dance with you?"

"Well, no. He thought I was nuts. But he will. See, I *am* getting more confident. Going up the stairs was my biggest thrill so far. A whole flight of them, and I was able to walk right up and down. No elevator. I just did it. Okay, I held onto the bannister for dear life, but soon I won't even need that."

"Now I'm jealous of you. If I could walk again, I'd give Claudia Schiffer and Elle MacPherson something to worry about. I don't think they're very threatened by my hands."

Gabby had been an up-and-coming model before the accident. Sometimes she still modeled, if only her hands or face were needed. She had the prettiest hands Maxine had ever seen. She gathered those hands in her own.

"Gabby, I want your opinion. Sam blames himself for my death. He tried to grab my hand as I fell, but he couldn't get a hold on me. I know he'll get over that. He probably feels sad about my dying, but he'll get over that, too. We were only friends. I want to start fresh with him. Well, not completely fresh, as it turns out. But he hasn't seen Maxine-the-first in two years, and that was only lunch. I've changed a lot. Am I doing the wrong thing?''

Gabby tilted her head. ''Aw, Jennie, I don't know. It's not something I've ever read about in 'Dear Abby,' that's for sure. Do you feel right about it?''

''Yes, very right.''

''Then I don't see anything wrong with it. Either way, he's lost somebody. But Jennie was closer to him. Here's another way to think about it. This happened to me, anyway. When I became . . . paralyzed, my life changed. Who I was changed. It was like getting a whole new identity, new friends, everything. What's so different about that compared to this?''

Maxine gave Gabby a harder hug. ''I never thought about it that way. Thank you so much. That's exactly what happened to me, too. Your old friends feel awkward around you. They don't know how to relate to you anymore. And after a while, you don't want to be around people who knew you as you were. You forge a new identity.''

A peppy knock made Maxine stand as Gabby went to the door. The owner of the building, Rick, wheeled in with his high-speed chair. ''So Gabby, are you going with me to the arcade?'' He stopped and looked up at Maxine with surprise. ''Oh, didn't know you had company.''

Maxine stepped forward and held out her hand. ''I'm Maxine, an old friend of Gabby's.''

Rick took her hand. ''Nice to meet you. I'm Rick.'' He looked a bit like a magical elf, with red hair and beard, and a twinkle in his eyes. Rick had been in a wheelchair for most of his thirty-odd years, after an accident left his legs unable to grow properly. He'd also had a crush on Gabby since she moved in.

''I don't know,'' she said to Rick, looking a little embarrassed at Maxine having caught her even considering a date. ''All those machines would be hard to get around. Besides, there's snow outside.''

Maxine smiled, because she knew Rick wasn't going to

let any such lame excuse fly. He didn't let her down, waving her words away.

"Ah, there's only an inch of snow out there. And it's not hard to get around in the arcade at all. It took me six months, but I finally nagged the owner into making the place accessible." Rick leaned his chair back against the island in the kitchen, his small legs dangling in midair. "Besides, you can walk." He drew those last words out in a taunting sing-song, snagging both of their attention.

"What do you mean?" Maxine asked.

"They have this booth with a virtual-reality device in it. It's the most awesome thing. Gabby, you put this headpiece on and you can see yourself walking. You can *feel* yourself walking." The excitement in his voice and wonder in his eyes made Maxine want to try it, and she already was walking. "We could dance," he added as extra incentive.

Gabby and Maxine traded looks. "Go, Gabby," Maxine heard herself saying. Not so much to discover virtual reality, but to get out and live life again. She'd spent far too much time hiding, sulking, and being angry at the world's injustice. "It sounds like a good time."

Rick gave his head a little twist. "Guarantee it."

Maxine could see the idea intrigued her, but Gabby was too stubborn to relent that easily. "Let it go, Gabby."

She looked at Maxine. "That's easy for you to say. Everything's different now."

Maxine knelt down beside her and spoke softly. "But don't think I'll ever forget. It's time for me to move on and accept my new life. And it's time for you, too." She nodded toward Rick, who was looking around the kitchen and pretending not to listen. "You always gave me advice about my life, about Sam. Now it's my turn. Go."

"But this is different. Sam was . . ." Gabby nodded subtly toward Rick and whispered, "He's not."

Maxine lifted an eyebrow. "No?"

"No." She glanced over at Rick again. "I don't know."

"You're welcome to come along, too," Rick said to Maxine.

And he meant it, though Maxine knew he'd rather be alone with Gabby. He'd be so good for her, an injection of life and determination. Nothing stopped Rick, not from driving, riding horses, or getting something on the top shelf in the supermarket. Maxine had seen him actually climb up the shelves and grab the item he wanted. Startled the heck out of one of the clerks, though. She grinned at the memory.

"Thank you, but I have some other things to take care of." She gave Gabby a pointed look, then grabbed up her purse. "I've got to get going. I'll keep in touch." She took Gabby's hand in hers and gave it a squeeze. "Have fun. I expect a full report on this virtual reality thing."

Maxine had gone to the club offices with the intention of questioning some of the employees about James's whereabouts the day of her supposed accident. She'd even gone to the door, phrasing the questions she'd ask in her mind, but she chickened out before walking inside. Armand was there somewhere, and she didn't feel like running into him. Just the thought had her hiding her hands in her pockets.

The problem was, even though she'd worked for a private investigator, she wasn't actually equipped to be one. And to start asking questions would only arouse suspicions. How did you ask about someone's whereabouts on a certain day and time without sounding like a cop?

It all came down to Sam. She needed him, and he didn't want to help her. She was going to have to appeal to him as a friend to take on her case. Maybe this was the big case he'd been after all those years. She frowned when she remembered his words about not wanting to go after the big case anymore because he couldn't deliver on his promises to Jennie. Well, she would make him want to fulfill those promises again.

The simple act of walking felt wonderful, and she filled

the rest of her day doing just that. She felt a little vain, pausing in window reflections admiring the way she walked and the sway of her hips. It was all wonderful; window shopping, easily dodging people, not having to search for the access ramp on the sidewalk. People didn't look at her curiously, or worse, in that sympathetic way. She blended in now. They didn't look at her at all. She was one of them.

Five o'clock filled the sidewalks with people rushing to get home. The crowd would have worried her before: would they see her down there? Bump into her chair or, worse, simply move her out of their way as if she were a piece of furniture? Now she plowed right through them. She headed to her car and drove past Sam's office building for the third time that afternoon. He still wasn't there. But she had a feeling where he might be on a Thursday after five: Bernard's.

Almost every Thursday he and Jennie had gone there after work for dinner, unless Sam was on a case. It was one of the few restaurants in the area that was wheelchair-accessible. Her heart did a little thump-de-thump when she saw his car outside. She parked next to him and walked up to the entrance feeling the cold air pinken her cheeks. The ramp had been built after the fact, always making her go several yards out of the way to where it started. This time she took the steps straight in. This time she could part the soft black curtain as she walked through instead of feeling it graze her face unless Sam moved it.

Bernard's was deep and narrow, filled with tables in close proximity with one another and wondrous aromas of beef and garlic. Sam was sitting there at their usual table, by himself. Pepe, their waiter, poured coffee and said something that made Sam smile a little before his thoughts absorbed back into the papers in front of him. Maxine realized it had been a long time since she'd seen him smile. Maybe it had been that last morning when he'd looked up from his desk and said good morning to Jennie. She wanted that Sam back. Her bossman. How she longed to call him that, but she knew it would spook him. He'd never call her kiddo again. But maybe, just maybe, she could make him laugh in that deep booming way again.

"Hi," she said softly from beside him.

He didn't look at her for a moment, but stared in front of him. Then, very slowly, he turned to face her. "I cannot be looking at you standing there. I refuse to believe that I'm not imagining it, so I'm just going to ignore you." And he did, going back to the papers spread out in front of him. Same old chicken-scratch writing, same long fingers with neat, trimmed nails.

She slid out of her coat and sat down opposite him, leaning forward. "Sam, I'm not your imagination. Sam?"

He looked up at her, his blue eyes filled with consternation. "How did you find me here?"

"Ah . . ." Did he come here when they were married? Probably not. She forced a smile. "I was driving by and saw your car out front."

He leaned across the table only inches from her face, and his voice was low and menacing. "You are out to make my life miserable, and I want to know why."

"Aw, Sam. I'm just sitting here."

She had the strongest urge to lean forward just a little bit and kiss those rigid lips of his. Maybe he sensed that, because his mustache twitched, and then he dropped back into his chair.

"My point exactly. What now? Did you find ketchup stains in the bedroom?"

She leaned her chin on her laced fingers. It was so strange to see this sarcastic side of Sam. "You have to take on my case. I can't do this investigation on my own."

"And here I was going to turn over my caseload to you. I already told you I'm not taking your case."

"But you said you'd give your business a couple more months."

He leaned back in his chair, running his finger along the rim of his coffee cup. "I said I'd think about it." After a moment of her worried expression, he added, "I asked for another month before starting the job. I figured I'd probably need it anyway. But it doesn't change anything. I told you I don't take on cases I have a personal interest in."

She lifted an eyebrow. "Are you saying you have an interest in me?"

"No," he answered too easily. "But we're friends, remember?"

"Ooh!" She tossed a sugar packet at him. "Shame on you, turning my words around on me." He only shrugged in his defense, if that's what you could call it. "Fine," she said, though she was far from giving up.

"Can I get you something to drink?" Pepe said from beside her.

"Yes, a coffee, please." When he brought it a minute later, she said, "Thank you, Pepe."

Both Pepe and Sam looked at her strangely. Pepe only nodded and returned to his duties. Sam didn't quite let it drop that easily.

"How did you know Pepe's name?"

"I've been here before. I remembered."

He glanced around. "This place isn't quite your style, Maxine. Dinners here cost less than twenty bucks. You on a downhill slide?"

She was ready to toss the whole container of sugar at him, but she tapped her fingers on the linen tablecloth instead. "Maybe my priorities have changed."

"I doubt that."

She'd just have to show him. She fixed her coffee with a large dose of cream and two packs of sugar. Sam was watching her.

"Since when do you put cream in your coffee? You always said it contaminated the true flavor of the coffee, or some such horse pucky."

"I changed my mind."

Sam chewed on the coffee stir stick he brought with him; he always said there was something not right about stirring coffee with a spoon. Although, she remembered with a shake of her head, he didn't have a problem stirring his coffee with a pen now and again.

He regarded her across the table. "So, where's your little Italian fellow? I'm surprised he let you go an inch from his grasp."

"You think it's funny, don't you?"

His mustache twitched. "Yep."

Her lips twitched back. "Well, it's not."

"Then why are you trying to hide a smile?"

"Ooh, you think you're such a great detective, don't you?"

He was smiling; not that sweet smile he used to give her, but close enough. "I have my moments."

For a second, she could pretend she was Jennie, and they were having their Thursday dinner together. But that didn't feel right anymore. She braced her chin on her upturned palm.

"Don't do that," Sam said.

She looked down at herself. "What?"

"Sit like that, with your chin in your palm. Just don't do it."

Why, she'd done that a thousand times, right there in that restaurant, listening to him talk and laugh that rumbly laugh of his. She laced her fingers instead.

"Better?"

"Fine."

When Pepe came to take the dinner order, Sam passed.

"Sam, you need to eat," she said.

Sam shook his head, looking up at Pepe. "You think you get rid of them when you divorce them." He shrugged, lifting his hands up. "It don't work that way. Don't let them tell you otherwise."

"He'll have chicken cordon bleu," Maxine said, ordering his favorite. "Me, too. That's all," she said when Pepe paused, waiting for Sam's approval.

Sam shrugged. "You heard the lady." When Pepe left,

he asked, "How do you know what I usually get here?"

"I knew you liked chicken. It was a lucky guess."

He chewed on his stir stick again. "Sure. Lucky. You ought to play the lottery, what with all your lucky guesses."

For so long, she'd kept her feelings from her eyes. Now she had to retrain them, just as she had to retrain her brain to talk to her legs. But not too soon on the first part.

"Sam, you don't think we can be friends, do you?"

He started to say something, but stopped. "No. Not us. I mean, we can be . . . polite. Anything beyond that would be inappropriate, not to mention impossible. Eating dinner together, for example, falls under the inappropriate category."

She tried to keep the twitch from her lips this time. "I suppose you're right. It was silly of me to think we could. So we're acquaintances, then?"

"I guess you could say that."

She finally allowed her smile to come to the surface. "Good. I'm hiring you to take on my case."

He opened his mouth, but held back the words. Instead he gave her a narrowed-eyed smile. "You're a conniver, just like I thought."

"Maybe. But you're in business, at least for now, and we're not friends. I'll pay you a retainer and we'll go from there."

For a moment, she thought he might still refuse her. But Sam had his integrity, that she would bet on.

"I'll be honest with you, Maxine. I think you're full of it. I think you're making an accident into something a lot more. I can't imagine why you'd want to retain me for the job. But you got me in a corner. If we haven't closed the case by the time I start working for Chuck, then it's back in your lap."

"Okay." She smiled, biting her lower lip. "Thanks, Sam."

For a moment he just stared at her. Then he shook his head. "No problem," he said, but she was sure he didn't mean it. He dug out the notepad beneath the other papers he'd been working on. "So, tell me what you know."

She was just another client. Well, that's what she'd worked out.

"I think James is behind it. He has the most animosity toward Ma—me. He thinks I'm marrying Armand for his money." By Sam's expression, she could tell he suspected as much, too. "Aida seems quite protective of her boss, as well."

"She looks like she could protect a boxer. Go ahead," he said when she gave him a stern look at interrupting her.

"And she was there when the supposed accident happened. Sally doesn't seem close enough to her father to try to get me out of the picture. Or ambitious enough. Those are my three suspects."

"I get the impression that Maxine—I mean, I'm sure they got the impression that I spent a lot of time in the greenhouse. I think someone worked on those brackets to make it look as though they'd corroded. They stood at the window and waited for me to walk beneath before dislodging the box. But there was something James said that first night after the incident. He asked if anyone was going to comment on how strange it was that the box fell the same way . . . and then Armand cut him off. Maybe there was another supposed accident."

Sam was scribbling as she spoke. After a moment, he looked up. "You mean before you started dating him? An accident that happened to someone else?"

"Er, yes."

"I noticed you're not including Armand in your list of suspects. Any reason?"

"Why would he try to kill me?" She forced a smile. "He hasn't even been married to me yet."

Sam grinned at that, and she felt warm inside. "Yeah, well. Let's not discount him entirely. And don't get defensive. I know you have feelings for the guy, but—"

"I'm thinking of postponing the wedding," she blurted out. Might as well start the demise of her engagement now.

Sam raised an eyebrow. "Don't go jumping to hasty decisions, Maxine. Just because I don't want to eliminate him as a suspect doesn't mean you should dump the little fellow."

She took a sip of her coffee. "No, it's not this or even the accident. I just don't know if he's the right man for me." Looking up at him, she asked, "Do you think he's my type?"

Sam raised his hands. "Oh, no, I'm not treading on *that* ground. I can't tell you that. All I can tell you is the kind of man who's not your type."

"Don't be so sure of that," she caught herself saying. "And I know what your type is."

"Oh, yeah? And what's that?"

Well, she'd gotten herself in it now. "Mostly blondes with large . . ."—she gestured to her chest—"and long legs."

He was grinning again, and her throat tightened. "Yeah, I like my women with legs that go all the way down to the floor."

Her lip twitched. "Don't they all do that?"

"Yeah, well, some do it the long way."

"Why don't you pick one with a brain once in a while?"

He lifted an eyebrow. "How do you know whether my women have brains or not?"

"It goes with the . . ." She made the long-legs big-chest gesture, though she knew she was being unfair to women with those attributes. That was the only way she could think of to get out of the tight spot she'd put herself in. "You want to know what I think?"

He rolled his eyes. "Uh-oh. Dare I?"

"I think you pick those women because you know you won't get involved with them."

"Whew. I thought you were going to get deep on me or something. And what's wrong with that?"

"What's wrong with that? Don't you wonder why you don't want a commitment? What if there's some not-so-gorgeous woman who could handle the demands of your job, but you're overlooking her because she's not your type?''

Pepe brought their food, but Sam only toyed with the green beans. She realized her own appetite wasn't hearty either. It was too strange, sitting here like usual, and yet not at all like usual.

"Actually," he said, setting his fork down. "One of the prettiest gals I ever knew didn't fit that description at all."

"Really?" She tried to remember if she'd seen any women without the long legs. Maybe a brunette. And of course, once a redhead. "Did it last long?"

His expression seemed far away. "Yeah, it did. For four years."

Four years? Her heart squeezed into a tiny ball. That had to have been during the time she worked for him, and yet he'd never let on there was anyone serious in his life.

She pushed the words out. "And are you seeing her now?"

He slowly shook his head. "She was my assistant, Jennie."

Maxine's heart went from hard and tiny to exploding into vibrations that shook her to the tips of her fingers and toes. "Jennie?" she sputtered in disbelief.

"Yeah. She was a brunette, wasn't real large in the chest, and was in a wheelchair, so I could never really tell how long her legs were. But it didn't matter; she was still the prettiest lady I ever knew."

Maxine had to put her fork down before her trembling gave her away. Sam focused in on her.

"What's the matter? Don't tell me you're so shallow you don't think I could find someone in a wheelchair pretty? Or are you mad because I didn't say she was the second prettiest?"

"I'm not mad," she said on a whisper. She could hardly swallow. "It's just that . . . I mean, did she know?"

"That I thought she was pretty?" He shrugged. "I don't

think I ever told her, no. We worked together. I didn't want her to think I was coming on to her or anything.''

Only then could she breathe fully. "She probably wouldn't have thought that." Maxine had to look away for a moment. Of all those women Sam had known, he'd thought she was the prettiest. Dull Jennie with her plain brown hair that wouldn't take a curl with a prayer; with her average body and average looks. With her wheelchair.

"Anyway," Sam was saying, picking up his fork and cutting into the chicken. "I'll do some background checking into the family tomorrow and find out what this other incident is. I'll keep in touch. Maxine, that means I'll call you, don't call me. Or pop in on my dinner."

"Yes, boss—boss," she finished. *Yes, bossman.*

Typically Sam met with the client once initially, often in a public place where they felt more comfortable. He might meet again with them once or twice during the course of a long investigation. And then the final meeting when he gave the client the report she'd typed up and the bill. Sam wasn't going to get rid of her that easily, though. And he didn't look all that convinced that she'd heed that request, either.

They ate in silence. She was just glad to see him eating. Later, when Pepe brought the bill, she snapped it up and put it on her credit card. He tried to shove money at her, but she wouldn't take it.

"Sam, I barged in on your dinner. Besides, you took my case. It's the least I can do."

"When did you become so darned stubborn? I mean, you were stubborn before, when it came to getting your way. But not in buying something for someone else."

She winked at him. "Told you I'd changed."

"Yeah, right."

She pulled a checkbook out of her bag and wrote a check for Sam's retainer. Luckily Maxine-the-first had a nice balance, even if she had no home of her own. Everything in her new life depended on Sam. She'd be content to work at the agency again doing what she'd done before.

"All right," he said, standing and running his palms down the front of his pants to smooth them out. "I'll let you know what I find out."

"What are you doing now?" She didn't want to just show up at the Houndog; he'd think she had hired somebody to investigate his habits.

He gave her an impatient look. "I'm going to unwind for a while. Alone."

"Aw, Sam. Don't you want some company? You look kind of down lately."

"Maybe I want to be down."

He did have his melancholy moods, and seemed to revel in feeling blue. That's when he put on the soul-ripping blues and sank into it. Sometimes he'd do that at the club, too, when a particular song came on.

"Listen, Maxine. Go home to your fiancé. That's where you belong, not hanging around with your ex-husband."

"I don't want to go home," she stated, dreading the thought of returning to that white place with the dummies. "Those things give me the creeps."

"Things?"

"You know. The dummies. They're always watching me. He even has them in the bedroom."

"All I can say is, you must have known about them before you agreed to marry the guy." He took her shoulders in hand and turned her to face him. "I know what your problem is."

"You do?" His fingers felt warm on her shoulders, and she had the urge to close the gap between them and bury herself against him.

"You're getting cold feet. And this flower box thing has made it worse. Soon you'll be as excited about marrying the guy as you were before. You're just a little confused."

This was the Sam she knew: compassionate, warm. At least a glimpse of that, anyway.

"Sam, hold me for a minute. Please?"

He met her gaze. "I don't think that's a good idea. I—"

She slipped her arms around him and pressed her cheek against his shoulder. Inside his open coat she felt warm and safe, like a worm in a cocoon. How could she convince him to let her stay there for a little while . . . say about three days or so? After a moment, Sam slipped his arms around her, though he didn't press her any closer. Then again, maybe that was impossible.

"Maxine," he murmured into her ear a moment later. "We're not supposed to be friends, remember? Acquaintances don't hug each other, not for more than maybe a brief hello or good-bye."

She opened her eyes. "I know." Reluctantly, she loosened herself from him. He let her go far too easily. "I'm sorry." The heck she was!

He touched her chin. "Everything will be all right. You're confused that's all. Come on; I'll walk you to your car."

She didn't want to go to her car, because that meant he wasn't letting her tag along with him to the Houndog. And sinking into some blues was sounding pretty darn good right about then. Throwing herself on him wasn't going to accomplish anything but alienate him.

Except for a car stopped farther up with its lights on, the street was quiet. Sam walked beside her to her car. They'd had to park nearly a block away from the restaurant. She was watching Sam, who was looking at the ground about a foot behind her.

"Thanks for letting me eat dinner with you, S—"

Headlights slashed across them. The sound of an engine roared through the air. The car bore down right at her.

"Maxine!" she heard Sam yell.

Her body was frozen as she stared at the lights coming at her. The terror of the car accident twelve years ago filled her. The regret of losing Sam again numbed her. *No, no, no!* she thought as adrenaline shot through her. She felt his hand on her arm as he pulled her out of the way.

The car jerked to the right, tires squealing on the asphalt as the driver tried to cut her off. She wasn't fast enough. The car nudged her backward. Sam's arm went around her shoulders, hauling her against his body. And then she felt the hard pavement as they both hit the road.

Chapter 6

"*I*'m all right, I'm all right," Maxine heard herself saying between deep breaths, though she had no idea why she was saying it. She certainly didn't feel all right. Her body was racked with waves of trembling. The black haze in front of her materialized into the night sky. She blinked, turning to find Sam crouched beside her and feeling his warm, deep breaths across her cheek. "What happened?"

"Someone tried to run you over." He looked around, probably making sure the driver wasn't coming back to finish the job. "Are you really all right?"

"I don't know, actually." The sounds of shattering glass and crunching metal still echoed in her head. That was another accident; another lifetime. She curled her fingers, then her toes. Thank God everything moved as it should though her muscles were tighter than stretched rubber bands. And the trembling was getting more violent. "Yes, I think I'm all right."

"I'm going to call the police."

"Do you really think the driver was trying to do this on purpose?"

"Just a little. When the driver missed the first time, he swerved to the right to get a second try. But I couldn't see who was behind the wheel, and I was too busy eating asphalt to get a look at the car's license plate. Did you recognize the car or see who was driving?''

''I didn't see anything but headlights. I felt like those deer probably do, frozen in fear. I couldn't move.''

Her body ached as she tried to get to her feet. Sam's fingers wrapped around hers as he helped her up, watching her carefully. He pulled her to the side of the road and the safety of the cars they stood between. ''You're shaking,'' he said, rubbing up and down her arms.

''I'll be all right.'' She willed the trembling to stop, but it kept coming, wave after wave of it. She scanned the road on either side. Had whoever done this parked the car and snuck back to see his handiwork?

''Come here,'' Sam mumbled softly, pulling her against him. ''You're safe now.'' His hand stroked down her hair in rhythm with her trembling.

She pressed closer, shutting her eyes against the warmth and solidness of his body. His chest still rose and fell heavily, and beneath the layers of his clothing she could faintly hear his heart hammering away. She felt safe right here. If only the rest of the world would leave them alone and let this moment ride into forever.

The hit-and-run scene played in her mind over and over, but she couldn't pick out any detail. Sam kissed the top of her head, then rested his cheek against that same spot. She realized she wasn't trembling anymore.

''Do you want me to take you to the hospital? Just to make sure everything's all right,'' he asked.

''No, I'm okay.'' To prove it, she reluctantly moved out of his embrace. Hopefully it wouldn't take nearly getting run over to get another one of those. ''You yanked me out of the way. You saved my life, Sam.''

''Not quite fast enough. I wasn't exactly planning to dodge hit-and-runs tonight. Maxine, you were right all along. Someone wants you dead.'' His voice was calm, but the undertone of dread was clear.

She looked in the direction the car had torn off into. ''I

could have died, just like that." Again. She turned to Sam. "I really am in danger, aren't I?"

"Yes." He held her hands in his. They were both shaking a little, though Sam had taken those terrible trembles away. "Maxine, I think you should go to the police. This is attempted murder."

"But the police won't believe me. You hardly believed me before. And what are they going to get from this? We can't identify the car. I see no one out here who could have seen it. And I have no evidence from the flower box. No, I want you to investigate this. And I want to hire you as my bodyguard."

His fingers tightened on hers before he let go abruptly. "No, Maxine. I'm not going to do this. For one thing, I'm not trained as a bodyguard. I'll refer you to someone who is."

"And for second thing?"

He looked at her. "What?"

"You said 'for one thing.' What's the other thing?"

He ducked his head, pressing his fingers to his temples. Finally he met her gaze, his eyes filled with pain. "I can't. I just can't."

She touched his arm. "Why, Sam? I need you."

His voice sounded raspy when he spoke. "I couldn't save Jennie; how can I take responsibility for your life?"

"Sam, that was an accident."

"It doesn't matter. She was right there, and I couldn't save her. How can I depend on myself to save yours? Or anybody else's?"

"That's why you want to work for someone else, doing paper trails, isn't it? Because you don't think you can handle it anymore."

He didn't answer for a moment. Finally he looked away and said, "Yes."

She inhaled deeply to calm her breathing once and for all. "Sam, you just saved my life right here. If you hadn't moved me out of the way, I would have been hit."

"I didn't do anything. I wasn't even looking." He shook his head wearily. "My instincts aren't there anymore. I used to be able to feel this kind of thing coming."

"But I felt your arm pulling me. You knew somehow." After a moment, she said, "Sam?"

He looked at her. "I'll investigate your case, but you're going to have to find someone else to look after you if you don't go to the police."

She didn't want to start all over again with the police. "They can't help me. Only you can."

"I told you I'd investigate. Don't ask me to do more than that."

She didn't want to push too hard, afraid he'd back out completely. "All right, Sam. If that's what you want."

"It's what has to be." He handed her his car keys. "Sit in my car for a minute. Lock the doors."

She watched him scout the area, walking to the roadway to look for potential witnesses. It was so dark out, no one in the restaurant would have seen the car, even if they had been looking through the curtained front window. He disappeared from her view, and she sat back against the vinyl seat and let out a long breath. Her back ached, and she stretched it. Her heart was still pounding a hundred beats per second, though she kept taking deep breaths to calm it. Now she knew how Maxine-the-first had felt as she'd driven to Sam's office: terrified. And because of Jennie's accident, Sam didn't feel competent to protect her.

A tap on the glass startled her. She breathed a sigh of relief to see Sam standing there. He slipped inside and closed the door.

"Are you all right?" he asked.

"Yes. Thanks to you."

He shook his head slightly, then pulled out a cellular phone from his coat pocket. "Call home now. See who's there and who isn't."

"Ah, good idea." She dialed the number. Aida answered. "Hi, Aida, it's Maxine. Is Armand home?"

"Yes, and he's been worried sick about you. You're a naughty girl to make him frantic this way, Ms. Lizbon. You ought to spend a few hours in the corner." She paused, as if expecting Maxine to actually have a response to that. "Hold on a moment and I'll get him," she finally said.

A second later, Armand picked up the phone. "Darling, where have you been? I was ready to call the police."

She remembered her vow to make him mad enough to break off their engagement, but she couldn't find it in her to do that right then. The truth would be enough anyway. "I'm with Sam." She heard a disgusted noise, but kept going. "Someone tried to run me over just now."

"What?"

"Armand, who's home right now?"

"What do you mean? No, you can't think anyone here would do that? You're wrong, darling. Sally has been home since noon, not feeling well. Aida just took some soup up to her. James walked in the door five minutes ago. Where are you?"

She could hardly answer, after being ready to find out who the murderer was. "In the city."

"Shall I come get you?"

"No, I'll be driving home. I'll see you shortly. Goodbye." She disconnected. "Everyone's there."

"Damn. If it is one of them, they could have hired someone to do the job. Believe me, there are enough punks around here that would pull off something like this for the right kind of money. I'll check with my contacts to see if anyone in the usual group was hired for a hit like this." His fingers tightened around the steering wheel. "Are you sure you're all right to drive? I can take you home."

"No, I'll be okay."

"I'm going to follow you home, just to make sure. I want you to call my friend tonight. He knows what he's doing."

"All right." Her voice sounded small and thin.

He walked her around to her car, gesturing with his finger for her to lock the doors. She looked up at him through the glass, wishing she was back in his arms again. Her gaze kept flashing to the rearview mirror, watching him as he followed her back out to Armand's mansion. It was the last place in the world she wanted to be. And possibly the most dangerous.

Armand was waiting outside when they pulled up. How he could look both worried and agitated was beyond her but he managed to pull it off. He rushed to her car when she stopped. She buried her hands in her coat pockets as soon as she closed the car door. He was looking for them as he spoke, but gave up and let his hands drop to his sides.

"Darling, please tell me what's going on." Armand turned to find Sam walking up behind him. His displeasure clearly won over his worry for a moment. At least until he heard about the car that had tried to run them over. Her particularly.

They all went inside, where Sam reverified the whereabouts of the family members and asked if anyone had received a call in the last hour. Except for her call, the phone had been silent.

"I was hoping the punk had called to let his client know the job was botched," Sam whispered to her, sending a little shiver down her neck with his warm breath. "Maybe whoever's behind this is smarter than we think."

Armand opened the door as soon as they reached the foyer, his incredibly subtle way of ushering Sam out. Sam didn't need any more of a hint, apparently, and walked directly out the door. Maxine followed him, taking a few steps onto the front porch.

Armand stepped out also, after giving her a pointed look which she ignored. He directed that annoyed expression at Sam. "I want to go on record that it's ridiculous to even think anyone in my house would have done this to Maxine."

Sam's fingers closed over her shoulders. "I want to go on record that your fiancée here is in danger, and you better damn well take this seriously or you're going to lose her."

Just that small touch made her feel more protected than a suit of armor or a platoon of soldiers acting as bodyguards. Despite his deadly tone of voice, she couldn't help but feel warm inside. Sam cared.

"Here's the name of the guy I told you about," Sam said, handing her a business card with a name and number scribbled on the back. "Call him as soon as you get inside." His words became puffs of fog in the cool night air.

Her fingers brushed his as she took the card, and she held his gaze, making her words more meaningful. "Thank you, Sam."

"So you think this is real now?" Armand asked Sam, pushing into their space.

"I would bet my life on it, but I wouldn't bet hers. Your girl's in danger, Armand. She won't go to the police, though I'm not sure how much help they would be, either. But she needs help." He turned to her. "I'll be in touch. Let me know if Mark can't help you."

She nodded, wishing like the first time that he would stay. He got back in the car and pulled away, taking a part of her with him and leaving an empty ache deep inside her. His taillights became smaller and smaller, then a spark in the distance. She crossed her arms in front of her and anchored her hands over her shoulders, wishing it were Sam's hands on her still.

"Maxine?" Armand cleared his throat. "Maxine," he said a little louder this time.

She finally dragged her gaze from the empty driveway and hoped she didn't look as bereft and alone as she felt. "Yes, Armand," she heard her tired voice say.

"I don't think I know you anymore."

She looked at him, trying to keep the frown off her face. "I don't know me anymore, either. But I can't live like this. I'm afraid to be here." She nodded toward the house. "I'm afraid to leave the house. I'm hiring a bodyguard."

"I won't allow it." He sounded firmer than she'd ever heard him. For a moment, despite the circumstances, she admired him. Then his voice went soft again. "Darling, this is crazy. Let me stay home and take care of you. If—and I think it's crazy—you think my family is doing this to you, then they wouldn't dare try to hurt you if I was with you. I'll stay by your side twenty-four hours a day." He actually found her hands inside her pockets and grasped them through the coat's material. "No one will hurt my kissums."

Claustrophobia set in at the mere thought of round-the-clock Armand. "No, I can't allow you to do that." She moved free of his grasp and walked toward the house. "Sam gave me the number of a guy who guards people for a living." She only hoped the guy couldn't do it.

"I'm surprised you're not hiring Sam. You seem awfully fond of him lately. But honestly, I feel like he's always been around us, haunting us like a ghost."

Maxine stopped so abruptly, Armand walked into her. "What did you say?"

He cringed a little, taking her surprised statement as an invitation to a fight. "All I'm saying is that it seems as though he's always been between us. You talked about him from the day we first met, how he didn't make you happy, how he'd done this, hadn't done that. At first I thought it was good that you obviously didn't have any lingering affection for the man you used to be married to. But you kept talking about him until I felt I knew him without ever setting eyes on the man. The banana shakes he ate for breakfast, the fact that he stirred his coffee with a pen, that his handwriting was an archeologist's challenge. Goodness, I felt as if *I'd* been married to him! Now he's in our lives physically. You were with him tonight." That last spoken with more accusation than the rest.

Maxine tilted her head, eyes widening. "You don't think it was possible that . . . I was in love with Sam before all this happened, do you?"

"What are you saying?"

"Just asking your opinion. Do you think I might have

been in love with him before all this? You know, like so deep inside I didn't even know it?''

His eyebrows wrinkled in thought and indecision. ''In my worst hours of insecurity maybe. But I didn't want to believe that, since you were marrying me. That's why I never said anything about it before. But now . . .'' He shook his head, giving her a disappointed look. ''You were seeing him tonight obviously.''

He wasn't going to let that one go.

''I was hiring him to investigate the first accident.''

''Let me hire someone else, someone not so personally involved with us.''

''No. I want Sam.'' She took a quick breath, those words fraught with other meanings that had nothing to do with his profession. ''Sam is the best. You can't tell me who to hire for my own murder. I mean, attempted murder.''

She stalked into the house and straight to the phone. Sam had tried to write the man's name and number down neatly. As the phone rang on the other end, she found herself tracing his numbers with her fingertip. Armand hovered behind her, looking ready to disconnect the phone at any moment.

'' 'Lo,'' a man's voice answered. The static on the line indicated he was on a cellular phone.

''I need to speak to a Mark Lohman.''

''You got 'im, honey. What can I do for you?''

She decided to let the honey thing pass without comment. ''You were referred to me by Sam Magee for your bodyguarding services. I guess that's the way you say it. You're not available to do that right now, I bet, are you?''

Silence greeted her for a moment. Okay, so she'd worded it in a strange way. ''Well, actually I'm on a case right now. I might be done in about a day or so when the trial's over. I can recommend someone else I know who's available if you'd like.''

''No, I know someone who can handle it. Thank you very much. Very, very much.'' She turned to Armand after placing the phone on the hook. ''I can't stay here another night.

I'll probably wake up with a knife up my nose."

She walked into the bedroom and pulled down a suitcase that looked like something Maxine-the-first might own. She started throwing clothing into it, including a drawerful of more lace panties. Armand watched in confusion.

"Well, let me come with you, then. Where are you going, anyway? Who do you know that can handle it? Are you going to tell me anything?"

She turned to Armand, putting her hands on his shoulders the way Sam had done to her earlier. "Telling you might put your life in danger," she said in a low, grave voice.

"What?"

"If you know, someone may try to kill you for the information. I can't put you at that kind of risk, Armand. I care about you too much. I know things are . . . tense between us right now. Maybe this time apart will be good for us." She tried to look upset at the prospect of leaving. "We can take this time to look inside ourselves and see if our lives are headed in the directions destiny has charted."

Armand blinked, then shook his head slightly. "But will I see you?"

"Of course." They had to keep investigating, after all. "I'll call you."

"When?"

Grabbing up her jammed suitcase, she hauled it to the door. "Soon. Mr. Wiggles will keep you company." And then she left, feeling both bad and great at the same time. Armand stood at the doorway and watched her pull away, probably looking as blue as she had looked watching Sam leave. Geez, was this all screwed up!

Maxine had never been to Sam's apartment, because he lived on the second floor of a building without an elevator. Once he'd invited her for dinner, and she'd actually been foolish enough to think of taking him up on it. But as usual, her first question had to be if his apartment had wheelchair access, and he'd had to think about it before admitting it did not. When he'd offered to carry her up the stairs, the thought of putting him out like that had sent her into a hundred babbling excuses about why she couldn't have dinner with him at his apartment. He'd never asked her again. She'd never give up a chance like that again.

Sam didn't know it yet, but he was going to guard her body. And he'd get her heart and soul in the bargain.

As it turned out, Sam didn't live in an apartment building at all. Maxine glanced at the address she'd written down, then back up to the warehouse-turned-shops-and-apartments. Not far from the office, this area too was going through renovation. Unfortunately, the old buildings hadn't complied with the Americans with Disabilities Act. Not a ramp in sight, nor an elevator.

Even now, she felt frustration boiling inside her. Locked out. Excluded. Now she took those stairs with a vengeance, hauling the large suitcase up with her. No matter the struggle, she relished each step. Music drifted beneath his door, buoying her heart with hope that he was home. Blues. She was tired of having the blues. Now she wanted the reds and the pinks. Anything but white!

She heard Romeo bark at her first tap-tap on the door, and then the music lowered. She knocked again. Sam opened the door and stared at her for a moment, as if he weren't sure she was really standing there. Probably hoping she wasn't. His hair was slightly damp, and he wore nothing but sweatpants. The sight of his bare skin, especially on a chilly night, stopped her words in her throat. His skin looked creamy and soft in the warm light, but the muscles of his chest looked hard and capable. The warmth inside his apartment gushed out and enveloped her, heating her cheeks even more.

"Hi, Sam," she said, not holding back the smile. She knelt down and scratched Romeo's head. "Hello, sweetie." Then she stood again.

Sam was not smiling, especially when he caught sight of her suitcase. "Running away from home?"

She remembered that wicked puppet asking her that in the closet. "In a manner of speaking. Your friend couldn't help me. Now I'm hiring you." Before he could say a word, she pushed forward with her bag in tow, forcing him to move out of the way. She met his flushed expression with a determined look. "Sam, I don't care what you say, I'm not leaving and I'm not talking to anyone else. You're the only person who can keep me safe."

"Maxine, I told you—"

"That you didn't feel able to protect me because you couldn't keep a woman from falling down the stairs? Sam, what are you, superhuman?" All those years of watching quietly were behind her. "So what if you can't fly at the speed of sound, see danger through a door, sense every catastrophe in the world? That makes you incapable of protecting one woman who needs you?"

He just stared at her for a moment. Finally he stuck his hands in his pockets. "My heart isn't in it anymore. That's what makes me a bad choice for protecting you."

She took a step closer, inhaling the scent of fresh soap and fresh male. "Then you'd better damn well put your heart into it, because I'm here, and you're not getting rid of me. Show Jennie that you're not going to let her death ruin your life. How do you think that would make her feel? Do you think you're honoring her somehow? Sam, you're the same man you were last month, last year. Maybe life will be different without her. But life will go on, and it will pass you right by if you let guilt drag you under." Her chest filled with determination and wonder that she could stand up to him like this. That she could risk his friendship and protection by pushing his buttons.

"You have no right to lecture me, Maxine," he said in a low voice.

"Caring about you gives me that right. Don't tell me not to care about you, Sam. I can't do that."

He slowly rubbed the back of his hand across his mouth, narrowing his eyes at her. "What is this really about?"

"It's about you keeping me alive. And in a way, it's about me keeping you alive, too," she said in a softer voice.

"What has gotten into you?"

Maxine smiled. If he only knew. But he couldn't, not ever. "Life has gotten into me." And love. She could feel it swelling inside her, pushing at the edges of her being. *Not too fast, girl.* "Thank you, Sam."

"I haven't said I'd do it yet."

"I wasn't giving you a choice, remember?"

"Hmm," he mumbled, lifting his eyebrow. Glancing at her luggage, he said, "Well, seeing as I don't have much choice, I suppose I'll take your case. I state right here for the record," he said derisively, using Armand's tone, "that I don't think this is a good idea." He pointed a finger at her. "And I don't want you lecturing me anymore. I recall all too well how you did that when we were married, and we're not married anymore. What are you doing?"

Maxine had moved forward and hugged him. "I think they call this a hug. As in thank you, your help means the world to me, I promise I won't be a pain in the butt."

She'd barely gotten comfortable when he moved away. "You're welcome, though I have a feeling I'll regret this, and I know you'll be a pain in the butt anyway."

Maxine had been so involved with Sam himself, she just now got a chance to look around at his place. It was basically one large room with high ceilings and open metal beams above, and natural-finish wood floors. A series of Art Deco screens surrounded what might be the bedroom. A bathroom was built out to the right of that, and the lower roof over that sported various items such as a neon cactus and a ceramic cowboy hat. The kitchen was only separated from the rest of the room by a long, curved counter with a granite surface.

In the overall sense, it was neat; neater than his office. But in the small places—the cabinets, corners, and shelves—his true self crept through.

"This is nice," she said, wondering if Maxine-the-first

had ever been there. She knew Sam had bought the place two years ago. Probably not, then. "I can sleep on the couch."

"No, take the bedroom." He picked up her suitcase and walked through a division in the screens. "It's got a little more privacy than the couch, and I remember how you are about having your space."

She followed him in, her stomach tightening at the sight of the large bed that dominated the area. It had no frame, so it sat directly on the floor. Sam slept there. Now she would. "No, Sam, I can't kick you out of your bed. I'll take the couch."

He dropped the suitcase on the bed where it sank in among the swampland of black sheets. "Maxine, don't argue with me. Take the bed," he enunciated.

"Yes, sir."

"I'm afraid I only have the one set of sheets. I wash them and put them right back on the bed. When they wear out, I buy another set. It's a little late to wash them now, though, so remind me to throw them in the washer tomorrow."

"That's fine. Really."

He nodded, then walked over to a wood contraption that served as an open-air closet with built-in drawers. With one arm, he compressed his clothes and made space for hers. "There's room in the bottom drawer, too. Would you like a glass of wine?"

"Sure." How many times had she dreamed of such an evening, lounging around sharing wine and talk? She'd never invited him to her place; the modifications emphasized how different she was, and how things had to be altered for her use.

Music drifted through the air, a low, sensual saxophone that reverberated inside her and coiled through her veins like a drug. Glasses clinked together as Sam opened a bottle of wine and poured a glass for her, a refill for himself. He walked over with the glasses.

"Have a seat. Seeing as you've already made yourself at

home, you might as well make yourself comfortable.''

She didn't detect any malice in his words, or even sarcasm, so she walked over to the living room. The wraparound black leather couch offered the sitter the opportunity to watch the large-screen television angled in the corner or the crackling fire. At the vee, it was wide enough to make a cozy place for two. She chose the fire, taking the glass from Sam as he sat down a couple of feet away from her and propped his bare feet on the glass coffee table. He had nice feet, and she wasn't particularly a foot person. But her gaze kept drifting to his chest and the light from the flames as it played over his skin.

''It's warm in here,'' she said, pulling her sweater away from her neck. ''I think I'll go change.'' She walked into the bedroom, noting the gaps between the screens that allowed little privacy in the bedroom despite Sam's intentions. Opening her suitcase, she hung up a few of the things she'd brought, then chose a soft turtleneck shirt and cream-colored leggings. Maxine had some nice stuff; she'd hated to leave so much behind in Armand's closet, but she'd go back to get it later.

She started to strip off her sweater, then looked up to see Sam's profile as he sat on the couch. Sheesh, he could just turn his head and see her. She shifted a few feet to the left, but that put her in the pseudodoorway. Finally she found a small place where he couldn't see her and quickly changed.

''Did you think I was going to peek?'' he asked, a slight smile on his face when she emerged.

''Why do you say that?''

''I saw you shifting back and forth, looking through the cracks. Through my peripheral vision,'' he added at her accusing look. ''Hey, it's in my blood. I can't help but notice things. Especially things that are out of the ordinary.''

Maxine sat down in her spot again. Romeo jumped up between her and Sam, curling up with his chin on his paw. She pulled her legs up and wrapped her arms around them. ''So, I'm out of the ordinary, am I?''

"Very." After taking a sip of wine, he set it down on the glass-block coffee table. He propped his arm on the back of the couch and faced her. "What bugs me is that I can't figure you out."

Just the way he looked at her made her heart tumble, and combined with his words and that bare chest of his, it was doing somersaults. "What do you mean?"

"During the time we were married, and in the years afterward, all you ever talked about was having things: status, money . . . stuff. I can't say that was the downfall of our marriage, but it sure didn't help in the compatibility department. I admit I wasn't perfect husband material, especially with the hours I put in at the agency. But now you have everything you want. That house . . ." He shook his head. "The decor leaves a lot to be desired, but it's big, in the right part of town, and has a maid to keep it clean. And I'm sure your little Italian fellow would let you put in ten flowered couches, as long as they weren't pink." He pinched the bridge of his nose like Armand had done. "He's a different sort, but he's rich, and he obviously adores you." He leaned his cheek against his hand. "And you're here with me. He can't be too happy about that."

Maxine shook her head. "No, he isn't. I've probably finished my relationship with him, actually."

"See, this is what I mean. Unless you think he's the one who's doing this."

"No, I don't. He wanted to be my bodyguard, but I declined." She paused for a moment, trying not to let her smile show. "He thinks I'm in love with you."

Sam laughed. *Laughed!* If he wasn't laughing at her expense, she'd have enjoyed the deep, booming sound of it. "Well, it's bound to put a strain on a relationship when your fiancée is hanging around her ex-husband."

"He thinks I was in love with you before all this. Because I talked about you a lot."

He laughed again, this time a little more softly. "Well, I'm sure you set him straight about that. Besides, you were probably talking about how my business was more important than our marriage, how I wouldn't give you a respectable life. And my bad habits.''

Maxine thought it was terribly ironic that Maxine-the-first had been in love with her ex-husband. She probably didn't even know it. Obviously Sam thought the prospect was out of the question. He'd pretty much shrugged off the words that represented her stunning realization of earlier.

''What are you smiling about?'' he asked, watching her with interest.

''Just how funny it is, Armand thinking that.'' She pulled her gaze from his, finding it harder to swallow with him so close and watching her.

The entertainment center took up most of the wall to her left. It was filled with electronic devices and stereo components, a few framed photographs, more knickknacks. Her gaze shot back to the photograph on the middle shelf, and before she knew it, she was walking across the space between and holding it in her hands. It was a picture of Jennie in the kitchen—her old kitchen—caught off guard but smiling, a spot of flour on her cheek. Her heart was up in her throat when she turned around to face Sam. She'd never given him a picture of herself.

That soft look on Sam's face from a moment before was replaced by something dull and lifeless. ''That's Jennie,'' he said in a voice that matched his expression.

Her fingers tightened on the frame. ''The prettiest woman you ever knew,'' she said in a whisper, staring down at her reflection mixed with the image below the glass. Jennie hadn't been all that pretty. For some reason Sam thought so.

But how had he gotten this picture? Gabby had taken it and included it in a collage of photos that took up half her bedroom wall. Maxine couldn't think of a tactful way to ask how he'd gotten that picture, so she set it gently down and walked back to the couch. Sam was someplace else, his gaze riveted to the flames in the fireplace.

She nudged the words out, not even sure why she was asking. "Do you miss her?"

Sam kept his gaze directed at the fire. "Yes. She was . . . great." He blinked, looking at her finally. "Tomorrow I've got some checking around to do on your case, but I also have some surveillance to do for Ned. I guess you'll be going with me. I get an early start in the morning, so maybe you'll want to get some sleep. Been a helluva day."

He was trying to get rid of her. It seemed that every time he talked about Jennie, he closed himself to her. It had to be the guilt of not saving her that ate away at him. She'd heal him of that, even if it took some time.

"It has been a long day," she said, trying to salvage some pride. Then she smiled. "You're taking me with you on your surveillance?"

"I guess I'll have to, if I'm going to do my job right."

"I promise I won't be any trouble."

His mouth came up in a half-smile. "That's what you said when you asked me to marry you."

"I asked *you* to marry me?"

"Well, you were there, weren't you?"

"Of course." Well, Maxine had more guts than Jennie ever had. "I just forgot, that's all."

"Did you ask Armand, or did he pop the question?"

She erased the blank look on her face. "He asked."

"Listen, if you want to call him and smooth things out, I can put on my headphones and give you some privacy. Or you can go in the bathroom with the portable phone."

She shook her head, maybe too quickly. "I'd better not. I—I'll call him tomorrow."

Sam shrugged. "Whatever. Just thought you'd want to call your little . . . kissums." Even he couldn't keep the grin from his face. Neither could she.

"It's silly, isn't it?"

"Yep."

"He's a nice guy, but . . . he's not for me."

"Don't make any rash decisions right now. Like I said

before, this is an emotional time in your life. You obviously loved him enough to say yes to his proposal of marriage.'' He reached over and touched the big diamond on her engagement ring. ''Wait till this all blows over before breaking his heart.'' He started to get up, but she wrapped her fingers around his arm.

''Sam, did . . . I break your heart? When we got divorced, I mean.'' She wasn't even sure who had initiated it.

He looked down at her. ''Maxine, you broke my heart long before we got divorced. Every time you asked me to be something I wasn't, or compared me with Ned, or asked for something you knew I couldn't give you. Every time you sounded like my family, it broke a little piece.'' He stood, letting her hand drop away. ''Until there wasn't anything left.'' At her stricken expression, he added, ''Don't worry about it now. I was young. I desperately wanted someone in my corner for a change. Then I figured out that no one was going to be there but me, so I became my own best supporter. We were just wrong for each other.'' He gave her a wink. ''Now we're old enough to know better, aren't we?''

She didn't know what to say, but it didn't matter. He walked to a closet in the bathroom and took out a pillow and blanket. Even Romeo deserted her, following his master. That was her signal to scram, and she did so gracefully. She paused in the doorway, watching Sam lay out the blanket and punch the pillow into compliance.

''Good night, Sam.''

He looked up and smiled. ''Good night, Maxine.'' Then he dropped down on the couch and disappeared from her sight.

She stayed there for a moment, listening to the music and accompanying crackle of the fire. A gnawing ache filled her as she pictured Sam as a young man in love, disappointed with his materialistic wife and maybe even the world in general. Did his family act the same way, trying to make him into something he wasn't? Sam was . . . well, Sam.

She'd always loved him just the way he was.

Loving someone didn't mean changing them. Sometimes he was a little too cynical, and now she knew why. But she loved his sloppy ways at work, his impulsiveness, and even the cynical side of him. She had been the kind of woman who would have given him the support and acceptance he'd once needed.

Her gaze went to the picture, although she could only see a dim reflection where the picture was. Jennie had been perfect for Sam, and she'd never let him know how much she respected him. She'd never known how important it was to him.

Wait a minute! Had she actually thought that, that Jennie was perfect for Sam? The truth of it slammed into her stomach. Sam never saw the wheelchair or her plain looks. He had seen only her; maybe he'd seen her respect, too. What a fool she'd been! If she'd told him how she felt back then . . . no, it was too late for that. If she kept thinking about the irony of it all, she'd drive herself crazy.

After taking off her bra the hard way, she removed her leggings and fell into bed with her shirt on. The light from the nightstand caught her diamond and made it glitter. She looked at it, turning it this way and that. It was nice, but not her style. She wanted to take it off permanently, but she didn't want to alienate herself from Armand yet. For now she could take it off and put it on the nightstand.

From the way the sheets were rumpled, she could tell which side of the bed Sam slept on. Snuggling under the sheets and blanket, she lay there wondering why it seemed he was right there next to her. It was like she was snuggled against his chest again. She rolled over on her side, burrowing down into the spongy pillow. That was why. These were Sam's sheets, and he had slept right where she was now. She inhaled, holding in the scent of him for as long as she could. Then she smiled. *Oh, Sam. Let me try again.*

Chapter 7

Sam had spent the night shifting and moving around more than a couple of mambo dancers during an all-night dance-a-thon. He'd wake up and wonder where he was. Then he'd figure that out and remember why he was on the couch. Then the awareness that Maxine was a few yards away crept over him, making him feel out of sorts. He'd drift back to sleep only to have the cycle happen all over again a while later.

He woke up at his usual time, six o'clock sharp. Through the cracks between the screens he could barely make out her form lying there in his bed. It had been a long time since she'd been in his bed. Sex had never been their problem. Something in his body warmed at that thought, but he squelched it. *It's Maxine, remember? Been there, done that, got the T-shirt. Not again.*

But there was something different about her, and he couldn't put his finger on it. That's what bugged him, more than her being there with him instead of wanting to be with her fiancé. She still wore the nice clothing, but she hadn't once commented on going shopping with Sharee or the lack of accommodations his place offered; she hadn't fussed with her face for hours before going to bed. She hadn't even complained about the prospect of riding around in his rattletrap all day today. In fact, she'd seemed thrilled at the prospect.

There was a light in her eyes that made him want to reach out and touch her cheek every time she aimed it at him. He hadn't even felt that way when they were married. And asking whether she'd broken his heart. Maxine didn't want to be bothered with knowing that kind of thing. It just didn't make sense, and his investigative mind was going nuts trying to figure it out.

But that speech she'd given him when she'd arrived. He shook his head. Now that wasn't Maxine at all. Because as much as he wanted to think she was doing all this for her protection, the fire in her eyes told him something much more.

He washed up, then tiptoed into his room to get his clothes. Romeo was lying on the floor by her side of the bed. Traitor. Well, half traitor. He had spent half the night out in the living room with Sam, and half the night here with her. Just like he'd done at the office, splitting his time between Sam and Jennie.

He cleared away that thought and looked at the woman Romeo—silly dog—seemed so crazy about. She was hugging one pillow, her hands tucked beneath her cheek. One long leg had escaped the sheets, and her red-tipped toes were slightly curled. Her red hair and creamy skin contrasted with the black sheets vividly, making her look like an art form someone had carefully arranged. Something twisted inside him at the sight of her lying there like that. Strangely, it was the same kind of feeling he'd had that day he'd walked out of his office to give something to Jennie. When she'd turned around with that beguiling smile of hers, he'd frozen up. It felt the same, yet that was Jennie and this was Maxine. Big difference.

He forced his gaze away and pulled down a shirt and pants from the hangers, then opened the bottom drawer for a pair of socks. That's when he found her underthings taking up half the drawer. There was something oddly intimate about his socks mingling with her panties. Maybe even something kinky about it.

He picked up a pair of pink lace things, trying to figure out which way was front. Neither side looked big enough to accommodate her rear. Unless . . . he shook away the image of her bare bottom with the lace strip going up the center and dropped the garment as if it had burned his fingers.

"Good morning," she said, making him jump to a standing position and feel like a teenager caught doing something illicit.

"Just getting my socks," he said, kicking the drawer closed. Good grief, had she seen him fondling her underwear? No, she'd have a cocky grin on her face. Instead she looked more like an . . . angel. It must be her tangled halo of red curls that surrounded her sleepy face.

"You're allowed. They are your drawers, after all." She leaned over the side of the bed. "Good morning, Romeo." Her fingers stroked beneath his chin, and the damned dog looked like he was in Heaven with his eyes rolled upward. Sam supposed he'd be doing the same thing if she was stroking him like that. Good grief, where were these thoughts coming from?

She slid from beneath the sheets, showing her nice legs beneath the long shirt that barely covered what might be another pair of those little lacy things. The white socks she wore gave her a girlish look that set his mind back on track. She stood beside him and went through the small section of her clothes. That was another un-Maxine-like thing: she never went anywhere without half her wardrobe, which had to be quadruple what it had been when he was supporting her. And she usually took half an hour just to get out of bed. Maxine had never been a morning person.

"I'm going to take a shower. When do you want to leave?" she asked.

Oh, no. He doubted her hour-long morning ritual had changed. "No more than thirty minutes from now." He readied himself for her whining.

"Okay." She gave him a sweet, sleepy smile and headed off to the bathroom.

He followed her out of the bedroom. "Okay, someone kidnapped Maxine and replaced her with an alien."

Her smile disappeared. "What do you mean?"

"I was kidding. I've never heard you agree to be ready in less than an hour."

He was rewarded with another of her smiles. "Told you I wouldn't be any trouble." She turned back around and closed the door behind her.

He absently rubbed his stomach with one hand, perhaps hoping to rub away the strange feeling churning inside him. This was absolutely, outrageously ridiculous. She was getting to him, or at least to his physical side. There was something about her. Something. Romeo stared up at him, panting with his tongue hanging out.

"Yeah, well, she's getting to you, too," he murmured softly, then turned and went into the kitchen to start a pot of coffee. He just hoped he had enough milk to support her new coffee-drinking preference. A ribbon of melancholy wrapped around his insides. Jennie had always put a lot of cream in her coffee. He'd teased her about it: "You like a little coffee with your cream, eh?" She'd even brought in those fancy creamers with French vanilla flavors. He pushed away the thought and set out two cups.

"Smells good," she said, coming around the corner towel-drying her hair. The wet curls framed her face, and in his large robe and without makeup on, she looked like a young girl. She reached for the carton of milk, then paused. "You don't happen to have any French vanilla or Irish Cream, do you? No, probably not, forget I asked."

She poured the milk in, leaving Sam to wonder if she'd somehow learned mind reading in the last few years. She stirred in some sugar, then looked up at him.

"What?"

"Nothing." He turned away, wondering if the ache would ever go away. Then he looked back at her. "Since when did you start using fancy creamers in your coffee? What's wrong with regular cream? Why cream at all? You used to drink the stuff black, and now, all of a sudden you want vanilla cream.'' He blew out a breath, knowing he sounded anal and also knowing he couldn't explain his irritation to her. Maybe someone sent her there to drive him crazy. Somebody who knew his inner torment, someone who—

She touched his shoulder, sending warmth through his veins the way a good shot of scotch did. ''What's wrong, Sam? Talk to me.''

He opened his mouth, then realized he was about to say something about Jennie. He couldn't share that with Maxine. Or with anyone. ''Do you ever wonder why some people are taken so far before their time? Kids, people on the edge of a great career . . .'' Jennie.

Her hand was still on his arm, fingers tightening when he spoke. How would she know that kind of pain? She'd never lost anyone close to her. She had drifted away from her parents long before they ever died.

She just stared at him for a moment, and when she spoke, it was carefully, with much thought. ''Yes, I wonder. But Sam . . . do you ever wonder if those people ever get to come back? In someone else's body maybe?''

He looked at her as if she were two straps away from a straitjacket. ''You're kidding.''

''I was just wondering. You're always wondering. So am I.'' She shrugged. ''You obviously think it's crazy.''

''Of course I do. What kind of world would this be if everyone jumped around from one body to another?''

She looked downward. ''Well, it wouldn't necessarily be everyone. Just a few people who maybe didn't get to realize their dreams the first time around. Oh, never mind, Sam. It was just something to say.''

Her hand was still on his. And she wasn't wearing that rock of an engagement ring.

''Don't forget your ring,'' he said.

She removed her hand staring at it as though she'd never

seen it before. "Oh. Maybe I'll leave it off today."

"Actually, I was thinking that you should have dinner with Armand and his family tonight." She honestly looked ill at that suggestion. "With me, of course. I want to meet James and Sally. Get a feel for the situation over there."

Her face relaxed. "Well, I guess. I suppose I should call him anyway."

He handed her the portable phone. "Do you want anything for breakfast?"

She was looking at the phone with a trace of dread. When she realized he was talking to her, she covered it with a smile. "Whatever you're having."

"Same thing I've always had."

"That's fine."

She punched in the numbers. "Hello, Aida. Let me speak to Armand, please. Yes, I know he's upset. I'm sure he appreciates that you're so protective of him. Now may I talk to him?"

A minute later he must have picked up. "Yes, I'm fine. Yes, I stayed at Sam's. Well, as a matter of fact, I did. But he wasn't in it. No, I can't do that. Listen, I'd like to have dinner with you tonight. And Sally and James. Of course I miss you." She pushed out the words. "Yes, he'll be there, too. He is my bodyguard. What good would he be if he's not guarding my . . . body." Sam swore her face flushed at that. "Okay, we'll see you tonight."

He busied himself with chopping up bananas and putting them into the blender along with a few other ingredients. Then he poured in the milk and let the blades fly. A minute later, he stopped the racket and poured the yellow mixture into two glasses. He turned around and handed one to her.

She held it up to the light, inspecting the contents. "What's in here?"

"Bananas, milk, honey, and wheat germ. Just like always."

"Oh, yeah," she said unconvincingly. "These were great." She took a drink.

He crossed his arms. "You hated it."

She took another sip, not meeting his gaze. "I know that. But I figured I'd try it again. And you know what? It's not too bad. Just a little . . . strange. What? Why are you grinning at me like that?"

"You have a milk mustache." He leaned over and ran his finger over the curve of her upper lip. Why'd he do that? Because he didn't know what else to do, he stuck his finger in his mouth. "You'd better get ready. We've got to head out."

She was looking at him, wavering a little. With a blink, she broke eye contact and walked back to the bedroom without saying anything. So he'd touched her lip. Big deal. He'd done that before. Hadn't he?

Maxine ran her finger over her lip the same way Sam had just done. For him, it probably meant nothing. But that simple act had touched her beyond belief. Her stomach still curled at the thought. She finished up the banana shake and went into the bathroom to get changed. The mirror had been steamy before, but now she could see herself clearly. Though Maxine's looks were completely different from Jennie's, one thing remained the same: that light in her eyes whenever she was around Sam. She leaned forward and put a little eyeliner on, then a bit of color on her cheeks. Maxine-the-first had enough makeup in her tote-bag purse to open a store, but the basics were enough. Even if Sam did go for those made-up dolls, Maxine couldn't force herself to be something she simply wasn't.

She layered a turtleneck, sweater, and another sweater. It was warm in the apartment, but not outside. The windows behind the sand-colored curtains were fogged up.

"Ready," she said as she emerged. Sam was on the phone.

It hadn't occurred to her, in her narrow-minded mission, to think that Sam might be seeing someone right now. Not Petula. But what about someone else? The thought secured her stomach into a neat little knot. Well, she didn't die and come back just to watch Sam marry someone else.

"Interesting," Sam was saying as he leaned over and jotted down a date. He was wearing blue jeans and a corded beige sweater. The jeans weren't tight, yet they molded his derriere just so. She sighed. Just so nice. Gabby had once commented that he had a model's butt, small and tight.

"Aren't you ever tempted to reach over and give it a squeeze?" she'd asked during the small Christmas party he'd given a few months back.

"Gabby!" Warmth had flushed over Jennie's cheeks. She took a sip of her eggnog and leaned closer. "Well, maybe once or twice in my wildest dreams."

Gabby had given her a friendly shove on the arm. "Yeah, right. I think you should go over right now and give it a try. Maybe you'll give yourself a little extra Christmas present this year. A bonus that's better than bankable. Go on."

"Right now?" Maxine heard herself answer, then realized she'd said it aloud and was staring at his butt. Luckily he was facing the other way and didn't see her. She hoped.

"Yep, that's exactly what I wanted," he was saying. "Thanks, I owe you one. I know, two. Bye."

"Ready," she said again. Well, that didn't sound like a girlfriend on the phone.

He turned to face her, and she found herself staring at him again. In that sweater, he looked like a football player with wide shoulders and a narrow waist. His blond hair waved down to the back of his neck, and it caught the light above him.

"What?" he asked.

She clamped her mouth shut. She was acting like a damned teenager. But then again, she'd lost most of those years; she had some time to make up for.

"Nothing. Nice sweater."

He glanced down, then shrugged. "Thanks." He folded up the paper and slid into his leather jacket. "We got our first lead. A friend of mine is on the force. I asked Dave if he could remember anything concerning the Santinis." Sam opened the door for her, and she wrapped her coat around her and walked onto the landing. Romeo stood in the doorway looking out hopefully. "Not today, buddy. It's too cold."

Maxine gave him a scratch on the head. "Bye, guy."

When they got into the car, she asked, "So, what did you find?" She rubbed her arms against the cold as the car slowly warmed up.

Sam's car might look like a rattletrap, but she could tell a highly refined engine when she heard one. It purred to life like a Mercedes.

"Apparently there was another accident at the Santini residence. Not the same house. This one had balconies with fancy concrete fixtures at the corners; one of those happened to break loose and fall when the first Mrs. Santini was walking under it."

Dread filled her chest. "Same type of thing?"

Sam nodded, rubbing his mustache thoughtfully. "The police checked it out, of course. But they couldn't find anything suspicious about it. No one could say that the Santinis were having marital or financial problems. She had a small insurance policy, not enough to murder her for. So it was deemed an accident."

"Sounds like what happened to me." She found herself duplicating his motion, rubbing her fingers over her upper lip. She stopped before he caught her. "So all we know for sure is it's not Mrs. Santini who's trying to get rid of me."

"No, but whoever did her is probably the same one trying to do you."

She shivered. "But why would James do his own mother in? She probably wasn't a threat to his inheriting the nightclubs, not like I am."

"That's what we're going to find out, after I take care of my other case."

Sam leaned in the back of the car, where a basket of laundry sat on the back seat. As he stretched, his sweater revealed an intriguing slice of his waist. He lifted the hinged top of the hamper, revealing a compartment beneath it.

"This guy I'm watching for Ned is getting suspicious. He gave me the evil eye the last time I walked past his house." He pulled his blond hair up into a baseball cap that already sported a light brown ponytail, then slipped on sunglasses. "I don't want to burn the surveillance. Maybe you'll throw him off; he's not expecting a PI to have a woman with him."

"I always wanted to go on a case with you," she said wistfully, then realized what she'd said.

As usual, Sam let nothing slide by. "You did?"

"Well, yeah. I never told you, but the thought fascinated me."

He gave her that skeptical look. "It's not like in the movies or in paperbacks. It's boring for the most part. I've spent hundreds of hours just sitting here watching this guy. He's suing one of the largest companies in the area because he claims he slipped on their lobby floor and permanently injured himself. I have a gut feeling the guy is lying, and his doctor's probably in it for a few bucks, too. Ned wanted me to lay low, but he's getting worried. The case comes up in three weeks. Besides, I want to wrap this up before I close the agency."

"Sam, you said you'd think about that. Weren't you the one telling me—twice—that I shouldn't make a rash decision during an emotional time?"

"It has nothing to do with emotions. My heart isn't in the business anymore. When your heart goes away, it doesn't come back."

"Oh, Sam, don't say that." He turned at the heartfelt plea in her voice. "Let me work for you, at least while you're protecting me. Since I'll be with you all the time, it only makes sense."

When he stopped at a light, he turned that skeptical look at her again. "You're kidding, right?"

"No, I'm not kidding. I can help."

"You can't read my handwriting. Can you transcribe?"
He laughed. "Type?"

"As a matter of fact, I can. I'll show you. Let me help."

"All right, if you want," he said, shaking his head as he
pulled away. "This ought to be good!"

"As long as you provide the coffee," she said, wishing
to take back the words the moment they left her mouth.

Sam's expression went dark, remembering Jennie's last
trip downstairs no doubt.

"So how much is this guy suing for?" She was trying to
get the conversation back to friendly again.

"Fourteen million dollars. But he won't get that much,
even if we couldn't prove anything. The worst part is, between his lawyer and his doctor, he probably won't net
much anyway. But it's going to hurt the company he's suing, especially with the publicity."

A while later they pulled into a nice residential neighborhood. Sam looked strange without the blond waves grac-
ing his collar. He reached into the hamper again and pulled
out what looked unnervingly like a gun.

"Sam, you're not going to shoot at his feet and make him
dance, are you?"

He smiled. "Now that's not a bad idea. But no. This is
a high-powered BB gun. I'm going to shoot his tire out."

Sam pulled out a camera and some tiny binoculars and
watched the house across the street. He set down the glasses
and turned off the engine. "Sorry, but I can't leave the engine on. One guy I knew died when exhaust fumes backed
up into his car." He opened the glove box and tossed her a
pair of knit gloves. "These'll help keep you warm."

A half hour later, she was starting to shiver. And trying
darn hard not to let him know about it. She wrapped her
gloved hands around her sides. "I'm surprised you don't
bring a thermos of coffee with you," she said, hoping he
didn't catch the tremor in her voice.

"You don't drink much of anything while you're on surveillance duty. 'Cause when you have to go, you have two

choices. You leave and hope the suspect doesn't decide to walk out at that moment, or you pee in a jar. Neither is especially appealing.''

"Oh. I guess I s-see your point."

"You're cold."

"Oh, just a little." She wanted to get out and jog around the block for a minute to get her blood going again. "Goes right to the t-teeth."

"Come here."

He pulled her over the bench seat so that her back pressed up against his chest. Then he slid his arms around her shoulders to anchor her even closer. Suddenly she wasn't cold anymore. Nope, not one tiny bit. Her blood was heating up in every extremity.

"Better?" he asked.

"Oh, yeah," she said on a sigh. She fought the urge to snuggle even closer. "What do you do to keep warm when you're by yourself?"

"I stick Romeo in my coat."

She turned to see if he was kidding. He was smiling, but not in a joking manner. "Hey, it works. And he doesn't mind, either. Even with his fur, it gets cold for him, too."

"The PI and his dog," she said with a laugh.

"I'll tell you what; Romeo has been worth his weight in dog biscuits. People aren't threatened when you have a dog with you. They usually pay more attention to the dog. Besides, what guy could be up to no good if he has a dog. It's so . . . American."

With the music playing softly in the background, and Sam pressed against her, she found herself with the sudden desire to neck in the car. She'd missed out on all that fun teenage stuff. And the adult stuff, too.

"Have you ever made out in a car, Sam?" Then she hoped Maxine-the-first hadn't made out with him.

"Don't you think that's a little personal?"

"Well, we were married once. If you can grab my thighs, I can ask you personal questions."

He laughed, and the vibrant sound filled her with bubbles of joy. That deep, sudden laugh she'd listened to for years. My, life was good.

"Well, I guess you have a point. And you still have nice thighs, by the way."

She felt her face flush. He'd looked so businesslike when his hands were moving up and down her legs. But maybe not . . .

She lifted one foot. If she thought hard enough, she could still imagine just how his hands felt on her. "Thank you. And you still have nice hands."

She hoped he couldn't tell how widely she was smiling at that statement. She felt those hands flex against her slightly. He made a deep-in-his-throat kind of sound and shifted back a little farther, bringing her with him.

After a moment, she said, "Sam, you never did answer my question about making out in a car."

"Ah, yes, we got a little sidetracked on hands and thighs, didn't we?" She could hear the lazy smile in his voice. "Sure I've made out in a car. It's been a while. If you'll remember, I tried to get frisky with you when we were dating. You wouldn't hear of fooling around in a car. Tacky, I think you called it. But it has its moments, like most tacky things do."

She heard herself sighing. "Someday I'd like to make out in a car. I think it's high time I gave it a try, tacky or no." She turned around to see his reaction, finding her forehead pressed against the bill of his cap. She shifted lower.

"Don't look at me. Ask your snookums."

"Kissums," she said, then shook her head. "No, I don't want to make out with him."

"Now that sounds like a little bit of a conflict to me. You want to make out in a car, but not with your fiancé."

When she turned around again, her cheek brushed against his. He'd shaved that morning, and his skin smelled of citrus and felt smooth. The tip of his mustache tickled her cheek. What would it be like to kiss him? Would those tiny hairs tickle her lips? She felt a tightness spreading through her insides, sitting here cheek to cheek with him like this. His warm breath washed over her chin, and she moved closer yet.

"Sam, are you seeing anyone right now?"

"Why, you wanna set me up with someone? A friend with a great personality maybe?"

She nudged him, but didn't move from her position. "No, I don't want to set you up with anybody." *Except me.* "Well, are you?" she prompted again when he still didn't answer.

"No, I'm not seeing anyone." He turned his head, pressing their cheeks even closer together. "Why are you asking?"

"I didn't know if my staying with you was going to put a strain on any . . . relationships you might have."

"The only strained relationship I have is ours."

She smiled, feeling their cheeks slide against each other with the movement. "Are you saying we have a relationship?"

"Oh, yeah, we have a relationship, all right. A client–private-investigator relationship."

"Oh."

"If I didn't know better, I'd think you sounded disappointed. What kind of relationship do you want us to have, exactly, Miss Snookums-to-be?"

Her heart jumped at the question. She decided to ignore the Snookums part. This was as good a time as any, and since he'd asked . . . "Sam, I want—"

Suddenly Sam lurched forward, setting her away from him. But his attention wasn't on her. It was on the man wheeling out of his house in a chair. He opened the door and transferred to the driver's seat, then folded his chair and pulled it in after him. The familiarity of that action made it hard to swallow.

Sam leaned across her and lowered the window. He aimed the BB gun and squeezed out a couple of shots.

"That tire should give out a few blocks from here," he said, rubbing his hands together after closing the window.

"Sam, he's in a wheelchair." Something dark swirled through her, a feeling of affinity with the man in the chair. "Maybe he's not faking it. He got in his car the same way I—I've seen other people do it." She covered her mouth, hoping he hadn't caught on to her gaffe.

"The schmuck's faking it, Maxine. Trust me." He glanced at her. "Why the look?"

It wouldn't sound right for her to be so upset, but still. She couldn't imagine someone following her around after the accident, waiting for her to get up on her own. Not that they'd had anyone to sue, but the thought of it sickened her.

The schmuck, as Sam so kindly called him, pulled out of his driveway. The tire was already a little flat. Maxine's fingers clutched the armrest on the car door. Sam was right on target; a few blocks away, the tire went completely flat. Sam pulled over to the side of the road a distance behind him. He got out and removed something from the trunk. Well, what was he going to do now? Bribe him to get out of the car with a jack? She looked through the misted windows, watching Sam put out a large sign by the roadside. He jumped back in the car, energy fairly crackling from him.

The man in the car had opened his door and was getting his wheelchair out when they passed by. He waved for them to stop, but Sam kept right on going.

"Aw, Sam, this is so unfair. What does that sign say?"

Sam was too busy watching in the rearview mirror. She turned around to see the man looking at his flat tire. Sam was already out of the car and placing another sign on the side of the road. It was blank on her side.

Then he pulled into a driveway and grabbed the camera. "They say 'Disabled person in training. Do not assist.' "

"Sam! I can't believe you're doing this. It's freezing out there."

"That's the point exactly. He's not going to want to wait around long, and no one's going to stop and help. See."

A car drove by, but didn't stop even when the man waved.

"I can't believe how unfair you're being."

He looked at her. "That sounds like something Jennie would say. I always wondered what she'd think about being with me on surveillance."

"You did? I mean, she probably wouldn't like it, not this part anyway." She tilted her head. "Do I remind you of Jennie?"

"No way. You're nothing like her."

He got out of the car and crept around to her side behind a tangle of leafless branches. From over Sam's shoulder she could see that poor man getting the jack out of the trunk of his car and struggling to turn the lug nuts. His chair kept rolling backward. Didn't he know to lock the wheels? He waved at another car, but they kept on going, courtesy of Sam's sign. What a heel. The poor man's shoulders slumped as he watched the taillights disappear. Then he looked around, desperate to find someone to help him.

And then he stood up and wrenched the lug nuts free.

Her hands tightened into fists as she watched him jack the car up and deftly change the tire as fast as he could. A couple of minutes later, he was back in his wheelchair, looking around to make sure no one had seen him.

Sam jumped in the car with a whoop. "Got the wascally wabbit!"

"Ooh! That man was faking it the whole time!" Her voice rose high in her anger.

He leaned over and winked. "Told you so."

"I know, but . . . Oh, Sam, how could someone pretend to be disabled like that? He probably takes the handicapped parking spaces away from someone who really needs them. He probably uses people's pity to get extra help. He makes everyone in wheelchairs look bad!"

"Geez, Maxine, get a grip. He's not victimizing other disabled people. He's a greedy opportunist. And an oaf. Let's get the signs and get out of here."

On the way back to the office, Maxine said, "I'm sorry I doubted you, Sam." She had transcribed reports about frauds before, but seeing it was far different.

"Aw, that's all right. It was kind of cute, the way you got all riled up like that. It's not like you to take up a cause that doesn't look good on you."

"Well, maybe it's about time I do. I'll just be careful about which cause I take up," she added with a wry grin.

"You do that."

They took the elevator up to the office; Sam hadn't even considered taking the stairs. It was strange to be back at the agency again with the purpose of working. She started a pot of coffee while Sam went in his office to call Ned.

"I got him," he said. "You're not going to believe how I did it."

Maxine pulled one of the sitting chairs behind her desk and blew off no less than half an inch of dust covering the surface of the desk. Sam's laughter filled the room with the same potency as the coffee. And just as comforting. She closed her eyes, feeling them tingle with threatening tears. This was her life, sitting here listening to Sam's deep laugh and wishing. But no more wishing. The listening part was fine, though.

She got up and walked around the office, then spotted the answering machine. Might as well check the messages. She jotted them down. Some were new jobs, some were people checking on their current cases. And two were from a Suzanne. Hmm. Maxine had the feeling that Sam didn't give out his home number to these women; they seemed to hunt him down wherever they could find him.

When the phone rang, she picked it up and answered cheerfully, "Good morning, Sam's Private Eye."

"Hi, this is Suzanne. Is Sam there? I really need to talk to him."

"Why yes, he is here, Suzanne." Maxine tapped her fingernails on the desktop. "But I'm afraid he's busy, and getting him between phone calls is tough." She put on her sweetest voice. "Can I help you with something? Anything at all?"

"Well . . . you're a woman, right?"

"Er, last time I checked."

"Sam and I met a few weeks ago at the Houndog. He looked kinda blue, you know, so I went up and talked to him and we hit it off. Or I thought we did, but he never called me. Is he, you know, seeing someone?"

Maxine smiled. "As a matter of fact, he is." And then Sam walked in, tilting his head at her conversation. She tried to wave him away, but he wouldn't go. "Very serious, actually."

"Oh. Well, is he gonna marry her or something?"

"He's investigating that right now. You know, licenses, that kind of thing. He's not taking on anything else right now. Yep, he's finished with that business. Well, thank you for your inquiry. Good-bye." She turned to meet Sam's curious gaze, trying awfully hard not to give her grin away.

"Are you sending my clients away?" he asked.

"You are going out of business, aren't you?"

"Maybe I am, but still . . ."

She chewed her lower lip for a second. "You were excited when you nabbed that schmuck today, weren't you?"

He smiled. "I always am."

"You should have seen your face, Sam. You were glowing. How could you give this up?"

He looked at her, shaking his head. "I'd really be glowing if I could figure out how you changed so much."

"Ooh, and would I like to make you glow. Er, what I mean is, time has changed me. Facing death has changed me."

He walked over and picked up the mug she'd bought him, the hound dog one. He looked at it, tracing the grooves with his finger. Slowly he filled it up and turned to her again.

"It's strange to see someone else sitting there. Jennie was the only woman to ever sit at that desk. Almost feels like I'm betraying her somehow."

"You're not. She'd be happy to know someone else is helping you. Now give me a bill or something to type, will you?" *Bossman*, she wanted to say. Oh, how she longed to hear him call her kiddo again.

Well, she got the bills anyway, a whole stack of them. Candy Dulfer's saxophone drifted in from Sam's office as he made phone calls and dictated reports. She let out a long sigh. Back in business. Now all she had to worry about was staying alive and making Sam fall in love with her. Shoot, no problem.

It was later in the day when Sam walked out of the office and propped himself on the edge of her desk. When he crossed his arms over his chest, he reminded her of a hulking football player again. He'd just gotten a call from someone named Sparky.

"What's wrong?" she asked when she saw his serious expression.

"That was one of my informants. I talked to him last night before you showed up, asked him to nose around about any hired hits. We may have found the guy. His name is Floyd, small-time hood in the area. I'm going to talk to him about his little job, but I doubt he'll come clean. Maybe I can get something out of him, like male or female. That'll narrow it down. Sparky says this guy hangs out at some sleazy club called the Pig's Tail. We'll hit it on the way over to Santini's, though I'd rather not have you in a place like that."

"I'd rather be in there with you than somewhere else without you."

He seemed to weigh her statement, then shook his head. "No way. You'll be safe in the car, and I'll make damned sure nobody follows us there. Besides, if this guy really was hired to take you out, don't you think he's going to recognize you the moment you walk in the place? No, it's out of the question."

He had a point. "Okay, you win. I'll stay in the car."

He'd opened his mouth to argue further, then closed it

when she acquiesced. "Really? That easily?"

"I admit I've been a little stubborn about all this. Okay, a lot stubborn. You just don't realize how important this is to me."

"Well, staying alive is important to most folks."

"It's a lot more than that. We'd better get going," she added, not wanting him to ask what she'd meant by the first statement.

"What time's dinner?"

"Six-thirty."

"Great. I can't wait."

The Pig's Tail was pretty sleazy, though Maxine could hardly grade it on any scale. After all, she'd limited her club experiences to the Houndog and . . . well, that was about it. A neon beer sign flickered in the large window that was painted black. Once the building had probably sported stores that attracted mothers with their children. Now it wasn't even fit for a streetwise man. Especially one as warm and wonderful as Sam, who made sure she locked the doors before he walked across the street to disappear inside. A puff of smoke snuck out the door and tainted the cold night air just before Sam pulled it closed. Worry gnawed at her insides. Her gaze only left that door long enough to take in the sign above it, with the name of the bar spelled out in a long neon-pink pig's tail. *Bet the owner thought he was clever on that one.*

Unfortunately the pig's tail only distracted her for a second before she returned her gaze to the door again. Sam was in there because of her. What if something happened to him? She reached for the door, but only curled her fingers around the handle. Even if he didn't have confidence in himself anymore, she still believed in him. If only she didn't have this feeling of dread that something was going to happen to him.

Chapter 8

When the door to the Pig's Tail finally swung open, Maxine lurched forward. But it wasn't Sam. A young man walked quickly through the darkness, his hands shoved in his pockets. Sam walked out right after him, watching the man for a second before looking at her. She waved, feeling relief sweep over her. He headed over to the car and got in when she unlocked the doors. She resisted the urge to hug him, instead pushing herself against the door behind her.

"Well?"

He smelled like smoke, but somehow it didn't offend her nose.

"The guy who walked out in front of me—he's the one who tried to run you over."

She sucked in a breath. "Did he admit that?"

"Not in any manner we could snag him with." Sam pulled the beeper she hadn't noticed off his belt and pressed a button that made a rewinding-tape sound. Then he hit another button and static music filled the car. "That's what I was afraid of. Floyd was sitting right next to the speakers." He listened, but the voices on the tape were nearly obliterated by the squawking of the music.

"Basically I told him the cops were onto him; I thought he might like to know about it. Of course, nobody does anything around here for nothing, so he asked me what I wanted for the generous tip-off. I told him I wanted to know who was behind it. He said someone hired him over the phone, left half the money and your picture and information in a designated place. He was to follow you around yesterday and take care of you however he deemed applicable. Swears he's never done anything like this before, but he couldn't turn the money down. Fifty thousand dollars.''

A chill ran through her, reviving that trembling. ''That's what my life was worth? Fifty grand?''

''People have been killed for less.''

''I know. But it's never been so close.'' She wrapped her arms around herself and looked at him. ''Did he say whether it was a man or a woman?''

''Oh, he was a big help there. He said it sounded like a woman trying to sound like a man. But then it could have been a man trying to sound like a woman. And he didn't have anything to do with the flower box incident. I think he was telling the truth. If my instincts are on.''

''Darn, that's no help. If we could only narrow it down. But I'm pretty sure it's James.''

''The person called him this morning; they knew he hadn't done his job. Floyd said he was pretty freaked about the whole thing, trying to run you down and all. He put the money back and told the person to shove their job.''

She let out a long sigh. ''Thank goodness.''

''Don't even think of relaxing yet. They could easily find someone else to finish the job, someone more, er, qualified. Everyone in the Santini household is still a suspect, though I wonder where Aida would get that kind of money.'' He put the key in and started the car. ''Let's go shake up the suspects.''

As they drove through the city, she watched the buildings around them, the cars passing. Anyone could be watching her, waiting for the right moment. And if they had a gun— she shivered. It could be over in an instant.

Sam's hand on her leg startled her. ''Maxine, you all right? You look a little spooked over there.''

"I am spooked. Everywhere I look I see someone trying to kill me, waiting. It could be over, just like that. I'm not ready to die." *I just got here.* Sure, she'd gotten a second chance, but there were no guarantees. She could still die without telling him how she felt. Her cautious side warned against pushing too hard. A desperation grew inside her, but she quelled it.

He stopped at a light and lifted the hand on her thigh to her chin, turning her face toward him. "I'll do my best to protect you. But if you want to hire someone more qualified, I'll understand."

She saw both determination and fear in his eyes. "I want you, Sam." She took his hand in hers and pressed it to her heart. "Only you."

He just looked at her, his gaze holding her captive until someone behind them pounded on their horn. Sam pulled out, staring straight ahead. Had he felt her heart speed up?

He didn't want her in his life, didn't want this job. Maxine had forced both. It struck her as ironic that as Jennie, she had tried so hard not to be a bother to anyone. With her disability, she was trouble enough. Even if it meant not having the one thing she wanted most: Sam's love. But as Maxine, she wasn't as concerned with bothering people to get what she wanted. How much of her life had she denied simply because she hadn't wanted to put anyone out? If Sam had cared about her, maybe she was worthy of a little bother after all.

"No dog, I see," Armand said as he let Maxine and Sam into the house. He would have probably preferred the dog to Sam.

"No, he had a previous engagement," Sam said, handing his jacket to Armand. "But he sends his regards."

"The *dog* had a previous engagement?"

Sam shrugged. "He's old enough to date. But I don't allow sleep-overs. I think it's important to instill some morals in them, don't you think?"

Sam looked so serious, and Armand so dumbfounded, Maxine had to try hard to stifle a giggle.

"I, ah . . . you're very strange, you know that?" Armand turned away from Sam and pulled her into his arms to give her a life-threatening hug. "I've missed you," he said softly, though she saw Sam tilt his head her way.

"I, ah . . . how are you doing?"

"I think you know."

The hurt in Armand's eyes tore into her conscience. *But she was marrying you for your money. You wouldn't have been happy with her. You would have probably driven her bonkers in the process. This is better, don't you see?* But he wouldn't, not ever. How could she explain something like this? Sam hadn't been open to it, though comparing the two men's reactions was like comparing a tiger to a mole.

Sam looked around as if he were cataloging everything. Armand watched him, scratching at his eyebrow as he shot a look of irritation at him. "Does he have to sit at the table with us?" he asked in that same low voice.

"What are we going to do, put a plate on the floor in the kitchen or something? Armand, he's protecting my life. Doesn't that mean anything to you?"

Guilt racked his expression, along with a few interesting wrinkle lines. "I know. But being apart from you is driving me crazy." He jerked her against his body. "Can't you feel how much I want you?"

Well, actually, she couldn't. That was a good thing.

Sam walked over, and she moved away from Armand and silently thanked Sam for his timing. He still smelled faintly of smoke, reviving the dread she'd felt when he was in the Pig's Tail.

At the dinner table, Maxine felt strange sitting next to Armand while Sam sat on the other side next to Sally. She kept stealing furtive glances at him, which Maxine knew he was wholly aware of. James was regarding him as more of a nuisance or intrusion. He paused, resting his arms on the table.

"Do you really think this bodyguarding thing is necessary?"

"If you'd seen the car coming at her, you'd think so," Sam answered.

"Okay, but don't you think it's a little inappropriate to have her ex-husband doing the job? I mean, isn't there some kind of conflict of interest or family thing?"

"I wanted him for the job," Maxine said, drawing James's sullen gaze to her. "He's good. Besides, if I'm going to be spending twenty-four hours a day with someone, it might as well be someone I know."

James regarded her for a moment before turning to Armand. "Dad, don't you see what's going on here? She's probably boinking her ex and laughing behind your back."

Armand's face went white. "James, we've been through this before. Please don't bring it up at the dinner table."

"Really," Sally said, rolling up her eyes. "It's so unappetizing."

So, James was working on his father while Maxine was out of the picture. But if he thought he had a chance of convincing Armand to dump her, why was he having her run over? Sam was sitting back in his chair watching everyone.

"Dad, don't you see what she's doing?" James persisted. "She probably put this whole thing together to get you so worried, you'd forget about that prenuptial contract I've been talking to you about. She probably hired the guy to almost run her over, and rigged up something so the flower box would come down on her. Heck, she probably put the cut on her forehead herself. And I wouldn't be surprised if her ex isn't in on the whole thing."

Armand's face now reddened, but it was Sam's voice Maxine heard from across the table.

"Maxine wouldn't do something like that."

"And you know her so well," Armand bit out. "Well, I guess you've had plenty of time to catch up lately."

Maxine glared at James. "You're just trying to accuse me to cover your own tracks."

Sally pushed her plate away with an exaggerated sigh.

"Are you planning on having Maxine sign a prenuptial agreement?" Sam asked Armand.

"Well, we had talked about it. She agreed, but she wasn't happy about it. But it's a moot point because once I marry her, I'm not letting her go." He lifted his chin, as if to challenge Sam.

Sam didn't quite pick up on that challenge. "You can have her. But first I need to find out who hired the guy to run her over last night. Who had access to twenty-five thousand dollars in cash?"

"We all could," Armand said. "James picks up the money from all the clubs every day and gives it to Sally to post and deposit."

"I don't," Aida said, bringing James another Coke. When everyone looked at her, she said, "Er, excuse me," and returned to the kitchen where she'd obviously been listening to their bizarre conversation.

"You mean someone actually paid some thug twenty-five thousand dollars to run over my kissums?" Armand asked, reaching for her hand.

"That was only the first half. He was due to get the second half after the deed was done."

"*If* that wasn't the deed itself," James added.

"Fifty thousand dollars," Armand was saying to no one in particular, shaking his head.

"You're crazy," Maxine retorted to James. Would Maxine-the-first do such a thing? Sam didn't think so, and he knew her better than she did. Gosh, she hoped he was right. But how would Maxine have rigged that box to fall on her? And who had wiped away those drops? No, it couldn't be Maxine. Still, the thought lingered.

"It's amazing what people will do to get their hands on a load of money," James said, gritting his teeth at her.

Sam spoke in an even tone. "Doesn't anyone think it's

rather strange that the first Mrs. Santini died in a similar manner?''

All conversation instantly ceased, and James's fork dropped to his plate and then to the white tile floor with a clatter. Everyone was staring at Sam, and he was shifting his gaze to each and every one of them.

''You've obviously been checking us out,'' James said in a sober voice.

''It's my job. Tell me about your mother.''

Sally spoke. ''She was a wonderful woman. We were devastated.''

Armand's fingers tightened around Maxine's until she wrenched free of them.

''You can't possibly think someone killed my first wife and is now behind the attempts on Maxine's life? There was nothing to be gained by her death. She had no money of her own. No enemies. I refuse to believe there is any connection.''

''Maybe it's just a coincidence, then,'' Sam said.

Sally leaned toward Sam. ''If you know there was a man hired to run Maxine over for fifty thousand dollars, then you must have talked with him.''

Maxine was watching James's reaction to this one. But Sam said, ''No, just the word on the streets.'' He shot Maxine a look that said ''Don't blow it.'' She nodded ever so slightly before turning to find Armand snatching up her hand again.

After dinner, James excused himself. ''Unless you're not done with your questioning.''

Sam waved him off. ''No, go right ahead.''

Maxine was trying to come up with a way to get more of her stuff out of the house without alarming Armand too much. Sally curled up on the white couch near where Sam had taken a seat in the matching chair. Armand sat down on the far end of the couch, and tugged her hand like a little fish caught on a fishing line.

"I'm going to get a couple of things I need," she said, loosening her hand. "I'll be back in a minute."

She ignored Mr. Wiggles who was sitting like a sentry by the door, and walked directly to the closet. Some of the outfits were things she wasn't likely to wear in her life with Sam, so she'd leave them there. Maybe Armand could burn them later and feel better about her leaving.

There were several boxes on the shelf above her clothing, and she reached up to take them down. Most were hats, some were papers and old checkbooks. She opened the last one to find her personal documents: birth certificate, passport, and some loose photos. Possibly it was Maxine's parents who smiled in the old picture. There was a newspaper clipping about her new decorating business. And a picture of Maxine and Sam in some sunny place. They looked young and in love, and she felt a pang of jealousy. Sam didn't have a mustache then, and he looked so cute. There wasn't a trace of that cynicism in his eyes.

And then there was a wedding ring.

Her heart felt funny, all tight and tingly. She picked up the plain gold band with the etched edges and put the cool metal to her lips. Sam's wedding ring—she could feel it. She closed her eyes, trying to imagine how it would be to face Sam before a minister and have him slip this ring on her finger.

"Maxine?"

Her lovely vision shattered, and she turned to find Armand standing there. His gaze had dropped to the ring she held in her fingers. He took her hands and sank slowly to the carpeted floor, crossing his legs. She had no choice but to go down with him, though she slipped the ring into the palm of her hand where it was safe.

"Maxine, what are you doing in here?"

She wanted to continue the charade, to have reason to stay in contact with these people and discover the killer among them. But she couldn't lead Armand on anymore. It was too hard on both of them.

"I was looking through my things," she said. She opened her palm to show him the ring.

"Maxine, let's get married tomorrow. No prenuptial. I don't care about that. I just want you to be my wife. Sam can even move in, if that will make you feel safe. But only after you and I go away for a few months on our honeymoon."

He wasn't even looking at the ring in her hand, only desperately pleading with his eyes. He was still holding the other hand, and she could feel his trembling. She knew that Armand was not behind the murder or the attempts. She suspected—and hoped—that what he felt was more like a profound loneliness, and not a deep love for Maxine. He was an unusual man who had overlooked his suspicions about Maxine's intentions and asked her to marry him anyway. Maxine had overlooked her feelings for Sam and agreed to marry Armand, because she wasn't willing to give up money for love. Or maybe she knew Sam would never take her back.

"I can't marry you," she said on a whisper.

"Why?" he asked in a high-pitched voice.

"Because I . . . I'm in love with Sam." There, that wasn't so bad.

Armand squeezed his eyes shut. "I don't believe this."

"But you knew. You're the one who told me. Armand, please look at me."

"I don't want to watch as you dump me."

"Armand."

Slowly he opened his eyes. "All right, go on, then."

"Armand, you're a nice guy." Without a clue, but nice. "I shouldn't marry you if I have feelings for someone else."

"Don't tell me you want to be my friend. Just don't."

"All right." She didn't. "I should get my things."

But he didn't let go of her hand. "Does he love you, Maxine?"

She pulled her lower lip between her teeth. "I don't know."

"If he doesn't . . . will you come back to me?"

"Armand, what I've done is unforgivable. How could you ever take me back?"

He took a quick breath. "Because I'm lonely."

She felt a twist in her stomach. "That's no reason to marry someone." She thought of Sam, sitting just two rooms away. "You marry them because you love them; because you want to be with them, not because you need to be with them. It's an entirely different thing."

"But what can he give you? You said yourself he doesn't make a lot of money, drives a rattletrap, doesn't appreciate the finer things in life."

She smiled. "Sam has qualities that go far beyond that. He's warm and compassionate and has a sense of duty. And he's a good friend."

Armand scratched his eyebrows again. "He's also right, you know."

"Hm?"

"Remember when he told me we all have bugs in our eyebrows and our eyelashes? We do. I can feel them crawling around. I looked it up in the library. They're awful creatures with claws and lots of legs." He shivered.

"Oh, Armand." She tried to stifle the laugh about to erupt. "They're too tiny to feel." She gave his hand a squeeze before rising to her feet. Sam's wedding ring was still in her other hand. She twisted off the rock and handed it to Armand. "Here is your ring."

"Keep it. You might change your mind."

She pushed it at him, and he finally took it. "I can't do that."

She took the clothes she'd picked and the box and walked back out to the living room. Sally was still talking to Sam, but turned around when she heard them walk in.

"Are you ready to go?" Maxine asked him.

He looked surprised. "If you want to spend more time with Armand, don't let me stop you."

"No, I'm ready to go."

Armand gave her a funny look, but she ignored it. Sam stood, stretching his shoulders. Sally was watching him with interest, though she finally dragged her gaze to her father.

"Daddy-kins, you should talk to James. You know, smooth his feathers."

Armand only nodded, watching Maxine slip into her coat as Sam held it.

"Thank you for dinner," she said to no one in particular. To Armand she said, "Thank you. Good-bye."

Walking out into the cold air had never felt so good before. She hadn't realized how warm and stuffy it had been in the house. The ring was still in her hand when she shoved her hands in the pockets of her coat. Maneuvering her fingers, she slipped it on her third finger.

When they got into the car, Sam said, "Well, you two seemed to have patched things up."

"What do you mean by that?"

"Just that you were both in the bedroom for a while."

"We were in the closet, if you must know." At Sam's grin, she flushed at the insinuation. "I was getting my things. See?" She lifted her hand to show him she wasn't wearing the engagement ring anymore. Then realized she *was* wearing Sam's wedding ring. She quickly put her hand back in the pocket.

"See what?"

Plucking the ring off, she held her hand up again. Fat chance that he hadn't seen the ring. "I gave him his ring back."

"That's what you were doing in the closet?"

"Yep. On the floor, no less. I couldn't keep stringing him along anymore."

He pulled to a stop at the end of the driveway. "What did I tell you about rash decisions?"

"Believe me, it's the right thing to do."

He lifted an eyebrow. "So, what was that other ring you were wearing? The one you took off real quick like?"

"What ring?" She gave him a sweet innocent look, which

he didn't buy for a second. She'd forgotten how cynical the man was.

He lunged for her pocket, grabbing her side and making her twist sideways as he tickled her. Her nose brushed his as they tussled, and her thigh pushed against the hardness of his thigh.

"Sam, you're tickling me," she said on a jerky laugh.

He was relentless in his pursuit of that ring. His soft hair brushed her cheek, and his shoulder pressed her against the door. She tried to close the pocket, but he was already pulling the ring out. Her fingers wrapped around his wrist just before he lifted his hand out of her pocket.

"Sam, don't be mad at me," she whispered as his face hovered above hers.

He remained there for a moment, his breathing a little quicker for their struggle. She wanted to kiss him, just lean right forward and plant her lips on his.

"Don't try to hide anything from me," he said.

And still he remained there, the shadows hiding what was in his eyes. Even with the darkness around them, she felt his gaze on her, holding her in a state of suspension.

"All right, Sam. Take it."

He leaned back in his seat again, taking an enormous amount of warmth with him. His eyes narrowed as he turned on the dome light and looked at the object in his fingers. Then he leveled a gaze at her.

"This is the ring I gave you when we got married."

She only hoped she wasn't giving anything away with her expression. "Is it? I found it in one of my boxes."

"Why were you wearing it?"

"I had taken it out when Armand came in. I just . . ."—she shrugged, trying to play it cool—"kept it in my hand while we talked. And then I realized I still had it and so I slipped it on my finger when we walked out here. I didn't want to lose it."

He handed it back to her and turned the car to the right.

"It's not worth much. Maybe you can melt it down and have something made out of it."

She sucked in an indignant breath. "Of course it's worth something!"

"Ah, don't get sentimental on me, Maxine. It doesn't suit you."

She hunkered down in her seat. And he'd accused *her* of being stubborn! Even though her instincts wanted her to throw herself at his mercy and come clean about being in love with him, she knew that would only scare Sam off. *Patience.*

"So, what were you and Sally talking about?" she asked.

He smiled. "She was flirting with me."

"Oh, really?" A spike of jealousy shot through her. She was this close; she wasn't about to let Sally lure him away.

"Actually, she was trying to convince me that James had nothing to do with your two incidents."

She narrowed her eyes at him, though he was busy watching the road ahead. Was he trying to get her jealous?

"And do you believe her?"

"That is one bizarre bunch you have there."

"I don't have them. Remember, I just severed ties."

"Okay, that's one bizarre bunch you *had*. I can't believe you were going to marry into that, even for the money."

"Me, neither. I mean, it wasn't the money. But I can't believe I was going to marry into it, either. I . . ." She tilted her head, measuring what she said. "I thought I loved him, you know. He was different." Sam sputtered a laugh, and she tried to keep her smile from showing. "But I now realize why I was attracted to him."

"You have a latent puppet fetish?"

"No." She gave him a nudge, which actually felt pretty good. "I was lonely. I was marrying him for the wrong reason."

"*You* were lonely? That's hard to believe."

"Well, what about you? You never remarried."

"No, I didn't. Once was enough."

She nudged him again. "Oh, come on. It wasn't that bad, was it?" She hoped not.

He was grinning. "No, Maxine, you didn't ruin me for all women. I just never found the right person." His smile disappeared so suddenly, she thought someone had run in front of the car. But he kept driving, staring ahead. "I thought I liked the solitary life. Nobody expects anything from you, there's no one pissed because you came home late. I figured it suited me."

"But?" She held her breath waiting for his answer. Was he ready to settle down?

His voice grew soft. "I realized I wasn't so solitary after all. I had Jennie. I mean, we only worked together, had dinner once a week. But I never realized she was a part of my life until she was gone." His throat worked as he swallowed. "She never tried to tell me what to do, or what I should be. She believed in me when no one else did. And she made me laugh."

Jennie again. Her heart tumbled. So he had cared about her, more than as an employee. The warmth of the heater vents washed over her face, making her feel overwarm. She was glad he'd cared about her, she really was. But Jennie was dead.

"Didn't I make you laugh?" she asked in a low voice.

He didn't look at her, but he was shaking his head. "No. Well, maybe in the beginning, when we were young and silly. Not much after that. Don't get me wrong. I probably didn't make you laugh much, either. Maxine, I never blamed you for the demise of our marriage. I don't want it to sound like that. We just weren't happy together, that's all. Happens all the time." He glanced over at her, touching her cheek. "Are you all right? I mean, with Armand and all?"

He let his fingers drop from her cheek too soon. She waved away his question. "Yes, I'm fine with it. Never better." Why did it bug her that he held Jennie in such reverence? She pushed the thought away. "Sam, why didn't you tell them that you had talked to the guy who was hired to run me over?''

"Sometimes it's good to force action, like I did with the wheelchair guy this morning. But sometimes it's dangerous. I'm not ready to play that card yet.''

"You really shocked them with the first Mrs. Santini thing.''

"Yeah, but they're hard to read. James looked the most shook, but Sally went absolutely white. Whiter. Armand looked a little shaken, too.''

"It's not Armand. I'm sure of it.'' At Sam's skeptical look, she said, "Just take my word on it. The man is smitten with me. He'd never try to kill me.''

Sam gave her a half-smile. "Smitten, huh?''

"Yes, smitten to the core.'' Too bad other people didn't follow suit. "My money's still on James. I don't think Aida could get her hands on that kind of cash.''

"Don't underestimate anyone. Armand probably pays pretty well. Or she could be stealing it. And there's Sally.''

"Sally? Ah, I don't know. What would she have to gain? She doesn't seem that close to her father, and she's not obsessive about the clubs like James is. He's the one who's been so hostile toward me since—well, since the beginning.''

"Don't trust anyone implicitly, all right?''

She smiled at the protective tone in his voice. "All right.''

Romeo's low woofs greeted them when Sam put the key in his apartment door. The phone was ringing, but he didn't hurry any to answer it. He helped her off with her coat and hung it on the coat rack by the door, then removed his coat. The answering machine picked up, and after the beep a woman's voice set Maxine on edge.

"Sam, darling. Are you there? You know better than to ignore your own mother.''

She let out a breath of relief and chastised herself for

feeling so threatened. Sam made a pained face and picked up the phone.

"Hello, Mother." He leaned against the counter, flattening one hand on the surface. "I know it's been a while. No, I'm not ignoring you, I've just been busy. I know that, but Ned's a mama's boy, and he lives closer. I don't want to live out there, I like it here. They just instituted a neighborhood watch, so you don't have to worry anymore."

He pulled the sweater loose from the waistband of his jeans and repositioned himself against the counter. His fingers were spread out on the granite surface. He had nice hands. She'd always admired his hands. They seemed capable of doing . . . well, they just seemed capable. Those hands had touched this body once. A warm flush washed over her at the thought, sending strange tingles throughout her body. This body had made love with Sam, too. For five years they had shared a bed, and probably much more.

"Tomorrow night? I can't; I'm on a case. Yes, that's the case I'm on. How did you find out? Oh, I should have figured. Well, I suppose I could bring her. I know, I know, don't put the guilt trip on me."

Her gaze traveled down his body, from the soft waves of his hair, over his shoulders and arms, down legs that looked strong and lean. She had always appreciated Sam's physical attributes, but she'd never let herself think about actually making love with him. Okay, maybe on one or two occasions when she'd let her guard down. Those fantasies soon turned to the grim reality of Sam having to lay her down on the bed, position her skinny legs . . . and then she'd have to explain that she couldn't feel anything down there, though she wanted to so very badly. That's where the fantasy fizzled. She knew she could never satisfy him the way other women could. Now she realized it was really her own lack of self-esteem rather than a lack of ability or feeling.

But now she wasn't paralyzed. Fingers of warmth spread into her stomach, then lower still. Oh, yes, she could definitely feel things.

She had only started getting interested in guys before the accident. Her parents had let her go on group dates once or twice. And then everything had changed, taking her sexuality along with it. It was coming back awfully darn fast. What was she going to do with it? She'd only seen naked men in the movies, what little they showed of them. And once a friend had shown her a photograph of her ex-boyfriend posing in the buff. He'd been long and lean like Sam. What did Sam look like naked? The top half looked awfully nice.

"Good Lord, Maxine, you're going to give me a hard-on if you keep staring at me like that."

With an audible gasp, she realized Sam had hung up the phone and was watching her . . . fantasize about his naked body. She ducked her head, feeling a flush overtake her own body.

"I'm sorry. I wasn't thinking."

"Mm, I think you were thinking too much, and I don't want to know exactly what about."

She continued to stare at the wooden floorboards, her face in flames. This was why she had been so restrained around Sam before. Gabby had talked about the games men and women play, the subtle glances, the come-on looks. All that was a whole new world for Maxine.

"I'm going to take a shower," he said, walking into the bathroom.

She found herself leaning against the wall by the door, listening to the way the sound of the water changed as it moved over his body. Yes, she had a lot of catching up to do, but did it have to be in the space of one evening? She pushed herself away from the wall and walked over to where Romeo lay sprawled out on the floor. Sitting next to him, she ran her hand over his smooth hair.

"Romeo, what am I going to do? I mean, if—no, when I get into, you know, that kind of situation, how am I going to pretend to know what I'm doing?" Anticipation and trepidation flowed through her. "It's easy enough to explain away changes in style over five years, but acting as though I know nothing . . .'' She shook her head, gently grasping the loose skin of his chin and leaning down into the sagging hound-dog face. ''That's not going to work. I'm going to be terrified.''

Romeo let out a sympathetic groan and rolled over to better position himself for her strokes. She listened for the sound of the water. Still going. She wasn't about to get caught spilling her guts to the dog.

''I need to talk to Gabby. How am I going to get away from Sam to do that? It's not exactly the kind of thing I can do on the phone, either. Romeo, Romeo, wherefore art thou, Romeo? Can't you give me some advice?''

He lifted his head, then laid it back down. ''I know, keep scratching.'' His ears were flopped outward, giving him the odd appearance of being caught mid-jump. ''How can one dog have so much skin? It hangs off you like an oversized suit. You look like you're melting.'' She picked up one ear and ran her fingers over the tiny hairs on one side, the smooth skin on the other.

She was still doing that, but not talking, when Sam emerged from the bathroom. He was wearing the jeans and nothing else. His clothes were balled up in his hands, and he walked into the door adjacent and threw them into a hamper next to the washer and dryer.

She remembered times she'd had to crawl from the floor to her chair and pull herself up into it. Now she struggled to get to her feet, relishing the act. Most people didn't appreciate simple actions like standing and walking.

''My turn,'' she said, not meeting his eyes.

After taking a cool shower, she slipped into a pair of forest-green leggings and a matching long shirt and walked out of the bathroom. Sam was standing in front of Romeo holding something in his hand, something Romeo was very interested in.

''Trick.'' Sam placed it on top of the dog's nose. Romeo's eyes crossed as he tried to see the little piece of meat.

"Okay." Romeo popped it up in the air and caught it in his mouth.

"Wow, that's neat," she said, leaning against the back of the couch.

He turned to her, his gaze drifting over her before he gave his attention back to the dog. "He's a smart dog. Watch this." Pointing at the dog, Sam fired off some "shots." Romeo dropped down, shoulder first, and lay on the floor, feet and ears sprawled out. The only thing that moved were his eyes, and they watched Sam for a sign of release. "Okay! Good boy." Sam tossed Romeo another piece of meat.

"What are you giving him?"

"Some leftover steak from dinner the other night. Romeo, come here. Sit." Romeo sat directly in front of his master, looking up with those solemn eyes. "Sniff it." Sam held out the piece of meat, and amazingly, Romeo only gave the meat a nose wiggle. "Stay there." She watched Sam walk around the couch where Romeo couldn't see him and tuck a piece in a corner of the entertainment center. Then he walked to the opposite side of the room. "Go find it."

Romeo lurched forward, nose to the ground. It amazed her that his paws looked so rubbery; they almost didn't clear the floor. But he made progress, covering the path Sam had taken a moment earlier and going right to the treat. Sam scratched his head. "Good boy." He looked up at her. "He's born to do more important things, like find missing children. I only keep him busy with finding treats. Don't laugh; he's a great sniffer dog."

She met his gaze. "I'm not laughing."

He looked at her, and his gaze softened. "No, I guess you're not. It just seemed like the type of thing you'd laugh at. Before."

She leaned down and rubbed the dog's head. "He's incredible." And in his ear, she whispered, "Don't give away any secrets, now."

Sam was leaning against the back of the couch, watching

her with raised eyebrows. "Is there something I should know about?"

She put her hand out, and Romeo held out his paw for her to shake. "Nah, we're just good friends."

Sam dropped back onto the couch, his legs dangling over the back. He took a blue racquetball from a glass dish on the coffee table and started tossing it up, catching it just before it would hit his face. She walked over and sat down near him on the part of the vee that was wider. Romeo settled down by her feet.

"No wonder he likes you. You've been whispering sweet nothings in his ear."

She leaned a little closer. "Would it work on you?"

He missed the ball, and it bounced off his forehead and onto the floor on the other side of the room. "Don't fool around like that and make me miss the ball, woman," he muttered, getting up to retrieve it. But he returned to his spot and took up his distraction again. "By the way, you get to return the favor tomorrow night."

"What do you mean?"

"You're coming to my parents' house for dinner. They're doing their biannual guilt-tripping me into having dinner with them thing. They already knew you were staying with me, so I couldn't use you as an excuse."

"Use me . . . wait a minute. How did they know I was here?"

"Sharee called Armand's to talk to you, and he told her you were staying with me." He laughed that deep, sudden laugh that made her insides tingle. "I'll bet that flipped her lid. Anyway, she'll be there, along with Ned, so you'll have someone to gab with all evening."

"Sharee's Ned's wife," she said, more to herself as she tried to put the pieces together.

"Last time I knew. The woman was a bad influence on you, in my opinion."

"What do you mean?"

"She's the one who put all those ideas into your head

about having fancy cars, million-dollar clothing allowances, a home by the lake . . . all that stuff that I didn't care about.''

"Oh.''

"She's going to think you're crazy giving up Armand.''

Maxine shrugged, not looking forward to someone confronting her about her decisions. "Well, she should understand that I'm not marrying him because I don't love him.''

"Oh, you think that's the way it works, huh?'' He was still tossing that ball, and she fought the urge to snatch it out of the air.

"Well, didn't she marry Ned for love?''

"Maxine, you know better. People in that stratum marry strategically. Her father owns several very large corporations. Customers for Ned, a lawyer in the family for them. You know the score—you're her friend.''

"I am?'' She hid the wrinkle in her nose. "Well, of course I am.''

He paused in his ball-tossing for a moment. "This whole situation has you on a different plane, doesn't it? You hardly sound like the Maxine I was married to.''

"Is that good?''

"What does it matter?''

She let out a sigh of frustration. The man was not cutting her any slack. "Maybe it does matter.'' She watched the muscles in his arm and chest as he continued tossing that darn ball. She found herself twisting the band of gold on her right finger, wondering if he'd notice—no, *when* he'd notice she was still wearing it. The right hand seemed safer, less presumptuous. "I found a picture of us. Want to see it?''

"Not particularly.''

She got up anyway, needing to expend some of the energy stemming from her irritation. She pulled out the picture and brought it to the living area. "See?''

He held the ball still for a moment and looked up at it. "Our honeymoon.'' He started tossing the ball again, making her pull the picture back out of the way.

"I found it in a box of my things. We looked like we were having fun."

"That's because we were drunk."

She glanced at the picture again. "No, we weren't. We were . . . in love."

"We were drunk."

Maxine looked over at the picture of Jennie and wished she could put this picture over that one. Fat chance. Why did it seem as though she were in competition with her old self? Perfect Jennie, who had been the prettiest woman he'd ever known, who transcribed perfectly, who made him laugh. Why hadn't she felt so perfect then?

She looked down over his upside-down face. Every time he moved, his hair touched her thigh. The ball zinged past her head; Sam's attention was on that and not her. Riveted to it, actually.

She let her gaze travel down his throat, over his chest to where his skin disappeared into the waistband of his jeans. A fine line of blond hair started over his stomach and traveled downward toward that mysterious region of the man's body. He was gorgeous, every inch of him. That warmth spread through her again, and she longed to touch him. Not intimately; she wanted to start somewhere safe and comfortable. Mm, nothing on Sam looked safe and comfortable. If women were able to get a hard-on, she'd have one now! Gawd, what a thought. Was this Maxine's body talking, or Jennie's heart? Maybe both.

She looked back at his face. If he noticed she'd been gawking at him, he gave no indication. Sam had never shut himself away from Jennie like this. That was because he'd obviously cared about her more than she imagined. But they'd never crossed over that barrier that opened up all kinds of deeper emotions the way he and Maxine had. And Jennie had never hurt him because she wanted more than he could give her. She inhaled a breath, steadying herself. It was time to start this . . . this seduction, if she did it well enough to call it that.

The ball went up, the ball came down. The ball went up, the ball came down. The ball went up—and Maxine caught it. She tucked it away and leaned down over him, her damp curls falling down over her cheeks. Maybe this wasn't such a good idea, starting this upside-down. But she was in it now.

She cleared her throat, but her voice came out all raspy anyway. "Sam, I want another chance. With you."

Chapter 9

Sam just sat there for a moment, his hand still at the ready to catch the wayward ball. She threaded her fingers through that hand and waited.

Finally he spoke. "Where's my ball?"

"Sam!"

She stood up and approached him from the back of the couch, leaning against his legs. With her weight against him, she lost her balance and braced herself on his thighs. Muscular thighs. Now she was farther away, but at least facing him.

"Didn't you hear me?"

"Yeah, I heard you."

She dropped her chin, then finally said, "And?"

"Either I'm delusional or you are. Or you're playing games."

"I'm not playing games, Sam. I want us to give this another try."

In one swift move, he grabbed her wrists and yanked her forward. She was now face-to-face with him, the tips of his mustache hairs tickling her nose. And she was lying on his body, being enveloped in the warmth of him. Hey, maybe this wasn't going to be so hard after all.

"You're out of your mind, Maxine."

"Maybe. No, I'm not. Just being around you has made

me realize what a fool I was to let you go.'' Ooh, Maxine-the-first *was* a fool, too. Sam's blue eyes sparkled, but it wasn't exactly with passion. She lowered her voice, meeting that gaze with honesty in her eyes. ''Sam, I never stopped loving you.''

''I think this danger thing has gotten to your head. It puts a new slant on your life when someone wants to end it. You'll get over it.''

''Sam, I don't want to get over it. Don't you see? Haven't you noticed the way I've been looking at you?''

He shrugged. ''Yeah, but at first I thought it was my imagination. Figured I'd gone a little too long without some female company. But when I out-and-out accused you of staring, you didn't deny it.''

She shook her head, lifting her mouth so that she felt those tiny hairs over her lip. ''I wasn't trying to be obvious. I just couldn't help it.'' Her heart was beating so fast, it pulsed in her ears. She wondered if he could feel it, too. She didn't quite like the smile he had as he narrowed his eyes and tilted his head.

''Well, I would have never thought in a million years I'd find myself in this position again.''

''It's not altogether bad, is it?''

''Parts of me aren't griping.''

And she could feel it! Slowly, beneath her stomach, that male mystique was growing. She had done that. Her cheeks burned at the pleasure of that knowledge.

''What about the rest of you?'' she chanced asking.

''The rest of me isn't too sure.''

The last thing Sam would have ever thought would happen was having Maxine sprawled over his body wanting a second chance. Or that he'd be getting a hard-on that she had inspired. He had to admit this situation intrigued him, if only in a this-will-never-really-work way. That's the only way he'd let himself think about it.

Her wrists felt tiny beneath his fingers, and he loosened

his grip and let his hands drop to the sides of his head. She twined her fingers through his. Her breath was warm and minty, tickling the hairs of his mustache with each exhale. There was something about her eyes, something soft and yearning that reminded him of Jennie. Well, he'd get rid of that, because Maxine was nothing like Jennie. Besides, it was probably his imagination. Had to be.

In one swift move, he rolled her over onto the wide section of the couch and pinned her beneath him. It worked. She didn't look soft and yielding—she looked terrified. He didn't much like that expression, either. So what if he kissed her? Big deal. And he did, rubbing his lips over hers, then running his tongue over them. Usually Maxine jumped right in, but now she was rigid and hesitant. This was strange. He slipped his tongue through her lips and ran it along her teeth. That prompted her to open her mouth a little, though it seemed more involuntary than invitation. But he didn't need an invitation.

He heard her suck in a breath as he plunged into her mouth. Her hands were on his shoulders then, fingers digging slightly into him. He had to coax her tongue into moving. It finally did cooperate some. Now, Sam didn't mind working at something, but this just wasn't right. She was trembling a little, and her breath was coming faster. But not in the way he was used to hearing.

He changed the kisses to lips-only, and she seemed to relax a bit. When he opened his eyes, he saw that hers were squeezed shut in concentration. This whole scene reminded him vividly of the first time he'd made love to Maxine. She had been a virgin, desperately wanting to please him and unsure how to do it. She'd clung to him, wholly concentrating on what she was doing instead of letting it happen.

But Maxine wasn't a virgin anymore. He stopped kissing her and rested his chin on his palm. She seemed startled, opening her eyes and looking at him with a dazed expression.

"What's wrong?" she asked in a strained voice.

He'd been so distracted by her strange behavior, he hadn't realized that kissing her had been a rather nice experience. She had some of the nicest lips he'd ever kissed. His own mouth still felt warm and tingly. Ah, forget that.

"Where is the woman who started all this?"

Her eyes widened, pushing away that sweet haze that had filled them. "What do you mean?" Her fingers tightened on his shoulders again.

"You give me this come-on, put your hands on my thighs and ask me for a second chance. When I put you to the test, you freeze up. What's the deal?"

"I, uh, I'm not very good at this."

He couldn't help the laugh that escaped him. "Since when?"

Her cheeks flushed even more than they had already been. "It's been a long time. A real long time." At his skeptical expression, she said, "Come on. I didn't doubt you when you said the same thing."

"But I haven't been engaged recently and living with that engagee."

"I never slept with Armand."

That seemed incredibly hard to believe, but he read nothing but honesty in her eyes. "Why?" he found himself asking.

She went blank for a second. "I, well, I just didn't want to. We were waiting until we got married."

He laughed again. "Since when did you become so virtuous? As I recall, you couldn't wait to get rid of your virginity."

"You were my first," she breathed, something odd lighting her eyes.

"Why do you keep repeating the obvious?"

She shrugged, chewing her lower lip and making his stomach squeeze with the action. "Try me again. I'll do better."

He ducked his head, shaking it. "Don't tell me you haven't kissed anyone in a while, either. I can't see Armand waiting until the marriage bed before getting a smooch out of you.''

''I'm trying,'' she said, giving him a look that went right to his heart.

He didn't want to kiss her again, but he found himself leaning forward and capturing her lips. She opened for him immediately, her breathing rate increasing already. Her tongue moved hesitantly with his at first, but in no time she matched his fervor.

He had kissed women—he'd kissed Maxine. But this was different. For one thing, she was trying. Really hard. And whatever she was trying at, she was succeeding at, because his insides were starting to warp and bend. He scooped his fingers up behind her head, positioning her better and feeling the softness of her red curls. She let out a small sigh, wrapping her hands up behind his neck.

Physically his body was responding to her every breath, to every movement of her mouth against his. But something else was happening inside. Behind that darkness of his eyes lurked a feeling he wasn't familiar with. His thoughts weren't telling him that this was his ex-wife, that they would never make it, that he'd only started this to bluff her. They were telling him that he wasn't kissing Maxine at all, that he was kissing . . .

He sat up so suddenly, his head spun. Running his fingers through his hair, he stood despite the dizziness and walked to the entertainment center to place his hand against it for support. His insides were shaking. What was wrong with him? It had to be all the stress of the past month, and then Maxine's strange reappearance in his life. He turned around, not sure what he'd find. Anger was probably what he expected; in fact, what he hoped to find. But the confusion on Maxine's face was worse than anger. She had one hand on her slender throat, the other bracing herself upright.

''I'm sorry,'' he said, surprised at how rough his voice sounded.

''But why? What did I do wrong?''

"You didn't do anything wrong, girl."

He was so drawn to her, though he couldn't explain it. He wanted to keep his distance, but he found himself perching on the coffee table opposite her. In fact, he had to plant his hands on his knees to keep them from taking hers. The Maxine he knew would have been storming around the room, but now she simply sat there and waited for him to explain. How could he explain when he didn't quite understand what had happened?

"This—" he waved to include both of them and the couch—"isn't right. We're different people, we want different things out of our lives. I'm . . . well, I'm surprised and flattered by your interest, but I think it's misplaced. A month ago, heck, technically a day ago, you were engaged to someone else. Now your life is in danger and you think I'm your savior. That's what this is all about. You're confused." As if he had any right to judge her! "Listen, I've seen it before. Women start to see the detective as the guy who found their missing . . . whatever. We're the hero, and they feel this urge to thank us. Or they see the pictures of their husband and his girlfriend, and reach out to us for a bit of vindication. It's just like the patient-doctor complex, that attachment thing. When you realize what's going on here, you'll see that it's all wrong."

She didn't appear to see that. "Sam, you have it all wrong. I made a mistake by agreeing to marry Armand. Maybe I knew it wasn't right the whole time, but was running from my feelings for you. And then fate threw us together. You don't have any idea how right this is."

Without thinking, he put his hands on her knees. "It's the danger, plain and simple. It has strange effects on people. You've put me up on a pedestal, see me as some knight in shining armor. But pretty soon you'll realize I'm just that same ole guy you married and divorced."

"No, Sam, it's different." He could hear the plea in her voice, could see the sincerity in her eyes.

"You can't tell me that after ten years, you suddenly

don't want a life filled with money, prestige, and parties."

She leaned forward, placing her hands over his. "Yes, I can."

Her touch was doing strange things to him. Maybe this danger business was affecting him, too. Damn, this was why he never took on cases for people he was personally involved with. Yet, he hadn't been, until tonight. She was looking at him, so close he could feel her breath. The taste of her was still in his mouth, on his lips. Okay, maybe he'd gone a little too long without the sexual company of a female. Fooling around with Maxine would be his worst mistake. And there was that other thing, the feelings and images when he'd kissed her.

She licked her lips, a subconscious act that riveted his attention to them. She could not have gone so long without kissing a man, Armand in particular. Yet, that's exactly what it had felt like.

"Stop looking at me like that," he said, maybe a little too gruffly.

"Then start kissing me."

He stood so suddenly, she jerked backward a bit. "You'll get over it. I'd like to get some sleep now." He pulled his blanket and pillow from the side of the couch.

At first her body stiffened, and she gave him a look of defiance. She pulled her lower lip into her mouth and seemed to struggle with what to do. Then she stood and walked up to him. Be angry, he thought.

But she disappointed him again. "I'm sorry if I pushed, Sam," she said softly, meeting his eyes with a mixture of vulnerability and honesty in hers. "I just wanted you to know how I felt."

Then she walked into the bedroom area, Romeo at her heels. She might as well have punched him in the gut. What had happened to the Maxine he knew from before? Could danger change a woman so drastically? For Pete's sake, she was wearing his wedding ring again, albeit on her right hand.

He watched her through the cracks in the screens, glimpses of skin and then the creamy thing she slept in. Maybe he was just losing his mind. Until the day she'd dropped on his doorstep—literally—he'd felt nothing for her beyond a general good will. Until today, he'd preferred she find someone else to protect her. But everything had changed, and he didn't like the way it had snuck right up on him. Something stirred inside him, something protective and determined to find her attempted killer. And he found himself curious about her, in a physical way. Watching through the cracks . . . *Come on, Magee. You've seen her naked before.* Yet his body was responding as though he'd never seen her, never touched her or made love to her. Those strange feelings swirled through him. He turned and picked up the picture of Jennie, running his finger along the grooves on the frame.

There was a simple explanation to all this: he was losing his mind.

The morning hadn't officially started yet, but as awake as Maxine was, it might as well have. The bank of windows that ran along the wall revealed only a hint of light through the curtains. She walked into the living room, holding herself against the slight chill. When she saw Sam lying there asleep, warmth inside overrode the chill outside. She'd heard him toss and turn for a while last night, the same thing she'd been doing. One of his bare legs was over the back of the couch, the other was planted on the floor. It was an interesting position to say the least. The blanket covered his midsection, making her wonder what he was wearing under there. She was sure she could spend hours standing there looking at him, studying everything about him from the lay of his hair to the contours of his chest.

Romeo was lying next to the couch. Strange, how he'd picked up his old habit of splitting his time between Jennie and Sam when they were all in the office. He was still asleep, as was his master.

She ran her finger over her lips, remembering their much too brief kisses. What an idiot she'd been, thinking she could fool him. And herself, for that matter. She wanted to be that worldly woman that Maxine had probably been, but she couldn't come close. As soon as Sam had leaned forward and touched his lips to hers, she'd frozen. She hadn't French-kissed a boy since she was fourteen years old, and that was during one date with one boy.

Damn you, Mother, for hiding me away. She shook her head, asking forgiveness for her outburst. Helplessness did that to her, and that was something Maxine had thought she'd never feel again. *I know you were protecting me from all the harshness in the world, but it made me feel so inadequate. It still does.*

That fear of taking a chance still clung to her. She glanced at the picture of Jennie, now at a different angle on the shelf than it had been last night. If she had had more guts, she might have at least kissed more guys. Then she wouldn't have made such a fool of herself with Sam. No wonder he backed away!

If only she could have read what was going on behind those eyes of his. Yet, he'd kissed her again, and that time she told herself to be relaxed no matter how much effort it took. As it turned out, it didn't take much effort at all. She'd opened her mouth to his and let some ingrained instinct take over. Her belly warmed at the memory. Kissing Sam had felt like making love did in her fantasies. She wanted more of it, even while Sam was intent on analyzing her actions and pushing her away. *Not in my lifetime, Sam. Not this time.*

"What are you doing?" Sam's hoarse voice asked.

She jumped at the intrusion in her thoughts and the silence. "Just thinking," she said with a shrug. *Standing here looking at you, and thinking.* He probably already knew that.

He ran his fingers along his scalp, coming to a sitting position. "What are you doing up so early?"

"Couldn't sleep."

He nodded in agreement with that. "Long night."

"Why don't you let me sleep out on the couch, Sam? This is your place, after all."

"Nope, can't do that. Wouldn't be right."

She twisted her lips. "Do you always do what's right?"

"Yep," he said, giving her a look that told her he knew exactly what she was talking about.

She couldn't imagine what it would be like to wake up next to him in the mornings. She shivered at the thought, knowing this body had done just that for five years. How did they fit together? How did their bodies react when they made love?

"I think you need some breakfast," Sam said, getting to his feet. "You've got that hungry look in your eyes." He stopped midway, glancing down at his white briefs. She was already staring at all that firm, bare skin. "Guess I should get dressed first." He slid into the jeans he'd discarded last night.

She started to turn away, but he was already in them by that time. She followed him to the kitchen, remembering Gabby's comment about his derriere. Just grab it, she'd once told Jennie. Very tempting, but she could still see that look in his eyes last night. Haunted almost. But by what, memories of their marriage? It couldn't have been that bad.

"Do you want another banana shake?" he asked, peeling one.

"What else do you have?"

"Cereal." He pulled down a box of Corn Pops.

"Sounds fine." She looked for a bowl and spoon while he fixed his shake. When she poured the cereal into the bowl, she stared at the round, colored circles mixed in with the yellow corn puffs. "Er, Sam? Why has the integrity of the Corn Pops been violated?"

"Oh, I forgot to tell you: you have to pour it just so. When I have several boxes of cereal with only a little bit left, I pour them in one box a layer at a time. Then I pour out one layer at a time." He shrugged at her questioning look. "It's what's nice about being a bachelor. Never having to explain all your quirky habits to anyone."

She looked down at her mixture of Fruit Loops and Corn Pops, shrugged, and poured the milk on. "When you love someone, it's those quirky habits that make them endearing."

"Until that initial infatuation wears off; then they're annoying."

"Was . . . I annoyed by your quirks?"

"Highly." He started the blender.

That wasn't true, but she couldn't say that. As Jennie, she'd always loved his quirks: stirring his coffee with a pen, throwing everything on his desk into a box when a client came in for an appointment. She smiled at the memories. Jennie was cool about things like that. It had never worn off, either, because she had been more than infatuated with Sam. And he had appreciated that in her, as he'd said at least once.

Yes, in some ways, she had been perfect for him. And she'd made him laugh, he'd said. He had thought she was beautiful. She'd only thought of herself as dull and ordinary, beyond the wheelchair and its requirements. The man she held in the highest esteem had thought much more of her. She felt a chill of realization wash over her as she glanced across the room at the picture he kept of Jennie.

Jennie hadn't been such a boring person after all. And though she hadn't been any great beauty, she had been pretty enough. To Sam, at least. She'd been competent, and valued as an employee and friend.

She got up and walked over to the picture, though pretended to look at the stereo. Jennie Carmichael grinned up at her. Maxine wrapped her fingers around her throat. She didn't know the woman in that picture anymore. Now she wondered if she'd known her even when she *was* her. Sam had shattered every self-perception she'd had.

"What's wrong?" Sam asked, turning the blender off and making her realize she hadn't even heard it.

"I wanted to . . . turn the television on."

"Those are the stereo controls there. The remote's on the coffee table."

She turned it on, and habit made her switch to the cooking channel she'd watched every Saturday. Somehow she wanted to connect to Jennie again, even in a small way. At the moment, she didn't know who she was.

Sam was looking at the screen when she returned to her cereal, now a little soggy.

"The cooking channel?"

"Uh-huh." She turned to Sam, who still watched with disbelief. "I want to make you dinner tomorrow night. Just you and me."

"You want to make *me* dinner? Not like those frozen dinners your ex-fiancé eats, I hope."

"No, a real honest-to-goodness dinner." That had been one of her fantasies, right after the kissing one—making Sam dinner.

He gave her that skeptical look she was getting used to, but it was still mixed with surprise. "And what are you going to make?"

She glanced at the television. "Let's see what I can find on these shows. I always do that on the weekends, find some interesting things to make on the cooking channel and have the ingredients delivered. . . ." She trailed off, realizing she was talking as Jennie. Maybe all of Jennie hadn't died after all.

"You hated cooking."

"That was before; this is now." She got up and searched for a pad of paper and pen, then sat back down at the table and watched the show. "Hm, how about poached salmon with an herb crust?"

He was shaking his head. "Whatever you want."

I rather like that sentence, she thought with a grin.

A tall, elegant woman opened a tall, elegant door where Maxine and Sam stood on the wide front veranda later that morning.

"Mrs. Sandman, I'm Sam Magee, and this is my assistant, Maxine Lizbon. I'd like to talk to you for a minute about a case I'm working on."

Maxine liked the sound of that: his assistant. The woman at the front door studied Sam's business card, then looked hesitantly up. "What does this concern?"

"A family that used to live next door about five years ago. The Santinis. There was an accident at their new home, and I was asked to investigate."

Maxine liked the way he insinuated that the Santinis had hired him.

The woman's expression darkened. "That was a long time ago. I'm not sure how much help I'll be."

"I'd like to try," he said, giving her a smile that made Maxine feel very cooperative, anyway.

"All right," Mrs. Sandman said, stepping aside. She led them to a sunny breakfast nook where she was having coffee and a croissant.

Sam declined a cup, and so did Maxine. "You remember the Santinis, then?" Sam asked, pulling out his notepad.

"Oh, yes. They were . . . an unusual family."

"Why do you say that?"

"He was a ventriloquist. He'd sit out there"—she nodded at the house next door—"and talk to himself for hours. He'd even speak with me, if I was out there weeding or planting. But he always did it through that creepy dummy. I haven't liked those things since that movie *Magic* came out. Anyway, I didn't like him that much. Mrs. Santini was pleasant enough. Very self-absorbed, though."

"Why do you say that?"

"I never saw them do anything as a family. She would be lying out in the sun, and her boy would come out to talk to her. She'd shoo him away, as if he were a bug. I felt so sad for him. He spent a lot of time by himself, wandering around the grounds. The daughter got more of her mother's attention, but she spent a lot of time with her brother. Typical adoring younger sister, I suppose. They were always climbing on things, or hanging from the balconies. Used to give me the willies watching them. Then they took to dropping things off the balcony or the roof of the shed.''

Maxine saw Sam perk up. ''Dropping things?''

''Like water balloons. They'd have targets below, and they'd yell 'bombs away' or something. Once they even dropped one on their father's head. He seemed to take it rather well.''

Sam crossed one leg over the other. ''What about the accident with Mrs. Santini?''

''What a shame that was.'' The woman rubbed her arms. ''Talk about horrible timing. They had these ornate concrete things at the corners of the balcony. The new owners removed all of them when they heard about the accident. They were attached with a metal rod, but one had come loose. I guess the rod had disintegrated with the weather, and the thing fell on Mrs. Santini just as she walked beneath.'' The woman shook her silver head. ''So sad.''

''How did the children react?''

''They seemed to withdraw. I never saw them apart after that.''

''And Mr. Santini?'' Maxine asked, getting into the spirit.

''He was a mess. Put the house on the market the next week for almost nothing. My husband wanted to buy it, just for investment purposes, but the new neighbors beat us to the punch.'' She shrugged. ''Is there anything else you wanted to know?''

''No, that'll do it.'' Sam stood and extended his hand. ''Thank you for your help. We'll find our way out.''

During the car ride back, Maxine asked, ''It still points to James, doesn't it?''

''His mother ignored him, and she died. You threatened his inheritance, and you almost died.'' He shook his head. ''But I get the feeling there's something we're missing here, and it's bugging the heck out of me. I need to talk to Floyd again. He's the only real link to the one behind this. Maybe he's remembered something else.''

The Pig's Tail didn't look any less dingy in the daylight than it did at night. She watched Sam walk in, praying that he would walk out in one piece again. As he'd instructed, she'd locked the doors and waited in the car, watching for signs of anything unusual. At the slightest suspicion, she was to honk the horn.

She breathed a sigh of relief when he walked out again, though his expression did not look hopeful. When he got in the car, the smell of cigarettes wafted through the air.

"What's wrong?" she asked.

He sat there for a moment, staring ahead at nothing. Finally he turned to her. "It seems as though our friend Floyd is dead. The cops were in earlier asking the barkeep about his habits and the company he kept. They think it was a mob hit; one shot to the back of his head, execution-style."

A grisly image formed in her mind, though she could hardly dredge up any real sympathy for the man. "But that doesn't sound like something James would do. I mean, he's more into hitting people with heavy objects."

"I know. The punk could have been involved in something else entirely. Or we could have scared someone at the dinner table last night."

Fear tunneled through her. "So he has a gun."

"I'm going to call my friend and find out the details."

"And I'll call Armand and find out who owns a gun in his household."

Sam looked at her. "Are you sure you're comfortable with that?"

"Yes. I want to put an end to this."

"Whoever is behind this probably hasn't advertised to the rest of the house that they have a gun. But it's worth a try."

"I thought breaking off my engagement would also make the killer's motivation null and void. I guess I was wrong. Just my luck, someone who likes to follow through."

"He—or she—probably thinks we got more information from Floyd than we did. With him dead, we don't have proof of anything, but that doesn't mean we can't find something if we're looking in the right place. Or maybe he wants to make sure you don't realize what an awful mistake you've made and run back to Armand.''

''If only they knew''—she met his gaze—''how determined I am to make this break with Armand clean and forever. James wants to make it even more permanent.''

The expression in his eyes turned to blue steel as he reached over and took her hand. ''I'm not going to let anything happen to you, Maxine. I swear it.''

''I know, Sam.'' She tried to smile, drawing strength from the tight hold on her hand. Somewhere in the heat of his gaze, she knew he was trying to atone for not saving Jennie. She let out a breath as he started the car and headed out. It always came back to Jennie, it seemed. Maybe by solving this, he could exorcise her from his life.

Sam leaned against his kitchen counter and watched Maxine pace as he talked with his friend Dave on the phone. She wore a long-sleeved green dress that set off her hair and swished pleasantly around her ankles. More pleasant, though, was the way it draped over her curves. He focused in on the conversation, chastising himself for getting distracted by her.

''So you think it was a mob hit, then?'' Sam asked.

''Don't know. Gut instinct tells me it's someone trying to make it look like a hit. This Floyd character was strictly small-time, drug peddler mostly. He had opened a drawer full of ammo; the perp nailed him in the back of the head. But get this: we think he was shot with one of his own guns. He had a stash of them, the ID numbers all scratched off. I think the perp was pretending to buy the gun and decided to make sure it was lethal. What's your interest in this Floyd character, anyway?''

Sam told him the story, complete with the lack of evidence and their main suspect.

''This why you were asking about Santini to begin with?''

"Yep. At first I thought this was all the product of my ex-wife's vivid imagination." Maxine looked up at him, and he smiled at her. "When Floyd tried to run her over, it became all too real. But I had no evidence at all. Still don't."

"Maybe you outta bring her in here being that whoever's trying to do her in now has a gun."

"I'll suggest it, but I don't think she'll go for it."

"Yeah, I know how that can be. I'm sure she's in good hands. I'll talk to this James guy, see what I can get out of him."

"I'll keep you updated on anything I find."

Maxine walked up to the kitchen counter when he hung up. "Anything new?"

"Santini's story checks out. No one there has a gun registered to them, though it hardly matters. Whoever's behind this took one of Floyd's unregistered guns."

Her face paled. "That means . . ."

He nodded. "Whoever tried to kill you, and did kill Floyd, intends to finish the job."

She wrapped her arms around herself, looking away for a moment before meeting his eyes. "Your friend wanted me to go in so they can protect me?"

"Yep."

"And you told him I wouldn't go for it."

"Yep. Though I'd feel better if you did."

"I'll bet you would. Then you'd be rid of me."

"Yep." He tempered the word with a soft smile. "But you'd be safer."

"No, I wouldn't."

He kneaded his forehead, feeling the tension rising. Not only because of this case, but because of dinner at his parents' looming ahead. He looked up to meet her concerned gaze. "You look nice." Hell, she looked gorgeous, but he wasn't going to tell her that. Maxine had a way of getting a big head mighty quick.

Except that she didn't. Her expression brightened into

something genuine and surprised. "Thanks." She glanced down. "Okay to go to your parents'?"

"Since when do you ask my opinion of what you wear?"

"Since now."

He used the excuse to let his gaze drop down over her dress again. "Looks fine to me."

Her smile faded as he held her gaze, turning to something else entirely. He cleared his throat and looked away. He had to find out who the wacko was and send Maxine on her way soon.

"Are you ready?" he asked, grabbing his jacket. Romeo walked to the door, tail wagging expectantly. "Nah, you don't want to go over to the Magees'." Romeo's tail stopped wagging, and he made his way to his pillow and sat down on it. Sam looked up at her. "He knows better. So do I."

She touched his arm. "We can just say I'm not feeling well and skip it. Order in a deep-dish pizza or something."

While that sounded appealing on several levels, it was for that reason he said, "We'd better go and get it over with. They're expecting us." Besides, she'd spend the evening with Sharee, and he could use some time away from her for a change. Maybe that's what all this confusion was: over-exposure. "Wait a minute. You actually don't want to go somewhere that Sharee is? You two are worse than a couple of giggling teenagers when you're together."

"Maybe I don't want to giggle tonight." She let out a small sigh. "All right. If that's what you want, we'll go." Her coat obliterated the view of that dress and her curves.

"That's what's best," he said, trying to keep the grumble from his voice. He was going to have to do something about this case real soon.

The Magees' mansion had a magnificent view of the lake, which reflected the last rays of the sun as they pulled down the driveway. Maxine took the structure in, finding it diffi-cult to reconcile this kind of wealth with Sam. He had dressed up tonight, which meant gray flannel pants and a nice striped shirt. That was as dressed up as she'd ever seen him.

She chewed her bottom lip as they approached the huge oak doors, hoping there weren't too many people she was going to have to know. She was half expecting a butler to swing the door open, but a beautifully dressed woman stood there with a smile. Her skin was flawless, her blond hair pulled up in a swirling bun. She hugged Sam, then gave Maxine a hug, too. Maxine was instantly lost in a cloud of rich, spicy perfume.

"I'm so glad I could talk you into coming for dinner, Sam, though really, it shouldn't take that much effort." After sending an admonishing look at Sam, the woman turned to Maxine. "And it's good to see you again, Maxine, though I must say it is strange to see you both together again. Nice, but strange."

She stepped aside to let them enter. Maxine tried not to look so awestruck, but it wasn't easy. Dark green Italian marble, ornate wood trim framing the doors and ceilings, and miles of house weren't easy to overlook. The rooms kept going, twisting and turning and making her want to explore them. Instead she followed Sam and his mother across the foyer, both women's heels click-clacking on the marble and filling the twenty-foot-high space with the noise.

They took three steps down into a large living room where she guessed Sam's father, his brother, Ned, and his wife—and Maxine's friend—Sharee sat. Maxine glanced at the steps, noting that if she had been in a wheelchair, as Sam's date for instance, she'd have had to be carried down those steps, chair and all. Unfortunately, she was paying attention to those steps when she slammed right into Sam's hard back.

"Oops, sorry," she said. "I didn't realize you'd stopped." She left her hand on his waist, however, simply because it felt good there.

Sam's father was tall and lean, with Sam's blue eyes and

silvery-blond hair. He wore a gray suit that his chest filled out nicely, but seemed awfully formal for dinner. He stood up from a high-backed gold chair and shook both Sam's and her hands. He held on to hers for a moment. "Maxine, I hear you've hired Sam here to guard you. This is the real thing, then?"

She didn't even know the man's name, but she gave him a smile. "Oh, yes, it's real. One man is already dead because of me. Whoever tried to kill me the first time probably plans to finish the job." She didn't want to get into the details. "But I'd rather not talk about it now, if you don't mind."

"Of course, dear, of course. How terribly upsetting," Sam's mother said, shaking her head.

Sharee was a dark-haired beauty with matching eyes and creamy skin. Ned looked like a smaller version of Sam, without the longish hair and mustache. They sat together on a stiff-looking couch that matched the gold chair. Sharee stood up and walked across the deep red carpet that was thankfully much quieter than the marble, giving her a hug and a cheek kiss.

"Maxine, how awfully terrible that this is happening to you! It's almost like one of those detective movies, only worse because . . . well, because it's for *real*. Come, sweetheart, let's talk."

Sharee led her by the hand back up those steps to the foyer, sitting down at a small sofa that looked more ornamental than practical. Definitely not comfortable. Even though the space was high and open, the silk trees, flowered runner carpet, and fancy wooden chest made the area seem cozier somehow.

Sharee didn't let go of her hand. "Are you sure you're all right?"

"Well, as good as anyone can be when their life is in danger. The whole experience has been nerve-racking."

"I'll bet. You can't imagine how surprised I was when I called for you at Armand's and he told me you were living with Sam." She put her hand over her heart and rolled her eyes. "At first I thought you'd left Armand for Sam, which would have been really crazy, until he explained about the hit-and-run." She smiled conspiratorially. "You know, it was strange to see you and Sam together again, walking in the room just like old times. Especially considering . . . well, you know."

Maxine nodded her head to coax the rest. Finally she said, "I know . . . what?"

Sharee wiggled her fingers in front of Maxine's face for a second. "The dreams, silly. Those erotic dreams you were having about Sam."

Maxine felt her fingers involuntarily tighten over Sharee's. "Oh, those dreams."

"Are you still having them? Like the ones where you're being held prisoner, and Sam saves you and makes love with you right there, untying the ropes with his teeth."

Maxine could hardly hide her laugh. "No, I haven't had any of those dreams lately." Gee, she wished she had. Maybe they would make her feel more comfortable than she was about that whole area. She looked at Sharee, knowing that some of her questions could be answered if she could word them right. "Maybe I subconsciously miss the sex life Sam and I had."

"Well, you used to say that he was the best lover you'd ever had. Especially after Armand."

"Shh," Maxine said, looking around to make sure Sam wasn't nearby. Maxine and Armand's sex life could well remain one of life's mysteries. "Did I say that? The best sex I'd ever had?" She grinned.

"Unless you were making it up to make me jealous."

"Oh, I'm sure I wasn't. What did I tell you, anyway?"

"Just that he was everything you ever wanted in the sex department: the right size, the right stamina, concerned about your pleasure, and very, very romantic." Sharee waved her hand rapidly in front of her face, as if to cool herself.

"Really?" Maxine felt her blood warming at the pictures

she was conjuring up. "I mean, really, it was truly . . . great."

Sharee leaned closer and whispered, "I wish he'd have a pep talk with Ned." She let out a long sigh, looking in the direction of the living room. "I was very jealous." Then she smiled. "Until you told me about Armand." She crooked her pinky and wiggled it.

"Forget Armand. That's over."

Sharee's eyes widened. "You can't be serious. You worked a long time to get his attention, hanging out in his clubs, learning about those dummies. You said besides in the bedroom, he had everything you could ever want."

"I'm in love with Sam," she said.

Sharee let out a soft squealing noise. "You're kidding! But what about having the right lifestyle, money, the cars . . . ?" She studied her friend, and her mouth dropped open. "You *are* in love with him, aren't you?"

"Is it that obvious?"

"More obvious than a new Lamborghini. But you know he's not going to give you what you want, moneywise anyway. How can you think of giving all that up?"

Sam's laughter filtered out of the living room, wrapping around her heart. "How could I have ever given up Sam for anything? And it's not the sex." She didn't know about that yet. "It's everything else about him. He's dedicated to what he does, and he enjoys it. You should see him when he finds a clue or wraps up a case. He glows."

Sharee placed her perfectly glossed nail to her perfectly glossed lips. They actually matched. "Ned used to be that way, early on. Now it's just another case to him, another check." She rubbed her hands together, smile glaring. "But they're big checks."

Sam's mother came out to join them, followed by that warm, spicy scent. "There you two are, lurking in the foyer." She placed a manicured hand on Maxine's shoulder. "Are you sure you're all right, dear?"

"I'm good, considering."

"Good enough for a little shopping?" Maxine caught the conspiratorial look that passed between Sharee and Sam's mother. "My friend at Lord and Taylor told me they're getting their new collection in this weekend. What do you say the three of us make a day of it at the Center up in Skokie? We haven't done that in a while. I love that place, and I've been in the mood for those mimosas we had last time."

Jennie had never been a big shopper. Mostly because clothing racks were too close together, giving her claustrophobia as she wheeled between them. But she couldn't find the idea appealing even without that problem. And she didn't even know what a mimosa was.

"I can't. I mean, Sam would have to go with me, and I'm sure he'd hate to go shopping with us." Maxine forced a smile.

"Oh, pooh," his mother said. "Who's paying his bill?"

"Well, I am." Though he hadn't asked for more than her initial retainer.

"See there. Drag him along. It'll be good for him to see how much work shopping is. You know, they think it's all fun."

Sharee rolled her eyes. "All that walking, the search for the perfect accessories, the right color." Her smile returned full force. "Let's do it! We can make Sam give us his opinions. Men hate that."

Maxine watched the two women glow with the prospect of torturing poor Sam. "No, I don't think so. But thank you for asking; maybe another time."

"Shoulda figured you all would be sitting out here talking about shopping," Sam said, walking into the foyer. Maxine was glad he hadn't come in any earlier when she and Sharee were talking about Maxine and Sam's sex life. But he must have heard the comments about dragging him shopping with them. He winked at her, as if thanking her for saving him that particular horror. "What do you want to drink?"

"Red wine would be nice," she said.

He turned to a woman standing by the living room entrance. "Red wine, please." He looked back at the three women. "Well, I'll mosey on back to the men. Never like to hang around too long when the conversation's about shopping or babies."

Sharee nudged Maxine. "Well, are you going to tell Abigail what you told me?"

Maxine flipped through their list of subjects: sex, Armand, shopping. She turned to Sharee. "You mean about Sam?"

"Of course, what else?"

Well, they seemed to be a close family. Maybe a little too close. "You tell her."

"She's in love with Sam," Sharee said in a high-pitched voice she was trying to keep down in volume.

Abigail looked surprised. "Is he giving up that agency of his?"

"No, I won't let him do that," Maxine said.

Abigail's finely tuned eyebrow lifted. "Then what is he promising you?"

Maxine slumped against the seat. His own mother didn't want him to follow his heart and keep his agency. "Actually, he's not promising me anything. He hasn't even agreed to a reconciliation yet."

Sharee's mouth dropped open. "You mean he didn't beg you to come back to him? No plea bargaining? No hanging him on the line before giving him an answer?"

"No, afraid not."

Sharee's hands went up in the air. "Where's the fun in that?"

Abigail touched her chin thoughtfully. "My dear, I find this rather out of character for you. I mean, I'm more than pleased to have you back in the family again, on an official basis. But I'm having a hard time understanding your motives. You want him back even though he's still going to be a private detective, even though he lives in the city in that detestable warehouse he calls an apartment, even though he hasn't even asked you to come back to him? What's in this for you?''

Maxine couldn't believe this came from his own mother. Now she knew why he'd hardly ever spoke about his parents before. "Sam is in it for me," she answered firmly, standing to find Sam walking over with her glass of wine. She didn't have to wonder what he'd heard, because the look on his face was a mixture of shock and pleasure. Maxine felt a warm flush rising from her chest to her forehead. "Thanks, Sam," she said softly, walking back into the living room where his father and Ned were having a lively discussion about some case.

She sat down on the love seat across from them, and Sam joined her. She could feel his gaze on her, but she knew if she looked at him, he'd see everything she felt for him right there in her eyes. He'd heard enough.

Later, his father turned to her and said, "Well, I guess you're rather happy he did go into private detecting. I mean, now that it's come in handy."

Maxine shot a look at Sharee and Abigail, then aimed a smile at his father. "You know what? I just want Sam to be happy about what he does for a living. Yes, it is nice that he can help me, and I can't think of a better man to do the job." She flashed Sam a quick smile. "I'm very proud of him, and you should be, too. He's a great detective."

The whole room went silent for a moment. His father finally said, "Really? Well, now, that's . . . nice. We are proud of him, of course. Even if he didn't choose the career most Magee men choose."

"Gee, thanks, Dad," Sam said, leaning his cheek against his hand. He didn't seem overly bothered by his parents' attitude. He was probably used to it by now.

When the maid announced that dinner was ready, everyone stood. Sam held her hand, though, keeping her in the room after everyone else had left. Unlike Armand's tugging, all Sam had to do was apply the slightest pressure to keep her there. He leaned closer and spoke in that low, rumbly voice that sent shivers down her spine.

"Now I'm sure an alien has abducted Maxine and replaced her with someone else."

"Why?" she whispered, feeling a warm rush at his closeness.

"Because you never, in all the years we were married, ever stuck up for my profession. And you never said you were proud of me."

"I'm sorry, Sam. I should have. But I meant what I said."

He looked at her, blue eyes studying hers. "I know you did. That's why I think someone abducted Maxine."

She shook her head, moving just close enough to feel the hairs of his mustache brush her lips. "It's me, Sam. Only better." She reached up and ran her finger across the hairs of his mustache. "Has anyone ever told you how soft your mustache is?"

That mustache twitched. "I put conditioner on it. And no, I don't think anyone's ever commented on it."

She kept her smile small and just a little coy, running her finger across the hairs one more time. "Conditioner, hm?"

She had the strongest urge to feel those soft hairs tickling her upper lip again, and there was only one way to accomplish that. She pushed up on her toes, moving closer.

"Sam, Maxine, are you coming?" Abigail's voice rang out sweetly.

Maxine let out a breath, smiling. "Not even breathing hard," she said so only Sam could hear.

He laughed, then shook his head and led her to the dining room. "Don't tempt me."

Dinner went better than Maxine would have imagined, meaning that she didn't have to talk much. Observing worked much better and got her into less trouble. She even got a childhood story, the one about Sam as a ten-year-old following a suspicious neighbor and finding him with his mistress. Since no one had brought it up, she had to assume

Sam hadn't told them about his plans to close his agency. Maybe he'd changed his mind after all.

She even got a glimpse or two of the kitchen as the doors swung to and fro. Just the sight of that huge gourmet vision had her fingers tingling to find something interesting to make. Why, she could whip up something as good as the braised quail and baby carrots their cook had prepared.

Later, as they drank coffee or brandy in the living room and talked about the big case Ned was working on, Maxine slipped down the hall to the bathroom. That's where she found the wall of photos, the Magees through time.

She pulled her lip between her teeth as she took in Sam's beguiling smile in a portrait of him as a five-year-old. He had a sprinkle of freckles that he'd outgrown. She found herself wishing she'd known him her whole life, wishing she could have shared in every moment. The one thing that did stand out among all the photos was that, well, Sam stood out. Not because she loved him, either. His hair was always a little longer, he looked a little shaggier, and his eyes sparkled more than the rest of the Magees. He was probably thinking something mischievous or naughty. Ned looked like a clone of his father, even in pictures of him when he was younger—formal, sedate.

"Told you I was adopted," Sam's low voice said from behind her, sending a chill up her neck.

"You are not," Abigail said on her way to the bathroom.

"But there are times when you'd like to think I am," he said with a wry grin.

"Of course not, darling," she answered before closing the door.

Sam made a tsking sound. "It's really sad when your own mother lies."

On the drive home, Maxine tried to ignore Sam's curious glances and focused on her thoughts. A sadness flowed through her at the observation that Sam's parents didn't seem to wholly accept him for who he was. In fact, Maxine-the-first seemed more accepted than he did. Sure, they loved him. But Sam had forged his own path from the beginning, and the pride in that thought overrode the sadness. Sam looked more at ease with himself than Ned did. Ned seemed to weigh each word he said to his father, using the ones he knew would impress him. Sam didn't bother with that stuff. Besides, a fancy law firm definitely wasn't Sam's style. And they wouldn't have hired Jennie.

When she looked over at him, he was concentrating on getting through traffic. She hadn't really known him, not the way she thought she did. The more she knew about him, the more she loved him.

"Sam, you seem a lot more relaxed than your brother."

"I have a lot less pressure on me. Not only does he have to live up to Dad, he has to live up to Sharee and all her bills." He shook his head. "I grew up with that 'you gotta be this and that' pressure. But I looked around and saw the men who fit that mold, and you know what? They weren't happy. Sure, they had the fancy homes and fancy cars, but the more they had, the more they wanted. Believe me, it was easy to train myself not to want more than I had. And why am I telling you this? You were one of the people in my life hounding me to become something I didn't want to be."

He looked at her, but she saw no malice in his expression.

"I was a different person then." If only he knew how true that statement was.

"And this flower box hits you over the head and you have a sudden epiphany about wanting something different in life? Wanting to be part of my life, particularly?"

"Exactly."

He faced ahead again. "You'll get over it."

She let out a muffled sigh. With Sam, it was one step forward, two steps back.

Chapter 10

Maxine watched Sam head to the shower when they got back to his place. *Want some company? No, that won't do. Can I join you? No. Need me to scrub your back? Oh, geez, this is awful!* She let the door click shut without uttering a word. She bet that if she looked up her sign in an astrology book, it would say something like: not a seductive sign; Aries women should keep their mouths closed and wait for the man to make the first move.

She needed help. And she had an idea of where to get it. As soon as she heard the water running, she snatched up the phone and perched on the couch, watching the door as if her life depended on it. She dialed the number.

"Gabby!" she said in a rushed whisper. "It's me." Then, because with her different voice, that didn't mean anything, she added, "Maxine. Jennie."

"What are you doing? Why are you whispering?"

"Listen, I don't have much time. I need your advice, and fast."

"My advice?"

"Yes. I know this is asking for a lot, but I need advice on how to make love to a man in ten minutes or less. I mean, the advice needs to be less than ten minutes, not the lovemaking."

Gabby laughed. "You're kidding me."

" 'Fraid not. And it's not that I'm planning on doing anything, well, real soon, but I want to be prepared.''

"Things are going well, then?"

Maxine grimaced. "*Well* would not be the word I'd use. I tried seducing him, but I'm just no good at it. I mean, I got a kiss out of him, but that was it. It was awful. Not the kiss, me." She let out a sigh. "The kiss was wonderful. The problem is, I'm supposed to be this experienced woman, and well, I'm not. That was painfully obvious during the kiss. So, tell me everything you know."

It was good to hear Gabby laugh, even if it was at Maxine's expense. "In less than eight minutes. Well, keep in mind that it's been a couple of years."

Maxine frowned. "This isn't a touchy subject, is it? I mean, I don't want to dredge up any painful thoughts or memories."

"Everything I can't do anymore is a painful thought, Jennie. Actually, I still can make love to a man and feel it. Not doing so has been my choice. Okay, what I remember. First, if it feels good, make a sound. Like a moan or something. Don't fake it, but if it really feels nice, you'll find yourself wanting to express it. Guys love that, so don't hold back."

"Okay. What do they like?" She ran her fingers back through her curls. "God, I sound so naïve. What am I talking about—I *am* naïve. I should have been reading books about sex or something. Okay, go on."

"Relax, Jennie."

"I'm trying."

"No, I mean, they like for you to relax. It's all right to be a little nervous, but you sound wigged out. And men like for you to touch them just about anywhere, but especially those, well, you know. *Those* areas. Jennie, you do know what they look like, don't you?"

Nervous laughter shot out of Maxine's mouth. "Of course. I've been around. I've seen plenty . . . Okay, I've seen a picture. Once."

She heard Gabby exhale. "You're almost hopeless, I hope

you know that. Okay, you can't be timid, because that will give you away. At least try to act like you've touched one before. A nice firm hold, like holding a pot handle, works best.''

"Oh, that sounds romantic.''

"It's just to give you a point of reference! You were . . . are a cook; I figured you could relate to that.''

Maxine kept one ear perked for the sound of the shower. Still going. If she kept up these furtive conversations, she was bound to get caught. "Okay, I got that. When we kissed, I felt so many things. Some of them I'm embarrassed to describe. Suffice it to say it was in areas where I've never felt anything before. Is that normal?''

"Oh, yeah.'' Gabby took a deep breath. "You're really making me wistful here. Let's see. Don't be too shy to meet his eyes. Trust him with every part of your body. Don't hold back. And don't be afraid to tell him what feels good and what doesn't. Ask him what he likes, too. Everybody's different.''

"Hold on a minute.'' Maxine was busily jotting everything down in a cryptic handwriting, because she knew she'd never remember it all.

"Jennie, are you actually writing this down?''

"Uh, yeah. You know me; I can't remember more than three items without writing them down. Go on.''

"I just hope he doesn't find your notes. He'll think you're crazy.''

"He already does. And he's still keeping me around, though reluctantly. What else? What about initiating this whole business?''

"Hm. With great modesty, I say I didn't have to worry about initiating most of the time. Music is good. Something slow and sexy.''

"Saxophone music,'' Maxine said with a nod. "He positively gets off on that.''

"That'll be a good start. Wear something provocative that shows some cleavage.''

"And I actually have cleavage now."

"I'm going to share the secret of being sexy with you, Jennie. Love your body."

"Isn't that a little vain?"

She laughed. "I don't mean worship it. I just mean, be happy with what you have. Most women are always down on their bodies: too much here, not enough there. Look at yourself, with your eyes and your hands, and be happy with what you have. Models learn this early on. We concentrate on our good points, and don't think about our bad points. When you see those runway models, you know they're not thinking about that little wrinkle or the nose that's a tad too big. They're comfortable with themselves. I used to be that way, too."

"But you're still beautiful, Gabby." Maxine meant that. "You still have it."

"Thanks, I appreciate that. But being paralyzed . . . being in a chair takes all that away."

"Take your own advice." The hum of the shower stopped. "Darn I have to go. Thanks so much. I'll let you know how your advice worked."

"Don't give me too many details. I might miss it too much."

"You don't have to miss it at all. I know someone who'd be happy to refresh your memory, I bet."

"You're bad."

"I hope so. I'm trying, anyway. Gotta go. Wait! There's something I have to know. Sam has a picture of me . . . Jennie, one you took when I was baking brownies."

"Oh, yeah, I forgot to tell you, what with all the excitement. He came by about a week after the accident. He wanted to know if I had any pictures of you. He only wanted one, and that was my favorite. I didn't think you'd mind."

Maxine sucked in a breath, glancing at the photo. "Of course not. Okay, I have to go. Bye."

"Who was that?" Sam's voice asked as he stepped out of the bathroom followed by a bank of steam. He towel-dried his hair as he spoke, distracting her completely as the muscles in his bare chest and arms pulsed with each movement. His white sweat pants hung a little low on his hips, giving her an inch or so more flesh to gander at than she'd seen before.

"It was, uh . . .," The lie came so easily, she was almost ashamed. Almost, but not quite. This was going to work out just fine. "Actually, it was Gabby. Jennie's roommate." Sam's expression darkened, and she went on. "She was calling to see how you were doing. And you want to know something funny? I know her. From a long time ago, before the maniac attacked her." That part definitely wasn't true.

Sam stopped mid-rub. "Someone attacked her?"

Maxine's voice lowered. "Yeah. Her boyfriend at the time, and the guy who photographed her the most. She wanted out of the relationship when he got too possessive. He ambushed her at her apartment. She ran out onto the balcony on the seventh floor and he pushed her off." She shivered at the image, and at the memory of the haunted look on Gabby's face whenever she talked about it. "He only got a year in prison. Now he's in New York photographing models again. She's very bitter."

He shook his head. "I don't blame her."

It seemed weird to mix Jennie's life and Maxine's, but this would allow her to visit Gabby without arousing suspicions.

"Did you know her roommate, Jennie?" Sam asked.

Maxine shivered. This was getting a little too close. "No." The last thing she wanted to do was start talking about her former self. But she broached one subject that bugged her. "Gabby said you came by and asked for that photograph of Jennie."

Sam looked over at the frame. "Yeah. When she . . . died, I realized all I had of her were my memories. I wanted something a little more tangible. She was a good friend."

Maxine swallowed the lump in her throat. She'd taken a

picture of Sam at one of their Christmas parties, and had cherished that picture above all else.

Sam went into the kitchen and poured two glasses of wine, walking around the couch and setting them down on the table. He dropped down on the cushions and flipped on the television. "All right, since I spent the morning watching those cooking shows of yours, it's your turn to watch some manly television."

She walked warily around, though the thought of sitting next to Sam watching anything sounded appealing. Until he turned on wrestling. She sat down not far from him, feeling the humidity emanating from his damp skin. He glanced over in time to catch her wrinkling her nose.

"Look, even Romeo likes wrestling." He pointed to the dog who did appear to be sitting there in front of the television watching the antics.

"I'm going to cook dinner for you from those cooking shows. What are you going to do, wrestle with me?" Her face flushed when she realized how nice that sounded.

He merely lifted an eyebrow at her, then turned to the show where grunting behemoths were lunging at each other.

"That's Cyclone Charlie in the pink tights," Sam was saying. "Mac the Pounder is in blue."

"How nice."

"These two have had a rivalry since nineteen eighty-nine."

"How nice."

"I'm rooting for Mac," Sam said with a nod, placing his bare feet on the coffee table.

She wondered if he was trying to turn her off by exposing her to sweating, grunting, very large men. Sam took a sip of his wine, and leaned back comfortably against the back of the couch.

She couldn't help grinning. "If you aren't a study in contrasts."

"Hmm?" he said, hardly taking his eyes off the screen.

"A PI sitting here watching wrestling and drinking wine."

"Mm-hm." When Mac pinned Charlie, Sam leaned forward, moving back and forth along with the men in the ring.

"You know they're faking it, don't you?" she asked finally.

His mouth dropped open and he gave her a look that reeked of shock. "No."

She honestly didn't know if he was kidding or not. "Sure. Everybody knows that."

"Oh, no. Why didn't anyone tell me? This is worse than finding out Santa Claus and the Easter bunny don't exist!" He buried his face in his hands murmuring, "Oh, no, oh, no." What he was really doing was muffling his laughter.

She nudged him, and he leaned away with her push, then rocked back against her arm, his face still down. "You've ruined it for me. It'll never be the same."

She found herself laughing despite the fact that he was having fun at her expense. "Oh, all right." But she rather liked having his head pressing against her arm like that.

He lifted his face into hers, a cocky grin in place. The scent of soap and clean male made it hard to concentrate on his words.

"See, here's the thing about watching these kinds of shows. It makes you feel smart when you watch those bozos running around in their underwear pretending to annihilate one another. Isn't America great, that you can do that *and* get paid for it?" He shook his head, sitting upright again. She was tempted to pull him back, but clasped her fingers together instead.

"Oh, America is great, indeed," she muttered. Sam was too busy moving with the action to pay much attention. She just concentrated on feeling the warmth of his arm whenever he leaned toward her.

Maxine might not know a lot about men, but she recognized one earnestly trying to ignore her when she saw one. After the wrestling, a movie came on that he became instantly engaged in, and he spent so much energy trying to pretend interest, he tired himself out. When she looked over at him, his cheek was lying against the leather couch and his eyes were closed. His breathing was even, and she could feel each exhale against her chin. She willed him to open his eyes and find her so close, but if he knew she was there, he wasn't giving anything away.

After a minute or two, she very gently kissed the tip of his nose, then pulled the piece of paper out from beneath the cushion. With her finger, she pushed him until he dropped back on the couch where he wouldn't have a kinked neck in the morning. The lights from the television played over the contours of his chest, and she was tempted to follow the lights with her fingers. Her splayed hand hovered over him, and she let the shadow of her hand do just that.

In her fantasies as Jennie, she'd always imagined they'd be married and acting pretty much the way they always did—as friends and partners. But being his ex-wife who had already been intimate with him, and living here with him put a new slant on those old fantasies. Warmth churned inside her, spreading to areas of her body that ached for him in a way she had never felt before. Her fingers curled at her sides. She wanted him and was scared to death of that at the same time.

In the pseudobedroom, she dropped down on the bed and reread her notes. Her writing looked as sloppy as Sam's, she thought with a smile. But what those notes represented left a knot of worry in her stomach. Sam would probably not initiate anything with her, not the way things stood. But pulling this off convincingly was going to take yet another miracle, and this one wasn't coming from God. She glanced over to find Romeo giving her a look that must have mirrored her own: hound dog all the way.

When she knew thinking about it another minute was going to drive her crazy, she got up and tucked the note in the drawer with her fancy underwear. Sam sure wouldn't find it in there.

*   *   *

The next morning, Sam found himself listening to the way
the sound of the shower changed as it hit Maxine's body.
He shook his head. This case had become way too personal,
despite his best efforts. Where had everything gone wrong?
When he'd taken the case, that's where. That's when he
realized it: this was the big case he'd been after for so long.
Murder, protection, a cast of suspects. Not that he was going
to make enough money to buy Jennie a copier—to buy the
agency a copier. He'd only charge Maxine his costs. After
all these years, and it had finally come. And it was too late.

He walked into the bedroom, finding the sheets and blanket still rumpled from Maxine's sleep. Something inside him
stirred, and he shook his head. Now he was getting off on
rumpled sheets. He opened the sock drawer and took out a
pair, still not used to seeing her panties in there. Lace and
silk did a lot to intrigue a man's imagination. Maxine had
always been into sexy little nothings, he thought, picking a
pair of thong panties out of the bunch. It was hard to reconcile that woman with the one who got nervous when he
kissed her the night before last. When he placed the panties
back in the drawer, something crinkled. Had he left something in there from aeons ago?

The note could have been his, as messy as the handwriting was. But he was quite sure he hadn't written it. Which
meant Maxine had. He read the first few words: *Moaning
good.* His eyebrows wrinkled. He was being a terrible
snoop, and he knew it. He went to the next words, which
he couldn't read, then the ones below that. *Don't fake.* He
really shouldn't be reading this. Aw, what the heck?
That's what he did for a living. *Nice, firm hold. Like pot
handle. ?* He shoved the note back in the drawer and left
the room. Maybe snooping wasn't in his best interest. It only
made him more curious about the stranger who used to be
his wife. And he was obviously reading a lot more into her
scribbles than she'd intended. Sheesh, everything reminded
him of sex nowadays.

When she emerged from the shower a little while later, he caught himself watching the way she sashayed to his bedroom to get her shoes. She wore a bulky green sweater and jeans and not a stitch of makeup. He busied himself with peeling the bananas for his shake. She leaned against the counter opposite him when she returned.

"I remember a day when you wouldn't even have your coffee before putting your makeup on," he said.

Her expression looked a little worried. "Do I look bad without it?"

"I think you look better without it." She used to do this little wave thing with her hand whenever he'd told her that before. It said: ah, what do you know?

She tilted her head and gave him a smile that wormed its way right to his stomach. "Really?"

His throat closed up for a second, and he cleared it. "Really. You want a shake?"

"Sure. It's better than your cereal hodgepodge. But I need to go to the store and get fixings for dinner, plus a few other things."

"Now why do you look happy at the prospect of going grocery shopping?"

"I'm just happy, Sam."

How could she be happy with some nutcase out there trying to do her in? He didn't want to know. But she looked happier than he'd ever seen her during their marriage.

He handed her the glass. "My friend Dave from the station called while you were in the shower. He said James has an alibi for the time of Floyd's murder. That alibi just happens to be his sister. The police figure Floyd was whacked about six o'clock in the morning. Sally said she and her brother were eating breakfast at the house at that time Aida was off that day."

"She'd lie for him," Maxine said. "Although they usually do eat breakfast together, and early."

"Maybe. Because James's alibi is his sister, they're not

writing him off as a suspect. He hadn't fired a gun recently, but he could have been wearing gloves.''

She took a sip of her shake, leaving a thin line of milk over her upper lip. He remembered that impulsive action he'd taken the last time that had happened, and he tried to ignore it.

"So we really don't have anything more to go on," she concluded.

He found himself licking his upper lip in response to her mustache. She caught the action and smiled.

"I have a mustache again, don't I?"

"Mm-hm."

She leaned forward on the counter and looked up at him. "Aren't you going to wipe it off for me again?"

The woman was absolutely positively going to drive him nuts before this was all over. And by the looks of it, she was going to enjoy it. Well, he wasn't going to let her get the best of him, no way. He leaned forward, watching that teasing glint leave her eyes.

In the lowest voice he could manage, he asked, "Would you like me to use my thumb again? Or do you want to leave that up to me?"

A spark lit her green eyes that started a fire deep inside him. She cleared her throat. "I . . . I'll leave that up to you."

He leaned so close, he could feel the heat of her, smell the mixture of shampoo and soap. It looked as though her chin trembled, just slightly, but he couldn't tell for sure. Why was he doing this? Because he was going to show himself that he could give as good as he got and not be affected by it. Heck, he'd kissed the woman enough times; once more wouldn't hurt anything.

His tongue snaked out and started the journey from one end of her lip to the other. Her eyes were closed, but she didn't look as uptight as she had last time they'd kissed. See, nothing to it, he told himself. So he ran his tongue over her bottom lip, the one she liked to pull between her teeth all the time.

He heard the slight catch in her breath, and that tiny sound made his chest tighten something fierce. When he paused, she opened her eyes and moved her lips ever so slightly against his, tickling his mustache. She'd never liked it before, but the pleasurable slant of her lips told him that had changed, too, along with her comment about how soft it was.

He just sat there and let her move her lips back and forth over his, amazed at how something so simple could send blood charging to all his outer regions. He rather liked being the recipient, rather liked doing nothing more than enjoying her touch. Enjoying? Hell, he was getting off on something that wasn't even a kiss, not in legal terms anyway.

Their eyes never broke contact. Mixed with the teasing glint in her green eyes was a seriousness that made it awfully hard to swallow. Then she captured the ends of his mustache hairs with her lips. Their noses brushed softly. If she kept this up, she was definitely going to succeed in driving him crazy. And at the moment, he wasn't feeling too awfully upset about it.

Until the phone rang. It jarred both of them, but he still saw that sensual haze in her eyes when he picked up the phone.

"Yes?" he answered, hearing the irritability in his voice. "Oh, it's you." His tone didn't soften as he handed the phone to Maxine. "It's your Italian Stallion."

He stepped away and finished his shake, rinsing out the glass and letting the water run loudly into a metal bowl in the sink. Since it wasn't the portable she was on, she couldn't walk away. Ah, what did he care anyway? This was crazy. This was Maxine he was thinking about. The ex-wife. The one who was never happy with him. He shut off the water and leaned against the sink.

"That's awfully nice of you," she was saying, twirling the phone cord over her fingers. "But remember what I told you. Yes, I still feel that way." She glanced at him, then looked away. "I can't change the way I feel."

The gold ring on her finger caught the light above them as she twisted and fidgeted. He took a deep breath, holding it in until his chest hurt. She was still wearing his wedding ring. Why? Maxine wasn't the right woman for him, but she'd never toyed with him. She'd always been straightforward about what she wanted. But it didn't make sense that what she wanted was him. When he lifted his gaze, she was looking at him with a curious expression. He had probably looked pretty surly. This whole thing was coming at him at the wrong time. He had too much going on in his head.

"Okay, I'll give you a call," she was saying with a certain reluctance in her voice as he walked into the bathroom.

He closed the door and stared at his mottled reflection on the steamy mirror. That's how he felt on the inside—half fogged up. Maxine's toothpaste and brush sat on the counter as though they belonged there. He picked up a strand of her red hair and ran his fingers down the length of it. It curled back into position when he let it drop back to the countertop. He rubbed his hand over his mouth, feeling her lips on his, seeing her expression of pure pleasure. No matter what, he was going to have to keep his distance until this case was solved. Then she'd see that he wasn't a savior or a hero, that he was just the same old Sam she hadn't wanted before. And then he could go on with his life and try to figure out what he was here for.

Chapter 11

One of the unexpected joys of being able to walk again was grocery shopping. It didn't sound especially exciting to Sam, for instance, but Maxine took joy every time she reached up to the top shelf and grabbed something. No grabber stick, no asking someone to get something for her. And, she thought, remembering Rick climbing up the shelves himself, not having to resort to doing something that made others stare. Not that Rick cared, she thought with a smile. She'd forgotten to ask Gabby if she'd tried that virtual-reality thing with him.

When they reached the apartment, she found a message from Armand on the answering machine. Please wouldn't she call him tonight? He really had to talk with her. Guilt made her sag with its weight, but she knew cutting ties with him was for the best.

Sam was watching her as he put the groceries away. "Having second thoughts?"

"No," she answered quickly. "Just feeling bad that he's taking it so hard." There was something disconcerting about hearing a man beg. Although if Sam begged, she'd probably enjoy it. But if anyone was going to do any begging around here, it would probably be her. And that was only as a last resort.

She joined him on the kitchen side of the counter, putting

away her French vanilla cream that had given Sam a strange look. A streak of sunlight across the counter pulled her attention to the window.

The apartment looked bright and airy with the bank of windows open to the late afternoon sunshine. Snow on some of the roofs nearby glistened with golden light, spraying bright reflections across the room. When she turned to Sam, he was looking outside, too. The light turned his eyes a brilliant blue and washed his face in warmth. He turned to her and smiled.

"I haven't appreciated that view in a long time." His voice sounded wistful. "Do you ever wonder how something so beautiful can blend right into your life so that you don't even realize what you have?"

Uh-oh, one of his "do you wonder" questions. She wished she could read what was going on in those eyes. "I never stopped appreciating the beauty in my life, Sam," she said softly. "It only gets better."

He shifted his gaze just to the right of her, staring hard at something and nothing at all. She stood beside him, wishing she could see what it was.

"Sam, what are you looking for?"

"I don't know." He shook his head slowly. "It's like, something isn't right and it's bugging the heck out of me."

"Since Jennie's death," she ventured.

"Before that. I mean, her leaving bugs me, too, but it started before that."

"You were restless," she remembered aloud.

He turned to look at her, making her gaffe worthwhile. "How did you know?"

"It was a guess." She shrugged, but inside that same feeling of helplessness washed over her, just as it had when she was Jennie, watching his struggle. "And I'm not helping, am I?"

"No." He ran his fingers through his hair as he walked around the counter. "Don't worry, I'll figure it out. I'm going to take a shower, then I'll help you with dinner." He smiled, but it wasn't quite all there. "I haven't had a home-cooked meal in a long time."

With her arms wrapped around herself, she walked over to the windows, grabbing the remote control on the way. Expecting the television to turn on, she was surprised when only music filtered through the room. Soft, seductive music. She pushed away all thoughts of a seduction that would never happen, because that part of Jennie still lived inside her. Scared, self-conscious.

Bathed in sunlight, she closed her eyes against the warmth and the sound of the music. The first few notes of "Nights in White Satin" by the Moody Blues slid over her like seductive fingers. She turned the volume way up, sure the song would be done before Sam got out of the shower.

She let her head roll back, her hands flexing on her sides. Love yourself, Gabby had said. Maxine lifted her hands, then left them drift down over her face, throat, over the curves of her chest and down her stomach. She pulled her bulky sweater over her head and flung it to the couch, then rolled her shoulders as the singer proclaimed his love.

Sam, I love you. She replaced the words to the song with her own. With the toes of one foot anchored on the back of the couch, she leaned back and watched her hands arch gracefully above her. She tested her hips, swinging them back and forth to the sensuous melody. She'd forgotten that she'd had rhythm. Oh, to dance again! The triumph filled her, making her feel as though she stood on top of a huge mountain looking out over the rest of the world. Her feet took her across the wooden floor where she jumped into the air. She spun until she got dizzy, laughing with the sheer joy of simply moving to the music.

Sam wasn't used to taking clothes into the bathroom with him when he took a shower. After starting the water and removing his shirt, he walked back out to get a pair of pants and a shirt. He heard the music first, filling the room with its powerful message of love. And then he saw her. It was as if he'd been socked in the stomach, pushing him back against the door. Maxine stood in the rays of sunshine beside the window, her hair lit to fire as she rolled her head back. He sucked in a breath, trying to let her know he was standing there. But the sound wouldn't come. Didn't want to come. She raised her hands, then ran them down the front of her body. His own body came to life so suddenly, so completely, he was filled with a longing he hadn't felt in forever.

She flung off her sweater and started dancing, swaying her hips, using her hands to caress the air. Sam couldn't tell where the music left off and Maxine began. God, she was beautiful. How had he forgotten how beautiful she was? But this wasn't the Maxine he'd been married to. That he knew, though he couldn't explain it. And at the moment, he didn't want to. He just wanted to drink her in, to absorb the scene to hold for eternity.

Her peach bra sculpted her breasts, and her jeans molded her bottom to perfection. But it was the way she moved, as though she lived to dance right there, to that song, for him. He was grateful that this song was so long. One of her bra straps slipped down over her shoulder, and the light glistened off her skin there. An urge to touch her overwhelmed him. He wanted her, not just sexually but . . . spiritually.

When he recognized the final part of the song, he crept to the stereo where his compacts were loaded for random play. He hit the repeat button, then waited until she was lost in a spin before walking back to the place he'd been watching her from. His knees felt wobbly. He felt light-headed, drugged with something he never wanted to give up. She belted out those final words of love, closing her eyes and putting her all into it. Slowly she rocked back and forth as the music turned into something lyrical and the deep voice recited a poem. She took a deep breath, her chest rising with the sound of her sigh as the song ended in a metallic bong. She didn't want the song to be over, either.

As if in a daze, she blinked, looking for her sweater. And

then the song started again. Her eyes widened as she tilted her head, then looked at the stereo. After a moment, she swung around to find him standing there. He didn't know what his expression was, and he didn't have the strength to slap on a grin or sheepish look. Her face, however, flushed a deep red as she snatched up her sweater.

"*Oh, God,* Sam, how long have you been standing there?" she asked in a breathless voice.

When he opened his mouth, nothing came out at first. He cleared his throat and started again. "Long enough."

Her flush deepened, but her eyes kept watching him. "Sam." She said it softly, and yet it vibrated through his entire body with the force of a bullhorn.

He walked over, running one hand up into her curls and tracing a finger over her lips. She let the sweater she was holding between them drop to the floor. His finger trailed down her throat, and he spread his hand when he reached the curve of her breasts. Her breath hitched as he traced around the side before exploring farther inward. His hand dropped down over her bare stomach, sliding over the soft, damp skin. Her muscles trembled slightly beneath his touch. He watched his fingers skim over her, watched her chest rise and fall, then raised his gaze to hers.

Her eyes were huge and full of some emotion he wasn't even familiar with. With his hands on her hips, he pulled her flush against him. He could feel his arousal pushing against her stomach. Her fingers slipped around his belt loops as if to keep him from escaping. No chance of that.

Maxine had never felt so many tumultuous feelings in one small space of time. Being lost in the music, then finding Sam standing there watching her . . . She could have died. Until she saw the fire in his eyes and realized he must have made the song play again. And now she was on the edge of teetering into an emotional minefield. As his hands slid over her body as though she were something precious and irreplaceable, she knew she would shatter if he stopped now.

"Sam," she said on a rushed whisper. "Please don't do this if you're going to stop before . . . before . . ."

His hands slipped back through her hair as he pulled her close for a kiss that seared her soul and left her hungry for more. He didn't tease her to get her mouth open, he just plunged right in and nearly knocked her off balance. She let go of his belt loops and found the more solid anchor of his hips.

Even through the silk of her bra, she could feel his skin making her ache for more of him. How could a body ache like this, when it felt *so* good? Her entire lower region pulsed where he rubbed against her pelvis, washing her in a warmth she'd never felt before. Thoughts of pretending she knew how to do all this, and Gabby's advice, flew from her mind. He swayed, taking her with him in the slow rhythm of the music. She didn't need to worry about what to do. All she had to do was go with it, just as she had when she'd heard the song the first time and let the music lead her. Now she would let Sam lead her.

He took one of her hands in his, holding it between them; the other hand held her close as they moved slowly over the floor. His eyes were closed, his forehead pressed against hers.

"You wanted to dance," he said in a low, hoarse voice. "What?"

"The day you came to my office. You wanted to dance."

She smiled, pulling him closer yet. "Yes, I did." She had dreamed of doing this for years, but she never imagined it would feel so right, and so good. She'd guessed close, but not quite. They moved in and out of the shards of sunlight, and she watched it play over his hair and skin.

He flattened the hand between them, and she followed suit, feeling so connected to him with that one simple act. After a moment, that hand slid down and unclasped her bra. She let it fall to the floor, feeling a little self-conscious. He cupped her shoulders first, sliding down her arms before gently running his hands beneath the lower curve of her breasts. Again she caught her breath, amazed at how his touch there could stir through her entire body. His thumbs ran over her sensitive nubs, making them tighten beneath his touch.

She wanted more, more. She wanted everything.

When she thought she would burst from some explosive force inside her, she leaned against him, her lips to his chest. She kissed across his skin, which felt warm and soft beneath her lips. To touch him, oh, how she'd dreamed of doing that. Just simple touches, like running her hands over his shoulders and into his silky hair. He leaned his head back and closed his eyes, and making him react filled her with more passion than the music had.

He leaned down and nibbled her neck and ears, making all kinds of interesting noises that sent erotic whispers through her veins. Noises! She was supposed to make sounds when it felt good. And, oh, it felt good. She felt the bubble rise within her, and she let it out with a long sigh. He responded by leaving a wet trail across her jaw as he plundered her mouth again.

And then he went lower, weaving damp lines down her throat and over and around and covering every inch of her chest. Her fingers found his hair, and she rocked back and clutched at the strands while he drove her crazy. He tugged at her jeans snaps and pulled them and her panties down in one fell swoop. After planting a kiss on her springy hair, he lifted her up. Instinctively, she wrapped her legs around his hips, and he walked into the bedroom where she'd spent those nights enveloped in his scent and her longings. He laid her down on the bed and took off his jeans.

She couldn't help staring. He was about to slip onto the bed with her, but she said, "Sam, stop."

"What's wrong?"

She smiled, to let him know nothing was wrong at all. Leaning back on her elbows, she said, "I want to look at you."

"I haven't changed that much," he said, lifting his arms

as her gaze swept him from head to toe and back up to his midsection.

She took a deep breath to balance herself, spreading her fingers on the bed to help. He was breathtaking, every inch of him. She couldn't avoid that most mysterious part of the male anatomy, though she tried not to gawk. He looked perfect, even that part. When she looked at his face, she realized he was doing the same thing to her, looking and appraising.

Without waiting for her word, he slid up along her body, stopping on the way to kiss and nibble. He took a long time over her stomach and chest, making her toes curl as the sensations rocked her. While she was busy going crazy at that, he captured her mouth in a kiss that was filled with both passion and restraint. As he knelt lower over her, she could feel his hair mingling with her own, and above that, his own maleness pressing between them.

After a few minutes, he slid halfway off her and ran his fingers lightly over her skin. He seemed to drink her in as he watched his hand move over her stomach and graze her inner thighs before slipping into her most private area. She inhaled sharply, wondering if that counted as a sound. He merely smiled as he continued his ministrations.

"Sam, my gosh, Sam, what are you doing?" she said in a breathy voice.

"Just wait and see."

If she thought the sensations already pulsing at her were too much, what he was doing now was absolutely too much to bear. This was what she'd been missing, what Sam couldn't have given her if she'd still been Jennie. She curled her fists and arched her body, feeling close to breaking into a million pieces. And then she did. A warm rush filled her, and the pulsing became a pinpoint that commanded her attention.

Through the haze she felt him slide back over her, covering every inch of her with his hot skin and solid strength. He ran his thumbs over her cheeks, then leaned down and rubbed his lips over hers before slipping his tongue inside.

She was still spiraling upward when she felt him glide inside her and start a delicious rhythm that began that building feeling all over again. Her fingers tightened on his shoulders as she closed her eyes and lost herself in the realization that Sam was making love to her at last. She hooked her legs over his buttocks and let all the sounds that wanted to escape out as he lifted her higher and higher until her body shuddered. He kept the rhythm going until she relaxed slightly. Then in one swift stroke he buried himself in her and exploded, pulling her in a tight embrace as his body clenched.

They remained there, closer than one, for a long time. She wanted to capture the feeling of being completely one with Sam to hold forever. But there would be more of this, more to cherish.

After a moment, he lowered his forehead against her chest. She could feel his heavy breathing against her skin, could almost see the waves of heat emanating from him. She ran her fingers up into his hair, wondering when the ringing in her ears would stop. His hands were holding her arms, and she felt his fingers tighten. But he remained there for the longest time, so long that she wondered if he'd fallen asleep.

"Sam?" she finally said.

He slowly raised himself, but his head was still lowered so she couldn't see his face. Suddenly she needed to see his face very badly.

"Sam?" she repeated. "Look at me."

His face was damp, and his eyes were squeezed shut. Was this normal? Did men go through . . . something when they finished? She lifted his chin, and he slowly opened his eyes and met hers. The pain in his eyes shot right through her, making every muscle seize in panic.

"Sam, what's wrong?"

He just shook his head, pulling himself free of her and staggering to the doorway. He grabbed up his jeans, but remained there for a moment with his hand covering his face.

She grabbed the sheet and covered herself as she sat up. "My gosh, Sam, did I hurt you?"

The sound that came out of him clutched at her heart. It sounded too much like a muffled sob. This could not be a normal reaction. He turned to her at last, that same pain lancing across his expression.

"I'm sorry," he said in a broken voice. "So sorry." And then he walked away. She heard the bathroom door close and realized the water had been on the entire time. It had to be cold by now, and yet she heard him moving beneath it. For some of the longest minutes she could ever remember, she sat there and waited for him to come out.

Without Sam gazing down at her, she felt very naked and not altogether attractive. She tried to ignore the trembling in her fingers as she pulled on her jeans and her sweater. Pacing outside the bathroom door didn't help, and neither did going over everything to find out where it went wrong. What was he sorry about? Making love with her in the first place? It was wonderful. And it wasn't like she'd looked regretful. For lack of nothing better to do, and to warm the chill building inside her, she started a pot of coffee and watched it brew.

When the door opened at last, she wasn't sure what to expect. He'd put his jeans back on, but he hadn't combed his damp hair. She sat at the counter where earlier she'd rubbed her lips over his. Now his head was lowered as he ran his fingers through his hair. Trails of water dripped down his back, and she fought the urge to get a towel and dry him properly. Instead she wrapped her arms around herself and pulled her knees up.

He knew she was there, but he hadn't looked over at her yet. She waited, watching his body tense.

"Sam, you're scaring me," she said at last, hating the tremble in her voice.

He opened his mouth to say something, exhaled nothing

more verbal than air, then said, "I'm sorry."

She tried, but failed, to force a laugh into her voice. "Listen, if it was that bad, just tell me. I can take it."

"It's not that," he said in a voice that was so low, she had to lean toward him to hear it.

Sam walked over to the windows, where the warmth had receded to leave a bleak, dying sky. He stretched his hands up against the glass and pressed his forehead against it. His body heat created a fog aura in front of him. Maxine got slowly up and walked over beside him. She pressed her hand against the glass, which was ice-cold. In fact, the whole room was colder now that the sun had gone down and the insulated curtains were all open. But she couldn't quite close them while he was leaning against the glass.

Finally she gripped his arm and pulled him away from the window. The pain was more deadened now, but she still saw it there as he met her gaze. She tried to keep her lower lip from quivering as she crossed her arms over her chest.

"Sam, what is going on? Please tell me."

He rubbed his hand down his face, then matched her stance with his arms. "I have been so stupid," he said, looking out the window and shaking his head.

"Sam, I'm an inch from either strangling you or throwing myself out the window. Either way, someone's going to have a death on their conscience."

When he looked at her again, he was even farther from her. Little by little he was shutting her away. And just when she felt the despair at that, he reached out and touched her cheek. She wrapped her fingers around his, still pressing his hand against her.

"Maxine, I . . . I didn't expect this."

"Is this about birth control? Protection?" She refused to believe their union could bring anything tragic, although having Sam's baby wouldn't be half bad.

"I haven't even started thrashing myself about that yet."

He was thrashing himself. Well, wasn't that obvious?

"Maxine, I never meant for—I mean, making love with

you was great." His fingers squeezed hers. "Better than it ever was."

That gave her some hope, but she could feel the "but" coming on. "I'm glad," she said carefully. "And do you always act this way after having a great time in bed?"

The edge of a smile formed at his mouth. "No, not usually. I'm an ass, Maxine. But it just happened."

"*What* just happened?"

His voice lowered, and all traces of that bittersweet smile disappeared. He would have pulled his hand away, but she wouldn't let him.

"When I made love to you, I saw . . . Jennie's face."

He may as well have pushed her right through that window. As it was, her knees weakened, and he caught her elbows to support her. Every trace of blood fled her face.

"J-Jennie?" she whispered.

"I know. It was like it was there all along, and I never saw it. Not until we made love."

"Saw what exactly?" she forced out.

He looked out into the grayness beyond the window. "That I was in love with Jennie."

And then she dropped.

Sam caught her just as her bottom reached the hardwood floor. She gained her balance, saying, "I'm all right, I'm all right." Then she remembered the last time she'd said that without quite meaning it. This didn't feel much different than nearly being run over by a car.

He led her to the corner of the couch, where she sat down on the overstuffed arm. Then he walked the few feet back to the window, holding on to the ledge and leaning his back against the glass. She saw him glance at the picture of Jennie, then look down at the floor, or maybe his bare feet. Despite the cushion beneath her, she still felt on the edge of a precipice. This could not be happening to her, she decided. She was merely dreaming this. But she'd thought that one other time, too, when she awoke in another woman's body.

He was in love with Jennie. Jennie! Feelings of elation battled with shock and heartbreak. Mostly the heartbreak was winning.

She found her voice, though she cringed at how desperate and thin it sounded. "Through how much of it were you picturing her?"

His voice was far away. "I don't know. It happened so subtly, like you just blended in with her. The way you were dancing, the way you reacted when I touched you, was so innocent and fresh, so honest. And suddenly I was making love with Jennie, and realizing I'd made love with her before."

The fist in her gut was twisting, grinding. "What do you mean, you made love with her before?" Surely she would have known!

"In my mind." At last he lifted his gaze to hers, and still that pain was visible. "I knew I cared about her. When she died, I was so consumed with guilt that I didn't realize how empty I felt without her. Until you came barging into my life. Sometimes the way you smile, the way you laugh and pull your bottom lip between your teeth, reminds me of Jennie.

"And every time I thought about her, I felt an ache that was worse than the emptiness. But I still kept ignoring it . . . until we made love. My eyes were closed and I slipped into this, I don't know, this place between reality and my subconscious. That's where Jennie was." He ran his fingers down his face, pressing them into his closed eyes for a moment. "And when I opened my eyes, it was a shock to see you there. That's when I realized what had happened. And how I felt." He leaned back against the glass again, tilting his head upward.

Sam had been in love with her. Sam. It stunned her, refusing to penetrate the layers of her soul. For how long? Why hadn't she noticed?

"Sam, do you think she felt the same way about you?"

He pressed his palms against the window, spreading his

fingers out. "Jennie needed a lot more than I could give her."

If he heard her swift intake of air, he didn't let on. "What are you talking about, Sam?"

"She was strong, but delicate at the same time. She needed a man who was stable, who could give her a good life. Not in the way you wanted, because she wasn't like that. But she deserved a guy who would be home for dinner every night, who could give her a nice home."

"Oh, Sam," she said in a voice that rang with regret and irony.

Enough so that he looked at her. "You're not mad?"

Her fingers tightened on the leather. "How can I be mad at you? God, Sam, if you only knew . . ."

"Knew what?"

More than anything she wanted to tell him the truth. But it was too late for that now. "How much I understand."

He walked closer, sliding his finger from her throat to beneath her chin. "I don't deserve that. And I never meant to hurt you, know that. I have never thought of another woman while making love to you before."

"I know." Somehow, she knew that.

His finger remained there, his gaze on her. He closed his eyes. "I'm lost," he whispered, and those two words melted through her skin and into her very soul.

She lifted her hand toward him. "Let me help you find your way home."

He ducked his head and moved away. "Maxine, I need some time alone. I'll be back in a little while, okay?"

She nodded, wishing she could take away both their aches. He would come around, she knew he would. "Okay, Sam."

He walked like a man with a heavy load on his shoulders and no strength to bear it anymore. Her eyes prickled, but she blinked back the tears threatening to rain down on her. He opened the door, then looked up at her. She turned to him, hoping that he would close the door and walk back into her arms.

"Put the chain on the door," he said, then pulled it closed behind him.

She watched that door for a long time, waiting for some miracle that never occurred. Her gaze drifted to the picture of Jennie. Why hadn't she seen it? Before her death or afterward? Afterward was easy: she didn't want to see that he was in love with someone else, that he ached for Jennie's loss. Looking back, it was so obvious, she felt foolish for not seeing it.

She had been in love with Sam and hadn't felt adequate for him. And all that time, he had been in love with her, holding back for the same reason. And not once did he mention her disability. Would they have ever discovered their mutual affection? Probably not. The irony danced through her. And to top it off, Maxine had been in love with Sam, too! All the twists and turns were manifesting themselves in her stomach, doubling her over.

The phone rang, though even the jarring sound hardly penetrated her wall of numbness. The answering machine picked up, and she closed her eyes as a happier Sam told the caller he would return their call at his earliest convenience.

"Maxine, this is Sally. I really need to talk to you."

Maxine picked up the phone. "Hi, Sally, I'm here." She perched against the counter, her back to the door.

"Oh, thank goodness you're there. I'm probably over-reacting, but, well, it's Daddy."

Maxine closed her eyes. She just didn't have the heart to discuss Armand right then. "What's wrong with him?" Now that was a loaded question.

"I know things aren't, well, good with you two right now. But you have to talk to him, maybe get him into counseling. He hasn't been the same since you moved out. All he does is pace and scratch his eyebrows and talk about getting you back. James has had to run the entire business, because

Daddy just isn't . . . there. I'm afraid I didn't help much, either. I was trying to get him to forget you, so I told him . . .'' Her voice lowered a little. "I told him that you and Sam were probably screwing each other's brains out five times a day. I'm afraid it put him over the edge."

Maxine heard the key slip into the lock, and elation shot through her. Sam was back. And soon, which was a good sign. She remained where she was, not wanting to appear anxious. "Okay, I'll talk to him," she said. "I gotta go."

Romeo let out a low, happy woof that Maxine agreed with. She wasn't sure what to expect, but at least he was home. Then she heard Romeo's low growl at the same time she heard the high-pitched voice.

"Maxine, Mr. Wiggles has come to get you."

Chapter 12

$\mathcal{M}$axine whirled around in disbelief to find Armand standing there with his dummy. He looked as pale as the creepy thing did, and nearly as sensible. His eyebrows were covered with red scratch marks. The bugs Sam had told him about. Dread curled around her as he closed the door behind him. She hadn't locked the chain. But Sam had locked the door itself. Her gaze dropped to the key ring he jangled nervously from one finger, then to the billy club he held.

"What did you do to Sam?" she asked in a rushed whisper, the words barely managing through her tight throat.

Anger rippled across Armand's face. "It's always him you're worried about, isn't it?" He lifted Mr. Wiggles. "Why aren't you worried about your kissums? He cares more about you than that PI does."

Romeo's dark growl raised the hairs on her arms. Armand held out the billy club, backing the dog away.

"Don't you touch that dog," she said.

When he looked at her, he was wearing a macabre smile. "I've come to bring you back to your senses, cherry lips." He glanced around the apartment. "He's got you brainwashed, ever since that accident at the house. But now I've come to rescue you, like one of those heroes in the movies. Your nightmare is over."

Her chin trembled so violently, she bit her tongue. "What

did you do to Sam?'' she asked again, fearing the answer lay in that billy club.

"Don't worry about him," Mr. Wiggles said, twisting his head in an unnatural way. "Armand made sure he was out of the picture."

She leaned against the counter for support. "Has it been you all along?"

"Just come with me, Maxine," he said in a deeper voice. "I'm going to tuck you away until you realize how brainwashed you've been. Then you'll see how much you love me, how happy you were with me. I got used to the idea of being married to you. I don't want to give it up."

"You'll find someone else." Her mind scrambled for a weapon. Romeo kept growling, but that club kept him from getting closer to Armand.

"There is no one else, Maxine. I waited all these years just to meet you. I can't wait any longer. I want you now. We're getting married, and I'm not going to leave your side until things are the way they were before."

She had to believe that Armand wouldn't hurt Sam, not badly anyway. But she didn't know Armand. She didn't even know the man she'd worked with and loved for four years, not really. Right now she had to get out of there and find Sam. And the only way to do that was to go with Armand.

"Okay. Let me get my coat." She knelt down and petted Romeo on the way. "It's going to be all right," she said more for her benefit than his. The blood pulsed against her temples, her insides wound so tight she could hardly breathe.

"I wouldn't hurt you, Maxine," Armand said. "You know that, don't you?"

She glanced down at the club then quickly back up to his eyes. "I know," she pushed out.

He did not look well. His face was pale between the blotches of red, and his eyes had a hazy quality to them. His smile seemed at odds with his rigid body posture. In fact, he looked more like his dummy than the other way around.

She slipped into her coat, moving away when he lifted a hand to help. Her hands were trembling. Armand gripped them before she could pull them away.

"Everything will work out for the best."

She was beginning to doubt that. "I hope so."

She opened the door and sucked in the cool air in the stairwell. Sam was out there somewhere. The door downstairs opened with the suction of air, then closed shut again. Gripping the handrail, she took the steps quickly. Armand was right behind her.

"I missed you."

She pushed open the door and looked around. Sam's car was parked halfway down the block. Suddenly someone grabbed her and pushed her down into a bank of snow.

"Sam!" she screamed out before getting a mouthful of the cold, wet stuff.

She gained her balance as he lunged at Armand. With a quick twist, Sam had Armand's arm bent behind his back. Sam shoved him against the door, sending a gush of air from Armand.

"Are you all right?" Sam asked. All she could do was nod. "Go up and call the police."

"Please don't murder me!" Armand cried out in a pained voice.

"And why shouldn't I return the favor?" Sam asked as Maxine slipped past them and up the stairs.

Her knees would hardly hold her up as she pulled herself up the stairs and into the apartment. Romeo's woof was a warm welcome as she made her wobbly way to the counter and the phone. It was like that first day when her mind didn't know she could walk yet. After calling the police, she made her careful way back downstairs to Sam. Armand was lying in a heap on the sidewalk, Mr. Wiggles sprawled out beside him.

"What happened?" she asked.

"Aw, he was annoying me, something about me brain-washing you into hating him. So I punched him out." He put his hand to the back of his head and grimaced.

"Did he hit you with the billy club?" she asked, moving closer.

"Just a little."

As soon as she got near him, he reached out and pulled her up against him. His hands framed her face and his expression became grave. "I screwed up, and you almost died because of it."

She burrowed against him, craving his warmth and his aliveness. At his words, though, she looked up at him. "Sam, this wasn't your fault. You told me to put the chain on the door. I was too . . . I didn't."

"I was supposed to keep you safe," he said in a low voice.

"You did, by telling me to put the chain on the door. Sam, this isn't your fault." When he rubbed the back of his neck, she said, "You should see a doctor. Sometimes head injuries can be . . . fatal."

"Ah, I'll be fine. I'll just have a whopper of a headache for a while. It's the least of my worries, believe me."

"What happened?"

"I walked out and this little garbanzo bean whacked me with the stick. I went out for a minute or two." He tightened his hold on her. "All I could think about was getting to you."

He rested his chin on her head, and she closed her eyes. She was safe again.

"I can't believe it's over."

"Do you think it was him behind everything?" Sam asked.

"It has to be. You didn't see that look in his eyes. It was like there was a demon in him, a strange glow of evil. Maybe he had some cockeyed notion of killing me to keep me with him." She shuddered. "Maybe he was going to keep my body in a freezer or something."

"God, Maxine, don't be so morbid." After a moment, sirens pierced the air from a distance. "The only thing that bugs me is, where is the gun he took from Floyd?"

She glanced down at Armand's figure. "Maybe it was his backup plan."

Sam sat on the couch while Maxine made a fresh pot of coffee. The aroma tweaked his stomach, and he remembered the great meal she was going to make that night. Another thing he'd screwed up.

After the police had put an unconscious Armand in the squad car and questioned Sam and Maxine, Armand had woken in a fit. Writhing and foaming at the mouth, he'd accused Sam of brainwashing Maxine into hating him. Sam had ushered Maxine upstairs at the start of the debacle, then returned to help the two officers subdue Armand.

As it turned out, that wasn't necessary. They'd said that as soon as Maxine had left his sight, he'd sunk into a cat-atonic state. They hadn't been able to get a confession about his owning a gun or whacking Floyd, not even a nod when they'd read him his rights. Later, Dave had told Sam that they were going to try to match DNA evidence found at Floyd's apartment to Armand. Even Sally and James had requested that Armand be evaluated by a psychiatrist.

Sam pushed all thoughts of that business away and sunk into the mellow, soul-easing music of Pink Floyd. Only two ornamental lamps were on, casting slanted slices of light over the carpet and coffee table. Maxine walked around the couch and handed him a cup. Her fingers lingered on his for a second before she turned and walked into the bath-room. When she emerged, she carried some supplies that looked suspiciously medical.

"What are those for?"

"You." She sat down on the couch and gestured. "Turn around." Her hands touched his side as he turned. "Now lean back. There, that's good."

It was very good, actually. She was kneeling sideways on

the couch, and he'd slid between her legs. They tightened around him, securing him there.

Her fingers glided through his hair, making the persistent throb dim. The sweet scent of her, the heat of her body and the feel of her surrounded him. He closed his eyes, blanking his mind of everything but those physical sensations. And then she swabbed on something that brought him swiftly back to reality. And to a whole new pain.

"Ouch! What is that?"

"Hydrogen peroxide. Hold still."

She was gentle. He wished she'd bang him around a little. God knew he deserved it. Getting hit by the garbanzo bean, however, was a different story.

"Is it bad?" he asked. "I'm imagining a huge red lump roughly the size of a football. Field."

She laughed softly, and the sound swirled through him and dulled the pain again. For a moment he believed that all the world's pain, unhappiness, and injustice could be solved with that sweet laugh.

"It's not as bad as mine was." She touched the small bandage still hidden beneath her curls. "You'll live."

"Right now that's not a comforting thought," he said in a low voice. Romeo settled his floppy chin on Sam's leg, giving him a woeful look. "It's all right, buddy," he said, rubbing his head. "I know you did the best you could. You're not exactly a pit bull, are you?"

Romeo whined softly, but kept his head there. Somehow dogs knew when their masters were hurting. Sam wondered which pain he was responding to, the one on the outside or the one inside.

"Sam, you shouldn't say that," Maxine said in a firm voice.

"What? He isn't a pit bull. Look at him."

"I mean about living not a comforting thought."

"I know. It just came out." He let out a sigh, wishing he could expel all that ugliness right out of him.

Maxine pulled at him until he leaned back against her.

She slipped her hands over his shoulders and rested her cheek against his back. He could feel her heartbeat, the rise and fall of her chest. He'd almost lost her. The thought made his head pound even harder.

"Why are you being so nice to me?" he asked.

"Because I—because you saved my life."

"I didn't save your life. Stop trying to make me out as some kind of hero."

Her hands tightened on his chest. "Yes, you did save my life."

He closed his eyes, feeling as though some great weight was pushing him into the couch cushion. "Been a helluva night," he murmured.

"You got that right."

For a moment he thought he was going to fall asleep. His thoughts drifted on the edge of the music, carrying him with them. And then he saw Jennie's face. He felt himself stiffen slightly and relaxed his muscles again. His heart still hadn't gotten over the shock. Jennie, his friend. Jennie, his partner at work. His heart had been holding back on him all that time. But why did making love with Maxine trip the realization? He would never forgive himself for that lousy timing any more than he'd forgive himself for not saving Jennie.

So why was Maxine still here? It looked like Armand would be treated for his mental ailments, and possibly connected to Floyd's murder. Maybe they would get him on attempted murder, though Sam knew it would be a hard one to prove. If she was safe now, she could go home. But she had no home to go to. That didn't answer why she was holding him, treating him as if he were some hero. He was nobody's hero. Especially not Maxine's.

He'd honestly thought her ego wouldn't withstand his confession. Maybe he even hoped she would get mad and leave. Some small part of him, though, was glad she stayed tonight. Because, despite his best efforts, Maxine had become something she had never been before—a friend. The sex, and Jennie, got in the way. Strangely enough, something in Maxine reminded him of Jennie. It was eerie, and it was messing with his head big-time.

She sighed, and the soft sound went right to his gut. "I suppose I should find a place to live tomorrow. Maybe I'll call Gabrielle and ask if I can room with her for a while. I've got a life to figure out what to do with."

He couldn't wait to get her out of his life so he could figure out where his head was. Yet he found himself saying, "I could use some help in the office for the next week or so." He wanted to think it was pity because she had nowhere else to go, no other job. Yeah, that's what he wanted to think.

Her fingers had tightened at his words. "I'd like that, Sam."

He waited for her to ask what the offer meant, but she didn't. Maybe she was only accepting out of pity for him. That thought irked him, but he wasn't in the mood to explore or validate it.

Still, he found himself wanting to know what her plans were for the future. And afraid to ask lest she think he was interested personally. Oh, geez, *was* he interested personally? No, not with Maxine. The timing was bad, the chemistry was bad—no, that was still good. Better, actually. Okay, the timing. Besides, she was bound to remember how much she loved shopping, loved having money and prestige and all that other stuff he couldn't give her. She'd get over this strange infatuation, and his life would be . . . well, it would still suck.

Sam felt like a zombie when he woke the next morning. He was almost used to sleeping on the couch, but he distinctly remembered having Maxine as a pillow. He reached behind him and felt something that was not Maxine. Sitting up, he gained his bearings and tracked down the sound he heard. He ran his fingers through his hair, grimacing at the painful knot. Not quite the size of a football field, but pretty darned close.

Walking to the bedroom opening, he found Maxine placing her clothing in her suitcase. She moved slowly, pausing to look at every item before folding it and putting it away. His blood ran bittersweet as he watched her. They couldn't live together anymore, so he should be happy she was leaving. On some level, he was not. What he needed was a vacation, a long one very far away by himself. Just the thought renewed him, though it didn't lift the melancholy haze hovering over him. He already knew he couldn't leave for long, not with the Armand thing still up in the air. But he could go away for a little while.

She opened the bottom drawer and lifted a handful of those delicate panties. The note slipped out and fluttered to the floor. He watched her kneel down and pick it up, looking over the strange words with a wry smile.

"I forgot about the handle," she said softly, tucking the note in her suitcase and closing it. That's when she jerked upward and let out a yelp. "Sam! Good grief, how long have you been standing there?"

Those words reminded him of when she'd said them before, when she'd been dancing. "Not long."

"Do you always sneak around watching people?"

He shrugged. "It's my job."

Her shoulders relaxed for a moment, then she tugged the suitcase off the bed.

"I'll get it," he said, walking it to the door. After he set it down, he turned to find her watching him. He knew why she was anxious to leave. Hopefully she'd changed her mind about wanting a second chance with him. In any case, his admission had probably done her libido in.

When she opened the fridge to get her French vanilla creamer for her coffee, she pulled out the package of shrimp. It seemed strange that something like that could cause a knot in his stomach. That one was definitely the size of a football field.

"Take it with you," he said. "I won't eat it."

Something darkened her green eyes. "Gabby always liked

when I cooked. Maybe I'll bribe her with shrimp scampi for a place to stay.''

''When did you cook? Was it only the time you weren't with me? It seems that before and afterward you were Wolf-gang Puck's sister or something.''

She did that thing with her lower lip. ''I go through phases.''

He leaned against the countertop, facing her across it. ''Is that what I am, Maxine? A phase?''

''No.'' Anger flickered through her eyes. ''And just be-cause I'm moving out doesn't mean I'm giving up on you. I think we both need some time to figure some things out.'' She glanced behind him, and he guessed it was at Jennie's picture. ''I wasn't counting on fighting a ghost, Sam. Es-pecially not Jennie's ghost.''

He nodded, not sure how he felt at her statement about not giving up. ''It's not going to work out between us.''

Her eyes narrowed. ''How can you say that after every-thing that's happened?''

''I can say it *because* of everything that's happened. It always worked against us.''

''What did?''

''Fate. Chemistry. Karma.'' He waved his hand. ''What-ever you call it.''

She leaned across the counter until she was only a few inches from him. Something about her smelled light and sweet, making him lick his lips before he could think better of it.

''Sam, you don't believe in fate and karma. You can't see it, you can't follow it or investigate it. Therefore, it doesn't exist.''

He felt his mustache involuntarily twitch. ''As I recall, those were the words you used when you asked for a di-vorce. Fate wasn't in our corner; our chemistry went bad; our karma wasn't right.''

She leaned even closer, and he fought the urge to lick his

lips again. She was so close, he'd probably lick her lips in the process.

"I don't believe in fate. I happen to know there's a higher force, and that force says we are meant to be together. You don't know what I went through to get another chance with you."

"You got hit on the head. Nearly run over. And almost got kidnapped. What did it all accomplish, really? It made me realize I was in love with someone else."

"She's dead, Sam."

"I know. I was there, remember?" His tone had gotten harsh on those last words, and he reined in his anger.

She opened her mouth, then closed it without saying anything. Her eyes never left his. "I have to go," she said finally.

"Let me take your suitcase to your car."

"No, I can manage."

He walked over and picked it up anyway, then followed her down to her car. She took a quick breath, expelling it in a puff of fog. The cold had pinkened her nose, and the wind blew her curls over her cheek. When she looked at him, her bare vulnerability stabbed him right in the gut.

"Do you still want me to work with you?" she asked.

"Yeah, I still want you to work with me." He looked away, then back at her. "Why don't you come in tomorrow? You'll need today to get settled." He pulled the office key off his ring. "Here's the key. I have an extra at home. The alarm code is—"

"Your birth date backward with a zero on either end," she said.

He narrowed his eyes at her. "How'd you know that?"

"A lucky guess."

"You know, Maxine, you have a lot of lucky guesses."

She gave him a sad smile. "Yeah, but not a lot of luck."

"Maxine, don't tell anyone where you're staying. Especially anyone in the Santini household."

"Okay, Sam. I'll see you tomorrow."

He nodded, then closed the door after she'd gotten inside. Her brake lights flashed in the distance before she turned the corner and disappeared. He had to push himself to go back inside. Even though Romeo greeted him with a low woof and wagging tail, it felt empty in his apartment. The coffee cup she'd used was still sitting on the counter, still half-filled with coffee. He inhaled the scent of vanilla, closing his eyes for a moment.

He could still smell Maxine herself, that light, sweet scent filling his head. The back of his head started throbbing again, a dull, pulsing ache. He walked to the window and pressed his forehead to the glass, looking out over the rooftops and the gray skies beyond. He wondered if the fates he didn't believe in were trying to drive him nuts. It was going to be a short trip at this rate.

Maxine took deep breaths as she pulled up to her old apartment building. Gabby usually slept in late, but Maxine would make it up to her if she woke her too early.

Sometimes when she wasn't expecting it, her future would stretch out before her like a great void. That vision filled her with a fear and loneliness that ran a spike of ice through her. Along with that image came the bleakness in Sam's eyes. The only thing that kept her from drowning was something else in his eyes when he'd watched her pack. She had herself almost fooled that he hadn't wanted her to leave. He was probably rejoicing now.

Maxine preached patience to herself as she kept knocking. *Remember how long everything took back then?* Finally Gabby came to the door, her face flushed with sleep.

"Jennie—" She glanced backward for a second. "Maxine, what's wrong?"

"Can I come in?"

That second's hesitation worried her, but Gabby rolled backward. "Sure."

Maxine found a seat at the kitchen table, curling and uncurling her fingers. Gabby glanced back toward the rooms again.

"Do you have someone here?" she asked, not sure whether to be happy or not.

Gabby's flush turned into a blush. "Yes. He's asleep right now."

For just one little moment, Maxine could forget her problems and smile. "Who?"

"Rick."

"Gabby!" she said in a whisper, hugging her friend. "It's about time."

Gabby didn't hide the smile. Wow, she was beautiful when she smiled like that, Maxine thought.

"I know. I'm sorry I waited so long."

Maxine knew that feeling. "Well, what finally turned on the light bulb for you? The pep talks he'd give you? Harassing you about your foul attitude? A promise to lower your rent?"

Gabby laughed, but that softness returned to her face. "Part of it was his attitude. I tried very hard to stay bitter and angry about my life and . . . well, him." Maxine knew she meant her ex-boyfriend. "Part of it was the pep talks you gave me, telling me how much he liked me, how good he'd be for me. But what really hit the switch was the virtual-reality thing he was telling me about last time you were here. His friend wrote a program just for Rick, and he scanned both our faces in. When we put the VR helmets on, I saw him standing there. I looked down and saw my legs again. And then he asked me to dance. Dancing with him was incredible."

Maxine's throat tightened at the mention of dancing, but her smile won over. "I'm so happy for you, I really am."

"Mostly what made me fall in love with him was that he didn't give up. You didn't give up on me, either, but you're not my type."

"Well, I'm glad of that." Maxine felt a new resolve. "No giving up."

Gabby's smile disappeared. "I take it by your expression that things aren't going as well on your end? I expected you to be glowing, too."

"I had my moment," she said quickly. She flattened her hands on the table, leaning closer to Gabby. "I hate to even talk about my problems when you're so happy."

"I'll be happier if you're happy. I know, you think I'm too selfish for that, but I owe you. Even if you do have legs that work again, for which I heap tons of jealousy on you." Gabby smiled the smile of a friend, reminding Maxine just how precious those were in a person's life. "Talk to me."

Maxine let out a long breath, watching her fingers tap on the table's surface. "You're not going to believe this."

"What?"

Another breath. "Sam was in love with Jennie. *Is* in love with her."

"No," she said, drawing the word out. "With Jennie?"

"Oh, yes. That plain, boring girl in a wheelchair who thought Sam would never see anything beautiful in her. I should have seen the warning signs. He told me that Jennie was the most beautiful woman he'd ever known."

"You were pretty . . ."

"Maybe I'd give myself pretty." Maxine shrugged her shoulders. "Maybe. But beautiful? Come on. You're beautiful. I wasn't."

"But Sam saw beautiful," Gabby said dreamily. "So did he just tell you how he felt about Jennie out of the blue?"

Maxine laughed, a strangled sound filled with anguish. "Not quite as simple as that. We had to make love before it finally came out. Oh, Gabby, it was the most exquisite thing I have ever felt. Physically and emotionally. I didn't remember everything you told me, but I didn't have to. It was . . . karma. It just happened, and it was so beautiful." The glow drifted from her expression. "And afterward he told me he saw Jennie when we made love."

Gabby put her hand over her mouth. "Oh-h-h . . ."

"He never knew he felt that way about her—me. But I

somehow reminded him of her when we made love, and now he feels guilty and probably a little messed up. As a matter of fact, I feel the same way."

"But it's easy."

"I can't tell him I'm Jennie. In fact, I tried to bring it up, and he rejected the idea immediately. I can't do that."

"I wasn't going to say that. I was going to say, just be Jennie. In every way you know how. Give him Jennie back."

Maxine pressed her hand to her forehead, feeling the edge of the bandage. "That's the problem, Gabby. I can't be Jennie anymore."

"Well, that's silly. I mean, technically you still are Jennie."

Maxine shook her head. "I was paralyzed at the time in my life when my individuality and self-image were forming. Everything Jennie was, was in that wheelchair, that lifestyle. Unlike you, I never knew who I really was without being Jennie-the-paraplegic. And now I'm not paralyzed, not even in the same body. I don't know who I am anymore. Some of Jennie is in me, and some of Maxine, too, I think. I like who I am now. But I'm not Jennie."

Gabby looked at her for a moment. "I don't know what to even tell you. I know what you mean about identity being wrapped up in who you are. But Sam is in love with the person you were inside. Surely there's enough of that in you to make him fall in love with you as Maxine."

"That must be what Sam sees, what reminds him of Jennie. But it's not drawing him to me, believe me. He's running fast in the opposite direction. You should have seen the pain in his eyes, Gabby. I wanted to take it away so badly, but I couldn't. I can't give him Jennie. And you know what's really weird? I'm jealous of Jennie now." She laughed, shaking her head. "I look at that picture he got from you and I want to throw it away. It's crazy! I'm competing with myself. Or with my ghost. I told him I wasn't counting on competing with a ghost."

"What did he say?"

"He said we weren't going to make it." Her throat tightened, and she squeezed her eyes shut against the tears she'd been fighting all morning. "I can't bear that thought."

"Maybe you didn't come back for him, Jen—Maxine. It could have been for some other reason."

Maxine shook her head. "No, it was for Sam. I know it was for Sam." She rubbed her nose. "I moved out of his apartment this morning."

"Why? I thought someone was after you."

"It was Armand, and he's in custody. He wacked out and tried to kidnap me." Maxine smiled wryly. "For my own good."

"What?"

"He thought Sam had brainwashed me and that's why I didn't love him anymore." At Gabby's horrified expression, she added, "It wasn't that big a deal. I mean, it was scary, but Sam was right there." She shook her head, not wanting to get into all the details. "Anyway, I don't have a reason to stay with him now, and he didn't ask. But he did ask me to work for him for a couple of weeks."

"That's a start."

"I think he just felt bad. And now I'm afraid he's still going to close up his agency, and all because of Jennie. All those years I thought I was so powerless, so unimportant. I had it all, and I never even knew it."

"You've gone through a lot in the past few days, haven't you?" she said softly.

"You don't know the half of it."

"Do you have a place to stay?" When Maxine woefully shook her head, Gabby said, "Your old room is still available if you'd like. It'd be kind of like old times."

Maxine smiled. "I brought shrimp for dinner."

"I've missed your cooking almost as much as I've missed you."

"Uh-oh, girl talk," a rusty voice said as Rick rolled into

the kitchen. His grin was one hundred watts. "Maxine, right?"

"Right." Maxine couldn't help returning his smile. He was proof that persistence paid off. "Good to see you again."

He had the decency to look a little sheepish. "Even if I look a little rough first thing in the morning?"

"Yeah, even then. It's good to know my friend is being well cared for."

Gabby blushed, then wheeled to the coffeemaker. "I can take care of myself, Maxine. I have been for a while now."

Maxine leaned her hip against the counter. "Yeah, but sometimes it's nice to let someone else pretend they're doing it. Remember, taking a chance is good for the soul."

It was a sweet melancholy that wrapped around Maxine as she took the steps up to the office the next morning. She twisted the gold band on her right hand, a habit she'd fallen into in the last day or so. That ring felt so right, even if it was on the wrong hand. Someday she wanted a new ring, and she wanted Sam to slide it on her finger. In her dreams, she had envisioned herself rolling down the aisle with her dress wadded up in her lap. Now she could dream of taking those monumental steps most brides got to take.

She pushed open the door and was engulfed by sweet familiarity. Sam's voice in the background, the aroma of coffee brewing, and Romeo tilting his head to see who was coming through the door. His tail wagged as she knelt down to rub her cheek against his head. Although she wasn't ready to see Sam yet, Romeo was almost as bad—he was part of Sam's life. She was on the outer fringes. *Gawd, now I'm even jealous of the dog!*

She pointed her finger at Romeo and made a soft exploding sound. Romeo instantly dropped down and "died" for her. She bit her lip, holding back the smile at winning over at least one member of Sam's little family.

"I just can't imagine that dog liking you so much,"

Sam's voice said from too near for him to be on the phone.
He was leaning against the door frame watching her.

From her kneeling position, she glanced up at him with
a sheepish look. "Am I that hard to like, Sam?" she asked
as she stood.

He ran his fingers down the hairs of his mustache. "Nah.
But you're awfully hard to tease. You take everything so
personally."

"I think you know why."

They stood there for a moment, looking at each other and
not knowing what else to say. She had plenty to say to him,
but right then wasn't the time to say it. All she knew was
that she had to stay in his life, one way or another. She had
to believe that Sam would eventually get over Jennie's loss.
And when he did, Maxine wanted to be close by.

Romeo was the one to break up the taut silence with a
flappy-lipped sigh, a subtle reminder that he was still
"dead" and waiting to be revived.

"Good boy!" she said in the same tone Sam had used.
It worked, because Romeo lurched upward and shook himself, sending his ears out straight. Maxine walked over to
her desk and opened the drawer that held the box of dog
treats. When she tossed one to Romeo, Sam was staring at
her in a strange way.

"How did you know there were treats in there?" he
asked, then raised his hand. "I know, a lucky guess, right?"

"I, uh, saw them when I was here before." She threw
another one at Romeo and put the box away. When she
turned back, Sam was still staring at her. "What?"

He shook his head. "I don't know." After a moment, he
glanced out the window. "You know, I almost envy Armand."

"You do?"

"Yeah. It must be nice to get it over with when you're
living on the edge of insanity."

"Oh, Sam. You'll be fine." She lowered her voice.
"You'll be better if you let me help."

"You're the reason I feel this way." He looked back at her. "Jennie's death was hard enough. Then you suddenly show up at my office and act completely different than what I remember, asking for a second chance, and . . ." He just stared at her. "I don't know." He walked over and handed her a tiny transcription tape. "There's a final report and bill on there. I know I said I'd need your help for a week or so, but everything is wrapped up for now and I need some time off. After today, I'm closed. For a while," he added at her panicked look. "And I'll pay you for two weeks."

"I'm not worried about the money. What about the business? That job you were going to take?"

"I haven't figured anything out yet. Maybe a couple of weeks away from all this will put it in perspective. Jennie was always nagging me to take a vacation. Now I am."

Jennie, Jennie, Jennie. She was sick of herself, if that was possible. But his words were making her stomach twist. "Want some company?" she pushed out. "I mean, I don't have anywhere to go, anything to do."

His half-smile didn't encourage her. "Seems to me you need to spend some time alone, too, finding out what you really want in life."

"I already know what I want, Sam."

He dismissed her with a shake of his head. "You're one of the most confused women I know. I'm not what you want." He winked at her. "Give yourself some time and you'll see what I mean. I've got one more report to wrap up and then we can both be outta here."

He headed back to his office, then paused and turned around. "By the way, Armand has been transferred to a psychiatric ward. He's still pretty out of reality. My friend Dave's got strict orders to let us know if he's released." Then he went into his office and turned up a Candy Dulfer compact disk.

An uncomfortable feeling slithered through her, though she couldn't pinpoint what it was. They—whoever *they* were—said letting go was the only way to keep someone you loved. Maybe Sam just needed some time to work through all this. She poured herself a cup of coffee and dropped down into her chair. What was she going to do with herself while he did that? Go crazy, that's what.

A while later when Sam brought the last tape to her, she said, "I've been thinking about what I want to do with my life now, you know, workwise and all."

"What's that?"

"I want to be your partner."

He lifted his eyebrows, a trace of amusement on his features. Well, that was worth getting up the nerve to say it just in itself.

"You want to be my partner? In what, exactly?"

"For starters . . ." She paused for innuendo, then finished, "In this business. We could be like Bruce and Cybil in *Moonlighting*. Just going with you that one day was so much fun. I could feel the excitement you felt. I can become just as jaded as you in no time at all. We could tail people better, working in tandem. And if you had to go to the bathroom, you wouldn't have to use a jar." Sam didn't seem convinced. "All I'm asking is that you think about it. I could still do this part of it"—she gestured toward the desk—"at least until we get successful enough to hire someone for both of us." The excitement was growing inside her at the thought of being Sam's partner.

"Maxine, you can't be a detective because you up and decide to be one," he said. She felt her hopes rise even more. He hadn't shot it down right away. "You'd have to get your license."

She nodded toward the certificate on the wall. "I know that. No problem. I know a lot from you already. When we were married, and from recently," she added at his skeptical look. "Just think about it, that's all I ask. I have some money in my savings, enough to maybe buy some of the things we need here in the office."

"All right, I'll think about it. But that's all I'm promising."

"That's all I'm asking."

*   *   *

An hour later, Sam rinsed out the coffeepot, and she made sure everything was in order before turning out the lights. He closed the door with a click that sounded too permanent to her.

Sam still wouldn't take the stairs, so she followed him down the hall to the elevator. Inside, she wanted to slam on the stop button and hold him captive. But what could she do to knock some sense into him? Patience, she told herself as the doors slid open. He held back so she could walk out first. Outside in the chilly air, he turned to her.

"Thanks for coming in today. I appreciate the help."

"Wish I could have helped more," she said honestly.

He only nodded. "Well, take care of yourself."

So many thoughts crowded into her mind: *Hold him! Tell him you're Jennie! Tell him you love him! Don't let him walk away!* She pushed them away, byproducts of panic all of them. Panic wasn't going to win Sam's heart. Persistence was.

"You, too, Sam. I mean that. Call me in a couple of weeks, okay? Just to let me know how you're doing?"

He slipped his hands in his pockets and nodded.

She knew Sam was as good as his word, or his nod as the case was. "Okay." Quickly, before she thought better of it, she leaned forward and hugged him.

He slipped his arms around her and held her briefly before letting go. Without another word, he walked toward his car. Her body was tense with the thoughts still bombarding her, but she forced herself to walk to her car. But why did she have this gnawing feeling something wasn't right?

Chapter 13

Gabby and Rick were out doing that virtual-reality dancing thing. They'd invited Maxine, but she didn't feel up to pretending to have fun or even managing a smile. She was as miserable as she'd predicted she'd be that morning. What was Sam doing right now? Was he thinking about her? Or worse, was he packing his bags and heading off for a vacation in the Bahamas? Sometimes she teased herself with the thought that he was heading over to her right now.

That's why her heart leaped up into her throat when the phone rang. Chances were slim that it was for her, being that no one but Sam knew she was living with Gabby, but Maxine still jumped out of her chair and grabbed the phone by the second ring.

"Hello?"

"Hi, Maxine."

"Sam." Her heart did a funny dance, and her voice came out all breathy. She chewed her lower lip, afraid to let herself smile.

"I just got a call from Sally. She wanted to talk to you, but I told her you weren't in. She sounded pretty . . . I don't know, tense. You should probably give her a call."

Disappointment weighed her down. "Yeah, I suppose I should. Is that . . . all you wanted, Sam?"

"How are you doing?"

"Do you want me to tell you I'm doing fine and dandy, or do you want to know how I'm really doing?"

Sam paused. "Maxine . . ."

"I'm sorry, Sam. I'm just . . . in a mood right now. Okay, I'll call Sally. Thanks for calling."

"No problem. Listen, call me back when you're done talking to her. Just to let me know what's going on."

She smiled. He did care. "All right, Sam. I will."

Sally answered the phone on the first ring, her "Hello" terse and anxious.

"Sally, it's Maxine. What's up?"

"They've got Daddy under some evaluation now, trying to figure out if he's insane or just devious."

"What do you think he is?" Maxine couldn't help asking.

"I don't think he was going to hurt you. He just . . . loved you too much."

"Then why was he trying to kill me?"

Sally paused. "The reason I called was because some investigators are here right now, asking about Daddy: the way he was acting before the attack, that kind of thing. They'd like you to come out and talk with them, too."

"They want me to come out to your house?"

"Well, they said they could go to where you are." Sally's voice went a little funny then. "But I'd really like to talk to you. I . . . I just don't have anyone to talk to about this, and you're . . . well, you were there."

"What about James? You and he seem very close."

"He's so busy trying to keep Daddy's businesses afloat. He's in the city now, working late again. Besides, I need a woman to talk to. Aida's off for the evening, and she doesn't count anyway."

Sally had never been anything but nice to her, Maxine thought with a cringing sensation. She didn't want to leave the house and her comfortable state of moping, but someone needed her more. And James wasn't there. Even if he wasn't the family wacko, he still wasn't on her list of favorite people. Besides, the police were there. What could be safer?

"All right, I'll come out."

"Oh, thank you, Maxine. It means so much to me. I won't keep you long, I promise. And the investigators said they only have a few questions for you, too. Just to tie up some loose ends."

"Okay, I'll leave in a few minutes."

She pressed the off button, then dialed Sam's number.

"Hi, Sam. Some of the investigators are out at Sally's house now, asking her questions. She said they wanted me to come out so they could talk to me, too."

"They wanted you to go there?"

"Yeah, I thought it was strange, too. Sally wants a friend; you know, for moral support. James and Aida aren't there. She probably feels all alone. She wants to talk to me afterward."

"Oh. Well, let me know if anything unusual happens. I'll be here all evening if you need me."

She caught the little sigh before it escaped. "I will." If she could only think of some way to keep him on the line a little longer. "It's probably just a girl-talk thing."

"I wonder what the police are asking her." He seemed to dismiss it. "Be careful, okay?"

She heard real concern in his voice, and closed her eyes to the sound of it. "Thanks, Sam. You, too."

"Me?" he said with a half-laugh. "Yeah, sure."

"Are you going away? Or have you decided yet?"

"I may take a flight down to Key West tomorrow for a few days. I'll let you know when I leave, okay? Bye, Maxine."

She heard the click, then the silence. Still she clutched the phone until the annoying tone started. Walking to her old closet, she pulled out a long red sweater and soft pants with a white and blue flower design on them. This should be cheerful, she thought, though it didn't lift her spirits any once she had them on.

Her thoughts were too wrapped up in Sam to think much about the visit ahead of her. She drove through the darkness once she left the city, trying to remember the route to the strange white mansion. A while later she pulled down the long drive and approached the house. It looked peaceful enough, and she felt less dread than other times she'd driven down this road. There was a car parked outside, but it didn't look like a police car, undercover or otherwise. But it had to be, she thought as she stepped out into the cold air and walked to the front door. She only hoped James hadn't returned early. Maybe she'd suggest going to a cafe to talk, rather than staying at the mansion once the police were done with them.

Sally opened the door, a look of relief across her features. ''I'm so glad you came out, Maxine. You just don't know how glad I am.''

''I don't mind helping out someone who needs a friend,'' Maxine said, stepping inside and looking around for the officers she expected to find. The room was dimly lit; even the puppet niches and displays weren't lit up. ''I know that feeling myself sometimes. But, where is everyone?''

''They left.''

Sally said it so matter-of-factly Maxine almost didn't catch the strangeness of their absence.

''But I thought they wanted to talk to me.''

Sally wore a bulky sweater jacket, and her hands were tucked in the pockets as she sat down on the couch and nodded for Maxine to follow suit. ''They decided they could talk to you in the morning. Don't be mad at me; I still wanted you to come over.''

Maxine sank down on the leather couch she had spent a night on. ''I'm not mad. Just . . . confused, I guess.''

Sally laughed. ''Confused. Boy, I know that feeling.''

''I can imagine this has been tough on you.''

Again Sally laughed in a sputtering way. ''You don't know the half of it.'' She moved closer to Maxine. ''Daddy didn't mean to hurt you or anything.''

Maxine could still see that glaze in his eyes as he tried to get her to leave with him. ''No, I don't suppose he did. He thought he was saving me from Sam.''

"Sometimes people do things they don't want to do. They . . . think they have to do it, you know?"

"I guess. I mean, I suppose Armand thought he had to kidnap me, for my own good."

"Exactly." Sally smiled. "I'm so glad you understand that."

Ah, so this was Sally's way of trying to make amends with her father, by winning Maxine back into the fold. "I do. In the same way that I couldn't stay with your father anymore. I realized I didn't love him the way I needed to."

"Yes, you had to leave, and Daddy had to try to get you back."

"But I still don't understand why he tried to kill me. Can you explain that to me?" Maxine asked, knowing the girl probably couldn't.

"Daddy didn't try to kill you."

"Well, I know he didn't mean to. But what drove him to think killing me would solve anything?"

"Daddy loved you too much to hurt you."

"Well, that's what I thought. Until this last incident that tied it all together." Or did it? That question always nagged at her. Maybe James was behind it after all. But now James wasn't being threatened by her marriage to Armand, so even he shouldn't be a danger anymore.

Sally looked down for a moment at the fingers kneading in the pockets of her sweater. "I'm afraid that was my fault. I got Daddy too riled up about you and Sam."

"I know, but you didn't mean to. Who would have thought he'd react like that?"

Sally met her eyes. "I did." The vulnerability of earlier was gone, replaced by something as dark and cold as the night air outside.

"What?"

"I knew Daddy was in a delicate state, so I goaded him into going berserk. I mean, I wasn't sure exactly what he'd do. But he wasn't acting right since you'd left. He wasn't doing his job, and he wouldn't let James take over. Daddy needed something to push him over that edge so James could save the company.''

An unpleasant chill fingered its way up Maxine's spine, but she tried to maintain a calm exterior. "That wasn't very nice.'' Understatement of the year. "Maybe we were all on the edge before this happened, what with the flower-box incident and everything else.'' She glanced around at the quietness of the house. Several pairs of glass and painted eyes looked back. "Did you say Aida was off tonight?''

"Yes, visiting her sister in Ohio this week, actually. I haven't even called to tell her about all this. I mean, why bother her, right?''

Maxine nodded, hoping she didn't look as stiff as she felt. "Sure, that's the nice thing to do.'' The cushions seemed to swallow her more than they had when she'd first sat down. She pushed herself to her feet, and Sally quickly joined her.

"Where are you going?'' she asked.

"Just standing,'' Maxine said, smoothing down the fabric of her pants. Her palms were sticky. "I thought we'd go to a coffee shop or someplace like that.'' Maxine glanced around again at all the dark corners and shadows that made even the white carpet and furniture look dim. "Don't take it personally, but I'd like to . . . get out of here. This place brings back too many memories.''

"Yes, I thought we'd go somewhere, too. James might be home soon.''

So, Sally understood Maxine's trepidation. Maybe she was reading the girl wrong. Sally moved closer, breaking into Maxine's personal zone. She took a step back, but Sally followed, looking right at her.

"Are you still afraid of James?'' Sally asked.

"Not afraid, exactly. But we're not friends, and seeing him doesn't make for a pleasant experience. So, where shall we go? You know this area better than I do.''

"James is a good man.''

Maxine stepped back again, feeling the glass of one of

the dummy displays press up behind her. "I'm sure he is, deep down inside. I'll bet there's a coffee shop back through that one area with the Italian restaurant . . . Ciao's I think it was."

Sally took another step closer. "Daddy never let James do anything. He never saw how smart James is. Neither did Mommy. James was a slow learner, and they were embarrassed by him. But he caught up to everyone else, just like the teachers said he would. He tried really, really hard. But Mommy and Daddy never did see that. They got it in their heads that he was dumb. It took him a long time to get over that. A long, long time. Sometimes I still think he feels that way, but he won't even admit it to me."

"You're . . . very close to your brother, aren't you?" Maxine managed through a dry throat.

Sally's eyes were distant and wide, her thick dark lashes blinking irregularly. "I love James, more than anyone in this family ever did. I am his family, his only real family. I believed in him, and I helped him get where he is today. It's what we were talking about before, doing what you have to do."

Maxine couldn't help the words that came out. "What exactly did you do for him?"

Sally clutched at Maxine sleeve. "I had to help him. Don't you see? That's all I knew, that I had to help him. Nobody else would have done that for him."

Maxine nodded, but fear clawed up from her stomach to her throat and mouth. Her lips trembled as she tried to form words, to play the game. "I understand. It's okay, really."

Sally had that same relief on her expression that she'd had when Maxine had arrived. "Oh, good. You have to know, it was nothing personal. I liked you, I really did."

Maxine tried to force a smile. "I . . . I appreciate that." *Liked?*

Sally's face became troubled again. "But James was so upset. He'd been trying to convince Daddy for months that he was capable of becoming President of Santini Enterprises. He deserves that position. And then Daddy started talking about you.'' She laughed. ''That's all he ever talked about. He ignored James's requests, and then one day he told James he was going to hire you for the position.''

''Me?''

''He said he was going to make you a partner. That everything he had, he was going to share with you. James was, of course, very upset. I hate to see him cry. Do you know how terrible it is for a man to cry out loud? I'm talking about that heartrending sobbing children do. Men don't do that unless they're really, really upset. That's when I knew I had to do something. I'd do anything for James. Anything.''

''So you dropped the flower box on me,'' Maxine said in a deadpan voice.

Sally didn't look remorseful in the least when she nodded agreement. ''Yes. I didn't think it would hurt too awfully much. Kabooey, and it would be over. But you went and lived. You're smarter than I thought, too, finding the drops of cola I missed. Good thing I saw you in my bedroom window. But then my plan really backfired. The accident made Daddy want to move everything up because you were acting so weird. That made James even more upset, more angry.''

Maxine felt chilled through, as if she'd been standing in a rainstorm in December. This was it. She'd been stupid enough not to look further than the obvious, and now she was facing a murderer. Maxine-the-first's murderer. But she still had hope.

''Sally, I can . . . understand why you did what you did. You must love James very much, and I understand loving someone enough to do what you have to do to make them happy. But I'm not in the picture anymore. I'm not marrying Armand. You've even succeeded in having him put away, at least for a while. Now James can prove he's capable of running the company. See, everything's worked out just fine.'' She cleared her throat as her voice had gone higher.

"We can leave this as it is, no harm done." At least until she could get out of here.

Sally was, unfortunately, shaking her head and making a tsking sound. "But it's not all right. You and your PI kept snooping around. Finding the guy I hired to run you down for instance. He was a chicken anyway, and that made me afraid of him going to the cops. Especially when I found out he'd said something to Sam about being hired. So I told him I wanted to finish the job myself, but since he'd wasted my time, he owed me a gun."

She pulled out the gun. "This one. And then I offed him. See, another one of those things I had to do. Don't think for even a minute that I enjoy this. Uh-uh." The gun wavered as she shook her head. "Our lawyer said something about using DNA testing to prove Daddy didn't kill Floyd. Technology sure does make it hard to get things done, doesn't it? Once Daddy's cleared, they'll be snooping in my backyard again. The police and your buddy. Sorry, Maxine, but I've got to get rid of you."

Maxine tried to swallow, but a large lump in her throat prohibited it. "Does James know about this?"

"No. And he's not going to, either. I take care of him, kind of like a guardian angel. If someone makes him unhappy, I get rid of them. Simple."

"Like your mother?" Maxine still found this whole thing unreal, though the fear pulsing through her felt real enough. And that gun looked real enough.

"Mommy was the worst of them, putting James down and ignoring him like he was some dog. Less than a dog. If you could have seen how her digs affected James, you'd have done anything to take away the pain, too."

"Maybe," she said, hoping to gain a bit of trust from Sally. She remembered in the movies how people in these situations would say, "Let me get you some help." That never seemed to work. "Let's go have a cup of coffee and talk about it."

The sound of the front door opening shot relief through

Maxine. Until she saw James walk in and look around the dim room.

"Don't say one word," Sally muttered, pushing the gun into Maxine's back. "I'll kill you before you can say the second word. Don't forget, I've had practice." Her face lightened in a smile that bore no resemblance to the sinister expression Sally had had on her face earlier. "Hi, James!"

He rubbed his neck, taking in both women standing close together. "What are you doing here?" he asked Maxine.

"Oh, Sally invited me over for coffee," Maxine answered, her voice unnaturally high. Not that James would care enough to notice.

"Did you have a good day?" Sally asked with a hopeful expression. She pressed the gun a little harder against her back.

"No. When I wanted this job, I thought Dad would be training me. Being thrown in like this sucks. Besides all the questions I have to answer about why he went crazy." He leveled a glare at Maxine, while she gave him an imploring look. He ignored it, shifting his gaze back to Sally. "How was your day?"

"All right. You know, same old, same old."

"The *police* were here," Maxine said, giving him a lifted eyebrow at the emphasized word.

James glanced back at Sally. "They were?"

Sally looked rather bored. "Yeah, but it was nothing. Just some routine questions about Daddy's behavior."

James nodded. "You'd better go get your coffee. Maxine seems to be having some kind of caffeine fit."

Sally shoved the gun harder against Maxine's spine, eliciting an *oof* from her. She tried to lamely cover it with a cough.

"Yes, we're going to some new coffee shop down the street. Maxine says it's great. I'll see you later?"

"Sure."

"James, you can do anything. Remember that." Sally's voice was filled with love. Perhaps she had taken on a motherly role, because their relationship didn't seem sexual.

"Would you like to come with us, James?" Maxine asked as they moved to the door.

He narrowed his eyes at her expression of fear. Just as Maxine thought he suspected something was a little strange, he said, "No, thanks. I'm going to sleep. I'm beat. Have fun, girls."

And he walked up those stairs and disappeared, making Maxine whimper. He really didn't know about Sally's machinations. Sally shoved her toward the door with the gun.

"Nice try. Don't you dare drag him into this. He's been through enough."

"It doesn't have to be this way, Sally. We can forget this whole thing right now. I won't say a word to anyone about it." Maxine remembered that saying being ineffectual in the movies, too.

"What's done is done." Sally urged her to Maxine's own car, and Maxine took the wheel as Sally slid in next to her, gun at the ready. "Suddenly I'm not in the mood for a coffee shop. Too bright, too crowded, don't you think? I have somewhere else in mind. Somewhere a little quieter."

"Sally, if . . . something happens to me, James will be a witness that you were the last one to see me . . . alive." She swallowed hard.

"I know. I was hoping we could get out of there before he got home. I'll figure something else out." She took a quick breath, as if it were only a small bother. "Besides, James won't say anything. We stick together. I'll just tell him we nixed the coffee idea and you went home. I'll ask him not to mention you were even out here because I don't want the police to be suspicious. He'll believe I'm innocent."

"But Sam knows I was here," Maxine said triumphantly, watching Sally's confidence crumble.

"You told him?"

"Yes." The only problem with that was he wouldn't be

missing her anytime soon. Especially if he flew to Florida in the morning. Unless Gabrielle thought to call him when she noted Maxine's absence. But she might think Maxine had stayed with Sam. It could be days before anyone knew she was really gone. Fear pulsed through her again, infringing on her vision as she drove down the driveway.

"Then I'll have to take care of him, too. I was afraid he might do some more snooping anyway."

Maxine's fingers clamped around the wheel. "No. No, you can't do anything to Sam. He doesn't know where I went. I swear, I was just bluffing you."

Sally ran the side of the gun's barrel over her lips in thought. "I don't believe you. I think you were telling the truth the first time. Think of it this way: you and your honey will be together in Heaven. What a lovely thought, very romantic. Keep driving," she ordered when Maxine had come to a stop in her fright. "Take a right up there, then a left."

They left the faint security of the fancy, lit homes and drove for miles into a different neighborhood that became more sparsely populated toward the back.

"Where are we going?" Maxine hesitantly asked.

Sally smiled. "Right here."

A large house sat back from the road a distance. There were no other houses around it, only a thicket of trees. The windows were dark eyes of shattered glass staring out of a charred exterior. The smell of smoke filtered into the car through the air vents.

"I followed an ambulance here one time, just to see where it went. Two people died in the fire. Flames were shooting out of every window, and a crowd of people stood around and watched with morbid fascination. Someday when they find you, they'll probably do the same thing. They'll string up that yellow tape, and reporters will flock around to get a glimpse of your decomposed body. Get out of the car."

Maxine surveyed the surrounding area and wondered how

far she'd get before getting mowed down by bullets if she made a run for it. No, she still had a chance to overpower the woman later without risking a wild bullet. Their breath was suspended in the cold night air, puffs of fog that indicated life.

"Do you have a flashlight?" Sally asked.

"No."

"Oh, come on, don't be so uncooperative. Let's look in your trunk."

Maxine popped open the trunk, not sure if she did have a flashlight in there or not.

"Oh, no you don't," Sally said as Maxine started to feel around for something that might work as a weapon. "I'll get it." Sally held the gun at her and pulled out a thin flashlight.

Maxine was prodded by the gun over flagstones to the stench and horror of the burned-out house. She glanced around to see if anyone was in sight, but the darkness swallowed up everything. They walked through the door, and Sally played the flashlight over the wiry skeleton of a couch and the black walls. The floor was soft and mushy beneath her feet. Maxine's heart was a dull thud inside her, pressing an aching pain throughout her body with each beat.

"I know exactly what I'm going to do," Sally was saying as though they were old friends discussing a mutual problem. "Since someone's been after you anyway, I'll just say that as we were going to a coffee shop, someone crawled out of the back seat of your car and hijacked us. He drove out here and threw me out of the car. He wanted you," she said in a sinister voice. "I was only a nuisance, trying to save our lives from the masked villain. I could even say it was Sam. Hmm, that's an interesting twist. I'll work that out later." She coughed as the ashes rose up in a vile dust that choked their throats. "Nasty place to die."

"I know, I know. You hate doing this, right?"

"Of course. But everything's going to work out just fine once you're gone. You'll probably be happier up there anyway. The world's a terrible place to live anymore.''

Maxine stepped over some unidentifiable objects, sure they'd probably taken out the bodies by then. She could almost feel the heat of the fire as the smell of smoke insinuated itself inside her. Her legs were wobbly, and she almost lost her balance. She grabbed the side of a wall, then pulled her hand back at the gritty feel of soot.

"There it is, just as I remembered. I came back here later, when the yellow tape was gone. Okay, I admit it; I'm one of those morbidly curious people. I never thought in a million years it would come in this handy.''

Maxine's bleary gaze took in the refrigerator, its doors hanging open to a yellowed interior. Her throat closed up as her eyes widened. "No, I won't go in there," she said on a raspy breath.

"Oh, yes you will," Sally answered, sticking the gun against her spine again. "Either you go in willingly or I shoot you someplace that will disable you and then put you in to die a slow, painful death.''

Some choice. Maxine looked at the coffin, trying not to breathe in the acrid smell of melted plastic. No one would find her in there, not in time. And who would be looking, anyway? Her breathing was already growing heavy at the thought of sucking her last breath in only to find there were no more.

"Take the racks out," Sally ordered. "Come on, I want to get out of here. This place gives me the creeps.''

Maxine walked slowly forward and grabbed onto the rack in the middle. With one hand, she pulled, and with the other, she pushed. She made the appropriate sounds, but the rack didn't budge.

"What's the problem?" Sally said, irritation lacing her voice. "What are you, a weakling?''

"I'm too terrified to be strong," Maxine said, watching from her side vision as Sally walked closer. She had one chance to make a grab for the gun. Once Sally realized what was happening, it would be easy for her to pull the trigger. One chance.

Sally set the flashlight down. "It's probably melted on there," she said, holding the gun in one hand and pulling on the rack with the other. Now Maxine pushed with both hands, and Sally pulled harder. Maxine let go, and Sally jerked backward with the change of power. Maxine lunged for the gun, falling on top of Sally and creating a black dust storm with their struggle. The flashlight cast an eerie glow across the floor.

"Give me th—" Sally pulled the gun away, trying to aim it at Maxine.

Maxine didn't have a good grip on the barrel, but she managed to press Sally's arm against the floor so she couldn't move it. The gun dropped to the floor. Just as Maxine was about to grab it, Sally shoved her away. Maxine landed against the front of an oven, grimacing with the pain that ripped along her back and head. Sally's breath was heaving as she stood in front of Maxine, gun aimed at her nose.

"Nice try," she said.

"I thought so." Maxine felt all hope drain away as she stared at Sally's wild face in the dim light. She sucked in deep breaths of her own, wasting it on the ashes that swirled in the air around them.

"Get in the refrigerator. Now. I don't care if that metal rack doesn't move. You'll just have to fold yourself in half."

Maxine slowly twisted the racks until they broke away from the brittle plastic. She took one last look at Sally, hoping for . . . what? Some kind of regret or tenderness on her blackened expression? Another chance to grab the gun that was now pointed at her face?

Even more slowly, she curled into the bottom half of the refrigerator. Sally wasted no time in slamming the door shut. Maxine closed her eyes, willing herself to stay calm and not use up any more precious air than necessary. Maybe when

Sally was gone, she could kick the door open again.

And then her whole world tilted as the refrigerator fell facedown. Maxine's shoulder ached where she landed hard against the grooved shelves in the door. Her nose was pressed up against the egg holder. She let out a yelp, but it was drowned out by the sound of something being pulled across the floor. Then she heard a muffled thump as another object was shoved against the refrigerator.

She could hear her heart beating in her ears, drumming away like the rattle of a snake fighting for its life. Beyond that, she could hear nothing else. Already it seemed the air was dwindling, and she again willed herself to calm down. For what, she didn't know.

Straining her ears, she could hear the faraway rumble of an engine. Her car, perhaps. Sally leaving. Maxine was sideways, and she rolled around so that her feet were braced against the back of the fridge, now her roof. She shoved hard, hearing herself grunt with the exertion. Again. And again. It didn't even budge.

"No, no, no. This can't be happening. I didn't come back only to die again!"

She shoved again, fear washing over her and pushing her on. Nothing moved. Not even a tiny movement to spur on her hopes. She started pushing on the walls around her, hoping for a weakness, a crack to work on. It was sealed tight, like a coffin. Her coffin.

With all her pushing and panicking, she now sucked in one huge breath after another, not getting enough oxygen in any of them. It was over. And she'd lost Sam again. She closed her eyes, feeling dizzy and faint. Her second chance was over, and she still hadn't told Sam she loved him. She'd gotten closer this time, but not close enough.

She slipped the gold band from her right finger to the one on her left hand. Maybe that would tell him, if and when they found her body. That was all she could do now.

Chapter 14

Sam was lying on his back on the couch, his feet propped up on the back. He tossed the racquetball up and down, up and down. The sensual sounds of saxophone filled the room, the lights were dim, and a glass of wine sat on the coffee table beside him. This was what Sam called a perfect moment, and even when he was really caught up in a messy case, he could drift from there and put it aside for a while. Except he wasn't on any case. And he was as restless as a hungry tiger.

It was the same kind of restlessness that had permeated him before Jennie's death, and it had started again after Maxine had left. It had really kicked in after talking to her. So maybe it was a sexual restlessness, then. He closed his eyes and tried to clear his thoughts.

Jennie appeared in his vision.

How could one man get so mixed up? There was Jennie, and there was Maxine. Two totally different women. One he had loved and divorced, knowing there was no future for them. One he hadn't even realized he loved, and now there was no future for them, either.

"Ah, Jennie," he muttered. "I was a damned fool. Knowing you was the best thing I ever had. Maybe I couldn't have made you happy, either, but I could have at least tried." He could see Jennie in his mind, encouraging him, impressed by how he'd handled some of his cases. She'd always believed in him.

And there was Maxine. He could see her at his parents' house defending him, saying how proud she was of him. He shook his head. Now he could see why he kept getting them confused. Maxine had somehow taken on some of those sweet traits and innocence Jennie had. Both women made him feel like a man worthy of love, worthy of them. But it still didn't make it any easier for him to forgive himself for seeing one woman when he was making love to another.

Jennie's face filled his vision again. But not that soft smile he usually pictured her with. Her expression was pure terror, enough to send Sam upright with his heart beating wildly. The racquetball bounced across the wood floor. Sam turned to Romeo, who also couldn't seem to relax tonight. He paced near the door, pausing to look at his master.

"Something's not right. Even you're restless, and you're the most easy going dog I ever knew."

He stood and walked over to the phone on the counter. The cool, smooth plastic felt good against his hand, but hot needles pricked his insides. "That phone call wasn't right." He dialed Maxine's number, but Gabriel's soft, recorded voice was all he got. "Maxine, this is Sam. Call me when you get back. I don't care how late it is, just call me. Thanks."

She should be all right, with Armand in some psychiatric ward somewhere. He knew his buddy at the station would have told him if they'd released him.

The fire needles increased. But what if it wasn't Armand who was after her? Maybe it was James after all. This was why he didn't handle cases he was personally involved with. He had been so anxious to send Maxine off so he could get his head straight, he'd been more than willing to believe Armand had been behind the murder attempts.

He dialed the number at the station and asked for Dave. "Hey, this is Sam," he said when Dave answered.

"Hey, Sam, how's it going?"

"I don't know, you tell me. What's going on with the Santini thing?"

"Not a thing. He won't say a word, still in an almost catatonic state. Won't eat, drink, or anything. He's not going anywhere, if that's what you're worried about."

Sam didn't feel any relief from the needles. "Why are your people out at the Santinis' tonight? Maxine said they wanted her to drive out there and talk to them."

Silence. "I don't think anyone's out there. Let me check." Sam heard him yell across a noisy room and ask someone who was obviously handling the case. "Nope, no action out there. Something wrong?"

"Maybe nothing. I don't know, maybe the Santini daughter just needed someone to talk to. I'll call down there and make sure everything's all right. Thanks for your help."

"Oh, Sam. One more thing. The DNA tests came back: doesn't look like Armand Santini went anywhere near Floyd's place." When Sam went silent, Dave added, "Maybe the murder had nothing to do with your case."

"Yeah, maybe not," Sam forced out at last. "I gotta go. Thanks."

And maybe James had put Sally up to inviting Maxine out. He looked up the number in his book and called the mansion. If something was wrong, and he could talk to Maxine, he could ask her some strategic questions to make sure everything was all right.

James answered.

"This is Sam Magee, Maxine's ex—I mean, her private investigator. I hear the police were out your way asking questions, wanted Maxine to come out."

"Sally said there were some people here, just asking routine questions. They were gone by the time I got home from the city."

"Was Maxine there?"

"Yeah. She and Sally went out for a cup of coffee. In fact, you missed them by about ten minutes. I can leave her a message if she comes back in when they return."

Out for a cup of coffee. That sounded safe and ordinary. "No, that's all right. Thanks a lot."

He should feel better. James didn't sound nervous, as though he were lying or in the middle of something. In fact, he'd sounded sleepy. But why hadn't Aida answered the phone? Maybe it was her night off. Ah, hell, he didn't know. All he did know was that no relaxing was going to happen at his apartment tonight anyway. He'd go out to the mansion to see for himself that everything was all right. Maybe he'd even spot the two women at a coffee shop on the way in. Just imagining the sight of Maxine safe and sound spread a rush of warmth through him. But that warmth wasn't relief. He slid into his jacket and headed out, Romeo on his heels.

"You feel it, too, don't you, buddy?" he said as Romeo jumped into the car before Sam got in. "What does it mean?"

Sally was exhausted when she arrived at the mansion. Exhausted, and thanks to that witch, covered in ashes. She'd dumped Maxine's car after wiping her prints off the steering wheel. Eventually somebody would find the body, but they'd never connect it to Sally. She had no motive to kill Maxine, nothing anyone could actually pinpoint. If only James would have stayed at work like he was supposed to so he'd have an alibi. But it didn't matter; he was innocent. No one would convict or even arrest an innocent man. Besides, she had a story that would seal everything as tightly as Maxine was sealed in that refrigerator. She'd even pulled the range out and tilted it against the box so Maxine couldn't push herself up. She was probably dead by now; it had been at least half an hour.

Sally approached the house, her heart thudding. She had to convince James first, and then she would have to put on the show again for the police. Drat, she hated to drag herself into all this, but with Sam knowing Maxine had gone out there and James seeing her at the house, there was nothing she could do. It was the kind of sacrifice that would earn her points in the Big Yonder someday.

She took a deep breath, putting a horrified expression on her face and slumping her body. For effect, she'd tossed her purse out on the street. The hassle of replacing everything would be a small price to pay for having an alibi. She banged weakly on the door.

"James? James, please come to the door!"

A few minutes later, he opened the door, annoyance turning to concern. "My God, Sally, what happened to you?"

She fell against him, fearing she was ruining the white shirt he'd had on with her ashes. Heck, he could sacrifice, too.

Those two years of drama in high school were going to come in handy after all, she thought as the tears formed in her eyes, and terror filled her voice.

"Oh, James, it was horrible! Please, just hold me for a second so I know I'm alive."

"Sally, what happened? Come inside." He led her into the house, on that pristine white tile with her dirty shoes. She removed them, then moved back into James's safe embrace as he said, "You've got to tell me what happened. Where's Maxine?"

It annoyed her that he was asking about Maxine of all people. He should only be concerned about her. She forced a tremor in her voice. "We were going for coffee . . . this guy was hiding in the back seat of her car. He made us go somewhere, I don't know where it was . . . he made us lie down in the car while he drove. He had a gun pointed at us."

The gun was still hidden in her coat pocket. She was going to put it in a plastic bag and bury it in the backyard, just in case she ever needed it again.

James's hold became tighter on her. "A gun? My gosh, Sally. And this is supposed to be such a safe neighborhood. Go on, then what happened?"

She really wished he wouldn't interrupt her. She wanted

to get it all out in one gush, done and over with. "And then he made me stay in the car and he took Maxine away. I . . . I never saw her again. He came back to the car a few minutes later, and I asked him what he was going to do to me. He said his orders were to get rid of Maxine, and that I was only in the way. We drove for a while—I don't know where we were. Then he stopped the car in some desolate area and told me to get out. Believe me, he didn't have to tell me twice. I was so scared! I thought I was going to die!" The more she screamed, the tighter James held her. "I couldn't save Maxine. I feel terrible that she died and I lived. It's so unfair!"

James pulled away. "So someone really was trying to kill her. Maybe she isn't dead. How are you so sure she is?"

"I . . . I just know it. The guy said he'd killed her."

James nodded, though not convincingly. "But he could have thought he killed her and left her there to die. She could be alive. We've got to call the police and start searching. You have to remember where this guy took you. Did you see what he looked like? Could you identify him?"

Something cold washed over her. "He was wearing a mask, one of those knitted ones." Her voice was losing that scared quality, turning dull and monotone. "Why are you so concerned about Maxine all of a sudden? I thought you hated her."

His eyes widened. "I don't like her, but I don't want her to die. If we can save her, I want to do it."

"You haven't even asked me if I'm all right."

"I can see that you're all right, even if you are shaken up. Maxine could be dying right now."

"She's already dead! Didn't you hear me? She's dead, gone!"

His eyes narrowed. "But you said you didn't see her die."

"I told you, I just know she's dead. Let me take a shower, and we'll go down to the police station." That would buy her more time, just in case. She also didn't want any of that pesky DNA evidence on her.

"Sally, you can't wash off. There might be some evidence on you, hairs or skin follicles, that could point to this creep."

Anger bubbled up inside her. Why was he making this so hard on her? She was doing all this for him, and he was turning on her. "Whose side are you on, anyway?" she heard herself scream out at him.

James took a step away, narrowing his eyes at her. "I'm not on a *side*. Cripes, I'm wondering the same of you. Don't you want to see this guy get caught? Don't you want to try to save Maxine? I thought you liked her."

"I don't like her because you don't like her!" Her voice was rising higher and higher, but she didn't care anymore. She felt betrayed by the one person she loved in the whole world. He didn't realize how much she'd done for him. Maybe it was time he knew. Then he'd take her side and help her destroy any evidence that needed destroying. They could stall on calling the police for a while, saying it took her longer to get home.

James took another step backward. "I'm calling the police. Don't touch anything on yourself."

"James!" she screamed shrilly. "Wait! Don't turn away from me!"

He kept going, walking to the phone in the kitchen, picking it up, not listening to her at all. Fear laced his expression as she walked toward him. He was afraid of her. No, this couldn't be happening! She didn't want to scare her beloved brother. But at the moment she had no choice. She had to make him understand why she'd done all this. Then he could help her. She pulled the gun out of her coat pocket and pointed it at him, keeping her fingers steady so she didn't accidentally pull the trigger. The phone dropped to the white tile with a loud thud.

"James, don't be afraid of me," she heard her voice

whimper. "You have to understand. Let me make you understand."

He stood there for a moment, his face as white as the countertop behind him, as white as the entire house. Finally he cleared his throat, staring at the gun and not her. "Okay, Sally. I want to understand."

She smiled, but kept the gun held up. "Come in the living room, then. I'll explain everything to you. It isn't as bad as it looks."

She followed him to the couch. "Stay there," she said, maneuvering out of her clothing. "No, light the fireplace up first. Now."

Slowly he started the fire, and she fed her clothing into it. If she could get James to lie about the ashes, she wouldn't even have to give the police that crucial clue that would help them find Maxine's body. Then she could say she was simply thrown from the car. Together they could put this together. She'd lied to protect him; he could do the same for her. She was now in her underwear and bra, shivering a little before the heat reached out to warm her.

"Sit down," she said, hoping he'd forgive her later for using the gun to force him. He sat, keeping a wary eye on her. She sat down next to him, setting the gun across her thighs. The cold metal made her suck in a breath. "Don't be mad at me, okay? Promise you won't be mad."

"I promise," he said thickly. "What have you done?"

"It was all for you, James. I knew Maxine was going to take away what was rightfully yours, so I planned to remove her from the picture. Only she didn't die the first time, or the second. And her boyfriend, or whatever that PI guy is, kept snooping around, and I was afraid I was going to get caught. Or afraid they were going to pin something on you. Believe me, I never wanted them to look at you as a suspect. I knew they wouldn't pin anything on you because you were innocent. But now we don't have to worry, unless that PI comes snooping around. I was going to say he was the guy who accosted us, but then I figured he might have an alibi, and I'd look like a liar.''

James's body sagged more with every word she uttered. He rubbed his hand over his face, an expression of shock and horror on it. ''Start over, Sally. You've lost me.''

So she did, right from the beginning. Not with their mother, of course, but with Maxine and everything James stood to lose and how she wanted to protect him. All of it, but no details about what she'd done with Maxine. Her body was on edge, waiting to see if he'd understand and take her side now.

''So that's how you know Maxine is dead. You killed her,'' he clarified.

He was trying to understand, she knew it. ''Yes, I killed her.''

''Where is she? How did you do it?''

She frowned. He was still too interested in Maxine. ''I just did, okay? Don't you worry about it. The less you know, the better. I didn't want you to know anything, but you kinda pushed me into it.''

''And you did all this . . . for me?''

''Because I love you. Because you deserve it. And look what's happened because of all this. You're now heading up Daddy's company. He'll be released soon and he'll see what a good job you're doing.''

He leaned closer and placed his palm on her cheek. She closed her eyes for a second and exhaled. He understood.

''I can't believe you did all this for me. You're wonderful, you're amazing—'' He grabbed the gun off her legs. ''And you're crazy!'' he said, standing up and holding the gun at her.

She felt more annoyed than scared. ''James, put that thing down. I know you're not going to use it. Give yourself some time to think it over and you'll see that I did the best thing I could have done.''

''By murdering people? Sally, you have really lost it. I'm going to call the police and get you some help. They'll probably only put you away for a little while. It'll probably be some nice place, very quiet and relaxing. Then you'll be all better again.''

"James, if they put me away, I can't be with you. What would you do without me? No, you can't let that happen. You're going to have to help me get out of this. It's really easy; I have it all worked out. Just sit down and listen to me."

Sam killed the lights as he pulled into the Santini drive. The living room light was on, a beacon in the darkness. The gentle lighting of the fancy globes along the road guided him right up to the house. Maxine's car wasn't there. Damn. He hadn't seen it on the way in, either. He'd passed one coffee shop that seemed a logical choice for them to go to, but no luck.

Sam got out of the car, gesturing for Romeo to stay put. He left the keys inside, just in case he needed to make a quick exit. The drapes in the front window were sheer, and he could see two figures inside sitting on the couch. Through a small crack in the drapes, if he tilted his head at an angle, he could see inside better.

His heart felt squeezed when he saw James holding the gun on a half-naked Sally. Her face was streaked with something black. Other than that, the whole scene looked serene, with the fireplace flickering behind them. He searched the room, but found no sign of Maxine. Her absence didn't make him feel any better.

So James was behind it after all. Sally must have found out, maybe discovered him doing something to Maxine. His chest was so tight at that thought, he could hardly breathe. He had to save Sally first, then find out what had happened to Maxine. Now he was sure she wasn't at any coffee shop, safe and sound.

Before crashing through the window, he at least had the logic left to try the front door. It was unlocked. Damn, why couldn't he have decided for violence and bought a gun?

He never thought he'd have such a dangerous case. And such an important case. He opened the door and slipped inside, just around the corner from the living room.

Sally's tremulous voice said, "James, you're making a big mistake. How can you do this to me?"

"Shut up and move to the kitchen, now."

Sam made his move as they walked into view. He lunged at James, knocking the gun across the floor. Sally gasped, but didn't hesitate as she grabbed the gun and fled. At least the weapon was out of reach now. He hardly had time to see where she went as the two men landed on the white tile and wrestled for control.

"You don't know what you're doing!" James screamed. "It's Sally. She's the one who murdered Maxine."

That word—"murdered"—pierced through Sam. He held James down, but ceased the struggle. "What are you talking about?"

"Sally's been behind it all. She came home covered in soot telling me how some guy had jumped her and Maxine. But something didn't sound right. I was going to call the police when she pulled out a gun and told me everything. Then I got the gun away from her until you barged in."

Sam had to make a split-second judgment. Sally behind it? It didn't make sense. But if she was behind it, she had the gun. And if James was bluffing, she still had the gun. And hopefully she'd call for help. Sam let him up.

"Why?"

James looked around the room for Sally. "For me. She did all this for me, so I'd get a chance to run the company. So Maxine wouldn't take that away from me. She's crazy, man."

The lights went out, surrounding them in eerie darkness. "She's turned off the circuit breaker," James's voice said through the black. "Now she's going to kill us."

Maxine crossed her arms over her chest and closed her eyes. It was dark no matter what she did anyway. Her breathing was growing more shallow, the knowledge of impending death now calming her instead of panicking her. Her lungs were tightening, though, aching with their deprivation. She started to say the Lord's Prayer, very softly. ". . . and if I die before I wake, I pray the Lord my soul to take. Unless, of course, You want to give me another chance."

That's when she felt it. At first she thought it was her imagination. Then she felt it again, a cool shaft of air. She turned to find the source of it, feeling along the edge of the door. Her finger moved through a tiny draft of air near the top of the door. She couldn't feel the opening, but somehow the seal had been damaged or melted and let in a tiny bit of air. She felt around the rest of the door, but didn't feel any other drafts. This was it.

She pushed her nose to the crack at the top of the door where the butter might have been kept and inhaled the crisp air, pulling it into her tightened lungs. It wasn't a lot of air, not enough to keep her alive for a long time. But maybe it was enough to make it until the morning when people might be out and she could scream for help. She tried to remember the area surrounding this house. There were a few other homes, but she doubted they were within screaming distance.

Tenuous hope swirled through her. But she could breathe. The chance was dim that anyone would happen across the house in the near future, but it was a chance nonetheless. She kept praying in her mind, saving her breath for that tiny inlet of air. Sam would never find her, and probably wasn't even looking for her. But maybe someone, somehow, would find her.

If, however, she did die before anyone found her, she had to let the police know who did this to her. Sally would be a free woman, living her life with her brother thinking she'd done nothing wrong in protecting him. Maxine felt along the doorway for the metal bar that kept the jelly jars from falling in. She yanked it, finding the metal brittle from the heat of the fire. It broke easily, leaving a sharp edge. All the while she kept going back for an inhale of air.

She felt the flatness of the side wall beside her and mapped out the space. With the edge she scraped the words *Sally Santini murdered me.* And then, on the opposite side, she scratched the words *Sam, I love you.* She went back to the other side and scraped in some more information, having no idea how legible it was. All she could feel were the slight scratches in the plastic. Hopefully the police wouldn't have to rely on that to find her killer. And Maxine's killer.

Sally's voice rang through the darkness. "James, get out of the way! I have to get rid of this guy so we can figure out what we're going to do. Don't worry; we're going to work this all out."

A shot exploded through the living room, but Sam was already rolling away from where he'd just been.

"Sally, please don't shoot anymore!" James yelled. "No more killing. Put the gun down, and we'll figure this out. I'll help you, okay?"

"No, James, we have to get rid of him. He's going to ruin everything. There's no way around it. Do you think I *like* killing people? Puh-lease. It's a hassle, but I have to do it."

The woman was mad, that much was certain. Sam crouched behind the sofa, making his way around behind it. If he lived long enough, he'd chastise himself for making a mistake later. Now he needed to take this woman down. He could see her silhouette in the kitchen doorway, jerking this way and that with the gun in her hand as she blabbed on about how she had to do this and that. If he could see what kind of gun she had, he could determine how many bullets she had left. That was impossible in the dark. But he could hear James's breathing as he hid behind the other end of the sofa.

"James, come over here so I don't shoot you accidentally," she was saying.

Sam made his way over to him and whispered into his

ear, "Tell her you're coming, but stay there."

"Okay, I'm coming out."

"Don't think about taking this gun away from me, James. I'm not letting you near me. I can't trust you anymore."

Sam stood up, hands out. If she suspected it was him, she'd cut him down in an instant. But he had to take that chance, because she was his only link to finding Maxine. He had to believe she was still alive. The silence gripped him as he took slow steps toward her silhouette.

"Go right over there," she ordered. She was watching him, tensed in preparation for any move he might make. She lifted the gun. "James, say something."

Heat rushed through him. His time was up. "I—" He bought his last second and lunged for her ankles. She shot straight out, expecting him to go for her hands and the gun. He knocked her off balance. The gun clattered over the tile floor of the kitchen behind her. She jerked out of his grasp and crawled over the floor.

She had the advantage of knowing the layout. He rolled out of the way, ready for a blast to shatter the air. Nothing. Did she have the gun? He saw her get to her feet. She was standing in front of a doorway. All he could see was a black square that pulsed with the sound of her deep breathing.

In a crouch, he made his way closer to her, feeling for the gun along the way. As he got closer he could see her shadow next to the open door. A bullet exploded from the gun, so close he heard its *zing* as it shot past his head.

He moved quietly behind the door—and shoved hard. He was only hoping to knock her off balance, but the sounds that followed (including a long scream) didn't coincide with her falling to the floor on the other side. He opened the door and felt, rather than saw, the gaping openness of the basement below. He took a tentative step forward, feeling the first step down. She'd fallen down the stairs.

James's labored breathing alerted Sam to his presence as he made his way through the kitchen. "What's going on?"

"She fell into the basement. Stay away from the opening,'' Sam said, pushing him out of the target area. ''I don't know if she's still got the gun.'' He hated the darkness. ''Where are the circuit breakers?''

''Down there,'' James said. ''Sally? Are you down there? Are you all right?''

No sound at all emerged from the inky darkness below. Either she'd scrambled away instantly, or she was hurt. Or maybe worse. Sam didn't want her dead. She was the only key to Maxine's whereabouts.

''I'm going down there,'' James said. ''She may be crazy, but she's my sister. And she did this for me. Because of me,'' his pained voice said as he descended the steps. ''She's down here,'' he said a moment later. ''I don't know if she's alive. Let me get the lights turned on again.'' Sam heard him fumbling with something, stepping around or tripping in the darkness before blissful light flooded the room.

Sally lay sprawled out on the concrete floor below. The fall wasn't very long, but the landing had to be hell. Sam was down at her side in a moment, feeling for a pulse.

''She's still alive. But she's not going to be very informative anytime soon.'' His gut churned. Time was running out. Without Sally's assistance, if she even provided that when she did regain consciousness, he had no way to find Maxine. The police could check the surrounding area, but Sally and Maxine had left in a car. They could have gone anywhere. ''How long were they gone?''

James shook his head. ''I don't know, an hour maybe. I didn't pay much attention.''

Sam's head dropped and he squeezed his eyes shut for a moment. In the darkness that still permeated his soul as hope drained away, one pinpoint of light shone through. It was a long shot—a hell of a long shot—but it was all he had.

He ran up the stairs. ''Call the police, tell them to get an ambulance.''

''Where are you going?''

''I'm going to find Maxine. If Sally says anything at all, try to get her to tell you where she took her. And tell the police. But I can't wait for her to come to. I'll be back."

In the foyer, a black splotch on the white tile caught his attention. He knelt and ran his fingers over it, lifting it to his nose. Ashes. Just like the black stuff on Sally's face.

Sam ran out to the car, opening the door to find his salvation waiting patiently on the front seat. Romeo's long tongue was hanging out, but his eyes were bright and alert among the saggy eyelids.

"You're going to be a hero," he said to Romeo. "But I've got to find something of Maxine's. Something—" He lifted his head, remembering the time they'd staked out the weasel in the wheelchair. She'd put his gloves on for a while. He opened the glove compartment, pulled out the brown knit gloves, and held them out to Romeo. "Sniff it," he commanded. The only scents on the gloves would be hers and his. Sam was easy to find. If Romeo showed no interest, then her scent wasn't enough.

"Find her!"

Romeo's brown nose wiggled, and he rose to his feet. His tail started moving back and forth, at first slowly, then faster. He kept sniffing, covering every inch of the gloves. Sam moved out of the way as Romeo jumped through the open doorway and started sniffing over the pavement. He made his way to the front door.

"No, she's not in there," Sam said. He pointed in the opposite direction. "She's out there. Somewhere."

Romeo wended his way to where the driveway started out into the darkness of the surrounding neighborhood. He stopped suddenly and lifted his head, then turned to look at Sam as if to say, "This way! She's this way!" Then he took off, tag jingling in the quiet darkness.

Sam didn't even bother closing his car door. He ran after Romeo, watching his breath turn to fog in front of him. At the edge of the driveway, the dog stopped and sniffed at the air. Then he turned right, keeping to the side of the road. Romeo could pick up her scent even if she was inside a car when she left. All he needed was the trail of her skin follicles that floated out of the car's ventilation system and landed near the road. Even if she was in the trunk, Romeo could pick up her scent.

Sam followed, praying the dog knew what he was doing. They were built for this kind of thing, but Romeo had only practiced finding dog treats. All those skin flaps, the ears, everything pushed the scent toward his nose, and that nose was to the ground as he walked along the swale beside the road.

Sam's heart was up in his throat as they made their way through the cold air and out of the fancy neighborhood. He looked around at the distant glow of the city and the thousand lights all around. She could be anywhere. Then he looked down at Romeo, relentlessly pursuing Maxine's scent. He had to hope that the dog knew what he was doing. He might be their only hope.

"If you find her, I'll buy you acreage," Sam promised. "And I'll build you the biggest doghouse any dog ever had. I'll get you a girlfriend. Five of them. Cats to chase. Anything you want."

Romeo didn't even look back at Sam, but kept moving along. Occasionally a car would pause next to them, and the driver would ask if they needed help.

"Just walking the dog," Sam would say, though it looked unlikely with the homes spreading farther apart. "Thanks, anyway."

He glanced up at the starlit sky, washed to the south by the city lights. "Please don't let her die again," he heard himself say. "I mean, don't let her die, too." After that, he didn't take his eyes off the dog's swinging tail.

Once in a while Romeo would pause, lift his head and wiggle his nose in all directions. Sam's heart would stop, scared to death that he'd lost the trail. Then Romeo would set off in a new direction. Doubts pummeled Sam. Maybe the dog was just enjoying a long stroll, or maybe he'd picked up the scent of another dog in heat. Romeo hadn't been formally trained for this, he just had his built-in instincts. Maxine could be a hundred miles in the opposite direction. But this dog was all he had. Hopefully the police were getting some answers from Sally. He didn't care who found Maxine, as long as they did. And as long as she was alive. *God, please let her be alive.* He'd cursed God for taking Jennie, but now it was time to plead for help.

He glanced at his watch. They'd been walking for almost two hours. Romeo pushed on, even though fatigue showed in the way he walked. His big, floppy paws barely cleared the ground. Sam knew that bloodhounds wouldn't give up, even if they pushed themselves into exhaustion.

Sam tried to lead him to a puddle for a drink, but Romeo wouldn't stop. The dog's harsh breathing worried Sam, but he couldn't give up, couldn't stop Romeo when the dog didn't want to stop any more than Sam did.

They entered a nice, middle-class neighborhood that still had empty lots with spindly trees covering them. Some developer had bought the acreage years ago and then had gone bankrupt. There were a few homes here and there. Nothing to interest a dog, unless . . .

Romeo had something going, and Sam knew it was important that he find it. Sam's muscles ached, and his legs felt like jelly. But like Romeo, he had to keep going. They could rest, he kept telling himself, when they found Maxine. His mouth was hot and dry, and he inhaled the cool air through his mouth until his teeth ached. Romeo's pace quickened, despite the wheezing breaths coming from him. Sam saw the foam forming on Romeo's floppy lips and knew the dog couldn't last much longer without hurting himself.

A man out walking his dog waved at him, but Sam was too tired to wave back. But he had enough strength to yell across the street, ''Did you see a teal-blue Sunbird in this area earlier?''

The man paused, though Sam kept up with Romeo. ''Nope, I don't think so. Something going on?''

''Just checking.'' Sam was now too far away to continue

talking. And too breathless. Romeo's ears were flapping and flopping with his jerky movements. Then he remembered something: the black ashes on the carpet. Keeping an eye on his dog, he backtracked to the neighbor. "One more question. Was there a fire in this area not long ago?"

"There was a house that went up about a year or so ago. It's at the end of the road there, about four blocks or so in. We all keep asking that somebody do something about it, but it just stays there looking creepy. The kids wanted to make it a haunted house last Halloween . . ."

Sam was already running to catch up with Romeo. It was a struggle, but he picked the dog up and kept going. Romeo twisted to get out of his grasp. "Take a rest, buddy. If this isn't it, we'll do it your way again."

His lungs were crushed beneath the physical strain. Tension stretched everything inside him tight. He sucked in one cold, painful breath after another, searching the darkness ahead. When he smelled the faint scent of smoke, he ran faster, sending Romeo's ears up into his face. His eyes watered, but he kept them on the forlorn house off to the right. Chills washed over him, making the sweat covering him feel like cold rain on his skin. He set Romeo down and ran inside, losing his balance on the uneven floor and bracing himself on the sooty walls. He couldn't see much, but kept groping through the darkness.

Pulling a painful breath, he yelled out, "Maxine! Maxine, please be alive."

Moonlight shone in through the windows on the left side of the house. He made his way through the rooms. And he heard the noise. Very faint, muffled to the point he couldn't hear the words. But he heard enough to know it was a voice. Strength surged through him when he saw the refrigerator lying facedown. An oven was tilted up against it. He heard Romeo shuffling through the debris behind him, but Sam knew it wasn't the dog he'd heard.

He felt it, felt she was in there. He shoved the range away and pulled on the refrigerator, not even knowing where the strength came from. The unwieldy box rolled to the side, and something inside rolled with the movement. He jerked the door open. And heard the sharp intake of breath and the cry of relief in her voice. He couldn't see much of her, but he saw her hands reach wildly out. He grabbed them, their warmth and life injecting him with such relief, he simply pulled her out and into his arms, squeezing her hard.

"Sam!" she breathed. And then the tears came, and her body was racked with them as she hugged him back.

"Maxine, oh, Maxine." He wanted to touch her everywhere, just to make sure she was really there and alive. Spots of darkness clouded his vision as his body struggled to calm him and the blood rushing through his veins. He felt her knees give out, and he held her closer. They were both sucking in large gulps of breath. "Let's get out of here." Hoisting her up into his arms, he walked gingerly around the debris and Romeo, who was hopping up and down in an attempt to get to his quarry.

Out in the fresh air, he set her down on the cracked sidewalk. Her body was trembling, and she wouldn't let go of him. Romeo sniffed and licked at her, his tail going so fast Sam couldn't see it. He'd never seen anything move that fast on Romeo.

"Do you need some help?" the neighbor asked from a short distance away.

"Call an ambulance, please!" Sam's hoarse voice shouted out.

Maxine kept sucking in one deep breath after another. Clean, pure air tinted only with the faint scent of Sam's sweat. She didn't want to close her eyes for a second, didn't want to lose sight of Sam holding her close.

"Please tell me I'm not dreaming this, that I'm not delirious."

He shook his head, a soft laugh escaping his throat. "You're not dreaming. You're alive, sweetheart. Thank God you're alive." He squeezed her close again.

"Sam, say my name," she whispered. She had to make sure she was still Maxine.

He ran his finger down her cheek. "Maxine."

It still seemed unreal. Romeo nuzzled her, and she pressed her cheek against his head. She looked up at Sam and asked, "How did you find me?" at the same moment he asked, "How did you stay alive in there?"

They shared a laugh that felt so good, she wanted to keep it in her heart forever. He squeezed her hand.

"Romeo found you. He tracked your scent all the way from the mansion."

"Oh, my gosh." She pulled the dog in for a hug, closing her eyes against his soft, damp fur. "How can I ever thank you?" Then she looked up at Sam. "It was Sally. She was behind this all along."

"I know. I went to the mansion after finding out the police weren't out there and . . ." He dropped his head for a moment. "It's a long story, but miraculously we managed to overpower her. She's unconscious, or was when we left. Romeo was our only hope, and he came through." He scratched the dog's head, but moved his hand right back to her arm. "You've been in that thing for what, almost three hours? How did you stay alive in there?"

"I prayed. And then I found a hole, a warp in the molding that let air in. Not a lot, but enough to keep me going . . . until you found me."

He pulled her close again. "I can't believe I was so stupid."

"Sam, don't blame yourself for this. Who would have thought Sally was behind it? I didn't. Please don't blame yourself."

He met her gaze, his eyes seeming to drink her in. He reached up and stroked his finger down her grimy cheek. "I'll try."

"You saved my life, Sam," she whispered. "You and Romeo. Don't ever forget that."

He was still holding her when the ambulance came and

seemed reluctant to let her go even then. She was checked over by the paramedics, but aside from a few scratches and bruises, she was all right. Her lungs felt tight, but each precious breath came easier. From the kindly neighbor's house, Sam contacted the police and let them know he'd found her. He seemed to argue with them, but insisted that he was going to take her to his place, and the police could go there to get their statements. The paramedics took them back to the Santini mansion to get Sam's car. And then he took her home.

Chapter 15

Sam brought Maxine a cup of coffee laced with brandy. She took it with both hands, wrapping her trembling fingers around the cup. Even though Sam's apartment was warm, the chill inside her hadn't quite left. He sat down beside her on the couch, the place he'd occupied throughout the entire questioning by the police. Now they were gone, and a comfortable numbness had set in.

She looked up at him, his hair still slightly damp from the shower he'd taken after she'd taken hers. "Do you want to know what I thought about most when I was in that refrigerator, Sam?"

"Getting out, I'd imagine."

"Well, that, too. I thought about you."

"It's natural to think about the people in your life when you think it's over."

She turned toward him. "Sam, I love you. That's why I was thinking about you. I was locked in that coffin and all I could think about was that I hadn't told you I loved you. You don't have to tell me you love me back. Not until you feel it, anyway. But I'm not letting another minute pass without telling you that. I almost lost all my chances." She didn't tell him she'd scratched the words into the refrigerator wall. She'd tell him that later.

He reached up and touched her cheek, stroking her skin

with his thumb. "I can't tell you I love you because I don't know what I feel for you." She could see the honesty in his eyes. "I know I was scared to death of losing you. Let's just give this time and see what happens, all right?"

"All right, Sam." She wrapped her fingers around his wrist. "I know I owe you my life, but I have a favor to ask you."

"Anything you want." That didn't include his heart, she knew.

"I need to feel alive all over, and I know of only one way to do that. I want you to make love to me."

Something sparked in his eyes, and a smile made his mustache twitch. "I can handle that."

"In your car."

His eyebrows lifted. "It's cold out there."

"Not with you beside me."

He nodded slowly, that smile returning. "You did say you wanted to make love in a car, didn't you?"

"Oh, yes. With you, but I didn't tell you that part then."

He regarded her for a moment, probably again wondering what had gotten into his old Maxine. But she was staying true to Maxine-the-first—the woman had loved Sam, too. No way was she giving Sam up, not for any reason. Give him space she could do, but not forever. If they could get past this Jennie thing, they'd be fine.

He stood up, extending his hand to hers. "Let's go." When her hand was snugly in his, he lifted it to his face. "You're still wearing your wedding ring," he said softly.

She'd forgotten that she'd put it on her left hand. "I switched it in the fridge. I thought maybe you'd know that I was leaving a message to you if . . . well, if I didn't make it."

He lifted her hand and kissed her fingers. In those eyes of his, she could see so many things. Sorrow, confusion, and a softness that gave her hope the same way that little crack had in the fridge.

He poured the remaining coffee into a thermos, brought

a soft blanket and a pillow. "It's not easy making love in a car," he warned.

Making love. She inhaled those words into her heart. "Sometimes the good things in life aren't easy."

"So they say."

He found a cozy place on a knoll just outside the city. She didn't ask how he knew about this place. She knew the past didn't matter; if only Sam could see that. He shut off the engine and put the radio station on something soft and romantic. He turned to her, running his fingers down the length of her arm. She had taken off her coat as they'd come to a stop, and Sam had taken off his jacket soon after.

"I want this to be . . . right," he said, his voice a little hoarse.

"No ghosts?" she dared to ask.

"No ghosts."

She saw his willingness, but also the fear that the ghosts would win. Jennie's ghost. He was going to love her for who she was now. She had to believe that. He pulled her close, his eyes drinking her in before he closed them and kissed her. His lips rubbed against hers, stirring warmth in tendrils throughout her body. Her own hunger for more than his gentle touch made her open her mouth, and Sam joined her in a wet, wonderful dance that went on and on.

His fingers grazed her cheek, slid through her curls, then down her neck. He unbuttoned her long shirt—Sam's long shirt, actually—and slid his hand down over the curves of her breasts. She lifted to his touch, feeling her breaths deepen and filling his hands with her. Her stomach quivered as his fingers danced over the surface, and then lower. She closed her eyes against the wild sensations that turned into a raging fire, licking at her senses.

His mustache tickled along the skin of her neck as he answered her every moan with a rumble of his own. She ran her fingers through his soft hair, relishing every sensation that rocked her, wanting it to go on forever. Her body instinctively moved in unison with his as his fingers slid over her slick surfaces. She felt herself rolling toward that edge, and with one final stroke, she fell over it. Her breath caught in one final catch as rockets exploded inside her. Sam continued to explore and perhaps revel in what he'd done to her, making her toes curl until she couldn't handle any more.

"Sam, you're driving me crazy," she said in a rush of words.

"Ah, then we're even," he said, his breath warm on her ear.

She knew there wouldn't be a problem keeping warm as the steamed windows indicated. With trembling fingers, she pulled his shirt over his head, then worked on the tight buttons on his pants. Finally he maneuvered out of them, and she put him through the same sweet torture until he said on a raspy breath, "If you don't stop, I won't be able to, either."

She didn't want that, but she ran her fingers over that velvety skin at his tip once more, reveling in the shudder that rocked his body. This time she'd remembered the pot-handle theory, and it had worked quite well according to Sam's labored breathing.

They shifted awkwardly, but she didn't care. This was a long-time fantasy, and Sam was the only man she wanted to fulfill it. She moved around the steering wheel, lying fully down on the bench seat with her feet tucked to the side.

"Told you this wasn't going to be easy," he said, holding himself above her as she slid into position.

"I don't care. It's an experience, and I want to experience everything life has to offer. With you."

His thumb stroked the very tip of her chin as he looked at her for a moment. He left a trail of kisses from her stomach to just beneath her chin where his thumb had been, then slid his tongue into her mouth at the same moment he plunged into her. Her legs slid naturally around his waist, anchoring him against her. She marveled at the sensations she would have missed out on in her earlier life. She wanted everything, and she wanted it with Sam.

She dared to open her eyes, but his face was in shadow above hers. His eyes were closed, and she felt a tug at wondering who he was seeing in his mind.

"Sam," she whispered, then smiled when he opened his eyes.

Did she imagine the haunted look in them? He ducked his head and continued the rhythmic slide that carried her upward despite her doubts. Her fingers tightened over his shoulders, and she let out several guttural breaths as the rockets exploded and rained sparks all around her.

A moment later, his body shuddered, then tightened. He rocked his head back, then leaned forward to kiss her silly. His mouth swept hers up time and again, relentlessly. Maybe it had been all right, then, she thought as his kiss deepened in the kind of passion that should preclude lovemaking, not wind it down.

She let him carry her up on a tide of passion until he ended it several minutes later with kisses that gentled. He leaned over to the glove box and pulled out some tissues, then helped her to sit up straight.

They sat there staring out through the streaks of fog on the windshield for a few moments as she tidied herself up and got dressed. The top button on his jeans was still undone, as was his shirt. He leaned over and ran his fingers beneath her chin, and though the gesture was touching, there was something missing. At first Maxine decided she didn't want to know. But the more Sam seemed to wrestle with something, pulling farther and farther away from her, the more she had to know.

"Jennie again?" she asked, feeling colder at the mere mention of the name.

He didn't meet her eyes, staring straight out at absolutely nothing. "Yes. Both of you, actually." Finally he did turn to face her. "It's too weird. And I'm such a jerk, a crumb . . ." He shook his head. "I can't even think of the right word to describe the way I feel. Something really nasty and vile—''

She reached over and touched his arm, silencing his recriminations. "You're none of those things. You'll get over this. I promise you will."

"But it's not fair to you in the meantime. I can't put either one of us through this anymore. I want you to stay with me tonight. But tomorrow . . . I just need some time alone, a few days to sort through things."

She bit her lower lip, meeting his pained gaze with a matching one of her own. "Whatever you need to do, Sam."

"You'll be okay, I promise. Sally's being charged with attempted murder and first-degree murder for Floyd. She's being sent to a psychiatric ward for evaluation, which should keep her in until her lawyer can work the insanity plea. Armand's getting treated for his own mental maladies. You should be safe. If either are released for any reason, Dave will come by and take you into protective custody. And I'll call you while I'm gone."

"Gone?" The word struck her right in the heart.

"I wasn't sure if I wanted to leave in the morning, but this made up my mind for me." His thumb stroked over her lower lip, forcing her to stop chewing it. "Maybe I can sort through this."

"Maybe?"

"That's all I can give you right now."

She nodded, though she had a hard time understanding. "I'll take that, then."

He leaned back against the seat. "You know what was strange? Earlier after you called, I was sitting there trying to relax. Trying because I couldn't. I was thinking about you, but suddenly Jennie's face appeared in my mind."

Maxine's heart ached at the name again. "Jennie," she said, resignation lacing her voice.

"But it wasn't the usual Jennie. She looked scared. That's when I decided to call Dave at the station to see why the police were out there questioning you and Sally. And I found out they weren't.''

"What do you think it means?" How bizarre could this get?

"I don't know." He shook his head. "I just don't know. Let's go home."

On the drive home, she kept trying to ignore that bad feeling that had haunted her before. It was all this bringing her down, nothing more. But it didn't feel like heartbreak. It just felt . . . bad.

Sam stood there the next morning and watched Maxine sleep in the tangle of sheets his bed now was. Her expression looked troubled—all his fault. She loved him. Something in that warmed him and stabbed him at the same time. He didn't deserve her love. But he didn't want to lose her, either. He'd come damned close to that. The last thing he wanted to do was leave her, but if he didn't work through this confusion, he'd go crazy and probably take her with him in the process. No, he had to leave for both their sakes. It was only for a few days.

He'd told her to stay at his place if she wanted and had given her a key. She'd already agreed to watch Romeo, which had taken no convincing at all. Her hero. His hero, too. That dog had saved the life of the woman he loved. He felt his heart skip a beat. Had he thought that? Maybe he'd get over this after all. He did love her, but it was all twisted up with Jennie, and that made it less than what Maxine deserved. He owed her a love that was as pure as her own.

He forced himself to get a duffel bag from the top shelf in the closet and throw some things into it. After one more glance at her, he walked to the kitchen and called the airline to book a flight. He wrote the flight information down on the pad and ripped the piece of paper to stuff in his pocket. Time to go so he could make that early flight to Miami, and then on to Key West after that. Some warmth and sunshine and maybe a few margaritas might do his soul a lot of good.

If he felt right about things, he could even fly Maxine down later to join him. That thought warmed him more than the thought of sunshine.

He gave Romeo a good-bye pat on the head. "Take good care of her, buddy," he whispered. He looked around the apartment. It felt good knowing she was here. Because she felt right here. He was close to conquering this, he could feel it. Just a little time away, that was all he needed. He walked down the stairs and headed out into the cold morning air.

Maxine heard the ringing of the phone in the distant corner of her dreams. She pushed through the cobwebs to the surface of consciousness, feeling the sharp disappointment at finding herself alone in bed. She was still wearing Sam's shirt, and she rolled out of bed and made her way to the phone sitting on the counter. The answering machine picked up as she reached for the phone. Then she realized this wasn't her place.

She let the machine get it, turning toward the bathroom in hopes of finding the light on to indicate Sam was in there. It felt too quiet, though. He was gone, just as he'd said he would be. Romeo padded over to her, his tail a sweet greeting on a bittersweet morning.

A man's voice interrupted her thoughts. "Sam, this is Dave down at the station. Sam, if you're there, pick up, man."

Maxine picked up the phone. "This is Maxine. Sam's gone."

"Already?"

"Yeah. What's up?"

"It's not good. The Santini woman escaped as she was being transferred to the psychiatric ward last night. There was a mix-up in communication, and the people at the ward thought she was coming in this morning, so they didn't miss her. We found her guard tied up in the van. Her gun is missing. Sally's been out there most of the night. We need to get you into custody for your own protection. Where is Sam?''

"I don't know, exactly." She felt so lame at those words. "He needed some time to sort things out."

"When did he leave?"

"This morning. You don't think . . ." She didn't even want to say the words.

"Yes, Sam could be in danger, though I think you're in more danger than he is. We're going to send a car over for you right now. Stay put until the officers get there, all right?"

"Okay." She wrapped her arms around herself. "I'll be here."

She paced after hanging up the phone. Where could he have gone? Train, plane, automobile. That's when she saw the note on the pad addressed to her. She lunged for it, hoping he'd told her where he was going. He hadn't.

> *Maxine,*
> *I left this morning, didn't want to wake you. Here are the keys to my car; thought you could use transportation until they find yours. Stay at my place as long as you want. I'll be in touch.*
> *Love, Sam.*

Her fingers wrapped around the keys, pushing the sharp edges into her skin. Then she remembered something Sam had once told her about a case he'd been on. He'd lightly penciled over the pad of paper to see what had last been written on it. He'd written this note to her, of course, but maybe there was something she could find. She made fine strokes over the ridges of the next sheet of paper, revealing the letters of his note to her. But there was something beneath that, meshing slightly with the last words of the note. *Delta, Flt 464.* She glanced at the phone, wondering whether to call Dave and let him know. But she didn't know exactly where he was. Still, she didn't have time to wait for the car, so the least she could do was leave a message for him, which she did.

"I'll be back," she said to Romeo, locking the door behind her and taking the steps two at a time. She watched carefully for anything that looked suspicious. She even checked the back seat of the car, but everything looked normal. Her hands slid over the seat where they'd made love the night before. She turned the car onto the street and headed for the airport thinking about that missing gun.

She got lucky with a good parking spot and ran into the airport, so glad for legs that worked. He was probably all right, she told herself. Sally was after her, not him. But that bad feeling still clung to her soul, and it sped her pace even more.

"Sam, be all right," she said as she passed through the crowds looking for his tall, blond frame.

And then she saw him standing off to himself near the windows. His hands were in his pockets as he stared out at the gray skies and the airplanes. Relief flooded through her, though she was too far away to call his name out yet. An elbow shoved her sideways, pushing her into a nearby column. When she looked to see who had been so rude, her heart stopped. It was Sally, holding the same gun she'd had last night—and it was aimed at Sam.

"Nooooo!" Maxine screamed, but it was drowned out by the sound of gunfire. She saw Sam lurch as a spray of blood covered the window in front of him. He fell forward without even looking back to see who had shot him. "Sam!"

Several people tackled Sally, but Maxine only cared about one person. She made her way to his form, shoving two other gawking people out of the way. Security guards had the area under control immediately. Maxine dropped down to the floor next to Sam, pulling his head into her lap. Her hand trembled as she smoothed the hair from his pale face.

"Sam. Sam, please talk to me." Her voice was choked with tears.

"Help is on the way, ma'am," someone said from behind her.

"Do you hear that, Sam? Hang in there." This couldn't be happening. She couldn't lose him this way. She wouldn't let him die. Somehow her strength would become his. She closed her eyes and prayed the way she had in the fridge. Then she looked down at Sam, and then at the blood that seeped through his shirt. She pressed the palm of her hand over the bleeding, so damned close to his heart. But it was still beating, she could feel it.

The sound of the gunshot still echoed through Sam's mind, but it was becoming overpowered by the pain in his chest. What had happened? Had the world exploded? He could hear his heartbeat, slow but steady. And a voice, a soft, sweet voice pleading with him. He opened his eyes, finding the simple motion very taxing.

First a blur. Then two eyes, round with fear. And then he saw . . . Jennie. Jennie, holding his head, her eyes filled with tears. She was crying, and he wanted to comfort her. But he didn't know how, not when the world was becoming dark and pain engulfed him. *Jennie*. What was she doing here? It was too dangerous. Or was she on the other side waiting to bring him home?

"Sam," she was saying, leaning closer. A smile filled her face, a scared smile. "Oh, Sam, don't leave me." Her voice was choked with tears and pain, and it penetrated the foggy mist threatening to surround him. "Don't die," she urged in a hoarse voice. She grabbed at his hand, and though he couldn't move, he could feel her fingers squeezing around his own. "Stay with me, Sam."

No, she wasn't calling to him. She didn't want him to leave this world. Slowly images from behind her became focused. People crowding around them, voices shouting in the distance. Sirens. He'd heard enough sirens lately. He was still at the airport. And he was looking at Jennie. When he thought he must surely be dreaming, one of her tears splashed down onto his cheek, as hot as fire on his cool skin.

It was Jennie. For real this time. Her voice trembling with fear, her face red-streaked through her tears. He reached out to her with his other hand, and her cold hand clamped onto that one.

"Jennie?" he asked, wishing his mind could put it all together. She only hesitated a moment, then he felt her hand squeezing his again.

"Yes, Sam. It's Jennie. I'm here," her choked voice said.

As he looked at her, she transformed. One second she was Jennie, the next, Maxine. Yet, beneath their very different faces lay the same . . . soul?

And then the crowd parted and someone made Maxine move aside. But she clung to his hand, holding tight as if that would keep him there with her. And he wanted to stay with her. He didn't know why exactly, but something inside him wanted very, very badly to stay there with her. His heart was squeezing with a new sensation now, pushing the pain away and leaving him with a feeling of peace.

He felt himself lifted onto something a little softer than the industrial carpet had been, then he moved swiftly through a sea of people craning their heads to see him. Little black spots showered his vision, but at that moment Maxine squeezed his hand tightly and made them go away.

"Can I ride with him?" he heard her ask someone. "I— I'm his wife."

"Sure, ma'am," a male voice said as Sam was slid into the back of an ambulance.

When he was settled and could feel the ambulance take off, he focused on Maxine again. She looked like his wife— his ex-wife. No, his wife. But he knew what she had said, knew it wasn't from the gunshot or the pain. She was Jennie. He felt it and realized he'd always felt it. He couldn't explain it. He tried to remember that first moment when he'd found Maxine sprawled out on the landing in front of his office, but someone was injecting him with something, and his thoughts turned to mud and stopped flowing altogether. And over it all, through the mud and pain and the flashing lights imprinted on his vision he heard Jennie.

"You can't leave me, Sam, do you hear me? I'm not done with you yet."

It felt like months had passed between the strange explosion in the airport and the next time he opened his eyes. Light filtered in from a window next to him, and he blinked as his eyes adjusted to the assault. He knew a hospital when he smelled one and saw one. He supposed that was better than other places he could have woken up at. He glanced down at himself, at where a dull, throbbing pain pulsed in his chest. A large white bandage swathed his shoulder.

"Sam." Maxine's soft exclamation brought his attention to her as she got up from the chair she'd obviously been dozing in. The sleepy expression in her eyes was overwhelmed by a light brighter than the sunshine outside.

He found himself smiling, though his face felt stiff. "How long have I been in here?" his voice croaked out.

"Since yesterday morning." She took his hand and squeezed it the way she had then. "The bullet went through your shoulder, but it missed the important stuff. The doctor can give you all the technical terms, but the main thing is, you're going to be all right, Sam."

He looked into Maxine's bright green eyes and said, "I know I will."

"Sally's not going anywhere anytime soon. She's the one who did this. She escaped from her guard, got her gun and got away. They figure she watched the apartment and saw you leave, then followed you."

He started putting the images together in his mind. The explosion, the pain in his chest. Immediately Maxine was there, holding his head in her lap and pleading for him to stay with her. "And you were there?"

"I went to the airport to warn you that Sally was on the

loose. I used one of your tricks, running the pencil over a notepad.''

He reached up and touched her cheek, still wrinkled where it had rested against the top of the chair in her sleep. ''You're pretty smart. Maybe you would make a good partner.''

Her face brightened even more. ''You mean it?''

His smile faltered as another image formed in his mind. Maxine . . . and Jennie. He knew what he'd heard. *Yes, Sam. It's Jennie. I'm here.* And though he was looking at Maxine now, with her green eyes and red hair, he could feel . . . Jennie. He couldn't explain it; he just knew it was real.

''I saw Jennie yesterday,'' he said. ''I thought it was because I was dying. That maybe she was coming to take me to Heaven. But she wasn't.'' She was watching him, a careful expression on her face. ''She was . . . you. And you were her.''

She swallowed, her fingers tensing on his. The sun behind her lit her hair to warm fire. He thought she was suddenly an angel, looking upon him with eyes watering with tears. She just looked at him for a moment. Her lips trembled as she opened them to say, ''Yes, it's Jennie. I'm here, Sam.''

He felt a chill wash over him. It seemed preposterous, but what else had made any sense since Jennie died? Or more specifically, since Maxine had come back into his life. He could see it so clearly now. Even though she looked like Maxine, Jennie was in her eyes. Jennie was in her soul.

''Jennie,'' he repeated softly.

She nodded, watching his eyes. ''But how did you know?''

''I saw you. I mean, as Jennie holding me. She was there, and then she turned into you. It seemed so obvious that you were the same person, as crazy as that sounds.''

She closed her eyes and dropped her forehead against their linked hands. The tears were flowing when she lifted her face to his a moment later, and the sunshine glittered off them. She was still smiling.

"Sam, you don't know how much I wanted to tell you. And I even tried once, but of course, how could I expect you to believe me? It's crazy, isn't it, just like you said?"

He shook his head. "No, it's not crazy. I mean, I thought I was going crazy."

"I wanted a second chance with you, a whole new start when I realized I'd come back in another woman's body." She rubbed her forehead, a slight smile on her face. "And then I found out I came back in your ex-wife's body. By the time I realized you were in love with Jennie, I couldn't be her anymore. So I just hoped you'd get over her and start over with me." She nudged him playfully. "And then you go and get shot on me."

"Yeah, well. But nearly dying opened my eyes. And cleared up a lot of things, too. The coffee, the change in your personality . . . and the way you believed in me." He squeezed her hand. "I want to make the most of my second chance, too. With my life, and with the woman I love. Or should I say women? It's going to be better the second time around, kiddo, believe me."

She laughed, though more tears rolled from her eyes. "Gosh, if I'd known all I had to do was shoot you to make you see the light, I would have done that last week."

"It would have been worth it. It *was* worth it." He reached up and touched her chin, feeling her damp skin. "No more tears between you and me, okay?"

"Okay, bossman." She nodded, but the tears kept coming. "But these are happy tears. Tears of relief. I can have those."

He reached for her other hand, her left hand. The gold ring sparkled there on her finger. He couldn't afford to buy her a diamond back then, but now he could. He pulled her hand to his mouth, kissing the smooth metal of the ring and her finger at once.

"Marry me. Again and for good."

More tears, and she pulled her lower lip between her teeth the way he loved. "I promise I won't be any trouble," she said, just as she'd said it when she'd asked him to marry her years ago. Or rather when Maxine had asked.

He yanked her up against him, hiding the grimace the action made. It didn't matter, not when she landed with her lips right up against his. "Lady, I want your kind of trouble. I have a feeling my life will never be dull with you around. Partner."

To contact the author, write to:
Post Office Box 10622
Naples, Florida 34101
(SASE Appreciated)

It only takes a second filled with the scream of twisting metal and shattering glass—and Chris Copestakes' young life is ending before it really began.

Then, against all odds, Chris wakes up in the hospital and discovers she's been given a second chance. But there's a catch. She's been returned to earth in the body of another woman—Hallie DiBarto, the selfish and beautiful socialite wife of a wealthy California resort-owner.

Suddenly, Chris is thrust into a world of prestige and secrets. As she struggles to hide her identity and make a new life for herself, she learns the terrible truth about Hallie DiBarto. And when she finds herself falling for Jamie DiBarto—a man both husband and stranger—she discovers that miracles really *can* happen.

ON THE WAY TO HEAVEN

TINA WAINSCOTT

ON THE WAY TO HEAVEN
Tina Wainscott
_____ 95417-4 $4.99 U.S./$5.99 CAN.

Publishers Book and Audio Mailing Service
P.O. Box 120159, Staten Island, NY 10312-0004
Please send me the book(s) I have checked above. I am enclosing $_____ (please add $1.50 for the first book, and $.50 for each additional book to cover postage and handling. Send check or money order only—no CODs or charge my VISA, MASTERCARD, DISCOVER or AMERICAN EXPRESS card.

Card Number_____

Expiration date_____Signature_____

Name_____

Address_____

City_____State/Zip _____
Please allow six weeks for delivery. Prices subject to change without notice. Payment in U.S. funds only. New York residents add applicable sales tax.